THE KINDER POISON

THE
KINDER
POISON

NATALIE MAE

RAZORBILL

RAZORBILL

An imprint of Penguin Random House LLC
New York

First published in the United States of America by Razorbill,
an imprint of Penguin Random House LLC, 2020

Copyright © 2020 by Natalie Mae
Map copyright © 2020 by Natalie Mae
Map illustration by Marisa Hopkins

Visit us online at penguinrandomhouse.com

LIBRARY OF CONGRESS CATALOGING-IN-PUBLICATION DATA
Names: Mae, Natalie, author.
Title: The kinder poison / Natalie Mae.
Description: New York : Razorbill, 2020. | Audience: Ages 12+. | Summary: In the magical
kingdom of Orkena, a teenage girl is chosen to be the human sacrifice in a deadly game
among three heirs who will do anything for the crown.
Identifiers: LCCN 2019051803 | ISBN 9781984835215 (hardcover) |
ISBN 9781984835239 (ebook)
Subjects: CYAC: Fantasy. | Magic—Fiction. | Kings, queens, rulers, etc.—Fiction. |
Human sacrifice—Fiction.
Classification: LCC PZ7.1.M295 Ki 2020 | DDC [Fic]—dc23
LC record available at https://lccn.loc.gov/2019051803

Printed in the United States of America

1 3 5 7 9 10 8 6 4 2

Design by Theresa Evangelista
Text set in Perrywood MT Std

For Eve,

so you may know that however wild your dreams,

you can achieve them.

ALL good stories start with bad decisions.

This is the questionable mantra I repeat in my head as we watch the boat come in. It's a beautiful vessel, so unlike the plain wooden canoes that always flock Atera's river docks. The hull is glass, and through it I can see the dawn and the orange sands of the desert; the water and the reed-choked shore. As it draws nearer, the sun ignites along its edges like fire, the deep blue canopy above seeming to flutter in the heat. Guards with golden leopard masks and sickle swords patrol its railings, and in the river, the magic propelling it glows like a trail of fading stars.

It is a ship where legends are made.

It's also a ship where poor choices will be made, but Hen said I have to stop focusing on that part. I've lain on this roof a thousand mornings, imagining myself sailing to all the incredible places the desert travelers speak of, and not once has playing it safe helped me follow in their footsteps. Their adventures never start with, "Well, I waited patiently at home for something to happen, and it did!" No—proper stories start with risks. Switching identities, drinking unlabeled potions, trusting mysterious strangers. I'm not sure any of them ever started with lying to a priest, but again— I'm not focusing on that right now.

"There he is," Hen says, pointing to said priest: a shirtless bald man standing near the front of the boat. We're lying atop the roof of her house, one of the many flat-topped homes that line the river's shore. The second story gives us a perfect vantage point of the ship without it being too obvious we're here. The priest's gaze stays low, on the children who whoop and run on the muddy bank, their colorful tunics like flags. The tattooed prayers circling his pale arms and the pure white of his *tergus* kilt would have given him away even if Hen hadn't pointed him out.

He's the one carrying the ledger we need. No one boards that boat if their name isn't listed, and if I don't get to the palace now . . .

Well, there won't be another chance. This is the first time a royal boat has ported in Atera in six hundred *years*.

"That's the one we'll really need to watch," Hen says, pointing to a woman in a stunning blue *jole*—a formal wrap dress favored by the nobility. Hers is embellished with pearls and real lilies, and I squint, trying to make sense of my friend's warning. There's absolutely nothing daunting about the woman. In fact, compared to the armed guards and the scowl I now see on the priest's face, she looks delightful.

"Who is that?" I whisper.

"Galena of Juvel," Hen growls. "Royal Materialist, and thorn in my side. She's the one who made lotus boots into a thing."

I glance at the woman's feet. Her sandals look no different from the ones Hen often wears, but instead of ending at her heel, black lotus flowers twist up her brown legs to her knees.

"I think they're cute," I admit.

"Of course they are! They were my idea!"

One of the guards looks toward the roof, and we both duck down.

"We've been over this," I whisper. "Just because you get a weekly update on the lives of famous people doesn't mean they have the slightest idea of who you are. I'm sure it was just a coincidence."

"Was it?" Hen says, glaring as the woman drifts past. "Or was it conspiracy?"

"Well, when *you're* the Royal Materialist, you can ask her."

"Oh, I will." She grits her teeth. "I will."

I snicker at her response. One of my favorite things about Hen is her absolute confidence, as if rising from a simple—albeit distinguished—young Materialist in Atera to the person who crafts the latest fashions for the queen is only a matter of time. Though really, she's already on her way. Now that we're sixteen, this summer marks our last as apprentices, and Hen has already received dozens of letters from Orkena's nobility, commending her creativity and requesting her services upon her transition to Master. Soon she'll be traveling the country, using her rare ability to combine unusual materials, even fire or light or a stream of starlit water, into clothing for the elite. She can make dresses out of moonglow, and cloaks infused with dew so they stay cool even during the hottest afternoons. Meanwhile, the number of people excited for me to become a Master is one: my father. Which I appreciate, but it's not the same.

Hen's name is already on that ledger. I'm trying not to think too hard about why mine isn't, and how that's one of the many ways our lives are about to diverge.

"Just please don't talk to her about the boots *today*," I say, recognizing the glint in Hen's eyes.

Her black hair swings as she looks over. "I make no promises when it comes to war."

"And I'd be happy to help you plot later. But can we focus right now on the bigger task I'll probably come to regret? They're almost at the dock."

Hen's brown eyes narrow, tracking her mark. She taps a finger against her lips and shoves to her feet. "Follow me."

She disappears down the ladder in the roof. I follow in haste, earning a splinter when I slide too fast down the wood, and drop to the tiled floor of the upstairs hallway. Cool air emanates from the enchanted mudbrick walls, the spell that chills them hidden beneath a layer of creamy plaster. Within the hour, the house will feel drastically cooler than the summer air outside. I try to absorb as much of it as I can through my thin working dress. The stable is never unbearably hot, but it definitely doesn't hold on to the cold like Hen's house.

Rainbow-hued mats line the floor, and I smile as we pass rooms I know as well as my own. Hen's bedroom with her towers of dark, shimmering fabric, and her mother's nearly as cluttered, its walls and dressers covered in the rare items she accepts in trade for her potions. A bright weaving from the river country ripples with the light; a giraffe carving made of sandalwood and ebony sits upon the nightstand. Before my mother got sick, she and Hen's mother used to travel all over, selling potions and drinking in the world. I used to tell her that would be Hen and me someday, before I understood the magic I was born with wasn't the kind that would help me leave Atera. Apparently the ability to talk to animals doesn't actually impress anyone—including most animals—hence the lack of my name on the ledger.

But even our mothers had never been to the *palace*. And though tonight's party will only encompass one glorious, wonder-filled

4

night, it will be my chance to experience a sliver of the life I thought Hen and I could never have.

I cannot miss that boat.

"We're going to go with the 'distract and dominate' plan," Hen says, the hem of her green wrap dress flaring as she starts down the rosewood stairs. "You're going to provide the distraction, while I sneak the ledger from the priest's bag. I'll slip out of view and add your fake name. Then I'll put it back, and when they go to check people in later, aha! You'll be there."

"And you're putting me down as a Potionmaker, right?" I ask. We decided it would be safest if I assumed a false identity to get onto the boat, to avoid anyone recognizing a Whisperer absolutely shouldn't be there. It seemed only natural to use my late mother's name, as well as her (and Hen's mother's) power. That way I know some basics about the magic if anyone asks, not to mention potionmaking would be entirely impractical to demonstrate on board, unlike the elemental magics that can be conjured from the air.

"Yes," Hen confirms.

"And you're sure they're not going to make me prove it?"

She waves me off. "Let me worry about the details. You worry about the fantastic party awaiting us. Jeweled gardens, live peacocks, a dance floor the size of a town . . ."

"Hen, if I end up as the human sacrifice because you were thinking about dance floors instead of contest regulations—"

Hen stops, leaning solemnly against the wall. "This is not my first time, Zahru." Meaning not her first time *breaking the law*, and I force myself to smile. It may appear I'm taking this all in stride, but I'm also the girl who had a moral crisis once after a merchant gave me too much change, and I'm ignoring that this lie will probably haunt me forever.

"My associate looked into it," she continues. "The officials have so much else to deal with that even if we're caught, we'll just be removed from the palace grounds. And you know the sacrifice is actually a holy honor, right?"

"Right," I say, fidgeting as Hen starts down the stairs again. But I'll admit some of my excitement is dampened by the reminder of what tonight actually is. Atera has been so abuzz since His Majesty, the Mestrah, announced the Crossing, it's easy to forget that after the parties and celebration, real people will risk their lives for the sake of Orkena's future. Today, the royal boats will bring much of the nation's upper class to the palace—one per household—including a select group of Master magicians who will actually participate in the contest. While these contenders split off to compete for a spot on a prince or princess's team, the others like Hen (and hopefully, me) will get the run of the palace, including a viewing area where we can watch the selection process.

Then tomorrow, their teams chosen, the royal heirs will start on a weeklong race across the desert, where they'll battle the elements and each other and gods know what else to reach the sacred Glass Caves. Where the winner, destined to be our new Mestrah, will have to secure their victory by taking a human life.

The gods haven't called for a Crossing in centuries. I know I must trust the Mestrah, and that I should feel nothing but pride for the contest's reinstatement. But I also can't forget that the very reason it was discontinued was because a prior Mestrah deemed the race too brutal. I wonder what changed the gods' minds.

"Going out?" calls Hen's mother as we reach the bottom of the stairs. As is typical for the mornings, Hen's *mora* sits on a cheery yellow carpet in the main room, eyes winged in lines of kohl, plump legs crossed as she readies her wares for the market. Potion ingredients spread around her like a rainbow: yellow vials of palm oil, blue scorpion claws and orange beetle wings, pink lotus petals and green desert sage. Focus dots circle her beige wrists, drops of liquid gold that steady her hands and center the magic she'll use in the potions.

"Oh, just heading out to lie to a priest and crash the palace banquet," I say, trying to sound clever. I want to embrace this daring new lifestyle, and Hen's mother seems like the best place to start because she won't take me seriously.

"Oh, good," she says—taking me completely seriously. "I've been scheming ever since that sour messenger told me only one of us could go."

"She told him she had *two* daughters," Hen says, glancing at me.

Her mother scowls. "And you know what he said? 'Send the prettiest one. You're too old.' The cod. I hope he doesn't find himself in need of my services anytime soon."

She smiles as she pours green liquid into a rounded vial, coating the dried tarantula at the bottom. I have to admit she's the one person in the world who scares me more than Hen, which is why I'm very glad that when my mother passed, and Hen's father decided he felt "too tied down" and left the country without them, the broken edges of our families sewed into one. I even call her Mora to honor what she means to me. I'm fairly certain this woman would poison someone for me.

"Be safe, my hearts," Mora says, pinching gold flake atop the now-bubbling potion. "And let me know if you need my help."

"We will," we promise, kissing her cheeks.

We duck around the sapphire curtain shading the doorway and into the morning sun—and into the backs of a massive crowd.

"Sorry," Hen says, slipping around two younger boys. I follow her between the richly dyed wrap dresses and gem-laden hair of Architects and Dreamwalkers, through a handful of sandy kilts and the dirt-streaked working slips of Gardeners and Weavers— lower magicians like me. It seems the entire town is converging on the shore for a glimpse of the priest and his magical boat. My bare feet press against polished brick as Hen guides us to a side street.

Not that it's much better. People cluster here, too, leaning over iron balconies to ask if the boat has arrived, placing bets on which Aterian contender will actually make a team. Our town has six of them, I think. The Mestrah declared that every upper-class Master aged sixteen to nineteen is eligible to contend, as they're in the prime of their magic and thus the heirs' strongest options. With just two moons of training left, Hen missed the cutoff by a hair.

Snippets of conversation flutter past me, and I hang hungrily on to their words.

"—thought the Mestrah was going to name Prince Kasta his heir," muses a man with rich brown skin and rings glittering across his fingers. "Strange the gods would call for a Crossing after so long. Do you think there's more to it?"

"—a human sacrifice! I thought we'd moved past that—"

"—really should clear these dirty peasants from the street," complains a woman with porcelain skin and a gaudy gold headdress. "Why are they even here? None of this is for them."

"Don't worry," Hen whispers when the woman curls her lip at me. "I have a lot of dirt on her. Want me to tell her husband about her boyfriend? Or her clients that she's only been erasing half their wrinkles so they have to hire her again the next week?"

I gape at Hen. "How do you *know* these things?"

"It's my business to know."

"It's your business to *design clothes*."

A shrug. "Rich people like to talk. I like to listen." She grins. "Hurry, we have to catch him before he gets to Numet's temple. After that, the list will be much better guarded."

Numet's temple: the grandest of Atera's three places of worship. I'd be suspicious of how she knows the priest's schedule as well, but it only makes sense a priest would want to spend time honoring our sky goddess—the deity from which our Mestrahs are descended—before taking the long ride back to Juvel.

We navigate around the baker's daughter pulling her cart of fresh breads, and past the Gemsmith's shop, though the Gemsmith herself isn't in—instead it's her wife who nods to us over displays of gold chains and jeweled dragonflies. Down an alley choked with barrels we go, where the tantalizing smells of spiced onions and cooking fish drift. Finally we stumble onto an empty street where the upper district meets the lower, and the ground changes from paving stones to packed dirt. Children play at the corner where the houses meet the road, but everyone else must be clustered toward the shore.

We hurry to the end to watch the procession coming up the road.

The priest and Royal Materialist are in front, flanked by their leopard-masked guards, and behind them, half the town. Maybe we *do* need to watch the woman. While the guards keep their gazes forward and stiff (though, who knows what they're looking at under those masks), her restless eyes shift to the streets and the celebratory flowers strung between buildings. As if she can sense Hen's irritation with her, her gaze suddenly moves to us.

"She knows," Hen says, crossing her arms. "Memorize this face, Galena. It'll be the last you see when the queen discovers you're a fraud."

"Keep your voice down," I say. "And your imaginary vendettas on hold. What do we do now?"

"How should I know? I'm just here to grab the ledger."

"All right, but I'm not used to this life of crime. Do I run at them like a religious fanatic? Scream in agony and pretend I broke my ankle?"

"Both good options. I'll see you in a few." She darts back the way we came.

"Wait!" I whisper. "Where are you going?"

And she's gone without an answer. Leaving the fate of the entire evening to me.

All right, Zahru, focus. If they were riding horses, I could have easily introduced myself as the town Whisperer and spent an excessive amount of time tending to their mounts. I could ask for the priest's blessing, but I think the guards would stop me before I could get close. They're almost here. Gods, maybe I *should* run out howling about my ankle.

I move for the street, imagining the look on my father's face when the priest's guards drag me home. *What am I always telling you, Zahru?* he'll say as the guards untie my hands. *You went in without a plan, didn't you?*

Yes, Fara. I went in without a plan.

"Are those lotus boots?" I shriek, praying the Royal Materialist is half as obsessed with going over the details of her work as a certain local one is. "Wait, you . . ." I put my hand to my heart. "You're Galena of Juvel."

The woman smiles. "Yes, I am."

"Move off," a guard snaps, shoving a spear at me.

"Oh, let the girl be," the woman says, beaming as she steps around him. "What's your name?"

Her tone is a little patronizing, but I have to say I'm impressed by her friendliness. "Zahru. I'm a huge fan of yours."

"Zahru, it's nice to meet you. I—"

"Galena," the priest grumbles.

"A minute, Mai. She's only a girl." She turns back to me, her pretty violet eyes—powdered with gold and lined with swirls of kohl—darting once down the plain linen of my dress to my bare feet. "You like fashion, Zahru?"

"Yes, *adel*. I know all about bronze eyelets and Luck shawls." Not a lie. I know too much about them, if she's really wondering.

"Another of my fine inventions. That Luck shawl got me this job." She winks, and over her shoulder I catch a flash of green.

"Where did you get the idea for the lotus boots?" I won't pretend I'm not fishing for an answer for Hen, and I think I see that green flash pause.

"On a summer walk under the stars. The palace has several beautiful pools covered with lotus flowers, and when I went wading, the idea came to me."

A whisper that sounds very much like "Lies" drifts through the crowd.

"That seems like a perfectly reasonable explanation," I say loudly.

"Did you know I'm from a town even smaller than Atera?" the woman continues, and now she has my true attention.

"You are?"

"My mother was a Materialist, but she passed when I was born. My father was a Gardener. Without her we had only his trade to live by, and I went many years of my life without any shoes at all."

I swallow and scrunch my toes in the sand. This just got much more personal than I ever intended it to, and I know I said I'd side with Hen on pretty much anything, but she didn't tell me Galena grew up without her mother, too.

"Here." She begins unlacing her boots. The crowd gasps, and when I understand what she's doing, my heart jerks. Oh gods, I hope Hen is finished—

"Take these," she says, handing me the boots, which are several times more expensive than anything I will ever own. "And remember, no matter what you're born to, you can be more."

She smiles and starts off, and I can only stare after her, my heart like a dragonfly in my chest. I should probably be taking an important life lesson away from this about honesty and hard work, but all I can think of is how similar our stories are, and how she now travels on a glass boat at the side of a priest. It has to be a sign. That I'm meant to do this, and everything will work out, and maybe it will be even more amazing than I first imagined.

It's only after the last guard has passed and the crowd wanders in, ogling the lotus boots and whispering, that I remember I'm on a mission. Someone asks to touch the shoes, and under normal circumstances I might have stayed and shared them, but now I clutch them to my chest and dash to the end of the street where I saw Hen disappear. My blood thrums through my body, fitful and restless. I pass through the alley and back into the upper district, around a corner—and right into the crossed arms of Hen.

"Gods!" I yelp, juggling the boots. "Hen! Did you get it?"

Her brown eyes narrow. "It's done."

I scream and throw my arms around her. I know exactly what she's going to say next, but I'm too thrilled to care. We're leaving. We're actually leaving Atera to go to the palace, where there are trees that bloom jewels and golden rooms as big as towns. We'll eat all the chocolate we can stomach. We'll trail mysterious strangers and find secret passages and witness at least one spectacular rescue, because in all of the travelers' best stories, someone is always saving *someone*.

And when we return, Hen and I will bring back with us a memory just like our mothers'. Maybe it'll be the last one we have before Hen leaves at harvest. *Or maybe*, I think, squeezing the boots, *it will be the first of many*.

"You are touching me with *her shoes*," Hen complains.

"Sorry," I say, pulling back. But I can't stop from grinning. "I did what the mission called for."

A sigh. "You were really very good."

"Convincing?"

"I suppose." But even with her enemy's contraband in my hands, she can't stop a small smile. She gives my shoulders a shake. "We're going to the banquets."

I let out another squeal, and this time she joins me.

"There's just one thing left to do," she says, a new gleam in her eyes.

"Don't tell me you're going after Galena *now*."

"Oh, she'll get hers, but there are more immediate needs at hand." Her smile quirks. "It's time for phase two."

I blink. "There's a phase two?"

"Yes. One your delicate conscience won't be able to handle." She smirks. "Say goodbye to your father, and I'll find you as soon as I can."

I'M very quiet as I slip in through the stable door. But as anxious as I am to admit to the man who raised me that I've turned into a petty con artist, my *fara* is not inside. The animals stir in their stalls; a camel chews noisily on her cud. My father must be in the pasture.

Gods, please let him give me his blessing.

I flex my grip on the small sack I'm holding and start down the aisle.

Fara's veterinary clinic is the biggest stable in town, not because we have the most money, but because we need the space. The Mestrah allows us free rent as long as we prioritize his soldiers' horses on the rare occasion they come through. Half the stalls are reserved for large animals like cattle, gazelles, and camels. We've converted the other half into keeps for small animals like cats, dogs, falcons—sometimes monkeys, when needed. Some of the animals simply need boarding while their owners travel, while others need medical care. Most of them have quite an opinion about being left here like, well, animals. But Fara is kind and patient, and I'd like to think I am, too, and after a day most of their complaints have subsided.

Twig girl, snorts a cow in the second stall. *This food. Bad.*

Except for the cows. Who seem to think they're entitled to royal treatment, and who find the stable and its caretakers infinitely lacking.

"I don't have time for you right now," I say. "It's fresh. Just eat what I gave you."

Sensitive thing, thinks her companion, eyeing me.

Human on bad food, too, remarks the first. *Can't make grain, can't make anything*.

I grit my teeth. "For the last time, you're on a *diet*. Your masters specifically told me not to give you honey."

The second snorts. *Always on diet when here. Food bad as chewed cud.*

"Oh, you ungrateful—"

"You know it's no use arguing," Fara says, squeezing in through the far doorway and making me jump. My father is dressed today in his usual working slip, a sandy fabric that nearly matches his skin in the mild winter months but is now several shades lighter than his summer tan. A herding dog wiggles in his arms, one leg wrapped in palm leaves where a salve covers a scorpion sting. The other three legs thrash when she sees me.

Human! Human human human, can I see her? Please please please! I need down. Down down!

She licks Fara's face with the last request, and he smiles and strokes her side. "Yes, you did very well. We'll go back outside again soon."

No, down! Human! Play! Play—cat? Cat! Cat cat!

My heart clenches as Fara lowers the dog into a converted stall. As with most magic in our world, his abilities have faded with age and use, the same way muscles weaken over time. Fara was lucky to make it twenty-nine years with his. That's the only advantage of the lesser magics: they take far less of a toll on our bodies, and so we can use them longer. But many would agree ten years as Orkena's most powerful Firespinner far outshines thirty as Orkena's best Whisperer.

Two moons ago, Fara went deaf to the animals completely, and they stopped being able to understand him as well. And while it hasn't affected his medical expertise, he can no longer ask his patients what ails them or sense their fear, and so the weight of the stable has slowly shifted to me.

"You've been gone awhile," Fara says, wiping his hands on an old rag. "Was the market very busy?"

"I—yes," I say, hastily handing over the bag. "But I found everything we needed. I even got acacia and aloe. And that snake bite salve we liked so well."

Fara stares. "Zahru, that salve is expensive. We can make do with the honey poultice."

"It's all right. Hen covered it."

A small lie. The lotus boots covered it. Hen wanted me to get rid of them, so I did.

Fara tsks. "She shouldn't have. She and her mother have already done far too much for us."

This is the point where I should move on to the reason I splurged on so many fine medicines, but being the awkward and half-ashamed daughter I am, I just stand there while Fara takes the bag to the dusty cabinet. I'm still not sure how to tell him what I've done. Oddly it's not even the priest-conning part of it I'm worried about. It's that I can see how diligently he's working despite the excited shouts outside the stable; how focused he is even as the rest of Atera leaves their work to blow horns in the streets. He isn't even annoyed with it, just . . . accepting. To him, our place is here, and the idea of me keeping company with Dreamwalkers and Airweavers is absurd at best. I couldn't stand to hear him say I don't belong with them at the palace.

But more than that, I don't want him to see how badly I want to leave.

"*Zahru*," Fara says in the tone he uses when he's been trying to get my attention for some time. He's holding a jar of numbing cream from the sack, another small treasure I splurged on.

"Yes?"

"Are you sad about Hen's invitation?"

My stomach clenches. I wasn't even sure he knew she'd been invited. "No. Well, I was at first, but then . . ."

"I'm sorry about it, too," Fara says, fidgeting with the cream. "I feel . . . it's my fault. If you had your mother's magic, maybe—"

"Fara!" My chest constricts, and I rush to him, shaken he believes *that's* the reason I'd be sad about not going. Fara has always taken pride in our abilities, even if our work is not as celebrated as others'. And it's not like he had any control over my fate—I inherited his Whisperer magic the same way I inherited my mother's fair skin and amber eyes.

"Don't say that," I say, leaning my head against his broad chest. "Our work is important, too."

He's quiet a moment, his hand warm on my back. Then he pulls me gently away and holds up the cream. "You're going to try to get in, aren't you?"

Heat flushes my neck. "I . . ."

"That was a very long hug, and these are a lot of expensive products."

How does he *do* that? "I was really close to telling you, I promise."

"Zahru, what if you get caught?"

"Hen looked into it. They'll just escort us out. It's only bad if you try to sneak in as a contender."

"And if you're in Juvel? Will they send you home?"

"Hen will be with me the whole time. She'll buy our passage back if they won't return us." I press my hands together. "Please, Fara? It's just a night. I'll be back in time for supper tomorrow, and then I'll be here. Forever." I don't mean to say that last word aloud, or in the ominous tone a priest would use to impart a deadly omen, but Fara understands. He kisses my head and sighs.

"You are my world, *kar-a*. I want you to be safe." His smile is sad. "I also want you to be happy. It's only for a night? You'll be protected?"

"They'll have guards. And literally all of the country's top magicians will be within a kilometer of us. If we're not safe there, we're not safe anywhere."

A grunt. Leave it to my father to consider even that might not be enough. "All right. You have my blessing."

I squeal and hug him again. "Thank you, Fara! I'll bring you something from the royal city."

He shakes his head. "Just bring *yourself* back." He pauses to think. "Though I wouldn't mind some chocolate, if you can manage it."

I smile. "Of course."

I help Fara put away the remaining salves, excitement bouncing through me. My fake name is on the ledger. I have Fara's blessing—now I just need to hear from Hen. But just as I'm starting to worry that "phase two" will involve me negotiating her release from jail, quick footsteps beat outside the stable, and she comes bouncing in.

"Zahru!" she wheezes.

She's in a green *jole*, her arms bare and her deep beige skin glowing with pearl dust. Swirling golden circles—Numet's symbol—curl around her bicep, and her short hair jingles with beads of gold and emeralds. She carries a bundle of garnet-red cloth wrapped over something that chimes as she moves.

"You look amazing," I say.

"Storeroom!" she says, jogging past me without a glance.

"Is everything all right?"

"No time to chat. Phase two is complete, and they're boarding the boat."

She disappears behind the storage room's tan curtain, and I nearly trip on the water jug as I hurry after her. "As in, boarding *now*?"

"Strip!"

"Has it been an hour already?" I pull my arms out of my sleeves and tug the slip off, while Hen sets the red bundle on a grain sack. "Wait. How did phase two take *you* an hour?"

"Less talking, more dressing!" Hen gathers the red dress into a loop and gestures for me to raise my arms, then pushes the bundle over my head. The shining fabric spills down my body, flaring from red to gold with the light. It's sleeveless like Hen's, but the top gathers in the center instead of the side, forming rippling pleats that overlay the dress all the way to the floor.

"Hen, this is . . . stunning," I say, looking over my shoulder. The back opens to the base of my spine, where fine chains connect the fabric on either side. Hen flits behind me and mends a torn chain with a press of her fingers.

"It's boring, is what it is," she says. "But Mora wouldn't let me dress you in only river reeds, so this is what I have to work with."

"Is this fire silk?"

"Look straight ahead."

I do. Hen grabs one of the things that had been bundled in the dress—a thin brush and a jar of black pigment—and holds my jaw with her free hand. "Close your eyes."

"I already lined them," I say as the brush kisses my eyelid.

"Mm hmm."

The brush trails out to the edge of my eye and loops beside it.

"You better not be drawing anything gross."

Hen snickers.

"Hen!"

"I'm not!"

The brush retracts, then starts on my other eyelid.

"There's no phase three, right?" I ask. "Remember when I asked if I'd have to prove I was a Potionmaker? And you didn't answer?"

This side of my face doesn't get the same loop as the first. Hen has me look up and starts lining the bottom lid.

"The others had to prove their identities at the temple," she says. "We don't."

"What does that mean?" The brush lifts, and I blink down at her. "You . . . made a deal with someone?"

Hen considers this, a small smile in her lips. "Yes?"

"See, when you give me an answer that sounds like a question, it makes me think you're lying."

"When you ask me a question you already know the answer to, it makes me want to lie."

"You blackmailed someone."

Hen just grins and lets down my hair, threading crystals into the brown waves around my face, then lifts a delicate tangle of chains from the grain sack. It separates into three fine loops in her fingers, a garnet pendant dangling from the place they connect. A protection rune flashes from the gem's face. I realize what it is just as she lowers it, and I grab her wrists.

"I can't accept this," I say.

"But it's yours."

"No, it was my mother's, and now it's *your* mother's, after mine gave it to her on her *deathbed*."

"Mora wants you to wear it." She secures the last hairpin so the jewel dangles by my left eye, and starts taming flyaway stands of my hair. A new wave of appreciation for everything she's done floods through me.

"I'll take care of it," I say.

"I know."

She grabs my hand and tows me from the storage room. Fara turns from where he's mixing a poultice, and smiles as he takes us in.

"You look royal, girls," he says. "But is everything all right? Did I hear the boat is boarding *now*?"

"Yes, Fara, sorry," I say, darting to peck his cheek. "I love you. See you tomorrow!"

"Love you, too," he calls.

I think he might also say something about making good choices,

22

but we're already out the door, me holding a hand to my head chain and Hen holding her skirt. The desert sun burns hot on our shoulders.

"*Rie*," I swear. "I can't believe we're doing this. I can't believe we're actually going!" I laugh as we turn a corner, as fleet as antelope. "Can you even imagine what the *contenders* are going through? I'm nervous just to watch! I bet they'll be judged on their every move. One wrong smile and that's it, no eternal glory for them."

Hen shrugs. "But also no untimely death."

"Death?" We swerve to avoid a mother holding a baby. "The royal siblings aren't supposed to *kill* each other, are they?"

"Oh, no. But I've been reading all about past contests, and sometimes death just happened. Rogue assassins, hungry hyenas, starvation . . ."

My stomach tightens in pity. I guess I assumed royalty would have divine protection against such things, especially considering the way people have been celebrating the contenders all week. Everyone seems much more concerned with the prizes for being chosen: their name in history, a suite at the palace. I never stopped to consider why the prizes were so grand.

"Gods, and they're out there at least a week, right?"

"If they don't get hopelessly lost."

"That would be awful," I say as we cross into the upper district. The road ahead is packed with people, and Hen tugs me toward a gap at the side. "Can you imagine? Going through all this fuss and stress, just to get buried under a sandstorm?"

"Well, they *will* have spells and such. But just think." Hen's eyes flash, and we press between a man in a brown tunic and a pigtailed girl. "If Gallus gets chosen, we can picture him being chased by all kinds of rabid things."

I snicker at the thought of my ex pompously fighting a rattlesnake while trying to keep his hair perfect. "I hope something bites him in the rear while he's sleeping."

"I hope it bites him in the—"

"Shh," I say, giggling and clasping my hand over her mouth. The ground under our feet has shifted from hot brick to cool wood. "You can't say that here. At least wait until we're on the boat."

The mesh of people thickens as we excuse ourselves through, until it suddenly yields to the dock, a long structure of waterproof wood and iron posts, upon which ropes tether all sizes of boats to the shore. Guards stand in a wide semicircle around the priest and his assistants, giving them space. The nearest guard takes one look at our elaborate *joles* and nods us through. The crowd grumbles in envy. I admit the attention sends a shiver of satisfaction down my spine—I'm usually the one watching everyone else leave.

Galena stands at the base of a wide plank, and it takes me a moment to realize that plank doesn't lead to the glass boat. It leads to one made of a strange wood instead, something swirled with black and golden tones that looks like an enormous version of the giraffe from Mora's collection. A deep red canopy shades its deck, under which dozens of people mingle in their finest, their small crowns of gold and gemmed rings glinting like sparks in the sun. I recognize a young man who tutored Hen in writing, and the Gemsmith—no wonder her wife is tending her wares. The plank to the glass boat is by the priest instead, blocked by a particularly burly guard.

The Mestrah must have sent one boat to carry spectators and another for the contenders. I'm slightly disappointed Hen and I won't be riding on glass, but honestly I'd be happy to take a leaky canoe at this point.

"Here's something we didn't think about," I mutter, looping my arm through Hen's. "The entire town is staring at us right now, including the Apothecarist I just bought salves from and your nemesis, who might remember *handing me her shoes* this morning. The punishment for getting caught is seriously 'go away,' right?"

"Don't worry. No one's going to recognize you. Your makeup has been done correctly for once."

I snort. "I can do my makeup correctly."

"Mm hmm." She adjusts her hair and smooths a pleat near my hip. "Like I said, they don't care about spectators. They only strip your name away and shame your family if you try to sneak in as a contender. So relax, you're wrinkling the silk."

I exhale, trying to draw on even a sliver of Hen's confidence. I don't need to be so nervous. This will either work or it won't, and if it doesn't, at least I will have tried. Maybe I'll even gain some semblance of infamy. I think I'd like people looking at me sidelong, worried I might do something unexpected and daring at any moment.

"Cutting it close, aren't we?" the priest says, his usual scowl in place. The words inked into his shoulders glisten with embedded gold. "Lucky for you, we're all happy to stand around in the heat while you decide whether you'll bother to show."

"Apologies, *adel*," Hen says, bowing with her arm over her chest. I do the same. "We lost track of time."

"Which of you is Hen, and which is Lia?"

"I'm Hen," Hen says.

Galena steps forward with a smile. She nods to me as well, but Hen must not be exaggerating about my makeup, because all Galena's gaze holds is curiosity, thank the gods. She's still shoeless, and I still have an undefinable urge to hug her.

"Hen, I'm Galena," she says, nodding in greeting.

"I know who you are," Hen says, crossing her arms. I clear my throat, and Hen mercifully says nothing more.

Galena raises a brow but gestures to the plank. "Would you come with me?"

I have to bite the inside of my cheek to keep from screaming *Yes!* I can't believe we did it. After the uncertainty of this week, after all our worrying, now we can finally relax. We're here. We're *here*, and with Hen having already done . . . whatever she did . . . to get our identities cleared, there are no more hurdles. We're going to the palace, and it'll be a night that's just ours; a treasure no one can take away.

A memory I can unfold anytime I'm missing her, and remember what we used to be.

We start for the plank—and the priest grabs my arm.

"Where do you think you're going?" he says.

My heart lurches. He knows. Gods, he knows, and of course he'd wait until the worst possible moment to reveal it—

"That boat's for the spectators," he says. "The contenders are over here."

III

FOR a moment, all the sound leaves the world. I'm sure I've misheard him. Or perhaps panicked my way into a subconscious state, where things mean the opposite of what they are.

"I'm sorry," I say. "I think you're confused."

His orange eyes narrow. This close up, I can see his pupils are slit like a cat's. "You are Lia, daughter of Rai?"

I swallow. "Yes."

"Then I think you need to learn to read. All elite Masters your age qualify for contention. It was written in the first line of your invitation."

The heat is like a fist around my throat. He thinks I'm a Master. I don't know how he could think that, but I have a dreadful, sinking feeling that Hen missed something when she added my name to the list.

"Is there a problem?" Hen says, popping up at my side.

"I've qualified for contention!" I say too joyfully. "Because I'm a Master. Isn't that great?"

All the confidence blanches from Hen's face. I'm not sure I've ever seen her afraid before, and it scares me more than what the priest is saying.

"Oh," she says weakly. "Because Lia was—" She coughs. "Are you sure? I'm really certain the invitation didn't say she was eligible."

Because Lia—my mother—*was a Master*. The heat pushes into my gut. Hen assured me they wouldn't look at the names again

27

this late in the process, but it seems very much like someone *did*, and sweat beads my neck as the priest checks the ledger.

"Hmm." He frowns. "Yes, there was something strange with your name. It was out of order, so it must have been added last minute. But my contact at the capital confirmed you're eligible. You must have gotten the wrong scroll." He mimes tossing a handful of confetti. "Sorry, surprise, and congratulations. Say goodbye, and let's go."

"Um, actually—" I start.

"She'll be right there!" Hen says before the priest can turn around.

"What are you doing?" I hiss as she pulls me aside. "We need to confess *now*. I can't be in the contention pool!"

"Do you remember when I mentioned eternal shame and your name being stripped for people who lie about being contenders?"

"Yes."

"That's what this is."

"That's not what this was *supposed* to be!"

"I know!" Hen pulls on the braids in her hair, eyes watering. If she cries, I will lose it entirely. "I'm sorry. Gods, I'm so sorry, I don't know what happened! Even if he checked your name, I thought— whoever looked at the records should have seen you were way too young to be your mother. End of story, you go on as a spectator. They must be so busy, they didn't look at her birthday—"

"What am I going to do?"

People are muttering and eyeing us. We're delaying too long, and now they aren't simply curious to see the boats off, but to see why this girl they don't recognize is holding up the glass boat. If I run, would they let me through?

"You can't run," Hen says, practically reading my mind. "I'm sorry, but you can't. Those guards will catch you in a second, and the contending families take this really seriously. If they think you're trying to sabotage their chances, they might hurt you, Zahru. They might hurt Fara."

"That's unsurprisingly not helpful!"

"I know! But listen, this can still be all right." She squeezes my shoulders, and I might've been encouraged by the calm settling over her face if I weren't imagining a mob descending on the stable. "I know this seems bad, but the proving part of the evening is done. The next step is the banquets. You know enough about potions to be passable, so as long as you're not bragging about it, you should be fine. And if you have to, faint. No heir's going to pick someone who can't even handle the stress of a banquet."

I exhale, trying to regain control of my nerves. Hen's right. No one has any reason to believe I'm not who I say I am, and the biggest danger now is actually being chosen for a team, for which my odds were low even if I *was* my mother. I can be a sparkling conversationalist. Then all I need to worry about is not drawing royal attention, and everything should be fine.

"All right," I say, swallowing. "Lie to people, faint if necessary. I can do that."

A tap on my shoulder makes me jump.

"Would you like me to announce you to the Mestrah as the reason we're late," the priest growls, "or would you like the chance to do it yourself?"

I turn at once. "Coming! Sorry."

I cast one more panicked look at Hen, who watches me with

something between guilt and helplessness, not even flinching when Galena touches her arm to guide her up the plank. The distance between us grows like a chasm. I know we're only going to be separated for a few hours, but this feels like a warning from the gods; a crack on the wrist for daring to want something above my station.

I move up the plank, feeling like I've crossed into the wrong side of a dream.

Hen watches me from the other side, her hands on the rail, reassurance in her eyes. The servants blow long, curved oxen horns, the sound vibrating through the glass in a dangerous hum, and the crowd bellows as the contenders cluster beside me on the rail. The boat shifts back from the shore. My home slides away bit by bit, faster and faster, and I'm even able to fake a smile and wave—until we slip past the rise where Fara's stable sits, and two familiar figures wave goodbye.

As the shoreline slips by, I think of Mora.

Hen's mother has many different strategies for dealing with stress. Some are as simple as a breathing exercise, and some involve plotting a cold revenge over many months until the customer who wronged her is sorry they ever lived. I've decided to employ my own strategy by embracing this as just another part of my tale. This is, after all, exactly the kind of unlucky circumstance that starts off the best of the travelers' stories, and just when it seems the hero is doomed to a tragic end, they're rescued by a brilliant twist of fate or gorgeous newcomer. I'd happily settle for being rescued by Hen, though I wouldn't mind the gorgeous newcomer, either. I just need to let the tale play out as it will.

And so I've found a place along the rail, beneath the misting fabric of the blue canopy and out of the way of the contenders, where I can stand and take in everything I thought I'd only ever experience in dreams. The gentle sway of the boat, the feel of a river breeze in my hair. The smooth glass under my fingers, rippling with bursts of reflected sunlight. Fish dart beneath the deck like jewels, and crocodiles swim like black fissures, alive and incredible below my feet. Even the desert seems more mysterious and infinite here, its low plateaus stretching to the horizon in every direction. When we pass a town, people cluster the banks to shout wishes of luck. I can almost believe I'm supposed to be here.

There's just one problem Hen and I didn't account for. When I arrive at the palace, I'll be one of hundreds, easily lost in the crowd. But here, I'm one of *seven*. Which wouldn't concern me so much, if one of those seven wasn't Gallus.

"Something to drink, *adel*?" a servant asks, offering me a tray bearing a single bronze chalice.

"Yes, thank you," I say, admiring the tiny white flowers on its surface. It smells like vanilla, and I'm taking a sip when the servant adds, "The boy in green wanted you to know he sent me."

And thus ends my happy time alone. But I knew I wouldn't be able to go the whole evening without speaking to anyone, and it *would* be good to get in some practice as my alter ego before I have to face one of the heirs. I scan the deck for the boy in green, looking past a petite girl with russet-brown skin and a pale, rosy-cheeked boy at the rail, past a silver-haired girl who stands at the prow, and finally risk a glance at the two boys sitting with Gallus on the benches. I'm snickering that one of his friends thinks I'm worthy of a drink when I realize the boy in green *is* Gallus, and I spit the juice over the rail. Gods, I can't believe that's still his move, or that this is the second time he's used it on me. I slam the drink back on the tray.

"Sorry. Can you tell him I'm not interested? And maybe that I have a contagious disease?"

The servant's eyes widen. "A contagious disease?"

"Like heatstrain. Or magipox. Oh! Or moldmouth!"

Her eyes shift to the drink I put back. "Of—of course, *adel* . . ."

Except it's too late. Gallus has pushed to his feet, obviously confused as to how anyone could resist his charms, and is making his way over. I pray to every god I can think of that his friends will laugh and call him back, or maybe the boat will capsize, but the gods must not be on speaking terms with me right now, because he keeps coming, unhindered.

This is not how this was supposed to happen. I've made it five moons pretending Gallus never existed, and I'd planned to go the rest of my life without talking to him again. Well, maybe not *ever* again, but definitely not until I'd done something fantastic and memorable, like this very event, after which I'd show up at his house and throw a cup of wine in his face, because that's what important people do to people who told them they're worthless.

I mean, Gallus didn't use that word exactly. But he said he needed to get "serious" and invest himself in relationships with marriageable women, by which he means girls who have interesting futures and "real" magic. And certainly not girls who thought that's what they had until he told them they didn't.

"I don't know what you've heard about me," Gallus says, swaggering to the rail. "But honestly, I just wanted to invite you to sit—"

I pull away and start for the front of the boat. The other two boys watch me, amused.

"Hey," Gallus says.

I keep moving. Gallus clearly doesn't recognize me under all this makeup—he'd have a lot more to say if he did—and if I can make it to the silver-haired girl, maybe we can form an instant and intimidating alliance that will scare Gallus off for good. Considering what could happen to me if I'm caught, I don't *think* Gallus would go so low as to reveal me to the priest, but I've been wrong about him before.

"Wait, were you at Kay's last night?" Gallus says, jogging to my side. "I feel like I'd remember you, but if I was a jerk or something . . ."

I imagine he's talking about some upper district party, and the urge to tell him that yes, he's a jerk always, dances at the tip of my tongue. Gods, will anyone notice if I jump over the side? I bite the edge of my thumb, reasoning that at least revealing my identity that way would mean not having this conversation, when Gallus pulls my hand from my mouth.

"*Zahru?*" he whispers.

He looks stricken, and I know it has nothing to do with the embarrassment of sending me a drink. But maybe I think more clearly with a dose of panic in my veins, because I suddenly determine I'm not going to let him be the one who ruins this. After all, *he* doesn't know I'm not a Master yet, or that I didn't get an invitation on some miraculous recommendation. And in actuality this is the perfect comeback for how he broke things off, because I'm definitely the last person he thought he'd see here.

"Oh," I say, barely glancing up. "Hello. Whatever your name is."

"Zahru, you know who I am. What are you doing here?"

He pulls me to the side, out of earshot of the others, which I have to say is a relief. At least he hasn't totally transformed into a self-righteous snob.

"Oh, you know," I say. "Just checking out the competition."

"What? *How?*" I might have been offended if I wasn't drawing so much pleasure from the shock on his face. "No, it has to be a mistake. Does the priest know you're only a Whisperer?"

"Don't be a cod," I say, like my heart isn't hammering in my chest. "Of course he knows."

"And you still came? Did you even think this through?"

"What's that supposed to mean?"

"This isn't one of your little fantasies, Zahru. The desert is dangerous. There are sandstorms, thieves, wild animals . . ."

If only I could believe his concern was for me and not what I lack. "And I don't stand a chance out there with all you 'real' magicians, right?"

"I'm serious. Just because we aren't—" He looks past me, and my heart jerks with the hope that maybe being away from me has been hard for him, too, when he lowers his voice and I realize he's just making sure no one else is listening. "Just because we aren't together doesn't mean I don't care about you."

My heart pinches. "Don't say that too loud. Your friends might hear."

"Zahru—"

"Anyway, as flattered as I am that you think I could be chosen, you don't have to worry about it. I know I don't stand a chance. I just want to see the palace."

"Ah."

I know he's itching to say he never thought I'd be chosen. Gallus never could resist an opportunity to lecture me about how naïve my dreams are, but he must have decided it's not worth pursuing, because he stays silent. I really want to leave it at this and let us devolve into awkward silence, but it's just occurred to me I can't have him going back to his friends and telling them who I am. If my real name circulates, the priest might decide he's irritated enough to look into it.

"And stop calling me Zahru," I whisper, eyeing said priest, who sits with his servants in the clear glass cabin. "I go by Lia now."

"*Ah*," he says again, understanding washing over his face. He presses his hand over his eyes, and exhales. "This is one of Hen's schemes."

"Yes, and you absolutely can't tell anyone about this, Gallus. I'm serious. They could whip me in the square, or lock Fara and me in prison, or . . . or worse!"

"So you *do* sometimes think of consequences."

"Of course I do! This wasn't supposed to go this way. Hen was trying to get me in with the spectators. But we used my mother's name, and they didn't check the dates . . ."

Gallus sighs, and I wish I could take the relief on his face as him knowing how to help me, but I know he's just glad he's made sense of how a Whisperer is at his level. He leans casually against the rail, his swagger returned with his control of the situation.

"I'm happy to do that for you," he says, his tone genuine. "Really. Just relax, be elusive if the heirs ask you questions, and this could be a great night for you."

"Thank you," I say, which is all I can manage with that kind of advice. But I am grateful he'll keep my secret, so I hold back any other retorts.

The water laps against the boat. A pair of spotted geese cackle at each other near the shore, and for reasons I don't understand, Gallus stays by my side.

"You look nice, by the way," he says.

I force a smile and study my hands. I hope he's not waiting for a compliment in return, because that's more than I'm capable of at the moment.

"Sorry I panicked there," he says, shifting. "It's just . . . the competition is really stiff for these positions. That goes for me, too. The chances of being chosen . . ."

"You'll do fine," I say, sighing. I hate that I know him well enough to know he's nervous, and even more that I can't stand to see him that way. "You're talented and smart. If the heirs are looking for a Firespinner, you're the best option they have."

He looks over. I keep my eyes on the bank, but from the corner of my vision I see him smile.

"Thank you," he says. "You know, I never meant to hurt you. It's just . . . you knew we had to grow up sometime, right?"

I push back from the rail. "I have to go."

He nods slowly. "All right. It was good to see you."

I turn, exhaling. If I survived *that*, maybe I really will be fine tonight. I'm starting toward the prow and the silver-haired girl when Gallus calls out again.

"Er, Lia?"

I stiffen but look over my shoulder. Standing there in his finest, I can almost remember him framed in the light of the stable door, breathless from running, from his impatience to see me.

"Maybe don't talk to anyone tonight," he says.

"That's very supportive. Thank you."

"I just mean . . . you know. Too candidly? Don't tell the princess you thought she'd be more mystical or something."

He may have a point, but coming from Gallus it only reminds me of the many ways in which he finds me lacking, and my bruised heart aches with believing that maybe he's right. *What a desperate move*, his eyes seem to say. *How sad she still can't accept her place.* But I've already wasted enough time fretting about what Gallus thinks, and I bury the bruise deeper and pretend again there was never anything between us. Today I am a Potionmaker and one of Orkena's elite, and no condescending Firespinner is going to ruin this night for me.

I square my shoulders and move on.

Gallus is soon shoved from my mind when I notice the others pointing at something I can't see at the front of the boat. Sometime during that conversation we entered the royal city, for people cluster the riverbanks now in the finest attire I've ever seen: gossamer shawls and crowns of red ivy; gold bangles and bright silks dripping with crystal. Shining collars flash from the necks of dogs and cats, and beyond them white-sand estates tower like thunderclouds, their iron balconies framing potted palms and flowering trees. Then we float around a bend, and I'm not the only one who gasps.

It's like spending your whole life knowing only candlelight, then looking upon your first wildfire. The royal palace is a sprawling giant against the sunset. Pale and tall, its many stone spires are the carved bodies of the gods: Numet's fiery torch juts above the palace's center, her eyes windows to the east; her brother Rie, the god of death, guards the west, his great wings folded. The nine lesser gods stand around them, gilded in real jewels. Apos, god of deceit; Rachella, goddess of love. Oka, Valen, and Sabil, gods of judgment, fate, and magic. Talqo, Aquila, and Tyda, goddesses of healing, learning, and patience. Brazen Cybil, goddess of war. Her falcon companion sits upon her gloved hand, wings stretched—his metal feathers are the same ones our soldiers wear on their armor.

Gold shines along the edges of the perimeter wall, and as our boat draws near, the protection spells carved into the wall hum and glow. A square tunnel rumbles open before us. Down a long, narrow passage we float, until we finally emerge within a grand indoor dock glittering with torches. A tiled shaft of porcelain and gold guides us between breathtaking trees with small, ruby-red leaves and brilliant white flowers, to a redwood platform flanked by guards. There are more plants in this entire enclosed dock than I've ever seen outside.

I'm so busy trying to take it all in, I don't notice the wall has slid shut behind us until a loud *boom* shakes me from my stupor.

The wooden boat did not follow. The spectators are going to a different dock.

Breathe, Zahru, I think as our boat slides to a stop. *Now you just need to blend in.*

"Welcome to Juvel," the priest says as the contenders jostle toward the plank. I linger toward the back, grateful even Gallus is too preoccupied to notice I'm here. "This way, please. And be quick about it—*someone* has us running behind."

His orange eyes lock on me, and I quickly find a point in the distance to focus on as everyone looks over their shoulders. So much for blending in. But soon we're moving again, and the contenders are nervously practicing small, complicated tricks that might prove their control and give them an edge. A boy curls a visible ball of wind above his palm; the silver-haired girl freezes her breath into an icy knife. I try not to watch with too much wonder, but aside from my time with Gallus, I don't often get to see higher magics at work. Anyone at this skill level leaves Atera soon after they master their craft. They are our soldiers and architects, palace entertainers and protectors. I can't help but find what they do beautiful.

When I catch myself watching Gallus shift a flame from blue to white, I turn my attention to the garden.

"This is how the evening will go," the priest says as we step between two of the strange trees and into a tall, triangular hallway. "You'll attend three banquets, one for each heir. As the eldest, Prince Kasta has priority in who he picks, so you will meet with him first. Once he chooses his escort, the rest of you will be taken to meet Prince Jet, and lastly Princess Sakira."

"One escort?" I whisper, a little too hopefully. I thought each heir was supposed to have two, but if they've changed it, I'm liking my chances for surviving this even more.

"The second is always a Healer," the silver-haired girl whispers, with a kind smile that makes me regret not talking to her sooner. "They're chosen in a different ceremony."

"Thanks," I say.

"*If* you're selected," the priest says, casting me a warning glance, "your name will be announced to the spectators, and you'll be prepared for the race. You'll meet the Mestrah first, who may award your team the advantage of starting with the sacrifice if he believes your pairing to be the strongest. Those of you who are not chosen by the end of the evening will be dismissed to enjoy the rest of the night. Just remember the boats depart exactly one hour after the festivities tomorrow, and if you're not on them, you'll be finding your own way home."

Of course he's looking at me for that last line.

"And do the heirs pick the sacrifice as well?" says the petite girl.

All remaining whispers fall silent. The priest's lips twitch.

"That choice is for the gods to make, not our esteemed heirs. In prior contests, it has always been one of the Forsaken, so there is no need to concern yourselves."

Murmurs ripple through the group, and my chest twinges. The Forsaken are those who were born in Orkena without magic— an indication of the gods' disapproval. It's a rare occurrence in a country brimming with magical blood, but any child who fails to show aptitude by age eleven must report to a dedicated orphanage, where they stay until they reach sixteen summers. After that, they'll have to decide whether to risk crossing the desert to start a life elsewhere, or attempt to find work in Orkena. Some will find kindness in the outlying towns, from people like Fara and me who know them to be as capable as anyone else. But many Orkenians believe Forsaken incompetent or unclean, and some towns—like the capital—won't employ them at all. And even though I know this is what the gods demand, it still seems unfair that a person who's already lost so much should have to literally lose their life, too.

The priest scans the contenders for further questions, but an uncomfortable energy pulses around us now, and when no one else speaks, he continues.

"You'll have a moment to compose yourselves in this next room before being introduced to Prince Kasta. He may ask you a question or two. Then he'll either dismiss you to enjoy refreshments or ask you to sit at the royal table. You can imagine which is the preferable outcome."

"Are our chances gone if we're dismissed?" asks one of Gallus's friends.

"Not entirely. The prince can send for you at any time and will likely sift through many contenders before coming to a final decision."

Gallus clears his throat. "But he can choose an escort whenever he wants, yes?"

We all know what the priest is really saying. If we aren't chosen to sit at the table, we're basically just there to eat the food.

"Yes," the priest says, not kindly. "The whole point of the evening is to select Orkena's best magicians. The strongest will be picked. The rest of you will go home. I suggest you make a good first impression." He raises his voice. "Any other questions?"

No one with the fear of the gods in their heart would dare ask something else. The priest smirks, satisfied, and we move down the hallway again, the only sound our sandaled feet on the stone.

Soon we enter a much smaller room, though by much smaller, I mean it's the size of Fara's entire stable. It has no windows and only a single plant in each corner, potted versions of the grasses from the dock. I imagine the room would be loud and overflowing with hopefuls if we hadn't been late—there must be a few hundred in the next room if our small town alone sent seven. Now only two contenders wait by the room's other door, a girl holding a blooming rose and a boy who stands head and shoulders above everyone else. An old woman fusses over the girl's hair as a guard ushers the boy through the exit. His name—Marcus, son of Bernab—is announced in the next room, and a burst of nerves simmers under my skin. It's just occurred to me that I'm about to speak to the Mestrah's children, who, with traces of Numet's blood in their veins, are the closest I'll ever get to the gods. Prince Kasta won't rise into divinity unless he wins the Crossing, of course, but I'm unreasonably panicked he'll have some innate sense for detecting liars.

But I can hardly decide what to do about that when ten servants stream into the room, one brushing a streak of dust from Gallus's tunic, another fixing a lily in a girl's hair. A third attacks my face with cotton and some kind of powder. While she's distracting me, another servant dusts my shoulders and chest with flecks of gold, and before I can ask if it's real, the servant in front of me grabs the jewel of my head chain.

"No!" I say as she moves to straighten it. "I want it like that. It's the style."

The servant stares at me, probably waiting for me to admit I'm joking, then shrugs and moves on to the next person.

"This one next," the old woman croaks, pulling Gallus to the front of the line. At some point in the chaos, the girl she was helping must have been called in. Gallus fidgets with his tunic, but with his square shoulders and proud chin, he already looks like he belongs at royalty's side. If he hadn't told me earlier I'm better off not speaking, I might have reassured him he'd be fine. The old woman sends him through the gold-plated doorway with an impatient flick of her wrist.

"Gallus, son of Bomani," comes the announcement on the other side of the wall.

"You, back of line," the old woman barks at me.

Well then.

I sway behind the others, rising up on my toes, trying to see around the white curtain separating our room from the party. Gallus has not been in there very long before the petite girl is called. A few more minutes, and the silver-haired girl steps through. Then a boy with sparks between his fingers. Then the first of Gallus's friends, then the second, and then I'm standing before the old woman, who straightens the top of my dress and brushes something off my chin with her finger before going for the jewel on the head chain.

"No," I say, jerking back. "That's how I want it."

"You look a fool," she snaps. "I fix it."

"Don't fix it, just leave it!"

She grabs for the gem again. "Let me fix!"

"This is the style!" I yell, breaking away from her.

"You think I don't know the style?" She reddens, her hands curling into fists. "I dress nobles for ages, girl. Before you were even a thought in your mother's head—"

"Panya," says a man, now peering around the curtain. "The next one, please."

The old woman huffs, jerking a hand toward the door like she wishes she was slapping my face instead. She *still* jumps for the chain when I speed past, but I'm onto her, and I dodge around her and through the curtain.

Into the party room.

Where everyone is looking my way: the contenders dipping fruits into chocolate, the harpist playing by the fountain, the entirety of Orkena's elite crowded on the balconies above.

And Prince Kasta, who stands only a few paces away, his gaze sharp and annoyed.

IV

I'VE never met royalty before. I'm expecting Prince Kasta to glow, or levitate, or to literally hum with power as the travelers' stories claim princes do. I'm relieved he has normal eyes—a deep blue, not mirrors that can look into my soul—and slightly disappointed his olive skin has no hint of inner sunlight. But for what he lacks in otherworldliness, he more than makes up for in looks. Hen did not prepare me for this. She told me Prince Kasta was the hardest to get information on, that he kept to himself and was very studious. Even his Deathbringer magic, as feared as it is, doesn't require more effort from him than simply touching whatever he wishes to weaken. Thus whenever Hen spoke of him, I pictured someone who spent a lot of time sitting down.

Prince Kasta clearly does not. He's tall and fit, his arms toned and strong, his black hair curling at his ears in the preferred style of soldiers. Kohl lines his eyes, enhancing their blue. A garnet-red sash drapes the shoulder of his white tunic, and a belt of golden rattlesnakes twists about his waist, their eyes glittering black jewels. The serpents of Valen, god of fate and fortune. More of the snakes crown his hair.

I worry I'll answer any question he asks with "yes," and remind myself I absolutely cannot survive the desert, even if he'd be at my side, even if I could watch him protect me with those arms . . . even if we'd be sharing a tent.

Gods, please let me answer his questions normally.

"Lia, daughter of Rai," says the announcer.

Murmuring resumes in the room. I at least have the sense to bow, though the prince barely inclines his chin in response.

"You're dismissed," he says, and looks past me. "Is that everyone?"

That's it. When I tell this story to people, and they hungrily ask what sparkling wisdom the prince imparted, I'll have two words for them. Obviously this is what I wanted, but I suddenly feel insulted.

"Yes, *aera*," the announcer says.

Without another word, the prince leaves for the rosewood table, where of course Gallus is sitting with three others. I have half a mind to loudly explain it doesn't matter because that was the reaction I wanted anyway, and I'm only here for the chocolate, but the man at the curtain must see the storm brewing in my face, because his hand locks around my arm.

"He didn't even ask me a question," I say.

"It is best to leave the prince to his methods," he hisses, towing me toward the fountain. I puff my bangs out of my eyes and let him take me, reminding myself it doesn't matter what Prince Kasta thinks, and that truly was the best-case scenario, in which I didn't even have a chance to reveal myself. I glance up at the balconies, hoping to see Hen's approving face, but spectators crowd the marble railings and jostle the grim-faced guards, a constant shuffle of bright dresses and glimmering headpieces. There are just too many people. I'm going to have to trust she's there and move on before someone asks why I'm gawking like a commoner.

Luckily there is plenty else to move on to. Now that I've survived the first prince, my tension drains as I take in walls embedded with gemstones and giant white pillars carved like palm trees. There is so much *color*. In everyone's dresses and tunics, of course, vibrant shades of red and orange and green, but also in the real sapphires rimming the fountain and the elegant crane curled around the cascade of water, its feathers painted all hues of purple and blue. Flecks of crystal shine in the floor, and torches hang like stars from the ceiling, bathing everyone in a warm, vibrant glow.

Oh yes. This will be a proper story yet, judgmental princes aside.

And the *food*. I don't know if it's more impressive because there's so much of it or because I don't know what half of it is. Two long golden tables are cluttered with platters of steaming meats, white cauldrons of soup, trays of puffed breads, cups brimming with butterscotch candies, and chocolate cakes topped in fruit. I need to find someone to identify it all. Hen will want details.

"Did *you* get asked a question?" I ask a boy who's twisting a slice of melon through a creamy dip. He looks at me like I asked if he'd like to contract an embarrassing rash and scuttles away.

I guess I know why he isn't sitting at the rosewood table.

A brunette in a peach *jole*, thumbing a gold bracelet around her bicep, approaches the cakes. I decide the rare dye of her dress and the sapphires in her hair mean she knows something about palace food.

"Do you know what those are?" I ask.

"Strawberries, raspberries, lemon," she says, pointing to the different cake toppings. She selects a raspberry slice and turns away.

"Wait!" I say. "What about the rest?"

"The rest of what?"

It dawns on me that my next request is slightly unreasonable. "Um. Everything."

She looks down the tables—which stretch the entire side of the room—and smiles.

"Ask a servant. That's what they're here for."

She leaves for the couches on the other side. Everyone else has collected into groups now, laughing and talking with the familiarity of people who know one another. A girl in purple toasts her friends by the fountain; a group on a couch roars in laughter at a story a huge young man is telling. Gallus is still sitting at the rosewood table, now holding a bright flame in his palm, and for a moment I wish he didn't have to be so important or overbearing, because he probably knows what all this food is. But Prince Kasta is watching him in his regal princely fashion, and I concede that asking a servant really would be best and grab a strawberry-topped cake on my way to find one.

I've only had chocolate one other time in my life, when one of Fara's richest clients traded it as payment for boarding his stallion. This is something else. This is like drifting through delicious, bittersweet clouds and being kissed by a god who has sugary strawberry lips while someone else massages your shoulders and whispers how perfect you are in your ear. I could die right now and have no regrets.

I swallow the rest of the cake in two bites, smiling at myself, and approach a guard.

"Excuse me," I say. "Can you explain all of this food to me?"

The guard gives me a very condescending look, considering that, for the night, I outrank him as the heirs' guest. His black hair is shaved close, and his armor reflects slips of torchlight along his dark brown skin, one hand resting atop the curved sword at his hip. Its ivory scabbard seems a strange treasure for a guard who looks my age. I thought only officers carried such swords, but maybe he just looks younger than he is.

"Shouldn't you be more worried about looking like you have *any* interest in the prince?" he asks.

"Oh, I'm not here to be an escort," I explain.

He scoffs. "What, you're just here for the cake?"

It does sound bad when he puts it like that. I bite my lip, trying to think of another way to phrase it.

"That was a joke," he says. "But now I'm concerned it's true."

"It's halfway true. I'm also here to see the palace."

"But not the prince."

"Right."

A smile slides onto his face, and though I usually prefer boys of Kasta's height to the guard's stockier build, there's something magnetic in the warmth he radiates.

"You want me to tell you about the food," he says.

"Yes, please."

He scrutinizes me, opens his mouth in what I fear will be a *no*, then shrugs and starts for the tables. "All right."

I shoot another glance at the rosewood table to check on Gallus. He's now one of two sitting with the prince, though his smile is gone, and the room looks emptier in general. I thought there were six people playing cards and crystals on the couches—now there are three. Both girls who'd been sitting on the fountain when I walked in are gone. A few still wander the food, and a short boy sways before the harp.

"I thought we were allowed to enjoy the party until he chose someone," I say. "Is he sending people out?"

The guard sneers. "Well, since you've already declared you're not here for *him* . . . you should know His Illustriousness doesn't like crowds, remembering names, or treating others with basic human decency. Kindness is hard for him. So yes, about five minutes ago, he started clearing out everyone he's deemed useless."

My jaw drops as we pass a white-robed servant. I would worry this means the prince still thinks I could be use*ful*, but after our first meeting, I'm fairly confident I can be dismissed again with little effort. "You can say that? Aren't you afraid someone will hear?"

"On the contrary," he says, giving me a smile I'm growing fonder of by the minute. "I hope they do."

Hen will be in Paradise when I tell her about the unrest between the eldest prince and his guards. At the table, a new girl in sunrise yellow sits with Gallus, one of the three who was playing cards a moment ago. The prince looks over her shoulder.

Right at me.

And like I was the one who spoke ill of him, my face grows hot.

"So, the food," I say, turning away.

"The food." The guard pauses at the end of the first table. "*Kryderi* soup. Rune soup. *Manne* and lentil soups."

The last two I'm familiar with, having made them with Fara. "Rune soup?"

"A recipe from our sister country Nadessa. It's made with

50

something called 'cucumbers.' The Mestrah imports them."

"I've heard of Nadessa," I say, grabbing a shallow bowl and scooping some of the green liquid into it. "They have palaces made of ice and birds that grant wishes."

The guard snickers. "You don't know what rune soup is, but you know all about another country?"

He's certainly cheeky for a palace guard. I decide his mouth is what landed him a night guarding a party instead of watching the north desert for threats.

"I don't know *all about* Nadessa," I say. "But I know some things, yes."

"How? Have you been there?"

His expression is disturbingly close to what I must look like when a traveler stops in from a new place. Hungry for the story, hungry for details. Hungry for a world that's not my own.

"No," I say. "But I hear the travelers speak of it at my—er, my friend's stable."

"What do they say? Tell me one of their stories."

I suppose palace guards don't have the chance to get out in the world any more than I do. I lift the spoon to my lips, pondering which story to tell him, and am entirely unprepared for the frigid, sweet liquid that follows. "Ugh, is it supposed to be cold?"

A laugh. "Yes."

"This is terrible!"

I say this louder than I should in a room that's rapidly declining in population. And of course Prince Kasta is looking at me when I glance over. I fake a smile and force myself to take another spoonful of gross, cold slime, hoping he'll think I was reacting to something other than the soup. I'm finding I don't want to be sent out just yet. I still have fifty food names to memorize, and I'd love to figure out what issue this guard has with his potential king.

The guard sees the prince watching, and his smile fades.

"Forgive me," he says. "I'm getting distracted. Behind the soups we have *citron*"—he points to a platter of fish and lemon slices—"*freya* bread"—a loaf covered in tiny seeds—"and *osta-fel*. It's a soft cheese made of buffalo milk. You eat it with crackers or the bread."

"Cheese?" I haven't heard of buffalo, either, and after the cold soup, am less eager to try something new.

"You've never had cheese?" The guard's gaze flickers to the jewel dangling by my eye, and then—rather boldly—down the red of my dress. "You said your friend owns a stable? Surely cheese and milk would be one of their most profitable trades?"

He assumes "my friend" owns livestock, as true nobles would. I'm wondering how I'm going to dig myself out of this one when a shriek sounds from the rosewood table. The spectators go silent. The guard's hand snaps to his sword, but two of the bigger, shirtless guards are already on the scene, each clasping an arm of the girl in yellow. Everything within a short radius of her trembles, cups and plates lifting into the air.

"No!" she yells. "I was made for this. I've studied war, I know how to survive the desert! You cannot possibly be so set on Atera *trash*." She jerks her head at Gallus, whose eyebrows rise. I admit I feel a pang of satisfaction at this—at someone considering *him* to be beneath them. "You need someone with true power. Who can do more than conjure what the Forsaken could with two sticks!"

The guards tug her closer to the room we entered from, and the girl thrashes in their arms. Cups crack and shatter, spilling wine onto the tile. "I was born to be remembered! I was born to be *yours!*"

The guards pull the girl from the room. The curtain smashes to the floor behind them and a crack splits up the wall, but the vibrations soften as her angry sobs drift farther away. The spectators burst into conversation, and this time I catch a flash of bronze from the balcony. *Hen!* She's moving a serving tray to catch the torches, and clasps a fist in victory when I see her. Followed by the quick motion of her hand across her neck and a gesture toward the door. I nod. It *is* time to see about getting dismissed, before the prince sends out so many I'm the only option left.

"Well," I say, setting my plate aside. "Safe to say he dodged an arrow with that one."

The guard grunts. "That would be assuming *he* wasn't the arrow." He glances at me. "Will you think me overly cruel if I say those he dismisses are the lucky ones?"

I pause in moving toward the table, a shiver running up my spine as I consider that the guard isn't talking about the contest and its challenges. In the travelers' tales, the mysterious prince isn't always quiet because he's shy. Sometimes he's quiet because he's hiding a side of himself that he doesn't want others to see.

"Is he really so bad?" I ask as the prince turns back to Gallus. "He's a little curt, I guess, but I would be, too, if my future rested on the shoulders of whoever I picked tonight. He handled that outburst quite well, I think."

"Handled it well?" The guard chuckles. "That would be the first time my brother handled—"

He covers his mouth and closes his eyes. My heart jerks into my throat. Brother?

Brother?

I search the room for the other guards, but none of them are dressed nearly as fine; they wear the traditional servants' garb of white tunics or *tergus* kilts, many shirtless, none in armor. Of all the people I could have asked for help, *why* did I choose the one with the ivory scabbard? I look in shock toward the balcony, where Hen is shaking her head. She wasn't telling me to get dismissed. She was telling me to *stop flirting with the second prince*.

Specifically Prince Jet: middle heir, Soundbender, and master swordsman of Orkena.

"Oh gods," I say. "I am so sorry, *aera*, to have wasted your time—"

"Please, don't," Jet says. "Leave that title for him. I wouldn't even be a part of this contest, except—"

A hush falls over the room. Prince Kasta has risen from his seat, his eyes locked on his brother's. And whether it's Jet's warnings or the strained quiet that simmers between them, the smile on his face looks suddenly predatory.

His blue eyes shift to me, and he starts toward us.

"My apologies," Jet says. "I should have been forthright with who I was. I should have directed you to a servant. He's going to disqualify you for talking to me out of turn."

It takes everything I have to keep from exhaling in relief. Thank the gods. Now I can join Hen and we can laugh at how close I was to sabotaging myself and enjoy the rest of the night without another care.

Though I can't deny part of me wishes this conversation didn't have to end—a dangerous thought indeed.

"It's no matter," I say, forcing a smile. "I wasn't here for that anyway. Thank you for your help."

"It was my pleasure . . . sorry, did you ever say your name?"

"It's—Lia," I say, bowing.

"Lia. Perhaps I'll see you tomorrow before you head home. You can tell me what you know of Nadessa."

He bows in turn, which I find so strange and flattering that I bow again, my heart soaring at his words. Maybe I chose poorly in who I talked to, but I spoke with a *prince*, for more than two words this time, who also wants to speak with me again. And there's still an entire night to come.

"Well," says a quiet voice behind me. "Isn't this a surprise." I feel the heat of Prince Kasta on my shoulder before I turn to look at him. "Remind me, Jet: weren't your exact words for tonight 'a gaggling group of desperate, power-crazed street rats' you had no interest taking part in?"

Jet straightens, a muscle twitching in his jaw. "It was an exaggeration to avoid attending."

"Yet here you are. You must have found someone who's changed your mind." Kasta's gaze shifts to me, his eyes calm and beautiful and unnerving. "Interesting."

"Don't take this out on her," Jet says. "Name your First and be done with it. Save your vengence for the race."

Kasta sighs. "I suppose you're right. I've delayed long enough."

He asks for my hand and I give it, again wondering if being

royal will mean his skin feels like warm silk, but . . . it's cold. Cold and rough. I may have to exaggerate some of these details when I tell this story. Kasta squeezes my fingers in dismissal, and I'm dipping my head to thank him when he steps to my side, raises our hands, and announces, "I have chosen my escort."

V

THE crowd waits in rapt silence. Hen's serving tray clatters to the ground, shock and confusion warring on her face, and Jet looks much the same, though the ghost of something darker flickers in his eyes. The announcer gives my mother's name and title. The spectators clap in recognition, and then they're a bundle of noise again, chattering and heading for the exits to refresh themselves before the next Choosing.

Kasta turns to Jet with a smile.

"Well, brother?" he asks, in the same quiet, calm manner. "Aren't you going to congratulate her?"

Jet shakes his head slowly, and my throat tightens at his silence. I know he assumes I can hold my own in the desert, but that doesn't discount his warnings. Surely he'll say something, even if it's to admit he'd been too harsh.

But he turns to me with an arm crossed over his chest, his smile guarded.

"Congratulations, Lia," he says. "You are more than worthy of your new station."

He bows and marches out without a glance back. I look at Kasta in disbelief. I know he *also* assumes that whatever my magic, I'm more than qualified to help him, but he's still choosing me blindly. I doubt he even remembers what type of magic I claimed to *have*.

I should probably say something refined and gracious, but I'm a little more panicked about what will happen when he finds out I'm a fraud.

"With all respect," I say. "Do you think I'm someone else? Because this is the fourth sentence I've ever said to you."

"I knew from the moment I saw you," he says. Which I might have found acceptable, even a little romantic, if he hadn't been watching Jet when he said it. He beckons over the nearest servants, two girls dressed in white and gold. "Prepare her."

"You should probably know I don't know anything about surviving outside," I say as the girls take my arms. "I didn't even know what cheese was before tonight!"

"Tell my father to expect us," the prince calls to the rosewood table, where a servant has appeared and is urging a distraught Gallus to his feet. If only Gallus knew how badly I want to trade places. I wanted the satisfaction of proving he was wrong about me, but *this*—

"This way," whispers the girl on my right arm. She's small and pretty, no older than twelve, and surprisingly strong. The other girl looks more my age and seems as anxious about this entire ordeal as I am. "My name is Elin," says the younger girl. "I'll be your primary attendant until your departure."

My departure. As a royal escort. To go into the desert where travelers have fought unthinkable horrors with magic infinitely stronger than mine, sometimes barely surviving, sometimes not coming back at all.

"There's been a mistake," I say as they tow me around the couches and into a hallway painted with shimmering glass boats. "I mean, I'm honored. Truly. But I'm not who he thinks I am. I can't help navigate the desert, I can't even read!"

Elin grumbles something that sounds like, "Typical."

"What did you say?" I ask.

"Nothing," she says, beaming at me. She has a beautiful smile that I have a feeling gets her out of a lot of trouble. "Prince Kasta will handle the finer aspects of the race."

Prince Kasta. I can't believe I was joking earlier of sharing a tent with him. I won't be going home. I won't be sharing any fantastical memories with Hen tonight, because I'll be saying goodbye. And as soon as we leave, the prince will expect I can assist him with *anything* related to surviving, and once he learns what I am . . .

I have to stop this. I have to admit I'm not supposed to be here. Despite the punishment, eternal shame is still far preferred to dying out there. As soon as we reach someone in charge, I'll explain myself and this will all be set right.

I practice what I'll say in my head as the servants rush me down a set of stairs and into a large room with an open ceiling, under which a shallow square pool glitters with the reflection of stars. The night air shivers over my arms as we weave through painted columns and into a smaller room, this one with a wide doorless balcony that overlooks a moonlit garden. Sandfire gems burn in the wall above a canopied bed, and a small steaming pool waits in the tiled floor to my side.

A bedroom.

A bedroom clearly absent of anyone with the power to dismiss me.

"There are supposed to be guards here," I say. "You were supposed to take me to someone in charge."

"I'm supposed to prepare you," Elin says, towing me toward the steaming bath.

"You don't need to. I'm not staying." I pull free of her grasp. "Look, I can't be here. Prince Kasta doesn't know it yet, but I'm not from the upper district. My name isn't Lia, it's—hey!"

Elin ducks behind me and pops the belt under my chest free. The other girl loosens my head chain and I jerk away, gripping it to my head.

"I feel like you're not listening," I say.

"I feel like you should have considered this before you came," Elin says, hands on her hips.

"I did, but this wasn't even in the realm of possibility. I'm a Whisperer! I came with my friend to see the palace . . . You have to help me fix it."

Elin considers this a moment, then whistles between her fingers. I exhale and look expectantly toward the doorway, willing myself not to lose my nerves when the guards enter—only to see three more girl-servants bustle into the room.

So that's how it's going to be.

My dress falls in seconds. Hands guide me to sit in the pool, and just as I resolve to get this over with quickly, Elin works her fingers into my hair and frees my mother's head chain.

"Wait!" I say. Four pairs of hands push me down when I reach for it. "Take whatever else you want. But not that."

"Relax. We're just adding amethysts to the chains," says Elin. "You'll get it back. In the meantime, give me your arm."

"For what?"

Someone pours a jar of warm water over my head. I sputter and clear it from my eyes as someone else scrubs my back. Elin gets ahold of me in the chaos, her nails digging into my wrist.

"What are you doing?" I yelp.

"It's a grooming spell," she says, tightening her grip. "It takes about three minutes. Just focus on the bath."

She draws the spell using a thin brush, the purple ink shining as she writes the enchantment on my wrist. It absorbs into my skin seconds after each stroke, sending pins and needles up my arm.

"You're *trielle*?" I ask as the spell crawls, fever-like, up my neck. The *trielle* are coveted magicians—their ability to manipulate many kinds of magic, instead of a single specialty, is incredibly valuable. Their magic is also the only one that can show in any family, though it never passes down to the next generation like normal. When I was young, I used to dream I'd be that rare exception. That when I came into my specialty, it wouldn't be one of my parents' common talents, but the shocking ability to create magic from mere words, proof I was made for more.

Elin could be from a small town like mine, but now she'll serve in the palace for her lifetime. Something I'd typically commend her for, except I think something is wrong with her magic. Spellwork isn't supposed to feel like this. Mora keeps a stash of prepackaged healing spells, little rice papers she'd set on our arms and pat with water, dissolving the paper, leaving the ink behind. The spell would sink in and spread like a warm beam of sunlight. This is not a warm beam of anything. This is fangs jabbing into my legs as the magic burns off my hair, and sandpaper taking off the top layer of my face. My fingernails ache as the spell smooths and shapes them.

"I'm in training," she says.

"Is this your first day?" I gasp.

"If you weren't wiggling around so much, I would've been able to draw a clean line."

She has a point, but it's disheartening to know my pain threshold is not much higher than a grooming spell. I endure more scrubbing and fussing, and when the three agonizing minutes of the spell are up, two girls help me out of the bath while another wraps a towel of downy cotton around my body. The fourth works an enchanted brush through my hair and pins my mother's head chain in place. The towel disappears. A two-piece dress, as red as mulled wine, is fitted first around my chest, then my waist, leaving my stomach bare. An elaborate golden necklace follows. As do heavy earrings. Garnet lipstick. Gold eyeliner.

I feel exhausted and I've barely moved. Another reason I absolutely cannot let this go on any longer.

"There," Elin says, having adjusted my mother's chain and leaving the jewel dangling to the side. "I like this style. Where did you get the idea?"

"From *a stable in Atera*. Now can you please fetch someone who's in charge?"

"I'm sorry, I can't. If I leave before I'm dismissed—"

"You're dismissed," says a familiar voice. Relief floods through me, my hair jangling as I turn. Prince Jet trains his eyes on Elin. "Why don't you get her something to eat in the meantime? She has a long night ahead, and she'll need her strength."

"She sampled half the buffet," Elin says. And, quieter—"And Prince Kasta would not like you to be here."

"Are you going to tell on me?"

"Maybe I will."

"Maybe I'll get you that scroll you've been wanting from the priests' guarded stash."

Elin chews the end of her scribing pen, considering, then waves her hands like an exasperated mother. "Fine. But she's expected in the throne room within the hour." She gestures to the other servants, who keep their heads low and drift past Jet like feathers. She's almost out the door when she adds, "The *hour*. Not hours, plural, and not tomorrow."

"When am I ever late to something I *want* to attend?" Jet says, grinning.

"Aren't you supposed to be at your own Choosing right now?"

"I'll get there eventually. Do you want the scroll or not?"

Elin narrows her eyes but finally disappears. Jet waits until her footsteps fade to rub his hand over his face, smearing one side of his eyeliner.

"I'm sorry," he says. "I don't even know where to start."

"How about the part when you said those who got dismissed were the lucky ones," I say, "and then stayed quiet when your brother chose me."

That . . . definitely came out bolder than I meant it to. I should have thanked him for coming. Apologized again for mistaking him as a servant. But the more stress I'm under, the less control I have of my mouth, and this is possibly what Gallus meant when he said I'm better off not speaking to anyone.

Jet snickers. "And here I was afraid your manner might change to something *respectful* now that you know who I am."

"Why didn't you say anything?"

"I couldn't. It would be much worse for both of us if I'd made a scene."

"But all we did was talk. He doesn't even know what I can do!"

Or what I claimed I can do, anyway. Jet thumbs the metal feathers on his armor. "A rational observation, if we were talking about a rational person. I used to joke that Kasta would drain the rivers if he thought I fancied them. Even so . . ." He sighs, and his eyes stray to the garden. "I never thought he'd *actually* go this far."

I scoff. "Well, of course he would. You're his biggest obstacle to the throne."

Jet looks at me, then laughs so loud he has to cover his mouth. He swaggers to the balcony, the torchlight casting him into shadow. "If I wanted it, maybe. Honestly I'd rather be eaten alive by rattlesnakes."

I blink, certain I didn't hear him right. "So naturally, you're about to take part in a death-defying race across the desert to . . . what? Cheer him on?"

Jet grunts, and it's a moment before he turns back to me.

"The Mestrah is very sick," he says, and the way his voice thickens makes me instantly regret the question. "It is his greatest wish I participate, even if I make no effort to win." His eyes harden. "All of that is information that stays in this room."

My heart tugs. "I'm sorry to hear that."

"Yes. Well. So are the Healers, who can reattach severed limbs but can't get rid of a simple cough." He shoves off the wall, scanning my outfit. "Can you run in that?"

"I guess, but . . . wait. If you aren't competing with your brother for the throne, why do you hate each other?"

"Half brother. And I never said I hated him, though it's true that he hates *me*." Jet paces, eyes lingering on different pieces of the room. "He's convinced himself that the Mestrah and I are plotting against him. That my reluctance to attend the war meetings is a ploy so we can speak in private later. And we do, except I'm only listening to how disappointing I am during such meetings. There was a time when my father asked me to usurp Kasta in succession. I declined." He rubs his face again, grimacing. "Kasta was not supposed to know about that conversation, but he employs half the servants as spies. He knows far more about what happens in this palace than he should."

"So he hates you because, if you weren't so averse to ruling, *you* would be the heir."

"If he weren't so bull-headed and rash, he'd already be king."

"So he takes every chance he can to outdo you." I look down at myself, at the bracelets circling my wrists like manacles.

"Which is why you need to get out of here," Jet says. "The drop to the garden isn't far. I can lower you down."

And of course a story-worthy rescue is exactly what I was hoping for, especially since this solution doesn't require admitting I'm here with a false identity, but it occurs to me that as earnest as Jet seems, I don't actually know him. He didn't tell me who he was when we met, but now wants me to speak to him like a prince. He wants to see other lands, but stays here for his father. He was raised to rule, but doesn't want to be king. So many contradictions. Hen says the nobles are always playing games, deceiving each other or pretending to like someone they hate, all for some ulterior motive.

"How do I know you're not doing the same thing?" I ask.

Jet, who'd been leaning over the rail to judge the distance, straightens. "What same thing?"

"Using me to outdo your brother. Denying him his choice of First."

Not that I suddenly believe I'm meant to be here, but for all I know, the princes play this game all the time. If Jet's lying, I could end up in a worse position than I already am.

Jet inhales, watching the open doorway, and closes the distance between us in a few strides. He stops an arm's length away, fingers folded.

"Lia," he says, voice low. "I know we are strangers. I know I've given you little reason to trust me. But hear me now, and trust your gut. There is something *wrong* with Kasta. A blackness that has clung to him since we were very small. It's not always there—there are days he consults with me, days he even seems to recognize I'm not a threat to him. I have no doubt that whatever your specialty, he would find value in it, at first. But then that darkness will whisper to him. It will tell him you spoke to me first at the party, that we're plotting behind his back, that you're holding back on your powers and you want him to fail. It won't matter if there's no evidence to support it. He'll turn on you as he turned on me, and the desert won't care to spare your life as my station here spares mine."

He looks earnest. Anxious, even. If he's putting on an act, it's a very convincing one.

"But you care to spare my life?" I whisper.

"Preferably."

"You really believe he'd turn on me?"

I watch for him to glance away, to fidget; some tell that he's lying. His gaze never wavers.

"Yes," he says.

I move away from him, to the balcony where the crickets sing loudest. It's a little farther from here to the ground than I like, but I decide even if Jet *is* lying, this is my ticket out. No more nobles' games. No more surprisingly painful spells. No more risk of the desert or the many ways in which it could kill me.

"How do we leave?" I ask.

Jet moves to my side and offers me his hands. "I'll lower you as far as I can, and when you're ready, I'll let go. It's a bit of a drop, but I've done this before." He smiles. "It's highly survivable."

"You often sneak girls out of high bedrooms?" I ask, grabbing his wrists as I back toward the rail. The dress is long and likes to slither under my feet, and I move slowly.

"Gods no," he says, laughing in surprise. "I mean I'm used to sneaking out of second-floor windows. What do you take me for?"

"My best friend says you royals are always canoodling where you shouldn't be."

"I'll have you know I am a modest canoodler, and I take offense to that."

"Yes, well—"

I freeze. Jet looks over his shoulder to see what's stopped me, and if I wasn't in trouble before, I certainly am now.

Prince Kasta stands in the doorway, a remorseful Elin by his side.

VI

IT can't look good to anyone, Jet and I holding each other on a starlit balcony. I'm tempted to keep moving like nothing happened and risk broken ankles if Jet isn't paying attention. Surely even a paranoid prince can't be mad at a girl with broken ankles.

Jet pulls out of my grasp. His glare falls on Elin, who won't look at us, but he doesn't call her out.

"Kasta," he says. "You know it's gone too far this time. Choose another."

I expect Kasta to be livid. To throw me into prison, and maybe even Elin, too, for leaving us to conspire when I'm supposed to be his.

But Kasta looks . . . delighted.

"No," he says, walking slowly forward. "I think this is the first time I've gone far enough. How difficult this must be for you, to lose something to *me*."

Kasta motions to Elin, who breezes around him and takes Jet's hand without looking at him.

"Don't you dare harm her for this," Jet says.

"It's within my right. You should not have come to her."

"The Mestrah will not abide it!"

"Worry about yourself. We'll see who the Mestrah sides with when he learns you're sabotaging my chances already with your lies." Kasta jerks his head at Elin. "Take him."

"Please just come," Elin says. Her free hand clutches her brush, ready to mark Jet with an Obedience spell if she has to.

"Don't cross this line." Jet's eyes plead with his brother as Elin pulls him forward. "This isn't you. Think about what you're doing. Think about *her*."

"Shut him up," Kasta says. He blocks my view of Jet now, but Elin must have marked him with silence, because the scuff of their feet down the stairs is the last I hear of him.

And then I am alone with Kasta. A boy who said it was within his right to harm me.

In none of the travelers' tales has the rescuer ever *failed*.

Kasta exhales, arms behind his back as he strolls the perimeter of the bedroom. He's changed since the party, his tunic traded for a white *tergus* belted in leather, the deep olive of his chest painted with gods' symbols in real liquid gold. A tattooed scorpion raises its deadly tail up the back of his neck: the symbol for Oka, the god of judgment.

I have a feeling admitting who I am is not going to go as well as I'd hoped.

"You can relax," Kasta says. "My threats were for him, not you. Sometimes the promise of something is more powerful than the act."

He turns, the torches casting shadows across his muscled torso, and I can't help but feel his reassurance is its own kind of threat. It's too generous of him to pardon me for what Jet and I tried to do. For what it looked like we were doing.

"Jet has always thought himself above me," Kasta says. He continues his stroll past the balcony, past the bed. Surveying his territory. "Since we were young, his sole motivation has been to best me. Whatever passion I took to, he made it his mission to beat me at it. Mathematics. Hunting. Swordplay. He has dedicated his life to making mine as miserable as possible." He pauses, his eyes wandering down my dress, lingering on my stomach. I resist the urge to cover it. "If you were wondering why I'm not surprised, or upset, to see him in your room."

Like he'd read my mind. An explanation I might have found reasonable if he hadn't looked so happy to catch us together. Fara says good men do not enjoy causing pain, even to their enemies.

"He fears you chose me for the wrong reasons," I say, circling the table as Kasta draws nearer.

"Is that his defense now?" He stops near the bath, eyes as blue as the sapphires glittering around its edge. "He humiliates and slanders me for my own good?"

I swallow. The open doorway waits to my side, and I glance at it, at how close and far I am from freedom.

"Don't," Kasta says, rushing forward. I jerk back in surprise, but he grabs my shoulders, and I'm not sure if I'm more confused by how careful his hands are or the pain in his face. "Don't believe what he's told you. You don't need to fear me. He has turned everyone I love against me." He looks sincere. Desperate. The heat of his body is like a fire. "This is my chance to start over. I will prove to you, to my father, that I am not the monster Jet makes me out to be. From this moment forward, you and I are partners. Equals. Anything you desire before we leave, name it, and you will have it."

For a moment, I can't breathe. That . . . was not at all what he was supposed to say. He's supposed to be furious. He's supposed to be throwing me out the door and calling the guards. He's supposed to do any of a million things that end with me going home or to jail, and he's certainly not supposed to say we're *partners*, as if I could be anything equal to a prince.

He's not supposed to *look* at me the way he is now, with such surety and conviction that I wonder if anyone has truly seen me before this, and it takes reminding myself that he thinks I'm someone worthy of that praise to shake myself from his spell. I'm not who he thinks I am, and those words aren't for me.

"Anything I desire?" I whisper. I'm no longer as worried that he'll hurt me, but I still need a way out. Maybe I can make him admit he made a rash choice and it's in both our interests to let me go.

"Name it," he says.

"I want to know why you chose me."

The prince's jaw tightens. He looks at his hands on my shoulders, releases me, and walks toward the door. Torchlight shadows the ridge of an old scar between his ribs. It looks like it was made by a blade.

"Because I knew it would hurt him," he says.

Another answer I wasn't expecting. "That contradicts everything you just told me."

"I'm *trying*," he says, turning, "to be better. I have lived my life having to react to my brother's successes. Trying to prove myself to a father who favors a whore's son over his queen's!" He shoves the nearby chair, and the screech of it against the floor makes me jump. "I knew . . ." He inhales, relaxing his fists. "I knew if you'd caught his attention, that you were extraordinary. I may despise my brother, but Jet's intuition is rarely wrong."

My heart squeezes, guilt fastening like a rope around my throat.

71

He's so sure. He's so *certain* I'm the answer to his prayers, and I know this will be the moment that haunts me long after I'm home, the moment I crushed a real person's hopes and dreams because I wanted to live one day in a fantasy world.

"I'm not who you think I am," I say, miserable. "I'm a *Whisperer*. I snuck into the palace under a false name. My real name is Zahru, and I work at a stable."

I brace myself for his face to change. For the anger to come; for the guards to be called.

He only looks at me like I'm the one who doesn't understand.

"I know," he says. "Elin told me." He offers his hand, and I'm so shocked by the answer, that everything he said pertains to *me*, that I take it. "But that's why this will work. You're an unexpected choice; an underappreciated talent. So much so that Jet is threatened by it." His lip twitches. "You'll see. My father will award me the advantage for choosing you, and together we'll win the crown. You are the key."

Underappreciated. Unexpected. Equals . . . My mind reels trying to make sense of what he's saying. He knows what I am. He knows, and *still* he would tell me I'm extraordinary, that I could be more. Where tradition says I'm not, where most of the nobility would dismiss me without a second glance, he sees something else.

And I can't deny that, as his fingers curl around mine and his beautiful eyes burn with my reflection, something within me flares in response. Maybe I've listened to the wrong brother. Maybe Jet did intend to choose me and now finds me a threat. It's an absurd thought. But Kasta's faith is infectious. I suddenly want nothing more than to impress him, to prove him right.

In the back of my mind, a rational voice is pleading with me to wake up.

Remember what Jet said. Remember you have duties at home! But the voice sounds like Gallus, and I shove it aside.

I swallow, and dare to keep my gaze on Kasta's. Like equals.

"All right," I say.

His smile sends a shiver down my spine.

Every step forward draws the heat from my skin. We move down marbled stairs, between towering statues of the gods, past more indoor pools and a room wrought in gold. The prince is urgent and quiet at my side. Servants move wordlessly out of our way, and with every step, I assure myself that the feeling churning through my chest is not panic, but excitement for what I'm about to prove. If a prince believes I can survive the desert, then surely I can. Maybe this is even what the gods intended for me all along: a chance to see I don't have to be born with earth-tipping magic to be worth as much as Gallus.

By the time we step into the throne room, I'm shivering. If Kasta notices, he says nothing.

The throne room should have been a place that took my breath away. I mean, it technically still does, but I'm not sure if it's a stressed gasp or fervent awe. The ceiling stretches as high as the sky. At least twenty massive columns support it, their bases painted deep hues of red and gold, blue and green. A marble floor gleams around us like poured milk, interrupted only by the freshly cut palm leaves that pave our way to the thrones.

The Mestrah and his queen wait at the end like statues. The queen in a flowing white gown that flatters her ivory complexion, her chestnut hair shining beneath a wreath of ivy and pearls, and the Mestrah in his ceremonial leather armor, *trielle* spells glistening along his deep olive skin. A blue cape encircles his neck. A thick crown, its tines the curled tails of scorpions, sits atop his black hair. An ornamental staff rests in his fist, its metal falcon wings glinting in the room's many torches.

His jaw tightens as we advance, and I feel myself shrinking with every step.

It's enough to be in the presence of a true god. Elevated to divinity upon his crowning, the Mestrah will not be as worshipped in death as the eleven primary gods we honor at our temples, but in life he is our bridge between the mortal world and theirs. It is their will he acts on, and their laws he upholds. It's why his family, and especially his children who might go on to rule, are born with the rarest powers of our world. His ability to read minds is proof of the gods' favor, and his wisdom is confirmation. Fara always speaks of him with respect. He provides our food, our home, our protection. His people love him, and his enemies fear him.

I can only pray falsifying my name hasn't put me in the latter category.

"*Valeed,*" Kasta says. The formal word for *father* tugs my heart even more. The separation between them is physical as well, the stone stairs raising the thrones above us. "My decision is made." He raises my hand in his and bows, and I quickly do the same.

The Mestrah doesn't speak. He clutches the arms of his golden throne, frowning, and evaluates me with eyes the same cold, deep blue as Kasta's.

"I told you to come alone," he says, his voice weaker than I'd imagined. Jet said he was unwell, but I thought surely he, being an actual god, would sound commanding and otherworldly. His skin does seem to glow more, though I suspect it's a reflection from the throne. "But as you insist on doing things your way over mine, then so be it."

"You needed to see her," Kasta says.

"*I* will determine what it is I need," the Mestrah snaps. He coughs twice, swallows, and shifts his gaze to me. "Elin told us about the girl. That you've not only pardoned her, but chosen her as yours." His knuckles tense on the throne. "Your decisions continue to appall me."

A stone drops in my stomach. Away from Kasta's arresting gaze, it's getting harder to remember why I agreed to this. The Mestrah's words snap me back to reality. Of course I'm a terrible decision. I even told *myself* that before we came, and I have a sinking feeling I'm going to be reminded of every reason why.

Kasta lowers our hands, his grip on me tightening. "I don't understand."

"That's the problem," the Mestrah says, rising. "You never take the time to understand. Of all the fine magicians I sent for, you choose an uneducated Whisperer? What use could her magic possibly serve? What will you do if a sandstorm threatens the horizon, or it's been days since you've eaten? What if you're attacked by bandits who'd rather hold you for ransom than see you crowned? How will she save you if the most she can do is insult their horses?"

I bite my cheek with each point but keep my eyes down and remind myself this is for the best. The prince will have to listen to his father. And then he'll have to let me go.

"*Your* priests let her through," Kasta says. "This is outrageous. How is it possible to please you when—"

"Perhaps by using your brain!" says the Mestrah. "When we present you with a choice of escort, perhaps you could consider who might be able to calm storms and build shelters, or who might excel in matters of combat, not who you'd first like to see naked!"

That the king thinks *that's* the reason Kasta chose me makes my blood heat, but though I expected as much, I can't believe this is what I'm being reduced to. I'll agree I'm not the best choice magic-wise, but it's entirely unfair to assume that's all I have to offer. I could be a master hunter or navigator. Or know about a secret oasis along the route.

Luckily the queen seems to realize this is too far. She touches a manicured hand to the king's arm.

"I saw the others," she says. "I don't think that's why."

Oh. Ouch.

"No," Kasta says, finally releasing me. "You cannot disapprove of her. She caught Jet's eye at the party. He has already come to her room to try to steal her away. If it was he standing in my place, you would rush down and kiss our cheeks!"

"You and Jet are very different," the Mestrah says, and the regret in his face is far crueler than anything he could speak. "He has mastered many skills that will aid him in the race, and his needs are not yours. How many times have I told you to forget him? To concentrate on what it is you say you want?"

"Because what I want is impossible! Everything I do is a disappointment to you. I could turn dust into fruit and you would

76

still find some way I'd done it wrong. Some way Jet would do it better!"

I have a feeling Kasta is no longer talking about the throne, and my heart cracks a little more.

"Because. You. Do. Not. Listen," the Mestrah says, punching each word into his palm with a finger. Sweat glistens on his brow despite the coolness of the room. "You do not ask questions. You do not take advisement. You do what you wish."

"Because I—"

"Kasta," the queen says softly.

"I do not award the advantage to this match," the Mestrah says, and a new cough rakes through him, so harsh he has to sink back on the throne. The queen touches his arm, and a boy-servant rushes over with a glass of tonic. The Mestrah takes a drink with a shaky hand. His voice is little more than a whisper when he adds, "And I will not be naming you *dõmmel* this night."

I cover my mouth with my hands to hold back the "*Oh.*" The title of crown prince or princess is usually given to the Mestrah's eldest by the time they're thirteen. It wouldn't do Kasta much good now that the Crossing's been invoked, but it's a symbol of approval and expectation, and if something happened and none of the heirs could complete the race, he'd be crowned by default. He can still win, of course, but I imagine the whole point of this— everything Kasta desperately wants—revolves around hearing the words from his father's mouth.

The prince has changed. The anger on his face has faded to something unreadable, something disturbingly calm.

"*Valeed,*" he says, bowing to the thrones before grabbing my arm. I flinch at his roughness but don't dare protest, eager to leave the court. The Mestrah's coughs fill the air as we go.

"I'm sorry," I say, though I'm relieved the king spoke sense. As much as I wanted what Kasta said to be true, this really is the best for both of us. Once he calms down, I'll remind him I wasn't a valid choice anyway. He should be able to hold another banquet. Choose a true First. Appeal to his father and at least gain the king's approval, if not a second chance at the advantage.

Kasta says nothing in reply, just tows me forward, a gathering storm beside me. It's not until we've left the throne room and are walking through a hallway singing with little fountains that I realize we're not going back to my room.

"Please!" I say, fearing we're headed to the whipping posts. "Don't give me to the enforcers. I was honest with you. I told you I was only a Whisperer." It no longer seems wise to mention I'm my father's only heir, or that he'd be eager to have me back.

"You think I'm letting you go?" Kasta chuckles and shakes his head. "No, Zahru. Our time together has only just begun."

And with that he shoves me over a threshold, slams a golden door behind us, and locks it with a bar of wood.

VII

I catch my balance on an ebony dresser. A huge room stretches into darkness before me, its corners hidden in shadow, where the silver-blue glow of the torches cannot reach. The weak light casts the thin-legged couches, the tall bookshelves, the massive bed—curtained by thick sheets of velvet—in an icy, eerie haze.

A royal bed.

Kasta's room.

Gods, I should have flown off that balcony with Jet. I should have begged Kasta to see reason before he presented me to the Mestrah. I should have stayed home with Fara, because it's looking less and less like I'll have any chance of seeing him again. I don't know what Kasta intends for me, but I have a sinking feeling this is the turning point Jet warned me about.

He was telling the truth. Kasta may *want* to be better, but Jet sees him for what he is. What was it that Kasta even admitted? *Jet's intuition is rarely wrong.*

Besides the door, the windows on the far side are the only exit.

"Bravo," Kasta says, clapping. I turn, backing away as he comes closer. "My brother has truly outdone himself this time. To make me think I was ahead of him . . ." The light glitters over the paint on his chest. "Did he promise you a station here? A house?" His eyes flash. "More?"

"I don't know what you're talking about," I say.

He grins like we're sharing a joke. "Of course not."

I circle around a couch clothed in white leather. He follows, unrushed.

"He said he had no interest in observing who I chose," he says. "That we'd be lucky if he showed up to his own Choosing. But he only told me that so I'd notice when he arrived, and observe whom he was talking to. That's why you came under a false name: he planted you. He knew I would select you to vex him, and I took the bait. When I caught you two speaking in the room . . ." He thinks for a moment and nods. "You were solidifying your plans. Going over what you'd say, how you'd win my trust by appearing honest. But it was all part of the act."

"What?" I say. "There is no act. I'm from the town of Atera. This is my first visit to the palace. Jet came to warn me—"

"No. He knew exactly what kind of person our father would disapprove of and wanted to be sure his own advantage was guaranteed." A muscle twitches in his jaw. "You should have told me. I would have paid twice his price."

"He didn't pay me!"

But my words don't move him. Kasta only scrutinizes me, as I did with Jet—looking for the tell, for the lie. Except his eyes look feverish.

I move a few steps more, putting the low table in front of the couch between us.

"I suppose for him," he says, sinking onto the cushions, "it wasn't enough the Mestrah resurrected an ancient contest to show his lack of confidence in me. Did you know, in the centuries since the Crossing last happened, not a single second- or third-born has ever taken the throne? All the Mestrahs have been firstborns. *All* of them."

The pain in his voice is a heavy, horrible thing, and I glance at the windows. "I thought the gods told the Mestrah to hold the contest."

"Did they?" Kasta snickers, and a shadow slips under his skin as he rises, like the face of another person beneath the surface. "Or did he bend their will for his own gain? I've done much research on the Crossing since my father reinstated it. Enough to know that even the holy sacrifice, supposedly chosen by Numet herself, is actually marked by a High Priest. Odd how Forsaken who'd spoken against the priests, or caused unrest in the towns, suddenly found themselves called to the highest of purposes." A knife of a smile. "Perhaps the gods are at our mercy, and not the other way around."

"But that's sacrilege," I say before I can stop myself.

"It's *progress*." His eyes harden. "And when I am Mestrah, it will be proven."

I shudder to think what that means. That he'll use the gods, as he believes his father has, to justify doing things that are against our laws? He starts for me again, and I twirl behind a carved chair.

"If you're not my brother's agent," he growls, "why are you running?"

"You're angry," I say. "And I just spent the longest ten minutes of my life hearing how terrible a choice I am for you. How do I know you're not going to throw me out of a window?"

"I told you, you do not need to fear me."

"But you can't see your face right now."

He lunges. I leap away, but he catches my wrist and pulls me to his chest, his other hand a lock around my bare side. He looks down at me, jaw tense, and I grimace at all the places our bodies touch. At all the places he could draw my life away, as easily as a flame from tinder. Jet's warnings rush through my head. *There is something* wrong *with Kasta. A blackness that has clung to him since we were very small . . .*

I can feel it blooming around us, as if the shadows are crawling from the walls.

"*Aera,*" I say. "Please."

"You know, I almost believed you," he says, running his thumb on the inside of my wrist. The touch crawls under my skin like scorpions. "That you could be this simple, detached girl from a simple, detached town. An ally. Someone not predisposed to hate me." His eyes wander to the jewel dangling near my eye. "That I had something that was only mine."

I shove his shoulder with my free hand, but he keeps me tight against him. "You might have," I say, swallowing the panic riddling through my chest. My only reassuring thought is that if he wanted to kill me, he'd probably have done it by now. Which means I still have a chance at getting out of here.

"You might still," I say. "But you have to believe I knew nothing about this before I came here. I'm not Jet's puppet. I'm not here to hurt you." I tug my captive arm. "Please. You're hurting me."

He considers my wrist, and whether it's the dim light or that I'm finally getting through to him, his face seems to soften. His grip loosens—but not enough to pull away.

"Might still?" he whispers. "You would . . . you would forgive me for how I've treated you?"

Someone pounds on the door, startling us both. "Kasta!"

Jet. Even before Kasta's fingers clench around my arm, my nerves turn to fire.

"Liar," he says.

"No!" I say. "I have nothing to do with—"

"We need to talk," Jet says. "Open the door."

Kasta ignores him, looking down as the shadows overtake his face, twisting his lips into a sneer.

"I'm done being made the fool," he says. "I will not sit by while you run us in circles in the desert, waiting for news of Jet's victory. The priests have yet to mark a sacrifice. Let me spare them the trouble of finding a traitor." His hand slips to the knife at his belt, the metal grating as he draws it from the sheath. "I wonder. Will your precious Jet try to save you? Or will it be his hand that slices your throat?"

He jerks my arm to the side, and for a second I consider that striking a god's son is its own kind of sacrilege—followed by the precise jab of my fingers into his eyes. Kasta swears and releases me. I spring away, but he grabs my hair, a musical *ting* sounding as the jewel from my mother's head chain snaps free. He throws me against the couch. Jet bangs on the door. I roll away, yelling for him, but Kasta jumps on top of me and wrenches my arm against the backrest, the blade hot on my wrist—

I twist and knee him in the side. Handling spooked horses has made me familiar with dead weight, but none of them were as agile or determined as the prince. He grunts, gets ahold of my wrist as I try to wiggle free, flips me onto my stomach, and twists my arm up my back—

Lights spark through my vision, my skin alive with panic. The knife sears my skin. I clench my teeth and whip my head back, a sickening *crunch* sounding as I collide with Kasta's face. He releases me with a snarl. I scramble away from him, around the low table, gasping and cradling my bleeding arm, trying to back into the farthest corner of the room.

I attacked a prince. *I attacked a prince* and there is no world in which this will end well for me.

Kasta stares at his hand, at the blood dripping onto it from his nose.

"You dare to strike me," he says, twisting the hilt of his knife. The blade glows and lengthens, and I shrink against the wall, edging toward the windows. "You'll pay dearly for that."

I bolt for the nearest window. Kasta flips a table aside, gaining on me, when the curtains burst open and I fear he's called on some higher form of his power, on corpses that will rend and rip and—

Jet leaps in instead, out of breath. I could sob for gratefulness as I rush behind him, and he draws his blade, torchlight dancing across his winged armor. He glances at my bleeding wrist and turns pained eyes on his brother.

"Kasta," he says, almost softly. "What are you doing?"

Kasta circles us like a jackal, his face wild with fury. "This is your fault," he spits. "You planted her. You knew Father would condemn me for it. You've humiliated me for the last time!"

He lunges forward, and Jet moves to meet him, their blades flashing like sparks. Kasta strikes, his blade singing off the metal of Jet's armor, who grunts and jerks back, only to find Kasta right on him again. He parries and twists; Kasta swings recklessly and overbalances, leaving his side open. I brace myself for Jet's strike—

84

It doesn't come. Jet backs away, and Kasta, seething, pursues. Metal shrieks against metal. Kasta is ruthless, his swings pointed and deadly, but though Jet gets another opportunity to cut him— and another—he doesn't.

He's not going to strike his brother. I don't know if it's because he blames himself for what's happened or it's some kind of personal honor, but I don't see this ending well for him either way.

I have to find a way to subdue Kasta.

I search the room for anything that could help. The chairs are too heavy and unwieldy. I try to lift a small falcon statue, only to find it's attached to the table. The perfume bottles are too small to do any damage, but if I can distract him . . .

The broken ends of my mother's head chain tap my brow, and with a jolt I remember the protection rune carved into the gem. I sprint for the couch and drop to the tile, searching around its clawed feet, pawing beneath the purple silk of an end table. I'm panicking that the stone's been lost when a torch flashes off something red by the table. I dive to retrieve it, clutching the precious garnet in my fingers.

Except I don't know how to use it to protect someone else. Does Jet need to be holding it? I only know it's supposed to work automatically—

The *screech* of grinding metal rips through the air, and I whirl to see Jet's sword clang across the tile and disappear under the bed. He backs away from Kasta, hands splayed.

I press my thumb into the gem's side, begging it to activate.

"You're not going to kill me," Jet says. "You're going to realize this plan you think I've concocted makes no sense, and you've put the blame on an innocent girl, and that tomorrow, you can change who your First will be. Our father will be pleased. You'll win the advantage, and your victory will be all but guaranteed."

Kasta stalks forward, his face as dark as stone.

"I'll forfeit the race," Jet says, backing toward the windows. "I was going to desert the second day anyway, but I'll make it official."

He's running out of space. I can't stand the thought of him getting hurt for me, of possibly *dying* for me, and I don't have a plan, of course, but I rush for them—

"I don't want to," Jet says, "because that will hurt Father deeply. But I will, for you. If you'll finally believe I want no part of this anymore."

"Shut up!" Kasta snaps. "I know the girl is yours. I know the first chance she gets, she'll kill me."

"What?" Jet bumps against the wall. "Never. I would never—"

Kasta strikes.

I'm still too far.

"No!" I yell, wishing I could rewind time, wishing I could go back to when I approached Jet at the party, and I could notice the way he was dressed, and ask someone—anyone—else for help with the food, and Kasta would raise Gallus's wrist, and the Mestrah would smile in the throne room, and I'd be on my way back to Hen, and Jet would be in his room, dreaming of other worlds—

Light bursts from the gem in my hand, a blinding flash in the darkness. My palm burns like ice. One of the princes cries out and something heavy hits the floor, and when my vision clears, Kasta lies on his back. Light gleams from his eyes, his mouth; drops of it glisten on his skin like rain.

The glow fades, and Jet stands plastered against the wall, glancing at me before dropping to his brother's side.

"Kasta," he says, tossing the prince's sword across the room before shaking his shoulders. "Kasta?"

I drop the gem, flinching as it hits the floor. No one warned me this is what true magic looked like. No one warned me this is what it *felt* like. Like something completely wild and unstable; like the world bending around me and cracking, feeding on my desperation and twisting it into something else. I only wanted to stop Kasta. I only wanted to protect Jet. And now . . .

"Zahru," Jet whispers, and I know I'll never forget the way he looks at me, with something between fear and regret. "He's not breathing."

VIII

NOT breathing.

I've killed a man. I've killed a *prince*. All this time I thought I was the one who needed rescue . . .

"I didn't know it could do that," I say, my throat tightening. "It's just a protection rune. I didn't mean . . . I didn't know!"

"Water," Jet orders. He pulls a paper spell from his tunic, and I hasten toward a marble basin, stumbling over a broken statue of Apos on my way. My hands tremble as I dip a golden cup into its depths. I spill half of it rushing back to them, but Jet takes it without a glance.

"I didn't mean to," I repeat as he applies the spell to Kasta's chest. "I mean, I did mean to, because I didn't want him to stab you, but I didn't mean . . ."

"It's working." Jet sits back on his heels and exhales, watching the ink sink in. I don't think I breathe at all until Kasta gasps, and Jet and I flinch, but Kasta settles back again, his chest moving quietly, his eyes closed.

I muffle a sob, both for the relief that I'm not a murderer . . . and the realization that someone who wants to kill *me* is still alive.

"The spell will keep him unconscious awhile," Jet says, rising. "But we need to get you out of here. Someone might have seen that light or heard the struggle. If they think you're even slightly involved, this will get messy."

A miserable numbness washes through me. "I'm more than slightly involved."

"No, you're not. I got the upper hand and knocked him cold. It was a brawl between brothers and nothing more, understood?"

My heart sinks at the new distance in his eyes, and I nod.

"I'm sorry," I say, but Jet looks away. Disgusted at how much force I used, maybe. I don't blame him.

"He was going to kill me," is his only reply.

He reaches under the bed for his lost sword, and I reluctantly lift the gem from where I dropped it, running my thumb over its burned front. I never imagined I would look at it with anything but fondness. Now I will only ever see the light, and Kasta on his back, his eyes staring as if dead. But leaving it is not an option. I promised Hen I'd return it, and so I will.

"I'll negotiate your release," Jet says, sheathing his sword. For as steady as his voice is, his hands tremble. "I would take you right out of the palace, but the Mestrah knows who you are now. We need Kasta to dismiss you or there will be serious charges for your abandonment." He exhales. "Even after Kasta does, I'd suggest you and your family stay with relatives until the race has finished. My brother . . . does not like when things don't go his way. But rest assured that once he's crowned, he'll be too busy gloating to remember you exist."

I wince, imagining Fara's face when I tell him I managed just fine at the palace . . . except that we now have to go into hiding.

"And if he comes for me tonight?" I ask.

Jet shakes his head. "He won't dare. Your room is guarded, and even princes aren't allowed to go about hurting whoever we please." He sighs. "It's not really you he's angry with, anyway."

"And you're all right with that?" I ask. "With me just . . . leaving?"

Jet glances at Kasta, his jaw clenched. "This isn't your fight."

But he won't look at me.

He lowers me into the garden as he'd tried earlier that night, and we sneak from shadow to shadow, pausing for laughing partygoers and yawning guards. When he hoists me on his shoulders to return me to my room, he nearly drops me for how fast he lets go.

And I wonder if this is why the travelers' tales are so spectacular. If, behind every story about a felled tiger or a supposed dragon, there is a real person, someone the storyteller wishes to forget in the only way she knows, which is to retell the story again and again until even she believes it was a dragon, and not a boy, who left her with so many scars.

I don't remember the cut on my arm until dawn.

I find it as the first rays of Numet's light pierce the balcony, bringing to focus the brick-red smears along the top of my bedsheet. I jerk against the golden headboard and gape at the mess, praying it looks worse than it is. Dried blood crusts my entire forearm. More of it stains my bare stomach and skirt. But the only pain I feel is a dull ache near my wrist, where the blood's thickest.

Kasta's words echo through my head. *The priests have yet to mark a sacrifice. Let me spare them the trouble* . . .

Dread climbs my throat as I run my thumb over the scab. I want to assure myself it's meaningless now—I can't imagine Kasta finished whatever he meant to carve—but I'm struck with the sudden conviction that no one should see it.

I'm deciding how to hide it, and how I'll dispose of the sheets, when a crash sounds from the door. Melon and bread slices cascade across the table. The servant bringing my breakfast tray stares, eyes widening, first at my arm and then the sheets, before muttering an apology and rushing back out.

I swallow and fight the urge to throw the sheets, and maybe myself, too, over the balcony.

It's all right, relax, you stopped him. I exhale and try to believe the words. It doesn't mean I'm going to be the sacrifice, and once a Healer mends it, it'll be like it never happened.

It's fine, I think. *This is going to be fine.*

But I still startle when the Healer bustles in.

"*Apos*, what happened?" she asks, moving to my side. Like all Healers, she's around my age and wears the sigil of Talqo around her arm, two golden hands pressed together in prayer. Unlike most Healers, she also looks like she could best both princes in a test of strength—at the same time. Her pale fingers take a gentle hold of my arm and turn it. Her magic is already tingling through my skin, asking my body where it's hurt.

"I . . . well . . ." I was really hoping she wouldn't ask questions. I wish I'd prepared a reasonable explanation in case she did, but I'm just going to have to face it that I'll never have a plan for anything.

"I fell?" I say, cursing myself for sounding strangled.

"It's all right," she says, pressing her thumbs against my skin. "You don't have to tell me if you don't want to." She smiles, her gray eyes knowing. "Did you do a lot of celebrating last night?"

I half laugh, half sob at how very wrong her assumption is. "No. I mean, I don't drink. Yet. Not that I'm going to start. Not that I'm opposed to it, but—well, I should stop talking now."

She snickers. "It's nothing to be ashamed of. We all have nights we wish we could undo."

I bite back another sob at how badly I wish that were possible. But I start to relax, too. The Healer seems kind and reasonable, and surely if Kasta had finished what he was carving, she'd have said something about it by now. Then I just need Jet to come, and this will finally be over.

It's fine, I repeat to myself. *It's fine, it's fine . . .*

The Healer pats my arm and wipes her hands on a towel. "There, good as new. Though there will be a scar for a moon or two."

"That's it?" I say, marveling at my wrist. I didn't feel a thing.

"I'm very good at what I do." The Healer winks and draws a small jug from her belt. She pours the glowing liquid onto a cloth before wrapping the fabric around my arm. The enchanted water itches, but in a pleasant way, and I start to relax.

She smiles. "This'll need just a moment."

"Do you do hair removal, too? Because they really need to replace the girl who does it now."

She chuckles. "Elin will be very good, one day. But we all go through a learning stage. When I first started—"

She frowns as she lifts the cloth, now rusty with blood. Beneath it my arm is clean and smooth, save for a red, raised patch near my wrist.

"When you first started?" I prompt.

"Mm."

She scrutinizes the mark, and a chill wraps me, stark as night. But just as I'm panicking that she'll call the guards in, she smiles. "When I first started, I accidentally fused a man's kneecap to his shin. I was only trying to mend a bruise." She folds the bloody towel and rises from the bed. "It was my pleasure to meet you."

"And you," I say, but she's already disappeared around the pearl-crusted doorway. Leaving her jug of enchanted water on the bedside table.

I swallow the knot in my throat as I move my arm into a beam of sunlight. And my heart sinks into my gut. Kasta *did* finish what he'd been drawing. The mark is only three simple lines, but with the blood gone their shape is unmistakable. A curved line like the bottom of a carriage; a straight line for its roof. A half circle for the sun setting atop it.

The symbol for Rie, the god of death.

I have a very bad feeling about this.

I know I shouldn't technically fret until it's past midmorning, but I've still not heard from Jet, and as soon as the Healer left, the guards posted outside my room moved *inside* instead. I'm certain the Healer recognized the mark. What I'm not certain of is whether she'd tell someone about it, and whether the guards changed positions because of that or if they would have moved either way. And as much as I'm trying to assure myself it doesn't matter—Jet should have secured my release long ago—the silence is wearing on me.

As is the worry Jet decided I wasn't worth it.

The latter thought makes my blood rush in my ears, and I push it away in haste. Jet spent the evening trying to help me escape. It would make no sense for him to abandon the plan now, especially when this gives him one last chance to stop Kasta from getting his way.

He'll come.

Please let him come.

"No, I don't think it's real," echoes a voice beyond the door. "Unless you think Lana acted without me?"

With a shudder, I recognize the voice as the priest who came to Atera. No one else has a tone that deep and irritated. I cast a desperate look at the balcony, but the guard there crosses her arms like she knows exactly what I'm thinking, and I can only pray the priest moves past without stopping.

"She wouldn't," a girl answers. "She's far too soft to deliver a mark herself."

The Healer definitely told someone. I wring my hands and glance around as if a secret door will pop open at any moment, but of course there's nothing but the smooth, gilded walls and a bust of Tyda, the goddess of patience, her silver-painted eyes silently judging me. *Easy, Zahru.* Maybe I'm getting worked up for no reason. Maybe the priest will recognize immediately that Kasta has unfairly interfered, and he'll be disqualified from the Crossing, and I'll be dismissed without an investigation.

I exhale, and smooth my gown as if I'm expecting them.

The priest steps through the pearled archway, scowl in place, trailed by a girl in schooling robes, holy oaths tattooed around the edges of her face. His apprentice. But though I know she can't be older than fifteen, she's somehow more intimidating. Her fairer skin is jaundiced, her blonde hair greased back like a helmet. There's a coldness to her expression that reminds me of a burial mask.

"Your arm, girl," the priest says.

"I'd really like to talk to Jet first," I say, covering my wrist.

"That's a request Prince Kasta will need to approve, since you and *Prince* Jet are currently rivals." His pupils sliver in warning. "The Healer said you cut yourself last night. I'm to ensure you haven't sealed anything into the wound."

So he *doesn't* believe it's a sacrificial mark, but a way for me to cheat. Which means he still thinks I'm Kasta's First.

Jet hasn't secured my release.

I don't move.

"Let me put it this way," the priest says. "If you don't show me your arm, Alise is going to paralyze you, and I'll take a look anyway. I should add that her poisons take a few hours to wear off."

The apprentice smiles, revealing a mouth full of stained teeth. I have the sudden thought she's been testing poisons on *herself*, and with a shudder, I pull my arm forward.

This will be fine. Kasta won't get away with this, this will be fine.

"Both, please," the priest says.

I swallow and draw my fists together, palms down. The priest orders me to turn them over—and I pray to every god that when I do, the scar will be unrecognizable.

"Talqo's blood," the priest swears. He exchanges a bewildered look with his apprentice, who covers her mouth.

The scar is not gone. With the swelling subsided, it's even clearer the scar is Rie's mark.

I wait for the priest's scowl to deepen. For his apprentice to cry *Sacrilege!* and a swarm of disbelieving officials to charge in, but the priest only grips the circle of Numet that dangles from his necklace, and the apprentice falls to her knees, begging Valen's forgiveness. With a growing sense of horror, I realize this is *exactly* what Kasta meant by having the gods at his mercy.

"Tell the Mestrah the sacrifice has been revealed," the priest says. "Prince Kasta will need to choose a different First."

"What?" I say as they turn. "No, no, no. This wasn't made by Numet, it was Prince Kasta!"

They stop. The priest looks over his shoulder, his gaze burning my skin. "What?"

"You ungrateful rat," the apprentice snaps. "Being marked as the sacrifice is the greatest honor you could pray for. It means the gods themselves find you sacred. The Forsaken will weep for jealousy when they hear of the news."

"Oh, no, I didn't mean it like that," I say, swallowing. Though I'm fairly certain the Forsaken will weep for joy when they hear this, not envy. "I would yield to the gods' wishes, if that's what they meant for me. But it wasn't them, it was the prince! He cut me. He thought I was working with Jet against him and cut me."

"Desperate words," mutters the apprentice. "I'll tell the servants to prepare her."

"No, please, I . . . Jet!" I say, doing a poor job of not sounding desperate. "Prince Jet will confirm my story."

The girl continues out, but the priest grabs her shoulder.

I can't believe that of all people, *he* might be the one who saves me.

"No," he says slowly. "Fetch the princes. Let us see what they have to say."

"*Adel*, with all respect, is that appropriate?" the apprentice says. "Questioning the integrity of royalty against a commoner—"

But the priest gives her a look, and she sets her jaw.

"Very well," she says, her black robes swaying as she strides out.

The priest sighs when her footsteps fade, but his focus slides past me when he turns back to the room. I can't tell if he believes me. I can't tell if the worry creasing his brow is for the possibility the mark on my arm is real, or that Kasta could be the one behind it. From the glance he and his apprentice shared, it doesn't seem like they'd put it past him. Maybe Kasta has done something like this before. Maybe this is a moment they knew would come, and now finally, with Jet *and* a strange peasant girl to speak against him, it's enough to reveal Kasta for who he is.

Unless Jet lied, whispers a nasty little voice in the back of my head. *Why hasn't he come? Why aren't you released?*

I shove the doubts away. Fara would tell me to be patient; to not make a thunderstorm from a single cloud, as he likes to say. After Kasta is arrested, Jet will explain himself. He'll have a good reason for not coming that will make me ashamed I ever doubted him. Tonight I'll be laughing about this with Hen, at how intense and ridiculous palace politics are, and how silly we were to ever envy them.

I pace the room, thinking about what I'll say when they ask me how I got the cut, if I resisted the prince's knife. But the minutes pass too quickly. Before I have a solid strategy, footsteps sound on the tile stairs, and the apprentice steps into the room.

Followed by the princes.

Impossibly, as if nothing earth-shattering has happened at all, they've both bathed and changed since last night. Kasta to a ceremonial white *tergus*, his chest bare, and Jet to a blue tunic beneath light armor, the metal so new it reflects slivers of the room in its feathered shoulders. Kasta's gaze hitches on me like an archer marking a target. But it's Jet's indifference that steals the feeling from my fingers. His eyes pass over me as if I'm invisible; as if I'm just another decoration in the room.

"*Aeras*," the priest says, rising. "I'm sorry to trouble you on such an important day. I won't keep you long. But something's come to my attention that will be of great interest to you." He gestures to me, and I wish I could melt into the rug. "Our esteemed guest woke this morning with a peculiar mark on her arm." He pauses, gaze flickering between them. "It seems the gods have named your sacrifice."

A muscle clenching in Jet's jaw is the only reaction from either prince. Kasta must have told him he cut me, but that's hardly the knowing smile or solemn nod I was hoping for. I'm desperate for Jet to look over, to reassure me with a glance that this is all part of our plan.

The priest folds his hands. "You're unusually quiet, Prince Kasta. Have you no concerns about losing your First?"

"It is the gods' will," he says. "I will not question it."

"The gods'?" the priest says, watching him. "Or yours?"

Kasta pulls his gaze from me, switching targets. "That's a dangerous accusation, priest."

"Indeed. Which is why I'm hoping your brother can enlighten us on the truth."

The attention in the room turns to Jet, who looks like he's swallowed a rattlesnake.

"The girl claims she was cut," the priest says. "She said you would support her story."

Kasta stays still as a statue, though his hands curl slowly into fists. I can barely breathe for how much I want this to be over. *Almost there*, I think. *Almost done—*

Jet exhales, and a decisive calm falls over his face.

"I'm afraid I don't know what she's talking about," he says. "She must still be in shock."

IX

WELL, I wasn't in shock before. But I am *now*.

"Jet!" I cry.

He excuses himself with a bow.

"You can't!" I say. "Jet! Wait!"

"That is enough," the priest snaps. "Don't dishonor yourself further."

He nods to his apprentice, who sniffs and makes space for Kasta with one arm crossed over her chest. Kasta seems as stunned as I am. He watches Jet retreat, then looks back at me.

Perhaps the gods are at our *mercy,* he'd said.

And as if he can hear me thinking it, he smiles.

Elin is no longer my primary attendant.

She's been given to Kasta's new First, of whom not a single one of my attendants will speak, as if doing so might soil their reputations. I listen to them chatter and gossip, but their words are slippery and muffled, their touch numb against my skin. I cannot possibly be here. These can't be my arms they're painting with white lanterns and ancient prayers, or my body they're wrapping in soft golden silk, or my neck upon which they're setting a jeweled necklace that rivals the queen's. It's not possible they could be discussing next season's parties and babies to be born when my world will be ending in a week.

"Please," I tell my new handmaiden as she dusts my temples

with real silver. "Can I at least send a message to my family?" I swallow and think of Fara at his morning chores, of Mora with her potions. Of Hen, anxious and possibly committing several crimes right now in trying to get to me. "I'd just like to tell them goodbye."

"I'm afraid there's no time to write one, *adel*."

"Can someone tell them I wanted to send a message?"

"Would pearls please you, *adel*?"

I blink at her, wondering if the numbness in my arms has reached my tongue. Maybe I didn't say what I thought I said. "Parchment would please me. And a scribe."

"Please, *adel*. It would honor me if you'd state your preference."

"My preference is to go home and get away from all you vicious people!"

Her lips purse. "Yes. I think the pearls will be best."

We're clearly not having the same conversation. I say nothing more as she beads pearls through my new haircut, the locks now short above my neck for the desert heat and left long in the front, where they drip with glistening garnets. My mother's head chain has been discarded, the golden links broken and empty. I clutch the dark jewel in my hand. My handmaiden clucked her tongue when I said I'd keep it, for the rune is powerless now that it's been used, but where last night it seemed dangerous, today it feels like my mother's hand in mine. As long as I have it, it means I intend to return it.

It's that single thought that keeps me from breaking into an inconsolable mess. I imagine it's Hen's fingers smoothing the powder on my cheeks, her expression serious as she asks when I'm planning to escape. As casually as if she were asking when I'd be done with my rounds at the stable. She would expect me to get out of this, and she would roll her eyes if I told her there wasn't a way. Hen always finds a way.

"Is she ready?" A copper-haired woman in a pink *jole* peers into the room, surveying me like a piece of art. "The ceremony is starting."

I'm not ready. I'll never be ready. What kind of person asks if a girl who's being sent to her death is ready?

"Yes, *adel*," says my handmaiden, folding my dress from last night into a square. "Isn't she lovely?"

The woman smiles. "That color is stunning on her. It makes her eyes look gold."

"Someone is going to stab me with a knife," I remind them, because I think they're missing the point.

"Oh yes," my handmaiden says, beaming. "Just like in all the legends!"

Touché.

I do my best to convince myself I'll find a way out of this as I walk beside the woman in pink, past the pool and the clouds reflected on its surface, through hallway after hallway painted with rivers and fields and armies. A guard follows, silent and watchful. Servants ogle me as they pass. The word *sacrifice* follows me like a persistent fly until I want to press my hands over my ears and scream. *That's her*, everyone whispers. *That's the girl.*

"Did you say a ceremony was starting?" I ask loudly, because I need something to drown out their voices.

"Yes," the woman answers. "The teams are being announced to the city, and then you'll depart."

My insides twist anew. I knew we'd be leaving soon from the urgent way the servants dressed me, but I imagined I'd have a little more time at the palace, a chance to cause a distraction or otherwise slip away. Now it seems the first chance I'll have to escape will be in the desert, which does not bode well for me and my inability to plan.

"Here we are, dear," my escort says as the murmurs of a crowd and the sharp voice of an announcer rattle the silence of the halls. A burst of desert heat overtakes us as we round a corner, and my breath catches in my chest.

The entire world waits outside. At least it may as well be the entire world, for people cluster the field-wide stairs leading up to the palace entrance, the grand fountain in the courtyard, the bridge that spans the river and every nook and cranny of the market streets. A platform has been built on a cleared section of the stairs, where the Mestrah and the queen sit on thrones facing the crowds. The heirs stand before them, each flanked by two teammates—their First and their Healer. Horns sound beside me, a deep, soul-shaking noise that could silence the gods.

A woman with light brown skin and a purple *jole* raises her arms from a corner of the platform. The jeweled berries in her ivy crown flash in the sun.

"It is now my pleasure to announce," she booms, her voice spelled to travel, "the royal heirs and their Chosen!"

Cheers shake the foundation of the palace, vibrating like a sickness to my core. I wish I could find Hen among the faces.

Gods, I hope she wasn't arrested for trying to get to me.

"May I first present the Mestrah's eldest, Deathbringer and His Royal Highness, the Prince of Orkena: Kasta, son of Isa."

Kasta makes no recognition of this introduction, but stands with his arms behind his back and his shoulders square while the crowd gives him their appreciation. A group of nearby girls swoons over him. I feel a jab of embarrassment that I ever felt the same. If they knew what he used that strength for, they wouldn't be so taken.

"As his Healer, the prince has selected Christos, son of Peroi." The crowd mutters in approval, though the Healer, a short, pale boy whose tunic hangs from his thin shoulders, only fidgets in response. "And as his First . . . Maia, daughter of none."

A chorus of gasps greets this announcement, my own included. No wonder the serving girls wouldn't speak of her. Maia is a Shifter, one of the most powerful creatures in Orkena, but her ability to shapeshift is a wild, horrible thing, not given to her by birth, but stolen by her murder of another Shifter. The stripping of her mother's name from hers is symbolic of the soul she traded for such power. For she's not only proven she'll kill for what she wants, but also acted in the worst defiance of the gods, rejecting the magic and the life she was born to. I have a hard time believing the Mestrah would allow such a choice, especially since Shifters lurk either deep in the desert or under intense enchantments in the service of the army, but maybe he's washed his hands of Kasta completely.

She's a shadow in the silence, dressed from head to foot in black armor, her masked face scanning the crowd like a falcon scans a field.

The announcer raises her hand to Jet. "The Mestrah's second, Soundbender and Master Swordsman, His Highness the Prince of Orkena: Jet, son of Nadia."

Jet is greeted with a roar that dwarfs the cheers I've heard so far, and Kasta's fists tighten behind his back. But like his brother, Jet makes no acknowledgment of his titles. He cringes against the noise, turning uncomfortably to look at his teammates. And summarily ignoring me, even though there's no way he can't see me at the top of these stairs, standing apart from everyone and boring holes into his head with my glare.

"As his Healer, the prince has selected Melia, daughter of Luladel." The crowd raises their voices again as a slender girl with deep umber skin raises her hand in an elegant wave. "And as his First, Master Enchanter Marcus, son of Bernab."

A huge man with beige skin raises both hands in the air, and the crowd roars nearly as loudly as they did for Jet. A group of soldiers near the front chants "Marcus! Marcus! Marcus!" His unique armor and occupation must mean he's from Greka, for though most Grekans have no magical abilities, the few who do are all Enchanters. He can craft weapons and armor imbued with powers that never wear off as spells eventually will. Enchanters are often as skilled with wielding such weapons as they are with crafting them, and I have to admit Jet has picked well, considering he probably chose last night in the span of minutes.

"And finally," bellows the announcer, "the Mestrah's third and youngest, *trielle* and Her Royal Highness, the Princess of Orkena: Sakira, daughter of Isa!"

I'm surprised to hear her cheers are the loudest of all. Not because she's the youngest, but because I thought Jet was the one everyone favored, and Hen says Sakira has been chasing trouble since she could walk. The servants always have something to report on the princess, whether it's another of her lavish parties in which unlikely people end up married or stabbed, or something more considerable, like the time she broke up the prince of Amian and the heiress of Constanta and started a war between their countries.

But maybe her infamy is the very thing that makes her popular, for the stairs rumble with applause. I have to stand on my tiptoes to see the far end of the platform, where a tall girl steps forward, her scribing brush raised high as she basks in the noise. Shining bronze armor wraps her back and chest in a metal X, mirroring stripes of sun along her fair skin. Her stomach is bare. A deep red sash forms a short skirt above long, fit legs, her leather belt glowing with enchantments that create an invisible armor over her exposed skin.

"As her Healer, the princess has selected Kita, daughter of Hanim." The strong Healer who visited me this morning (gods, was it only this morning?) nods and waves to the crowd. "And as her First, the priest Alette, daughter of Nicola."

The cheers elevate again, and a gorgeous girl with long black hair steps beside Sakira, her tawny shoulders gleaming with sunlight as she blows kisses to the crowd. I can't say I quite understand Sakira's choice. Priests are certainly powerful—they can dream of the future and pray for favors or natural disasters—but they don't always dream when they sleep, and the gods sometimes take days to answer their prayers, if at all. Alette won't be trained for combat, either. But I suppose being *trielle* means Sakira has a wide arsenal of spells at her disposal, so maybe that doesn't matter.

"The heirs are permitted to take any route they please to reach the Glass Caves," the announcer says as the cheers subside. "With the exception that they must pass through two checkpoints along the way. These checkpoints will both force the teams into close proximity and provide different challenges in getting through them, whether a team seeks to gain or keep the sacrifice. As a reminder, outside support is permitted at these checkpoints—and only these checkpoints—but any action that risks the safety of a team will result in lifelong imprisonment. It is for the gods to challenge our heirs, not the people."

Murmurs of agreement flit from the audience, intermingled with praise for Numet and Rie. Others indicate their obedience with bowed heads, fingers rubbing luck charms and tokens that represent their favored god.

"The team in possession of the sacrifice will have four days to reach the first checkpoint, four more to reach the second, and two to reach the finish, or a default will be called, and the race will restart. This is to prevent the contest from extending indefinitely, as in order to win, an heir needn't be the fastest to reach the caves—but they do need to perform one critical rite."

"The sacrifice," echoes the crowd, their excitement building. Heads and hairpieces turn left and right, seeking the Forsaken she's referring to. Many of their eyes catch on me, and I feel the weight of them like a gathering rain.

"The gods have woken Sabil's knife, signaling their desire for this contest, and the promise of unmatched power for the heir who would win it. As it did for the Mestrahs of old, this knife grants an ability to a new leader above and beyond the magic they already possess: the divine gift of Influence, the power to bend the will of enemies and allies alike. That said, the Mestrah would remind anyone who would desire this magic for themselves that though the knife has been reunited with its altar, it is heavily guarded, and its spell will only work for those of royal blood." She casts a purposeful look across the crowd, who snicker and whisper. "But this power is not free." She waits for the muttering to quiet. "Representing the many difficult decisions a ruler must make, taking a human life is a seal between gods and leader. A promise to do whatever is commanded, and to realize that with each gain is a cost." She turns to me, sweeping a dramatic hand at the stairs. "Our sacrifice."

Reverent silence falls over the crowd. I'm not given a name. I'm a symbol, and I know they think I was chosen for this, but it's eerie to see them look at me with such blind conviction. I can't help but feel it was too easy to fool them.

"Go on," whispers the woman in pink.

Like I'm being too shy in *marching to my death*. Gods, everyone is watching. Do I go like I've accepted this? Do I run? I don't think I'd get far in the crowd. The nobles won't risk disobeying the Mestrah to help me, if there's even anyone here who would. I can't go back the way I came. My guard will drag me screaming down the stairs or mark me to walk against my will. I can't stomach the thought of either.

And I really can't believe that yesterday, I was watching a glass boat come down the river and dreaming of being here.

Breathe, I tell myself. This isn't over yet. Jet may have failed epically as my rescuer, and Hen may have finally met a challenge she can't overcome, but maybe that means that in this story, I have to rescue myself. It's at least a week's ride to the finish. That's plenty of time to get used to the desert and whatever team I'm with, and make Fara proud by coming up with a plan.

I can do that. Of course I can do that.

I take a troubled step forward. The pressure of a thousand eyes on me thickens the air, but I force myself to keep my chin high, my shoulders straight. People bow their heads and cross their arms over their chests as I pass. I almost choke at the irony of being surrounded by so many people when there are only three I want to see in the entire world.

"The Mestrah has awarded the advantage to Princess Sakira," the announcer says. "She will be the first to leave, and shall begin with the sacrifice in her possession. Following her, after the span of an hourglass, shall be Prince Jet, and an hour after, Prince Kasta."

I've reached the platform. I don't want to walk past Kasta and his monstrous First any more than I want to walk through fire, but I grit my teeth and move without looking at them, though I feel Kasta's gaze as I go. Jet *still* won't look at me, no more than a glance and back at the crowd, and I bite back some choice words for him as I pass. At last I take my place beside Sakira, who glances at my dress and then has the decency to look sorry for me. And gives me hope my chances of escape are better than I thought. Maybe once I tell her what happened, she'll be horrified and let me go. You would think that among three siblings, one of them has to be reasonable.

Her Healer looks as uncomfortable to be here as I am. She also looks like she wants to say something, but I have to confess I'm rather irritated with her right now, too, and I turn away before she can speak.

"So by the will of Numet, Rie, and Sabil," booms the announcer, "and all the gods who have called for this occasion, we wish luck to the heirs and everlasting life to our future Mestrah!"

The horns blast again, and the people cheer and roar, chanting the name of their favored heir. The platform vibrates with stomping, the air with sparks and light and water, and I startle when enchanted fire bursts overhead, blasting us with heat as the flames swirl into the shapes of grinning jackals and charging horses. And then it doesn't matter what else is happening, because Sakira has snatched my wrist and yanked me toward the front of the platform.

"Jump!" she shouts.

"Gods!" I yelp.

We plunge into the masses, who clear for us at the last second, my ankle rolling painfully as I land. Sakira drags me down the stairs, through the parting crowd, and toward a fountain where three desert horses toss their heads: two bay geldings and a buckskin mare the color of wheat, who tries to pull her handler's arm out of its socket when she rears. And by that I mean that's literally what she was thinking when she did it.

The mare sees us coming and swivels her head, ears flat against her skull.

You, she thinks, her dark eye on Sakira. She's harder to read than the cows at the stable—I'm not as familiar with her movements as theirs—but her anger is so strong, my magic translates it to words easily enough.

No ride, she thinks. *I'll kick. I'll kick and hurt!*

I dig my heels into the sand and jerk out of Sakira's grasp.

"Up!" Sakira yells, pointing toward the mare.

"Are you drunk?" I shout. "She clearly wants to hurt us!"

"I know. That's part of the fun."

"You realize I'm not allowed to die until we reach the caves?"

Sakira turns around, gripping my shoulders. She's practically a twin of her mother, though her sleek hair is black like the Mestrah's, and her blue eyes are her father's, too.

"You have a week left to live," she says. "You want to spend it plodding along on an old nag?"

"That would be ideal, yes."

"Sorry." She shoves me at the mare. "If you're with me, you're going to have fun."

Two servants hold the mare now, one on each side of her bridle. They're trying to look cheerful about it, but I think they're just hoping I'll be fast and they can leave.

"All right," I tell the mare, pushing back the heat of her anger with every thread of calm I can summon. "I know you're not excited about this—"

Whisperer, the mare spits. *Let me go. Let go!*

"Look, I told them I didn't want to ride you, but this is the princess. She's like our alpha. And she's saying—"

"Are you talking to a horse?" Sakira asks.

"I'm a Whisperer," I say. And to the mare, "Just don't kill us for the first few minutes, and you'll be out of here. No more crowd."

Mm, the mare snorts. *No crowd?*

"No crowd, no noise. Just the desert. Wide, open desert."

The mare trembles and looks around, but she finally lowers her head. *Fast. Be fast.*

"You have magic?" Sakira studies the side of my head, but I don't dare look away from the mare. "You just speak Orkenian to her? That's seriously all you do?"

"We communicate through emotion," I say, grimacing as I take hold of the saddle. "My magic turns the words into something she can understand, and likewise."

The mare stays still, but now that I'm touching her I can feel her impatience and fear flood my body as strongly as if I'd been doused in water. It amplifies my own nerves, and I try to ignore the shiver in my fingers as I push onto her back. Oiled leather gleams beneath my hands. Lilies and swords decorate the saddle's neck, and the small hope that I might get my own horse dies when I see the seat's long enough for another rider.

"That's the most useless talent I've ever heard of," Sakira says, pulling into the saddle behind me. "No wonder the gods are sacrificing you. Yah!"

Off we plunge, the mare cursing, Sakira whooping in my ear, and me clinging to the front of the saddle, my mother's jewel clutched in my hand. People dart out of our way, small animals fear for their lives, and I try to think of the path ahead as the first part of my escape, away from the royal city, away from Kasta. The desert rises before us like the back of a slumbering beast. The crowd thins. Shops yield to houses and then huts, and the beat of the mare's hooves overtakes the shouts. A glance back reveals Alette and the Healer are close behind, the priest's shining hair whipping behind her cloth headband, the Healer's face slicked in sweat. Sakira whoops again in my ear, and the mare whinnies in response.

Freedom, she's thinking. *Freedom. Freedom.*

The last of the huts slides by, and the path changes from paving stones to packed clay.

Freedom, I agree as the royal city shrinks into the haze.

X

THE desert shifts around us like an orange sea.

Outposts and villages drift among its plateaus like islands, small clusters of palm-thatched huts and low square buildings gleaming white in the sun. Mud-packed roads form currents between them, crowded with colorfully dressed travelers and merchants guiding oxen and carts. I imagine many of them are disappointed if they came to watch the heirs gallop past. But Sakira says the roads are more dangerous than the desert. Aside from none of them taking a direct enough route to the first checkpoint, she worries about the spectators getting involved: stepping in front of the horses, snatching the saddlebags. And even though the Mestrah has threatened life in prison for anyone who hinders a team's progress, Sakira knows— from personal experience—that the threat of punishment only works against people who think they'll get caught.

Which does not make me feel better about riding in front of her.

To keep the horses fresh, Sakira slowed them to a jog a few kilometers outside the royal city, a steady pace we've kept ever since. But Numet rides steadily across the sky, and heat sears any skin not covered by our cooling cloaks. The horses begin to tire after just a few hours. Not that Sakira or her team can hear them, but I notice the geldings thinking more about how deep the sand is, and the mare of water. A good opportunity to ask for a break . . . and to see what I'm dealing with when it comes to the third heir.

"How long are we going to ride?" I ask. "I think the horses need a rest."

I expect resistance. I imagine Sakira wants to get as much distance as possible from her brothers in these first hours, but to my surprise, reins are drawn in and Sakira helps me to the ground, using only one arm to do so. The horses' sides glisten with sweat and the glow of the Ice spell painted onto their shoulders. The ink is already wearing, half faded from their efforts.

Sakira lifts a square of glass to the sky, a compass that shows the night stars at any time of day, and moves it until she finds the constellation she's following. I unlatch the saddlebag and have barely reached inside when the Healer—Kita, I think—rushes to my side.

"Can I help, *adel*?" she asks. "What are you looking for?"

The formal address makes my stomach lurch. She must feel guilty for reporting me. I would politely decline her help, except she's already rifling through the bag and she's not the kind of person you can share a small space with.

"Er . . ." I step back as she shoulders me even more out of the way. "Water spells. The horses are thirsty."

"I'll tend them," she says, pulling out a waterskin with a long nozzle. It looks flat and empty, but a blue Water enchantment gleams on its side, and the bag swells as soon as she touches it. It's dripping by the time she offers it to the mare.

"She can talk to them," Sakira says, leaning against Alette's gelding. "As in, she can ask my mare who the biggest jerk in the stable is."

"Wow, really?" says Alette, adjusting her headband. "Who is it?"

"That's not really what I do," I say.

"I bet it's Montu," Alette says. "Every time I see him, he's kicking someone."

"Montu *is* nasty," Sakira agrees. "But as fast as rain. I actually requested him, but of course *Kasta* is firstborn, *Kasta* gets first pick." She sneers and chews a black-lacquered nail. "Then again, if today goes well, he'll be the jealous one, not us."

She shares a sly look with Alette, and I can only hope whatever they're referring to has nothing to do with me.

"What else can I get for you?" Kita asks, intercepting me as I approach the bag again. I don't know how she even noticed. She was offering water to one of the geldings.

"I'm just a little hot. I was going to—"

"Here, I'll get your drinking skin and a fresh ice shawl. One moment."

"Are you doing this to make up for reporting me?" I ask, confused. "Because it's going to take way more than this."

"What? Oh." She turns, a sapphire shawl in one hand and shame written so strongly on her face that she looks like she's in pain. "That's not why I'm doing this. You're the sacrifice. The gods' holy Chosen. Anything you need, we're here to serve you."

I look between the three girls, and even Sakira nods in agreement.

"But . . ." Heat crawls up my neck that has nothing to do with the desert. I know it's ridiculous to be opposed to being doted on, but accepting their help feels like accepting this as my fate, and that sends needles of panic under my skin. But here's the perfect opportunity to tell them what happened. Please, gods, let them be normal people and believe me.

"You really don't need to. It wasn't the gods who chose me."

"What, did you lose at straws?" Sakira asks.

"No, your brother cut my wrist open."

Kita gasps. Sakira and Alette share a look like neither of them is surprised.

"That's why you aren't Forsaken," Sakira says, frowning. "Oh. I'm so sorry."

"By 'so sorry' you mean you're going to drop me off at the nearest town, right?"

Sakira gives me a pitying smile and saunters to my side. She wraps a casual arm around my shoulders and guides me toward her teammates. "Tell us everything."

I recount every event of the last day (a little too thoroughly—I'm told at least once that yes, they *know* about the pool in the foyer, and they don't need a borderline-disturbing description of the chocolate), skipping the part where I almost killed a prince and instead claiming Jet knocked Kasta out with the hilt of his sword. Sakira remains distinctly unfazed throughout. She nods and frowns at the right moments, but more like someone impatient for me to finish, as though this is a story she's already heard.

"Is this a story you've already heard?" I ask when a sigh is the only reaction I get for explaining Kasta is the entire reason I'm here.

"No," she says. "And yes. I guess it just sounds like exactly what they'd do. Kasta's obsessed with outshining Jet, Jet tries to be the hero, Father's disappointed in everyone. And I'm nowhere to be seen. That's my entire life."

"You're not surprised your brother is *committing sacrilege* to enact revenge on people?"

Sakira smiles. "Darling. I may look like a pretty face, but I know exactly what determined men are capable of. I'm not surprised he marked you, no."

I'm so relieved she believes me, I nearly hug her. "Then we can go back now, right? You can tell the Mestrah what happened. He'll call off the contest. Kasta will be exiled, Jet will confirm he doesn't want to rule, and you'll be named!"

Sakira laughs. A small, amused thing at first that tapers into something bitter.

"Sweet Zahru," she says, nodding to her teammates to mount up. She guides me toward the buckskin, and I get the uncomfortable feeling she's not going to say anything supportive or understanding. "I wish I could. I really do. But proving your story will be next to impossible. Jet's already shown he has no interest in helping you, and my word will make no difference. My father will think I'm only looking for the easy way out and disqualify me for lying. Don't you see?"

I hold back a frustrated sob. "No. Is this really how easy it is to kill someone below you?"

Her brow softens, but my shoulders sink at the steadiness in her eyes. She's already made up her mind. Sakira's not going to be my ally, and my first plan for escape has already failed. Now I have to figure out another way to get out of this, which means just me against the desert, alone, without the slightest sense of where I'm going.

And every day I'm away, Fara will struggle more and more to keep up with his work, until one of the travelers figures out his magic is gone and his only child isn't returning. He'll lose the stable. He'll lose our *home*.

"Oh, love." Sakira squeezes my shoulders. "Don't look so sad. I'll be quick about it. You'll barely feel a thing."

I glare at her. "Meaning, you're still going to kill me even though you know I'm not supposed to be here."

She shakes her head. "I'm sorry you're mixed up in this. But regardless of how it happened, you *are* the sacrifice." Alette approaches with the buckskin's reins, and Sakira takes them, looking over at me as she checks the saddlebags. "And I have to consider Orkena's future over yours. Kasta would be a disastrous king. He's impulsive. He's angry. He'll start wars just to prove he can win them, because that's what he thinks ruling is about: power." She tilts her head. "Think about it. If this is what Kasta will do to get his way *before* he's crowned, what do you think he'll do with armies at his command? Orkena will bleed for his insecurities. He can't win. And I can't risk losing on a technicality."

"But there has to be another way to beat him."

Sakira's skirt flashes red as she mounts up, the fabric dripping around her leg as she settles in. "Maybe, if we weren't so far into this already. We don't have the luxury of time anymore."

She reaches for me, but I don't move.

"What do you even have to do to prove you killed me? Can't you just dip the knife in sheep's blood or something?"

Something in her eyes glints; a mask slipping out of and back into place. "Let me tell you a story." She beckons me forward, and because the alternative is trying to outrun horses on foot, I sigh and take her hand. The mare tosses her head as I pull up. "Once upon a time there was a king with three children." She urges the buckskin forward. "The first two were sons, but the last was a daughter, and he loved her the most. He saw she was given everything she wanted, and often reminded her how she was his little girl, how she was gentle and sweet and soft. Even when she grew. Even when she trained and sweated and bled, and especially when she begged him to teach her about war, he only shook his head and said, 'Little star, you are too young to worry about such things.' And when the question of the crown arose, and the Crossing was to take place, he told her she wouldn't go."

"What?" I say, turning. "But why?"

"Because I'll always be his little girl." She smiles; a humorless, crooked thing. "I'm a painter. An artist. My magic is beautiful and refined; it creates and protects. Gods forbid I be curious about how to draw curses or set cities on fire. Or worse—break bones with my own hands. How could a sweet thing like me even think of that? I'm safest when I'm at home, throwing parties and winning hearts, because it's not right I should have to make the sacrifices hardened men make. Even if I want to. Even if I *have*." Her eyes burn with memories, and she grits her teeth. "You know, I don't think I even have the heart to harm a sheep, the poor, soft little dear."

Great. I've traded the prince who'd kill for his father's affection for the princess who'd kill to escape it. I imagine that's why she causes the trouble she has, too—to prove she isn't the demure little girl the Mestrah wants her to be. And here I am again, the tool to prove her efforts.

"Being compassionate doesn't make you weak," I grumble.

"I'm sorry," Sakira says. "But in the court, yes, it does."

She raises the compass and adjusts our route, and pushes the buckskin into a jog.

"Besides," she says. "Even if I dared oppose the gods, I can't afford to throw away the magic that comes with the sacrifice. The world sees *trielle* the same as my father. If I want our allies to take me seriously, I have to have that power."

I hate that I understand that part of her argument. I don't think the world's view of me as a useless Whisperer would change regardless of the position I held.

"So is that how you convinced the Mestrah to let you come?" I ask, feeling more than a little bitter with my new situation. "You stabbed someone in front of him?"

She laughs and rests her chin on my shoulder. "Oh, no. I snuck into the archives and charmed the Crossing scrolls to add a rule: all heirs of fifteen years and older are required to participate."

I twist around. "You rewrote the word of the *gods*?" No wonder she wasn't shocked about what Kasta had done.

"Now, now," she says, smirking. "The Mestrah's little star would never use her powers in such a way."

I'm quiet the rest of the day. Not only because I doubt anything I say will convince Sakira to free me, but because I can't get one of the things she said out of my head: *Regardless of how it happened, you are the sacrifice.* I don't want to believe it's true. I mean, yes, I'm here and everyone *thinks* I was chosen by the gods, but that doesn't make me a real sacrifice. I was simply in the wrong place at the wrong time, and the real person who's meant to be here got luckier than they'll ever know. But Sakira makes it sound like the gods have and are allowing me to remain in this position. That maybe, despite Kasta's spitefulness, I was meant for nothing more than this after all.

But I think of Fara, waiting for me at home, and Hen, who might very well be mounting a rescue party of her own. I shake the thought from my mind. I won't believe I'm meant to die. And I'm going to prove it right now by coming up with a plan even Fara would be proud of.

First things first: timing. The farther Sakira and her team ride, the harder it will be to find my way home. If I'm going to make my move, it has to be tonight.

Second: strategy. I know . . . absolutely nothing about surviving on my own. I don't know how to hunt. I don't know how to find water that doesn't come out of a river. I could take a horse after everyone's gone to sleep and run for one of the town-shaped silhouettes on the horizon, but I've seen more than one of those vanish after just a few steps, and I'm not sure what I'll do if the one I pick turns out to be a mirage. Being stranded alone in the desert is hardly an improvement from my current situation. So maybe all I've learned from thinking through this is that I need to think it through more.

I'll come back to that one.

Third: backup plan. I realize I don't technically have a first plan, but being ripped away from my home and everyone I love has inspired me to be thorough. I've hidden my mother's gem under the pearled belt of my gown, where it presses into the soft flesh above my stomach. The rune carved into it is powerless now, but most towns have a designated Runemaster, and I could get it recharged at one of the checkpoints. I'd just have to steal something valuable from Sakira to pay for the enchantment. And sneak away long enough to make the deal before anyone noticed. And hope no other life-threatening events trigger the rune's magic before we get to the caves.

It's the start of a plan. If I can figure out how to increase my chances of surviving on my own, it could work.

"Something to drink?" Sakira asks, passing me the waterskin.

I nod and take it, the water frigid when I swallow. This is the third time we've slowed our pace. *Trielle* spells can't last more than a few hours, and though Sakira's repainted the Ice spell on the horses' shoulders more than once, her magic can only keep them from overheating, not tiring. She also uses this pause to write something on a scroll she keeps holstered to her thigh, and to look for Kasta.

She's not worried about Jet at all. Which makes me anxious for silly reasons, because clearly I'd wanted to believe more of the things Jet told me last night than I thought. Especially the one about caring to spare my life. But maybe I need to accept the reason I'm in this mess is because I look gullible or desperate or both, and Kasta was right all along. All Jet cares about is making his brother miserable, and I was never more than a playing piece in their game.

"What are you writing?" I ask. If I keep thinking about Jet I'll get angry, and the angrier I get the less time I have to figure out how I'm going to fix this.

"Just checking our course," Sakira says, moving a small quill over the parchment. It's only then I notice how small the scroll is, and that it's attached to the wooden rolling bar at the top. I can't read the words, but whatever she's writing will nearly fill the page.

"How many of those did you bring?" She can't plan to fill one out every time we stop. She'd need dozens.

"Hmm?" Sakira looks up, sunlight shimmering over her blue eyeshadow. "Oh. No, it's a listening scroll. See?"

She turns it on her leg—like that will help me read it—but in moments, I understand what she means. The ink on the top is fading with the seconds, sinking into the parchment like it's leaking through. The ink on the bottom follows as it dries, and soon it's blank again.

"Every listening scroll has a partner," Sakira explains. "It lets me share my thoughts with someone like they're here."

"Oh," I say as new writing bleeds up into the scroll. The scrawl is sharper than hers; messier. "Who's on the other side?"

Sakira is quiet as she reads, then she laughs and marks the paper with a diagonal line, signaling the text to disappear. She rolls it into a handsome redwood case and shoves it into the leg holster next to her scribing brush.

"Someone who would be an absolute killjoy if he were here," she says, winking at Alette, but her grin soon fades. "Though I really will miss him trying to talk me out of things. I told him he could lose on purpose and stay on as my advisor, but he says he'd rather live with jackals than in the court."

"Jet?" I say in disbelief. "What is he saying?"

I curse the hope unfurling in my chest. A minute ago I was ready to paint him as villainous as his brother, and now at the first mention of his name, I'm imagining him charging up the dunes on a white horse, an army at his back as he rushes to save me. Well, I suppose it wouldn't be *that* dramatic, but some form of that would be preferred. But I bite back on the image, scolding myself for even considering it. All the hope in the world never changed Gallus's mind about me, and I can't expect it to work here.

Sakira's brow wrinkles in pity. "Nothing about you, dear. Though I'm sure he regrets what happened. Even when he and Kasta were at their worst, he was never the type to bring other people into it." She motions for me to turn, and I comply as she urges the mare into a walk. "He's just reminding me about the bandit camp we're passing tomorrow, and plotting where I can build my shrine near the Old Temples. He says they could definitely do with some updating."

The Old Temples, where the first Mestrahs are buried . . . directly east of the palace and not at all in the southern direction we're headed. If he's deserting the race, as he told Kasta he would, that's a direct route to Nadessa. I assure myself that of course he'd tell Sakira the wrong thing if he was planning a rescue mission, but the logical side of me burns with resentment. Imagining him starting a new life while mine comes to a close seems the most unfair of all.

"And Kasta?" I ask, not sure I want to know.

"What about him?"

"Has he written to you yet?"

Not that I remember seeing a second scroll, but maybe she keeps his in her saddlebag.

This time even Kita laughs with Sakira.

"Are you serious?" Sakira says. "You've met him. Do you think being his sister makes any difference when it comes to him winning this?"

I shrug.

"He would have cut *me* to be the sacrifice, if it weren't too suspicious. Well, probably Jet first, but then me." She shakes her head. "No. There is no lifetime in which I'd share anything with Kasta on a listening scroll."

That resentment burns brighter in my chest. I should have known. Jet and Sakira are obviously close, and of course he'd choose her future over mine. That's what I would do for Hen, even if I can't imagine Hen killing anyone, ever, no matter what tradition or point she was supposed to be making.

"So Jet's helping you because he's already gone," I say, reminding myself it doesn't matter. I don't need Jet to be able to steal a horse and run. "Is that how you won the advantage, too? With his help?"

"Mm," Sakira says, the bitterness back in her tone. "I shouldn't have needed his help, because I *do* have the best team, not that Father would ever admit it. But technically yes, he helped by being an absolute cod with Kasta."

Alette snickers.

"That fight last night?" Sakira says. "Father was furious. I wasn't even in the room when he awarded me the advantage. My handmaiden came to tell me."

"But officially," Alette says, "it's because I'm the greatest power Sakira could have on her side. The very gods will hear my cries. We're protected implicitly."

"Not the first time they've heard her cries," Sakira mutters.

"Oh, hush," Alette says, though her smile is shameless. "She's only just joined us. Ease her into the waters, at least."

"Just as you eased that Imanian duke into the baths?"

"I did *not* know he was engaged," Alette says, pointing a defiant finger. "And I like to think I saved his fiancée from what would have been a terrible marriage. Besides, I wasn't the only one locking lips that night with someone I shouldn't have."

"He told me he was from Greka! How was I supposed to know he was a waiter? He wasn't dressed like one."

"This happened at the *Choosing*?" I say.

"Oh, no," Sakira says. "Though I did meet someone very interesting last night." She and Alette share a smirk. "This happened on my birthday."

"Her second boy of that day, too," Alette says, winking. "The first one was prettier, but weirder."

"He kept trying to turn me into a poem. Then when I marked him to stop, he had nothing else to say. Great arms, though. Gods, he had great arms."

My level of concern for being at the mercy of this team has just elevated. "So . . . you picked a friend as your escort."

"Alette and I have been friends since our schooling started," Sakira says.

"I prefer the term *sisters*," Alette injects.

"I knew she'd be my First as soon as Father told us about the contest. He only put on the Choosing banquets because he felt sorry for Kasta, who has no friends. Jet already had Marcus in mind, too."

"But weren't you supposed to pick someone who would help you?"

I realize only after asking that my question came out rather bluntly. Neither girl says anything, but Alette looks like I slapped her.

"I just mean . . . it takes time for your magic to work. And sometimes the gods don't answer like you want them to, right? You could pray for us if we run out of food or get lost, but what if we're attacked?"

"We're not going to be attacked," Sakira says. "Alette is going to pray Kasta away. Even if he gets close, I can ward myself against his filthy Shifter. Then it's down to him and a sword, and I'm not afraid to play dirty."

I blink. "I mean like hyenas or rattlesnakes. Or rabid jackals. Or that bandit hideout you mentioned?"

This is not a question I wanted answered with complete silence. Not that I'm trying to help Sakira get us closer to the finish by thinking of these things, but my safety is currently entwined with hers.

"You know, you worry too much." Alette urges her gelding into a jog. "None of that matters, because no one's going to catch us. We can see both horizons. The horses will warn us about animals. And the wrath of the gods will come down on anyone who tries to stand in our way."

"By 'wrath of the gods,' you mean you're confident they'll actually interfere, right?" I say hopefully.

"Alette's right. Stop worrying." Sakira pushes the mare back into a jog. "I have everything sorted out."

Which is exactly what I would say if I hadn't actually thought things through yet. I don't point out that whatever her strategy, she still needs time to paint whatever spells she intends to use, time she may or may not have, depending on the threat. And what will she do if she loses the brush? Or runs out of ink? I don't really know how *trielle* spells work, but I know those two things are crucial.

I'm starting to think I'm not the only one without a plan.

XI

SAKIRA makes her first bad decision before twilight.

There is a moment, when she takes out her glass compass to check the stars and says, "There it is," to a small, plain outpost in the distance, that I think she's simply marking an occupied place we need to avoid. I should probably have found it strange we'd otherwise stayed far from other people until this point, and that I'd seen no other towns or roads on the horizon that would force us to choose between moving close to a populous area or this one. It certainly didn't look like a place for making regrettable decisions. The outpost is small and isolated and, as we move closer, appears to be only two buildings: a high-ceilinged stable flanked by a mudbrick fence, and a long, wide residence behind it, pocketed with dozens of small windows. Brown canopies shade a third of the fenced area, and I surmise this must be a very rich person's estate, since the barn is nearly the size of the house.

The buckskin raises her nose to the smell of hay. *Friends?* she thinks. *Rest? Home?*

"We're switching mounts?" I ask, my throat tightening. Fresh mounts obviously make sense, as we could then ride on through the night. But this is very bad for solidifying my escape plan, which I'd have much more time to prepare if my captors stopped to sleep.

"Maybe," Sakira says, drawing her brush from her leg holster. "Bring your horses here," she says to her team.

"Maybe?" I echo. "What does that mean?"

Sakira ignores me and uncaps the third item threaded through her holster: a long glass jar whose liquid contents shimmer gold. She paints a dot beneath an arc on both horses' shoulders, then adds two crossed arrows before painting the same spells onto the buckskin.

"Mirage spells," she explains. "And Silence. Can't have the horses alerting our position, can we?"

As if on cue, the buckskin raises her head and whistles a greeting—or she would have, if the spell let her make any sound. She snaps her ears to her skull in annoyance. *Rude*, she thinks. *Why? Rest.*

She paws the sand, and Sakira slides off behind me.

"Why does it seem like they don't know we're coming?" I ask as Kita and Alette dismount in turn.

"Because they don't." Sakira grins. "Here."

She grips my hand in a way I think is meant to help me to the ground, until she flips my wrist over and marks it with a broken line.

"Gods," I say, jerking away. The memory of Elin's grooming spell is still too fresh. "I thought I was sacred and holy. Don't you warn sacred and holy people before you mark them?"

Sakira snickers. "Relax, it's just a Follow spell. Means you can't be more than a few hundred meters from me. One less thing to worry about while we're here."

One less opportunity to sneak away. I rub the ink hard, but the gold sinks into my skin, thankfully leaving behind no more than a cold prickle. Judging by how fast the Ice spells on the horses fade, this one should be gone by tonight. But I'm going to have to be more careful around Sakira and that brush.

"And why *are* we here?" I grumble.

"To make history."

I don't like the look in Sakira's eyes. It's not too unlike the expression Hen wears before sabotaging someone, and I have a feeling I'm about to experience firsthand one of Sakira's infamous exploits.

"Let's go, Your Holiness," she says, and to Kita, "If you need us, or you see Kasta, wet this." She hands Kita a paper spell with a double loop on its face, then marks the Healer's hand with the same arc and dot as the horses. "It'll burn a symbol on my arm. But remember, unless someone gets close, they can't see you. We shouldn't be long."

"Yes, *aera*," Kita says, bowing her head.

Sakira marks herself and Alette with Mirage, and I sigh and dismount as she adds the symbol to my shoulder. And then we're walking toward an unsuspecting building, our cloak hoods around our heads like we're miscreants, shattering every expectation I had about liars and thieves. Maybe grisly vagabonds exist in better stories, but in mine the criminals are Materialists and princesses.

"Do I really need to come?" I ask. "Can't I stay with Kita?"

Sakira loops her arm through mine. "Now, I know that's not something you would have asked yesterday. You're still the same girl who snuck into a palace banquet, yes?"

I groan. "Yes. And look where it landed me."

"Forget what happens at the end of this week. Right now it's just you and us, and an entire desert full of opportunities. I have a *lot* planned for us over the next few days. It's going to be the time of your life."

I look pointedly over. "Seriously? The *time of my life?*"

"Until you die honorably and painlessly." But despite the cavalier way she says it, I catch a flash of sadness in her eyes. "A queen must obey the gods first and foremost. But let's not think about that. Let's think about . . . presents."

"Presents?"

We're within shouting distance of the stable now. The familiar shape of its dome, despite the canopies sheltering the paddocks, pulls at something in me so hard I almost can't breathe. Someone whistles a song within the aisle of the stable, and I hear the familiar scrape of a broom against straw. The stable Whisperer, probably. Though I wouldn't be surprised if there was more than one, considering the size of the place.

My heart pinches thinking about Fara being alone without me, and I remind myself that even if someone discovers his magic is gone, at least he won't be cast out like the Forsaken. I still need to get back quickly, because all lower class magicians are required to serve Orkena until their sixtieth summer, and if I'm not there to say I need Fara to help me, he'll be sent wherever the Mestrah needs him. To harvest crops in a neighboring town, or to assist a rich Earthmover halfway across the country. He wouldn't have a choice in what he was assigned to, and we certainly couldn't regain the stable once that's done. But at least I wouldn't have to wonder where he'd gone.

"I know what you're thinking," Sakira says.

I look over. "I really doubt that."

"You're thinking this is a careless mistake. That I'm not staying focused. But see, that's where you and my father are wrong. A good leader doesn't have to be business all the time." She pokes my shoulder, like I'm about to disagree. "All Father ever worries about are taxes and trade contracts, and I'm not saying he hasn't done well with that, but he's the world's *worst* conversationalist. People pull away from him because he doesn't seem real, you know?" She nudges me. "Think about it. Who do you want to be sitting next to during a boring realm meeting? The stuffy prince who spends his days locked away or the princess who stole a priceless magical horse?"

I would note she should be *paying attention* during a "boring realm meeting," but I'm a little too caught up on that last part. "I'm sorry, we're going to steal a *what*?"

The gold lining Sakira's eyes crinkles. "This will be so much fun!"

"You do know you need a special license to keep an animal with magic?" I say, stopping. Not like it's a typical issue—animals born with magic are about as common as blood moons—but I remember Fara warning me about treating them, even though we never have. A fearful animal might bite, but a fearful *magical* animal might flood a town. "What if it levels the stable?"

"Now you're sounding like Jet. 'But laws, and consequences!'" Sakira releases me and walks backward, her edges already blurring with the sand and the plaster sides of the building behind her. In two more steps, I can't see her at all. "Relax. An experienced Whisperer has been working with this mare since she was a foal. She's well-trained."

Of which I'm sure, considering the grandeur of this estate, but somehow I doubt that control extends to being stolen by a loud, thrill-seeking stranger. But I don't see Sakira listening to that reasoning any more than she's listened to anything else, and with a sigh I start forward until she and Alette flash back into view.

"Wait," Sakira says as we near the stable's open archway. The person who'd been sweeping and whistling turns out to be a young man dressed in a simple working tunic, who looks toward the back of the stable when we stop. The thoughts of the animals within reach me in a murmured buzz. Like it's a distant conversation, I'm not close enough to make out full phrases, but I catch snippets of *warm* and *food* and *out*.

The man pauses his work, and snickers. "Yeah, food is coming. Hold on."

Definitely a Whisperer. He sets the reed-headed broom against the aisle wall and disappears into a room on the side.

"All right, this is the plan," Sakira whispers. "Alette is lookout. If whistler-boy gets suspicious, she'll get close enough for him to see her, and provide a distraction."

Alette grins and pulls the neckline of her *jole* a bit lower, which honestly is even distracting for me right now.

"We're going to sneak in and find the mare," Sakira continues. "I'm going to mark her with Mirage, and we're going to walk her right out of here."

I wait for her to expand on that. When she doesn't, I blink. "Just like that? Aren't there guards?"

Sakira grins. "Just like that, because I happen to have a friend who's a Whisperer." She slings an arm around me. "You worked your charms on the buckskin. I know this will be just as easy for you."

Even though I'm sure she's only saying that to win my

cooperation, I can't stop the stir of pride in my chest. I *have* worked with a lot of different animals, and in far more stressful situations. Maybe this will even help Sakira see I'd be far more valuable to her alive.

It's not like things could end any worse than yesterday, anyway.

"I can't believe I'm saying this," I say. "But fine."

Sakira beams. "That's my girl. Now, let's get this done quickly. The stable's enchanted to alert the barracks if Ashra's stall opens without permission. We won't have much time after that."

And my prior confidence dies. "That building is a barracks?"

We must be at one of the cavalry reserves. Not that I'm familiar with the Mestrah's military, but I remember a traveler talking about "secret stables" across Orkena, places soldiers and horses were kept in case the capital was taken by surprise.

Another realization hits me. "You're stealing from your *father?*"

Sakira does not answer, nor does she seem concerned by the possibility of a small army coming down on us. She's already crept into the sand-dusted aisle, past the columned doorway where the Whisperer is mixing feed, where she vanishes beside the first stall. I suppose she has no true reason to worry. Once her father's guards recognize her, they'll still try to stop her, but they won't hurt her. Of course, they certainly won't recognize me.

I swear under my breath and dart forward. The horse in the first stall jerks his head up as Sakira flashes into my vision—and as I flash into his. He lets out a long whinny, and I wince.

Food? he thinks. *You, give food?*

"I'm working on it," yells the man in the feed room.

Thank the gods for horses and their appetites.

"There she is," Sakira whispers, pointing to a stall across from us. The entire stable is ridiculously lavish considering its tenants, but this one especially looks more like a suite. Polished stone frames the walls, and a spout pours a trickling stream of water into a porcelain trough. The iron gates that bar both the stall entry and the opening to the paddock are shaped in intricate gods' symbols.

And still, all of this pales in comparison to the horse inside.

The mare is a deep, blood-red bay, and where the dying sun stripes her back, her coat shimmers like a living ember. Black colors her mane and legs from the knees down, small flames running their edges as if looking for tinder to catch. But her eyes make it hardest to look away. Flames crawl within them, burning green then blue then red, like a shifting sunset.

A Firespinner. She's the most incredible creature I've ever seen, and I get the impression I'm looking at something much older and more sacred than even her magic would indicate.

"Ashra," Sakira whispers, drawing closer. The mare jerks her head when we come into sight, her golden halter jingling, and I'm not sure whether to be impressed or alarmed she doesn't otherwise move.

Hidden ones, she thinks, reaching her nose over the polished wall. *Devious ones*.

I snicker that she already knows we're up to no good, until I remember there's another Whisperer here who could hear her. But when I look toward the far aisle, the man is leaning against the wall, a jar of grain under one arm and his head tilted toward someone I can't see. Alette appears to be succeeding at her part in this. A pulse of nerves runs through me, but I press them down, turning back to the stunning creature.

"Ashra," I say. Animals always feel more comfortable when someone knows their name. The mare stretches her nose to me, and after a moment's hesitation, I push my fingers up the bridge of her silken face. Her fur is soft and cool. I'd half expected it to burn. Instead, relief and familiarity warm my blood, like being reunited with an old friend.

Whisperer, Ashra rumbles. She looks young, but in my head her voice sounds old. *You do not belong.*

I swallow. "I feel like you don't belong here, either. Do they not let you out?"

The mare swings her head to see the gate barring the paddock. A shiver runs under her skin that I take to be longing, until red fire flashes across her shoulder, and the unfortunate fly that dared land on her drops to the ground with a sizzle.

It occurs to me riding her is going to be a little more complicated than Sakira anticipates.

Others, she thinks. *Afraid.*

"They don't like your magic." I suddenly feel sorry for her. I mean, fear was also *my* reaction when Sakira told me about her, but a wave of her loneliness floods through me, and I consider what it must be like to be so different. In her lifetime, she will not meet another like her.

"Hurry it up, Your Holiness," Sakira says, her eyes on the Whisperer.

"Will you come with us?" I ask. "Out somewhere you can run. No more walls."

Out? There's an eagerness in her tone that I don't like. She's been kept inside too long. *Yes*, she thinks, pawing the straw near the gate. *Out. After food.*

Curse horses and their appetites.

"What's taking so long?" Sakira grumbles.

"She wants dinner," I say.

"I have dinner for you," Sakira says, turning to the mare. "It's out there."

The mare doesn't even glance her way. She nickers to the man, who ignores her for whatever Alette is saying.

I shake my head. "She can't understand you."

Sakira frowns. "Why not? I'm doing the same thing as you."

"Look, you may think my magic is 'lesser,' but it works the same way as yours. I could pick up your brush and draw a spell, but it's not going to do anything. You need me to translate." Emphasis on the *need me*.

"Fine," Sakira says. "Then tell her we have food, and we need to go *now*."

"We have food for you," I tell the mare. "But we have to get away from the stable. Otherwise they won't let you go with us."

No, the mare thinks. *Grain.*

"Do you have grain?" I ask Sakira.

"All right, this is ridiculous," Sakira says, pulling out her brush. "New plan. I'm going to jump in there and paint her with Mirage. You're going to open the gate, and I'm going to ride her out."

"That's a terrible plan!" I whisper as loudly as I dare. "One, she'll probably roast you like that fly, and two, how am *I* going to get out of here?"

"Do you want to ride, too?"

I gape at her. "No! If you'd give me just two minutes—"

"Then I guess you'll need to compromise."

She swings a pale leg over the wall before I can protest, and the mare tosses her head and backs away, startled. The Whisperer turns around. I hear Alette ask loudly about a nearby horse to regain his attention, but he puts a hand up and starts toward us. Ashra is clearly too important to put aside even for Alette.

In a few more steps, he'll be able to see us.

"Sakira!" I snap.

I feel the change in the mare the second Sakira pulls onto her back. One moment it's annoyance at having a stranger in her stall, the next it's full irritation this person would be bold enough to sit on her. The Whisperer stumbles when Sakira draws the spell on Ashra's shoulder, the mare vanishing before his eyes, and the grain jar shatters to the ground four steps later, when he's close enough that all three of us flash into his view.

If he recognizes Sakira, it doesn't register on his face.

"Thieves!" he bellows, lunging for me. "Thieves in the stable!"

Off! screams the mare, rearing.

I try not to think about how many Earthmovers and Waterweavers are throwing down their cards right now to come after us. I do the only thing I can, and rip the metal gate open.

"Run!" I yell.

The mare plunges forward. The man curses and lurches back, falling over his feet to the ground.

"Ashra!" he calls. "Ashra, stop!"

But with nothing between her and the open door, Ashra

doesn't even notice the grain she tramples on the way out. *Run*, she thinks. *Open. Out!* I dart after them, hoping the man isn't as fast as he looks. But though he's back on his feet, he doesn't pursue me. He turns to the trio of armored soldiers who've entered on the far side.

"One of them is *trielle*," he says. "They're using Mirage!"

Metal footsteps clack behind me. Sakira is already out of sight, the sand flying eerily where Ashra's hooves hit it. I reach the edge of the barn and shriek when someone comes at me, but it's only Alette, her long hair flying wildly from her headband.

"This way!" she says, grabbing my hand.

We bolt into the desert. One soldier follows us on foot, his gaze low where our steps kick up sand, and I hear others drawing horses from their stalls. The Whisperer stops at the edge of the barn, shouting Ashra's name. Behind the stable, a low horn bellows the alarm.

I would like to revisit the moment I said this little adventure couldn't be worse than my last one.

"We're not going to make it!" I yell as the soldier gains on us.

"Yes we are!" Alette says, singsong. I have a feeling she does this way too often, and much too successfully. "There!"

She points to a large area of moving, churning sand, and Kita bursts into view on one of the geldings, the buckskin and the other bay in tow. The horses slide to a stop, and Alette is on the bay in an instant. I clamber up on the buckskin. The foot soldier is reaching for me when a shot of my fear must go right into the mare, because she whirls and strikes him, sending him flying to his back. We bolt after the others. I cling to the saddle, cursing Sakira's rashness. The mounted soldiers are approaching fast, their horses fresh and trained for speed.

"Where's Sakira?" I yell.

A blast of sand next to us is the reply. One of the pursuing soldiers is an Airweaver, and I imagine if he could see us better, that shot wouldn't have missed.

There, says the buckskin.

"What?" She was the last person—er, creature I was expecting a reply from.

Fire smell, says the buckskin. *Follow?*

A hysterical laugh bubbles up my throat. She can smell the other horse! "Yes! Geldings, follow the fire!"

All the horses shift direction, and if we weren't at a full gallop, I would hug the mare for this revelation. Of course, that means the other horses can smell us, too, but their riders aren't Whisperers. If we can lose the soldiers, they'll have no way to find us.

"Ah, she's brilliant," Alette exclaims, pointing ahead of us. Meaning Sakira and the route she chose, I assume. After what just happened, I'm not sure I agree, but this latest move does look hopeful. Ahead lies a hill spread with tall desert bushes and nettled grass, footing the horses will have to slow for; footing that will hide the shift of sand beneath invisible feet. The horses slide on their hooves and jog when we reach the first bushes, and we urge them quickly around. The soldiers are close behind. But as unnerving as it is to look over our shoulders and see them reaching the bushes we just passed, they're forced to slow as well. The three of them look wildly up the hill, their eyes sliding past us. In moments they spread out, trying to find hoofprints in the grass.

We press our horses on, until Sakira and the blood-red mare flash into view.

Nice work, Sakira mouths, her eyes locking approvingly first on Kita, then Alette—then me. She nods and moves Ashra on, a fresh spell I don't recognize sinking into the mare's haunches.

"They're here somewhere," grumbles a soldier.

"Hold," says another soldier.

Sakira raises her hand, and we stop, too.

The soldiers listen for our footsteps, but all that passes between us is the occasional rustle of wind through dead brush.

"We can't have lost them," says the third soldier, his black mare dancing sideways.

Up, she's thinking. *Fire*.

But of course he can't hear her, and since they left the Whisperer behind, they won't.

Move, Ashra thinks. *No stand. Move*.

"Easy," Sakira mutters as the mare shifts and tosses her head. If she makes much more noise, the soldiers will hear her.

"Quiet," I whisper, laying a hand carefully on Ashra's neck. A blast of impatience and nerves surges through my fingers, so strong I gasp and jerk back.

"Get off," I snap, turning to Sakira.

"What? No!"

"She's going to bolt. She's been locked up way too long in there, and—"

BOOM. The entire hill erupts into geysers of sand, the

Earthmover below us lifting his arms in effort. The buckskin lurches beneath me, and I barely hold on as she slams into Kita's horse to avoid the surging earth. Sand showers around us, revealing our position—

Ashra's scream cuts through the chaos. Anger flows off her in waves, and fire billows on her hocks and in her hair, streaming down her back where Sakira clings. She's turned to *face* the soldiers, and for once Sakira doesn't look amused or confident. She looks young and afraid, and when Ashra rears, she finally loses her grip and falls.

Burn, Ashra thinks.

Sakira rolls out of the way as the mare crashes back down. Every plant in the area flares up in scalding shades of yellow and red, and Alette shrieks as the bush next to her engulfs the side of her *jole*. It must scald the gelding, too, because he screams and charges up the hill.

"Alette!" Sakira cries. She lurches for her friend—at the same time that Ashra, once easily in her reach, bolts into the heat.

"No!" Sakira yells, whirling.

"Let her go!" I shout, reaching for Sakira. I won't go into the thoughts I have about leaving her, because she really could be our future Mestrah and the gods would frown on that, but I will admit the Follow spell on my wrist is a big inspiration in wanting to get her out. Sakira grabs my arm and swings behind me just as fear and pain overtake the buckskin's thoughts. The entire world is aflame. The soldiers shout in alarm and retreat, and the buckskin's thoughts surge with getting free, getting *out*, but I catch sight of a moving slip of flame and push the mare after it. Alette flashes into view, small flames crawling up her side from foot to shoulder. We charge after, heat searing our arms, our faces; blistering against our legs, until finally the foliage yields to open sand. Alette dives into it to extinguish her side. The gelding, his left flank still smoking, charges on with a pained whinny. Sakira reaches around me and yanks our mare to a stop.

"I'll get him," Kita calls, pushing her horse on.

Sakira is already on the ground, painting symbols on Alette's arms. Alette's once beautiful *jole* is charred along the side, but the fire is out, and her tawny skin looks red and tender but not scalded. She turns on her back, and for a moment the friends look at each other, Sakira with something next to panic, Alette with the stunned look of someone who doesn't entirely believe what's happened. Her pink irises glance past Sakira to the wall of black smoke.

And then, impossibly, she *laughs*.

"*That*," she says, giggling and holding her side, "was the most epic thing we've ever done."

Sakira sits back on her heels, her shoulders relaxing as a smile cuts her face. Soon she's giggling, too, and like that they're back to themselves, as untouchable by danger as they've ever been. Or so it would seem.

But I remember the panic in Sakira's face when she saw Alette catch fire. She could have reached for Ashra and gained an unprecedented advantage in the race. Between her skillset and a horse trained to use magic, she'd be nearly untouchable.

She reached for Alette.

XII

"OH, I had that boy going," Alette says, tossing her half-burnt locks. "I was a soldier's daughter, visiting for the week, bored and looking for something to do. He asked if I'd like to go riding later, under the stars . . . you should have seen him blush when I said yes, then asked if he meant on horses."

We've only just met up with Kita, who luckily had Alette's healed gelding in tow, and already Sakira and Alette are laughing over the details of their story, molding it into the tale the servants will whisper about in the palace.

"You really do have a talent for innuendo," Sakira says, shifting in the saddle behind me. "You should give classes."

"I wish I could give classes. Do you think you could make that a position when you're Mestrah? 'Alette: High Priest and Mistress of Seduction.'"

"I think I'd be robbing the world of a treasure if I didn't."

"And you on that wild horse! What was it like to ride her?"

I would remind them Ashra isn't actually a wild horse, and that Sakira's recklessness made her that way, but I hold my tongue.

"Like a dream," Sakira says, stretching behind me. "She's much smoother in stride than these street rats. And so much faster. If I hadn't stopped her to wait for you, we'd be at the caves by now."

I roll my eyes. Ashra's stride looked pretty much like that of every other horse I've seen.

"Too bad the guards spooked her," Alette says, frowning. "It would have been much more impressive to finish the race with her."

"Well, we didn't know we'd be locked in an epic battle." I hear the smirk in Sakira's voice. "There we were, the four of us against a whole barracks of soldiers. They had Airweavers and Earthmovers. Stormshrikes and Dominators. But they were no match for Ashra and a queen."

"There were three of them," I remind her.

"You mean thirty-three," Sakira says, winking when I look back.

"And you lost the mare."

"Don't be a killjoy," Alette says, fussing with a burnt hole in her cooling cloak. "Obviously Sakira felt such a beautiful, powerful creature belonged to no one, and after subduing the soldiers, set her free."

"Yes," Sakira agrees. "We'll say it was a rescue mission."

Is this how all travelers spin their stories? Has nothing I've ever known been true?

"But *you* did very well, too, my dear," Sakira says, nudging my shoulder. "Especially for your maiden mission. The others will be much easier."

I turn to look at her. "You have *more* of these planned?"

Sakira laughs. "I had everything under control. Give it time. Tonight, you'll remember you successfully stole a legendary animal from a fully stocked barracks, and soon you'll be saying you convinced *all* the horses to run free."

I wish I could show her the face she made when Ashra turned to the soldiers. She certainly didn't look like someone who was in control. And how would she feel if any of those soldiers were hurt because of it? Or if Alette's burns had been worse? Maybe having limitless access to Healers means she doesn't think about those kinds of details. But I have a feeling her father—and her potential future soldiers—wouldn't be so amused by her disregard for their safety.

But I sigh and remind myself to go along with it, because even though "the mission" ended poorly, it could have been worse. And Sakira recognizing I did well is a good thing. It's exactly what I was hoping for, even if I *am* still planning to leave as soon as viably possible, because if I'm not able to get away, I want it in the back of her mind.

Because whether she meant to or not, she showed me a different part of her today. Someone human. Someone who feared she'd gone too far.

Someone who might, if it came down to just us and the knife, choose a friend over the promise of power.

Twilight settles across the dunes like a silver sheet.

My nerves amplify with the darkness. It's been an hour since we crossed a road or skirted the distant shadow of huts, and here, where the meager spring rains have coaxed brush and patchy grass from their slumber, there are only animals. Overprotective rattlesnakes; herds of pale gazelles and sandy sheep. Soon, summer's rainless heat will drive them back to the riverbanks. But seeing them brings me to an interesting thought. The animals aren't foolish enough to wander far from a large source of water, and many of Orkena's towns are built along our two rivers' shores. If I can make it to a river, I'll find people. And if I cover my scar, I may even find someone kind enough to help me get home.

Which brings me to a realization I can actually thank Sakira for. Before, I wasn't sure how I'd find the main river once I took a horse into the sand. But thanks to Sakira's fire horse, I know I don't have to know exactly where it is. I just have to be close enough for the buckskin to smell it, and she'll guide us there herself.

Now I just need the opportunity to leave.

"All right, that's as long as this gorgeous body can stand riding," Sakira says, dismounting before the buckskin has stopped. "We're still a day from the first checkpoint, and I want to arrive as fresh as rain. Which means tonight . . ." Jars clank, and I turn to see her lifting jeweled flasks from the saddlebag. "We relax."

"How are you even still standing?" I ask, stretching my aching back. "Don't you ever sleep?"

"Darling, this isn't even half of what I can accomplish in a day." She shoves a flask into my hand. "Alette dreamed this night would go smoothly. Do you want to lie awake fretting about your future, or enjoy my infamous hospitality?"

She winks and twirls away, her red skirt flaring on her hips. I want to point out she could easily make my future not something to fret about, but I'm far too anxious about my pending escape to reason with her right now.

"I'll set up the tent, *aera*," Kita says, though she, too, is given a flask.

"To our new Mestrah," Alette says, raising her flask to the sky. Sakira clanks hers against it.

"To change," she says.

They drink. I slide off the buckskin and apologize again to her for the fire, but the wonderful thing about animals is they seldom stress about anything not immediately in front of them, and she only nibbles my shoulder and asks for food. I smile and rub her neck, feeling guilty that in another couple hours I'll be asking her to leave again. I'll have to take along an extra handful of grain, if I can find it. For now, I need to make sure there's enough in her saddlebags to last us both a couple of days.

I peer over the saddle, where the team is settling in. Sakira and Alette are definitely not paying attention to what I'm doing, but the Healer and her falcon eyes might be a problem. I wait until Kita wets a Build spell against the side of a large fabric square before shifting behind the bulky saddlebag and sliding my fingers beneath the latch. No sooner have I lifted the flap when Kita bursts into view and bustles me out of the way.

"What can I get for you?" she says.

"How did you even see me?" I ask.

"My son is two. I see everything." She beams. "Are you hungry? I'll make supper as soon as the tent is up, but we have a few snacks if you need them."

"It's the horses again," I hedge, sighing. "They need to eat."

"Of course. I'll grow them some grass."

She lifts a blue potion from the bag, but because I haven't moved, she turns and smiles, like she knows exactly what I'm up to.

"Anything else, *adel*?"

I shrug. "No, thank you."

She doesn't go. I shift in place and try a new tactic. "You have a son?"

"Yes." Her smile widens, her eyes growing fond and distant. "He's brilliant. And a terror. But at least he sleeps better than his sister."

"You have *two* children?" I say this with a bit more surprise than I intend.

"Yes. Well. I know it seems early, but I wanted to have a family before . . . you know."

Oh. Shame heats my cheeks. I'd completely forgotten that, as angry as I am at Fara's magic for leaving him, the cost of his power is minimal compared to some. Retired Firespinners find it difficult to keep warm; even Mora's Potionmaking magic will soon fade, leaving her without a sense of smell. Healers who give life do so at the expense of their own. Thus they rarely live past twenty, and I feel another jolt of irritation toward Sakira about the unnecessary magic Kita had to use today. "I'm sorry."

"Don't be. I'm not." Another smile.

"You're really not going to leave until I tell you what else I want, are you?"

"No."

"But you know I'm not the real sacrifice. You don't have to cater to me."

Her smile falters. "You're going through it all the same. Assisting you is the least I can do."

I sigh. "Fine. I just want water."

She digs a waterskin out and hands it to me with a nod. I take it and move away from the mare, yielding her the win. This time.

"There you are," Sakira says, running over and slinging an arm around my shoulders. "We thought you might try to make a break for it. We were taking bets on how far you'd make it before the hyenas found you."

"Did you already drink that whole flask?" I ask.

"I gave you six kilometers. Alette only gave you two."

"*Two?*"

"Where's your drink?" she asks.

I show her the waterskin.

"Not that one, the real one."

"Look, I'm already dying at the end of this," I say, ducking out from under her arm. "I don't need you pressuring me into all this other stuff."

"It's wine, um . . . what was your name again?"

How strong *is* that stuff? "Zahru."

"Zahru." She grins. "It's wine, Zahru."

"Yes. You told me."

"No. You don't understand." She shakes her head, the powdered gold on her temples glimmering in the twilight. "Have you ever had palace wine? This isn't the bile they scrape out of the ditches in your hometown."

I find that more than a little offensive, but I let it slide. "I'm sure it's excellent."

"Just try it." She produces another flask from gods-know-where. "You don't have to have more than a sip. But at least give it a chance."

It does smell divine. Like a breath of a summer orchard and something earthy, like cedar. I consider the emeralds ringing the flask, a new idea forming in my head. If everyone else is drunk, it will be very difficult to race after me in the dark. I just need to play along long enough that they stop caring where I am, and then I'll make my move.

I take a drink and try not to make a face while Sakira watches me with anxious eyes.

"Well?" she asks.

It's both sweet and bitter, and after I've swallowed I feel like I've licked a rug, but there's something undeniably pleasing about it.

"It's . . . not bad," I say.

"See?"

"How strong is it?"

"Stronger than some, weaker than others." She smiles and takes my hand. "Sit with us, Zahru. It's time I got to know the girl who got under my brothers' skin."

She guides me to sit beside Alette. The fire crackles before us, and Sakira lets go of my hand, but it's clear from how close she sits she doesn't entirely trust me. I pray she forgets how long it's been since she drew the Follow spell. The ink has all but faded from my wrist, and every other piece of my plan is falling into place.

"I want to know you, Zahru," Sakira says. "What makes you happy, what makes you sad. When people ask about you, I want to do you justice."

I take a minuscule drink from the flask. "I'm not really that interesting. I'm just a girl with bad judgment and questionable taste in men."

"And yet you ended up here. Competing with the best magicians in Orkena for a station even nobles dream of."

I shrug. When I told them my poor-little-stable-girl-becomes-a-human-sacrifice story, I skipped all parts involving Hen or the priest, and basically started with Kasta choosing me out of spite. I was really hoping they wouldn't think too hard about how a

Whisperer was there in the first place. I've made it this far without implicating Hen, and I don't plan to ruin that now.

"You must know someone of influence," Alette says, sliding her headband free and jostling a hand through her hair. "A count? A captain?"

"I really don't. I just got lucky."

"How lucky?" Sakira says, her grin widening. "I think you're holding back on your story. On what happened after the Choosing?"

My skin prickles. There's something calculating beneath her curiosity, and I wonder what she's really asking. Would Jet have mentioned the protection gem to her? Panic flushes through me at the thought. Gods, I hope not. If she suspects I still have it, I'll lose my best chance of staying alive.

I clear my throat. "I told you, there was this pool—"

"Enough about the pool!" calls Kita from somewhere in the dark.

"After the pool. After the *bath*." Sakira's watching me carefully now, her smile sharp. "Doesn't it seem strange Jet would come to your rescue when you'd only just met? And to say hardly anything to me after! That's not like him at all."

I bristle. "He thought Kasta was going to kill me. He was just doing what anyone would."

Sakira laughs. "Was he? Have another drink. And think about that. You're telling me a boy who was eager to be your hero one night won't even look at you the next morning . . ."

And here's where I realize there's a strategic side to Sakira's charm. She definitely has an honest interest in people—the way she spoke of wanting to connect with others, and her planning an entire week of adventures for me when she could drag me straight across the desert—she's reckless and doesn't think about consequences, but she wants to make me happy. But I don't think that's the only reason she goes through this effort. Even now I can feel the wine loosening my tongue, my worries softening under the warmth in her smile. I wonder how many people have let their guard down after a few drinks, spilling information about themselves or their countries without thinking of how she might use it. Regrets. Fears. Desires.

Secrets.

"Look," I say, "I don't know what Jet's deal is—"

"You kissed him, didn't you?" Sakira asks.

"What?" Alette says.

"*What?*" I say.

"I'm right, aren't I?" Sakira laughs. "That's why he's being so weird when I write him about you. I mean, he's weird about courting in general, but you must have been irresistible. And that's what happened. You and Jet were getting serious, and then Kasta walked in—"

"That is—!" I want to say that's not how fast I move, but this is the perfect opportunity to bury all thoughts of the protection gem, and I groan. "Yes," I say slowly. "That's exactly what happened."

"Wow," Alette says, straightening. "I didn't think him that forward. He courted a Pe heiress for an entire summer, and I can't even remember now if I ever saw them kiss."

"Oh, no, it wasn't him!" I say, panicking that they're already unraveling my lie. "I . . ." Gods help me. "It was me. I get a little carried away sometimes."

Alette bursts out laughing. Sakira joins in, and even Kita, who's still doing something with the tent, snickers.

"Stop it," Sakira says, taking another drink. "I'm going to start *really* liking you, and I can't be thinking about that in the caves."

"Yup, it's just one of those things." I shrug. "Quiet stable girl on the outside, lioness on the inside."

Alette is now rolling in the sand from laughing so hard. I can't help but grin, too, because anyone who knows me would know how ludicrous this all sounds, but if I fail to make it out of here, I feel like I should be remembered for something. This isn't exactly what I had in mind, but I'll take what I can get.

"Oh gods," Sakira says, wiping her eyes. It smears her liner on one side, smudging her knuckle in gold. "I hope I'm drunk enough to forget you said that in the morning."

"So how about you two?" I ask, eager to change the subject. "Any dark, hopefully embarrassing secrets that will make me feel better about myself?"

"Nothing like that," Alette says, giggling.

"Plenty," Sakira says, tapping my flask. "Finish this one. You'll feel like a child when we're done."

XIII

IN retrospect, there was a fundamental flaw with my plan.

I discover this as I sway before the buckskin, as the world tilts under me and I have to catch my balance on the mare's shoulder. Behind me, the fire burns low where Sakira lies asleep in the sand, her head resting on Alette's stomach. Kita is singing an old lullaby beside them, but she hasn't opened her eyes in a long time. She didn't even twitch when I rose, and as I command the world to stop tilting, her hand relaxes into the sand and the last notes die on her lips.

Actually, there were two flaws. One: Sakira kept checking my flask, making sure I kept drinking, making sure I always had more. Two: this is the first time I've ever drunk, which is resulting in unexpected consequences. Which brings me to three: I can't hear what the horses are thinking.

I think I started that off by saying there were only two things.

"Pull yourself together," I mutter, gripping the mare's mane to stay upright. Fara's and Hen's faces flit through my mind like fish, colorful flashes that slip away as fast as they appear. My muscles feel as heavy as clay. *Sleep*, my body says. *It would be so good to lie down, to rest . . .*

I puff my hair out of my eyes and start for the saddles. I'm not far enough gone to believe anything good would come of sleeping right now; though, as I fall in the sand before the first saddle, I'm not sure much good will come of me being awake, either. I breathe out and push back to my knees. The stars slip and reset in my vision. I grab Kita's saddle, its tall leather pommel crisscrossed with strips of scarlet, and heave it back to the buckskin. I miss her back the first time I raise it but center it the second. The mare rumbles in her throat. I don't need a translation to know she thinks this is a bad idea.

"I know," I say, hoping she can understand me even if I can't understand her. "But I can't stay. She may seem like fun, but she's still going to kill me."

She snorts. I check the girth—I think I check the girth—and go back to the side of the tent, where the bridles hang from hooks in the fabric. It occurs to me Kita went through a lot of unnecessary effort to raise the tent when all of them are sleeping outside, and I have a feeling I'm looking at a small-scale model of how Sakira would rule: dangerous missions, wine and excess, parties and secrets. Things built and labored over but not put to use. While the most important things—like me—are left to their own devices.

In this case, thank the gods.

Sakira mumbles and turns in her sleep, and I grab the bridle and stumble to the mare in haste. I lift it onto her head with an apology and promise we'll go easy. An annoyed flick of her tail is my response. I pull myself into the saddle—

And realize I did not check the girth.

The entire thing comes off in my hands. I land hard on my back, pain slamming through my lungs as the fall knocks the air from me. A gasp escapes my mouth before I can stop it—

Except it makes no noise. I cover my mouth with my hands as I cough, my lungs demanding air, but this makes no noise, either. Neither does the saddle sliding off me into the sand. My panicked movements as I jump to my feet and look at the fire. A stumble to the side as I take in gulps of air, both to recover and for the feeling of dread closing around me like a tomb.

I drank myself deaf. Gods, *I drank myself deaf.*

"Zahru?"

A whisper in my ear. I shriek and spin (luckily neither of these make noise, either), but when I strike at the person who should be behind me, I meet air and fall back to the sand. A horse and a rider cloaked in deep blue stand several paces away. Far too far for someone to have dismounted, whispered, and mounted again.

I decide this is the last time I'm ever drinking.

I should also possibly be more concerned about who this person is.

"Thank Numet," the boy whispers, dismounting. He glances at the sleeping figures around the fire and strides for me, the light dancing in a familiar pair of worried eyes.

"Jet!"

I almost sob in relief. Of course it's him—Soundbenders control noise, and Jet can redirect the commotion I'm making as easily as an oar shifts water. But more than that, he *came*. I'd hoped he would, I wanted so badly to believe he would, and here he is, proving good people do still exist in the world—

And then I remember he's half the reason I'm here. And there was an entire morning he could have told me what was going on.

"Go away," I say, knowing—hoping—he's keeping our conversation contained. I turn and lift the saddle again. "You're the last person I want to see right now." I think of Kasta. "The second-to-last person."

"I can explain."

"What, so you can lie to me again about how you'll get me out of this? Well, I've heard enough. I'm escaping on my own now."

A statement that would have had much more credibility if, when I set the saddle on the buckskin for the second time, it didn't slide right off the other side.

It falls soundlessly to the sand, and the mare, tired of humoring me, moves away.

"Are you . . . drunk?"

I whirl on him. "Yes, actually. Do you want to know why? Because after you left me to become a *human sacrifice*, I had to walk out in front of the entire country dressed in *this*, then be forced onto the back of a panicking animal and taken hours away from my home, into a *guarded barracks* to steal a horse who almost set me on fire, only to realize that at the end of the day, do I get to rest? No! I get a flask of wine, Jet. Your sister, who knows Kasta cut me and is going to kill me anyway, gave me a flask of wine."

He pinches the bridge of his nose. "Gods. I'm so sorry, Zahru. I know it's been terrible—"

"Oh, terrible doesn't even skim the surface. 'Terrible' is when you find yourself in a fight between two strangers that almost costs your life. But this . . ." I open my arms to the desert, to the horses and the dying fire, and laugh. The sound is both sad and wild, and whether it's too loud for Jet to contain or he doesn't like the sound of it, it's soon silenced. "This is worse," I say. "This is so much worse."

"I'll make it up to you, I swear."

"By making my death painless and easy? I'd rather stay with Sakira."

He flinches. "No. Gods, no. If you believe nothing else about me, believe that even if I had an interest in the crown, which I do *not*, I would never hurt anyone to win it."

"Then what is it you want, Jet? Because I'm a little busy right now."

I turn to look for the saddle, but he moves in front of it.

"Forgiveness," he says, his eyes anguished. "At least, eventually. I know things got out of hand, but I also have a plan to get you out of here."

"Is it as good as the one you had to secure my release?"

He winces. "Admittedly, that one failed. But *this* one won't. We only need to ride a day east, and we'll be back at the main river. We'll sneak you onto a boat. It'll take a day or two for my siblings to realize what's happened, and by then it will be too late. The race will default, and they'll have to start over. This time, without you."

He sounds earnest. Like he's thought this through and truly feels guilty, and I feel myself wanting to believe him again, even if my heart twists at the mention of someone else taking my place.

But as lovely as his plan sounds, I can't help but feel it's too familiar.

"Which would be amazing, except I've heard this all before," I say, shaking my head. "You *lied* to me, Jet. You said you'd get me out, that you'd protect me, but when the priests asked you to confirm my story, you acted as if we'd never met! How do I know this isn't another lie? How do I know you aren't saying this so I'll go quietly, and tomorrow we'll wake up at the caves?"

"Because I—" His jaw clenches, and pain works itself across his brow. His gaze cuts to the fire. "I told you, if I wanted the throne,

I could have had it. My father would have given it to me without this race."

"Maybe that was a lie, too."

"Except I told you that in confidence, before I knew you being marked as a sacrifice was even possible." He looks over again, eyes steady. "I had nothing to gain then by freeing you, and I have nothing to gain now but a clear conscience. I'll let you choose which town. You'll have your own horse. You can take a boat, or a merchant's caravan, or whatever you're most comfortable with. I have more than enough to cover your expenses." His shoulders drop. If he's lying, he's very good at it. "I truly never meant to deceive you. If you don't believe me, you can stay with Sakira. With the express warning that I don't know if the next opportunity to leave will be so peaceful."

I blink, wondering if he phrased that right. "So, if I stayed, instead of heading for Nadessa, you would keep following us in case I changed my mind?"

He nods, and I want to tell myself that of course he'd keep following us if he intended to kill me in the caves, but there's something in his expression that looks too raw to be false. But then I felt that same honesty after we subdued Kasta, too.

My mind aches trying to make sense of him, and I press my fingers into my temples. "I don't understand you at all. If this is really how you feel, then what happened at the palace? You sided with Kasta! Why didn't you tell the Mestrah what he did? Or the priest, when he asked you right in front of me!"

"I—"

"You could have stopped all of this. If you'd exposed Kasta, he'd

162

be disqualified. Then it's only you and Sakira, and you could have stepped down right then and there. No Crossing, no sacrifice, and Sakira is queen."

He clenches his jaw and looks down, but offers no answer.

"So what are you leaving out?" I challenge. "*You* were the one who said how awful Kasta is. Sakira trusts you so much she probably told you exactly where we are, and now you're sabotaging her Crossing chances *and* you could have made her queen without all this. Or have you been lying to her all along, too?"

I nod to Sakira's prone form, and I know the girl almost got me killed today, but I feel strangely protective of her in this moment. Maybe because I know all too well about being used, and I refuse to be instrumental in doing the same to anyone else.

But where I expect Jet to be angry or defensive, he just looks . . . tired.

He runs his hand down his face. "What you're missing," he says quietly, "is that I used to be the kind of person who *would* tell on my brother."

I can only stare in response. "I don't know what that means."

"You're speaking like I spared him a slap on the wrist. He faked a *gods' mark*, Zahru. If I'd confirmed your story, he wouldn't have just been disqualified from the race. My father would have disowned him and thrown him into the streets."

"So?"

"So it's *my fault*," he snaps. Now he looks at me, but it's shame, not anger, that darkens his eyes. "Everything Kasta does. Everyone he hurts. I made him what he is."

My heart tugs at the pain in his voice, and despite this entire mess, I feel my anger slipping. I know this guilt. Not in the same way, but when a wasting disease killed my mother, I spent weeks agonizing that somehow, it was my doing. That the gods had looked into my future and decided I didn't deserve her, and that if I was a better person, a worthier person, she'd still be alive.

"That's not being fair," I say. "Kasta makes his own decisions. He could have reacted to your success by studying more or working harder. Turning on the world and marking people for death is not normal."

"You don't understand." His smile is tortured. "I used to be *just like that*. There was a short time I thought I wanted to rule, and that I could do it better than him. So whatever he told you—yes, I did it. I embarrassed him. If I couldn't beat him at something, I cheated to do it. But I will *never* go back to that." His eyes flash with a memory, and I shiver to think what might have happened that inspired him to change. "I made a vow a year ago that I would never again put my interests before others. I'm already the reason Father never named him *dõmmel*. By Numet's blood I won't be the reason he's exiled."

His voice cracks, and my suspicion softens. He really does seem sorry, and I think back on everything he's done since I've met him: his pleading with Kasta when I was chosen as a First; his reluctance to cut his brother during their fight. The agony in his face when the priest asked him to confirm my story, not only because he feared what would happen to his brother—but because of what it would mean for me.

A cruel, manipulative person wouldn't have a problem tossing me or his family to a terrible fate. Jet has suffered for it. And ultimately, though I don't appreciate being on this side of things, I can't pretend it would be easy for me to send someone into exile, either.

"All right, fine," I say, sighing. I'm still not sure I can trust him, but I've decided that if he *is* after the throne, this is a strange way to go about it. "I really wish you would have told me this earlier, but I'll let you rescue me. I suppose."

He brightens, and I realize how much I've missed that smile. "Oh, good, because I was starting to worry I'd be a failure at this, too. My team is waiting over the next ridge. Shall we go before Sakira and I have to have a very awkward conversation?"

I nod and glance at the fire. I certainly won't miss wondering what epic, terrifying thing Sakira had planned for us next, but I find that despite it all, a small part of me is actually going to miss her. I'm fairly sure the wine is to blame for this sentiment, but if we'd met under different circumstances, I think I would have liked her. Obviously I still have concerns about her ruling a country. But if she'd care about Orkena half as much as she cares about her friends, we might not be too bad off.

I sniffle, and must stumble, because Jet's there in an instant to steady me.

"Are you all right?" he asks, the firelight turning his eyes to amber.

"Yes," I say, wiping my eyes. "But I'd really like to take a nap now."

"Zahru—"

"Just a quick one. I promise I'll be awake when we get to the horse."

I lean into him, but Jet rights me, his eyes looking between mine. "I'm not sure it's safe for you to ride alone right now."

"Oh, so your story is already changing? I see how it is. All you are is broken promises, Jet, and I—"

He lets go of me, and the world spirals left. The sand is surging for my face when he catches me again, and I laugh at myself, at how ridiculous the entire situation is.

"Maybe I can't ride alone right now," I agree as he sets me upright.

"We'll change as soon as you feel better. Melia will ride with me, and you can ride her mare."

"Melia?"

"My Healer. You'll like her. She disapproves of just about everything I do."

I snort. "We'll have a lot to talk about."

"Up you go."

He places my hands on the saddle, and though my grip slips off the pommel the first time, I grab it the second. Jet boosts me up and settles behind me, comfortable and sturdy at my back. We turn toward the darkness, and I cast one more look at the fire.

"I don't think you're going to be her favorite sibling after this," I say.

Jet follows my gaze and sighs. "She'll forgive me, eventually. She'll still have the advantage when they restart the race, and I'll still help her, as I did this time. Besides, I left her a gift."

"A gift? You really think some trinket can make up for her having to start over?"

"You don't know my sister." There's a smile in his voice. "Or how long she's wanted the Illesa."

"You gave her your *sword?*" I don't follow sword fighting as closely as Fara, but I know the enchanted sword, the only in our world that can hone and weaponize light, is a legend all its own. Its wielders are allowed to keep it until they're beat in competition, and Jet has owned it for years.

"Well, I certainly won't need it anymore. And it's much stronger than her air saber."

"Huh."

Jet moves the gelding into a jog. The stars blur and dip overhead, and I cling to the pommel, logging this newest bit of information against the rest.

"Jet?" I say.

"Mm?"

"I want to believe you. I don't yet, but I want to."

Jet chuckles sadly. "And that will be the very thing they write on my tomb."

XIV

JET'S team waits for us in a bowl-like hollow beneath a windswept dune, just out of view of Sakira's tent. And I *do* like his Healer, almost immediately. Melia is from Amian, a country west of us that has as few magical people as Orkena has unmagical, and thus she's finishing her apprenticeship under Orkenian Healers. Her skin is a deep ebony, and her hair falls in black braids so long they reach her saddle. Maybe it's the way she accentuates words, or the way she holds herself perfectly erect, but she gives off the impression of royalty far more than any actual royal I've met. She's also perfected the art of looking down her lashes at people, and it's clear that even with Jet in company, she's the one in charge.

Jet's First, Marcus, is her opposite. He's indeed a Grekan Enchanter, with fair skin and hazel eyes, and blond hair that grows in thick, short curls. He's as huge as he looked onstage—not in a sculpted, muscly way, but in that every part of him is solid and strong. He could possibly move a small house unassisted. As such he's not riding a desert horse but some kind of war gelding that's bred to carry weight. But where I assumed he'd only scowl into the distance with grim, battle-ready determination, he instead looks as though he's perpetually thinking about buying sweets for small children, and I have yet to catch him without a smile on his face.

"It was easy, then?" he asks, after we've put distance on Sakira's tent.

"Too easy." Jet sighs. "I told her to leave a lookout, at the least. You've made sure the area's clear?"

"Yes." He pats a brass telescope on his lap, the white runes on its side still glowing. "Only a small town and a caravan within fifty kilometers of us. The bandit camp is too far for them to spot her, and even if Kasta can find her this far off route, it'll take him the better part of the night to make the distance. They should be awake by then."

Jet exhales through his nose, but I feel him turn around.

"He'll have little interest in her without Zahru," Marcus adds.

"I know. I only wish . . ."

"She will be fine," Melia says, moving beside us on her white mare. "She can handle herself. And if she's not ready, then this is a good lesson."

"I just don't want it to be a *permanent* lesson."

"If she is going to be Mestrah, these are the things she must learn."

Jet stays quiet. So does Melia, though I think the stars begin to collapse between their glares.

"Alette said this night would go well," I inject, remembering. "They should be safe. The gods will ensure it."

Jet scoffs. "Yes. I'm sure Sakira will agree in the morning that the night went well."

I look back at him. "You don't believe their prayers work?"

"Oh, I believe they work, like any other magic. The priests ask for something, and if they're powerful enough, their magic answers. As to the gods themselves getting involved . . ."

"Ignore him," Melia says, though the edge has faded from her voice. "His faith has been slipping with his father's health."

"If I'm wrong," Jet says, "then you have to admit *you're* wrong, too. If I was meant to have the crown, shouldn't the gods have stepped in already to change my mind? Or maybe I should ask them myself, as my father supposedly does." He raises his arms. "Oh great gods, if I am meant to win, turn the sky to yellow—"

"I do not think that's how it works," Melia snaps. "*A-mah*, it's a wonder they didn't smite you already."

"It's because they agree with me."

"Oh, you—"

"As much as I'd love to hear this conversation continue into eternity," Marcus says, "may I suggest a change in topic? Where or if we're sleeping tonight, possibly. Or meat pie."

"Meat pie?" I ask.

"I was promised meat pie."

"I say we ride to dawn," Melia says. "Even that might not be far enough."

"You think Sakira will track us?" I ask, wincing as the world tilts again. "If she feels even twice as good as I do, she's not going to be moving anytime soon."

"Ah," Jet says, shifting behind me. "It's not Sakira we're worried about."

No one says anything to that, and understanding drops like a stone in my stomach.

"Dawn, then," says Marcus.

"Dawn," Melia agrees.

I'm not sure how long we ride. I only know that at some point I fall asleep, and when I wake, the world is no longer tilting and spinning, because the movement has shifted inside of me instead. It presses through my head, churns through my stomach. The rhythmic movements of the horse don't help. I try to focus on the solidness of Jet's arms and the hope I'm finally free, but all my mind can think about is how it would like to free the contents of my stomach.

"She's not looking good," Melia says beside us.

"Zahru?" Jet asks. "How are you doing?"

I open my mouth to answer—and have to cover it instead. Jet pulls the horse to a stop and helps me to the ground, and I retch up everything that was inside me until my stomach stops twisting. The night air is a welcome chill across my face. I sit back on my heels and let the breeze cool me, relishing a moment's peace, a moment when nothing is moving.

"It's near enough to dawn," Jet says. "Let's set up camp."

"I'll get the tent," Marcus says.

"I'll tend the horses," Melia says.

"Have some water." Jet kneels beside me. "It'll help flush the wine out."

I give him a look to remind him of his part in this, but I take the waterskin and drink. My stomach isn't thrilled with me filling it with something new, but it settles enough that I feel I can move again. If only there were something this simple for the pounding in my head. I'm sure Melia could help, but that makes me think of the sadness in Kita's eyes when she talked about her family, and I decide this is easy enough to bear on its own.

"I'm going to help with the tent," Jet says. "Unless I can get you something else?"

"A new body," I say, pressing the waterskin to my throbbing forehead. "This one is ruined."

Jet snickers. "There's nothing wrong with this body." The moment the words leave his lips, he seems to realize how forward that sounds, because he immediately stands. "And I'm going to go help Marcus now."

Warmth floods my veins at the slip, but I can't help but laugh at the absurdity of the situation, something I quickly regret when the sound splits through my head. I grit my teeth and suppress another snicker as I adjust the waterskin. If Jet can say something like that after he watched me retch, I really haven't given him enough credit.

I watch him work with Marcus, his movements strong and sure as the pair unfolds a billowing rectangle of fabric. Marcus gives him no instruction. Jet knows what he needs to do, and does so as if he didn't have twenty servants to prepare his bedchambers every night. Nearby, Melia hums as she works her hands down the legs of her white mare, rubbing the muscles, drawing out their fatigue. *Better*, thinks the mare, nuzzling Melia's shoulder. *Better*.

At least my magic's working again.

I sigh and take another sip of water. I'm still processing everything Jet told me, and wondering how seriously I should be thinking about taking a horse into the night again, but no one has laughed maniacally at how easy I was to fool, and we're definitely headed east. Not that I'm suddenly a directional genius, but I know Numet rises in the east, and her light has been steadily growing on the horizon in front of us. If I'm given Melia's horse after we sleep, I might have to start believing this is real.

Melia moves to the war gelding, one perfect eyebrow raised. "So. How long have you two been courting?"

I choke on a sip of water. Jet had to have heard her, but he's suddenly very interested in the stake he's already driven into the ground.

"Sorry," I say. "I thought you just asked if we were courting."

Melia smiles, though it looks cold. "Ah. My mistake. As the three of us are risking treason to free you, I assumed there was a good reason."

My stomach churns again, not only for the confirmation that Jet's team also believes they're freeing me, but for a risk I hadn't even considered: that doing so comes with very real consequences. Not just for Jet, but his team as well.

"There is a good reason," Jet says. "She's a person who deserves her life. My brother put her in this position, and I'm getting her out of it."

"And I empathize with that, until the point I consider all three of us could be put to death for tampering with the gods' will. It is too late to claim your brother cut her."

"Which is why I must do this instead. We'll be careful. Once she's on a boat—"

"We still have to sneak into a city to do that. People will recognize us. If they catch you freeing her, the Mestrah will know within the hour."

Jet pulls the edges of his hood. "Then we'll stay back and watch Zahru from a distance. No one knows her face. She can wear your clothes."

"And if your brother or sister have trailed us? She'll be an easy target." Melia crosses her arms. "There is an easier way to do this, *aera*, with much less risk to our lives."

Jet's face hardens. "Not a possibility."

"Win the race and refuse the sacrifice. Stand up for what you believe in, for once."

"This *is* what I believe in!"

His voice echoes in the space, louder than should be possible with the desert so open around us. Melia stays stiff and still, though her glare never wavers. Jet exhales and presses a hand through his shaved hair, dropping his hood back.

"We'll stay hidden," he says, quieter. "If we're caught, I'll tell them I ordered you to go along with it. You and Marcus will be pardoned."

He turns for the darkness. Marcus slowly returns to the tent, brow high, and shares a look with me like we've narrowly dodged a storm.

Melia sighs and turns to the war horse, her lips pursed.

"And that," she says angrily, "is exactly the kind of thing a good king would say."

By the time the tent is up, my headache is manageable and the buzz of the wine is wearing off. Melia disappears inside the tent with the sleeping mats, and Marcus whistles as he starts a smokeless fire with some kind of enchanted metal kindling. The scene is a drastic contrast to being with Sakira. Even the tent is more subtle, being sloped and a deep orange to match the sand, unlike the white monstrosity Sakira packed.

Marcus places four pitas wrapped in palm leaves into the fire, and the rods glow red.

"Meat pie," he says, grinning.

I won't lie that I'm as excited to taste meat pie as I am to be sleeping, which is considerable. But as the sky lightens, and a lone jackal peers down at us from a rocky hill, I can't stop looking over my shoulder. Jet sits a stone's throw away, on a slight rise where he can see the coming sunrise. He's removed his armor and balances a scroll on his knee, though I don't think he's reading it.

"So, Zahru," Marcus says, pulling his crossbow into his lap. "Where is home for you?"

"Atera," I say, watching the careful way his fingers slip over the barrel. The weapon is a handsome thing, a dark red wood inlaid with gold, with a sinewy string resting in the mouth of a sliding lion head. The lion's shining body forms the back of the bow, its haunches and tail the shoulder rest. "If I ever get back there."

"Ah, don't let them get to you." He nods at the tent. "They may bicker like a married couple, but we'll sort it out. I've led reconnaissance missions in Wyrim. I think I can secure you safe passage home."

He winks and starts polishing the weapon with a soft white cloth. The rectangular stones at the front glow red at his touch. I remember Fara talking with a traveler once about the similarities between Grekan Enchanters and our own *trielle*, how the magic shows up and skips generations in a similar way, except Enchanters can only imbue their will into stone. They're also limited to elemental spells, unlike our *trielle*, who can call on most types of magic. But also unlike *trielle* magic, Grekan enchantments never wear off.

"Do you like her?" Marcus asks, lifting the crossbow.

"It's . . . she's nice," I say. "My father would want to know everything about her."

"You can tell him she's ironwood and gold, with Etherstone enhancements. Means her bolts fly true even in high winds and water. If I can aim at it, she can hit it."

"And you don't have to charge her?"

"Nah. She uses me for an energy source." His grin turns mischievous. "Just like her namesake, actually."

I'd heard of soldiers naming their weapons in tribute to loved ones. "Oh? Who is she named for?"

"I call her Adoni, after my grandmother. Meanest and sharpest woman I know."

I snicker, picturing him at the mercy of a tiny, wrinkly old lady who wears too many cloaks. "Wow. I hope someday I'm memorable enough for my grandson to name a crossbow after me."

"Just get on his case about marrying his boyfriend already and chase off a horse thief with a pitchfork. You'll be halfway there."

I laugh. "She chased off a thief with a pitchfork?"

"And a few well-aimed rocks. You don't mess with my grandmother." He smiles, his gaze fond as he cleans sand from the arrow groove. "I take it yours are tamer?"

"Oh. Mine are dead." Marcus blanches, and I rush to explain. "No, it's fine. I mean, obviously I'd prefer if they were alive, but all my grandparents passed when I was really young. I didn't really know them."

"Ah. I'm still sorry to hear it."

"It's all right. I've started adopting random townsfolk as my grandparents now."

Marcus snorts. "If you're looking for more, I'd be happy to send you my grandfather. He's gotten considerably mouthier these past few years, but he can out-cook any palace chef."

I smile, imagining a fifth setting at our dinner table, with Marcus's grandfather assisting Hen and me in heckling Fara and Mora about what "just good friends" really means. "I'll take him."

Marcus laughs, a loud, welcome sound that booms around the little camp. It draws Melia from the tent, her long braids falling over her shoulder as she emerges.

"What have you got him on about?" she asks.

"He's going to send me his grandfather," I say.

Melia shoots Marcus a strange look as she settles next to me.

"Zahru's grandparents passed when she was far too young," Marcus says. "Do you have an extra you can spare?"

"Ha! You can have two of mine," she says, throwing up her hands. "My *stefar* snores like a falling mountain, and my *mam* thinks I'm a demon."

"A *demon*?" I say.

"She believes magic belongs to the gods only, and anyone who has it does so not because we are the gods' children, but because we are cursed." She sucks on her lower lip. "It is the way of the elders. They are not my beliefs, clearly."

A memory returns to me of a traveling family from Pe, the mountainous kingdom that borders Orkena's southwestern side, and the uncomfortable way they watched me when I spoke to their camels. Magic is such a normal part of my life, I've never considered what it would be like to grow up without it. A terrible part of me wonders if that means I could have been anything in her world, if I could have gone to school and chosen any number of futures besides the one I was born into, and I chide myself for thinking it. Fara says our magic indeed marks our lineage to the gods, and we must honor the life they've set for us.

Even so, I believe years of being looked down on by people like Gallus have prepared me for a grandmother just like this one. "Does she make good sweets?"

Melia frowns. "Yes, actually."

"Would she sing me to sleep at night?"

A smile. "She is a very good singer."

"Good. Then she's in, too."

Now Melia laughs. "Listen to this girl! Such simple, honest needs." She smiles. "Maybe I'm understanding why Jet could not leave you to that fate."

She points to the scar on my wrist, and I rub it with my thumb, suddenly self-conscious. A few moments sober with these two, and I'm already picturing their families at my table, laughing like there's not a doubt in my mind they mean what they say. Hen would tell me I'm not being nearly suspicious enough, but I miss her, and I'm so far out of my comfort zone I can't help but try to replace the bits of normalcy I used to have: people to trust, friends to laugh with. Maybe it's not a smart strategy, but it's what I know how to do.

I shake my hand out and scoot closer to the fire. "But you . . ." I hesitate, then decide I have to know the answer. "You still think Jet should try to win."

It's not just Melia who nods.

"Yes," Melia says, with a look at Marcus. "But not the way you think. Centuries ago, when Mestrah Adit was the first to refuse to hold a Crossing, it was revolutionary. Her legacy began the custom of naming firstborns as heir, the first of many revolutionary changes she would make for Orkena. We believe Jet could do the same. Prove he is resourceful enough to finish first but compassionate enough to show you mercy."

"He's already proven far more forgiving than I would be," Marcus grumbles.

"Ah, Kasta." Melia tsks. "How far he has fallen."

A heavy silence drapes us. Marcus leans over his crossbow and reaches into the fire, the rods automatically extinguishing. He presses the top of a wrapped pita before drawing back.

"Almost ready," he says, grinning.

"Have you known Jet long?" I ask.

"A few years," Marcus says, his smile turning smug. "I taught him everything useful he knows how to do with a sword."

"You did not," Jet calls.

"All right, all right," Marcus replies, snickering. "He taught me a few things, too. We trained together under a haggard old wasp named Jana who makes Kasta seem like a delight."

"And I have patched them up from those sessions more times than I care to count," Melia says, rubbing a smear of dust from her silver armor. "Still, this past day has revealed much I did not know. I thought this would be an easy journey to Nadessa, and then I would return to my parents." She frowns. "But now I find my energy desires a new focus."

"You believe in him so truly?" I ask.

"Yes. But I will also yield to his wishes, if that is not where his heart lies." She sighs. "I will not be quiet about it, but I will respect it."

Marcus grunts in agreement, and from the corner of my eye, I see Jet look over.

"Here," Melia says, sliding a warm wrapped pie into my hands. "Eat and take a few hours' rest. We need to keep moving if we hope to stay ahead of the others."

She rises to take a pie to Jet, but I touch her hand. If I'm going to decide to trust Jet again, I need more answers. "Can I take it?"

Melia nods. I slip the second pie over mine and move slowly for the edge of camp, toward the confusing boy who both betrayed and saved me; the boy who everyone seems to believe in, except for Jet himself.

"Dinner," I say, handing a pie over his shoulder. Jet looks up, eyes widening when he sees it's me. He takes it as I settle next to him.

"Thank you," he says.

He looks very different with his armor off. The deep blue of his tunic and his silver bracelets still leave no doubt of his rank, but under a layer of sand they look faded and older, and at a glance he could be any number of boys in Atera. The farmer's nephew, who brings us baled grass each week. Or the shy apothecaries' son, who ties wildflowers around the necks of the tonics I pick up. Someone approachable. Someone normal.

"I'm sorry again," he says, thumbing the wrapping of his pie. "I'm not sure I can say it enough to make it up to you, but I'm going to try."

I let a small smile onto my lips. "You're definitely going to have to say it more than that."

"I'm sorry, I'm sorry, I'm sorry. I'm sorry?"

"Getting there."

"I'm sorry—"

"New rule: you can't do them all at once, either."

"All right." His smile is sly. "Sorry."

I shoot him a look, but the smell of fresh bread and spiced meat wafts up from the pie, and I let his cheekiness slide as my fingers slip under the steaming leaves. The first bite is so hot it burns my tongue, but I can't even care as I chew through thick, savory beef and peppered cabbage. Jet only holds on to his, watching me with what might be thoughtfulness or concern.

"This is really good," I say through a mouthful. "This makes up for a few of those *sorries*."

His grin widens. He peels back his own leaves, and I notice the scroll he'd been studying earlier half-open at his feet. The smaller size of the parchment and the polished redwood roller look very familiar.

"Sakira?" I guess, nodding to it.

"Yes, and she's not very happy with me." He sighs. "Well, she's very happy about the sword. But she says she'd better win the restart, or she's going to turn my desertion into an actual death."

I swallow in alarm. "Would she?"

He snorts. "She's being dramatic." He hesitates. "Mostly."

"At least you know she's safe," I say. "What will she do until the race defaults?"

"She *should* head to the first checkpoint and wait there. That's where our father will send the boats that will take her home."

He takes a small bite of meat pie, and I know all too well the doubtful look on his face.

"But we both know she's not going to do that," I say, feeling extremely posh I know a royal so well.

"No, she's not going to do that," he agrees. "She'll wait until she hears of the default, and in the meantime she'll continue to 'see the countryside,' as she called your expedition yesterday."

"You knew about that?"

"Not until she told me she'd set a hill on fire, and would I please help her to get back on route from the northern barracks?" He scoffs and wipes his mouth with a knuckle. "Luckily I can still worry every hour of my life about what she's doing, even from hundreds of kilometers away."

I smile and take another bite, but I can see the sadness in his eyes. He will miss Sakira's antics as much as she will miss his warnings.

Which reminds me there's a second scroll that should be here but isn't.

"I don't get it," I say, setting the pie in my lap. "You and Sakira seem so close. What happened with Kasta? If firstborns are supposed to rule, how did this even start?"

"That," he says, breaking off a burnt corner of palm wrapping, "is the golden question. Most of it is my fault, though Sakira blames her mother."

"The queen?" This I didn't expect. "Why would she want you challenging her son?"

"No, she didn't want that, but . . ." Jet grunts bitterly. "You realize what my existence means?"

Heat flushes my cheeks. "Oh."

"We'll just say the queen didn't like my mother before she became a general, and she outright hated her after I was born. A sentiment she was happy to share with anyone who'd listen. Especially her son."

My heart pulls at the thought of what it must have been like for Jet growing up. "That must have been awful."

He shrugs. "I just avoided her and her friends as much as possible. My father made it clear early on that I was a prince, nothing less, so most were wise enough to leave me alone. But you can imagine what Kasta thought of me when he was old enough to understand." Jet rubs his fingers along his chin, his eyes distant. "Though honestly, at the beginning, I don't know if he cared. Gods, that feels like a thousand years ago."

"He was different then."

"Very. Maybe because he never thought I'd be a threat . . ." Jet winces. "I don't know. He used to like me, I think. He would help me with my schoolwork, and I'd bring him food when I knew he'd been working all day." A glance at me. "He was always tinkering with something or other. Some magical theory; some tonic he hoped could ease the effects of magic on the body. For instance, he didn't like that Healers had to give their lives for their magic. He said he was going to fix it." He draws his hand across his brow. "I thought he was brilliant."

"Huh," I say, trying to work this inquisitive image of Kasta over the one with the shadows in his eyes. "And then . . . you got competitive?"

Jet looks over, torment pulling the lines of his frown. "That's the thing. We were that close, and I *still don't know* what happened. I know our father was putting pressure on him to focus on war and economics, but one day I walked into Kasta's rooms, and his laboratory was trashed. All his experiments, all his tonics, ruined. And he was just sitting there in the mess, crying." Jet swallows. "I can't imagine my father doing that, but they'd been fighting more, and Kasta must have been ignoring his other studies. I only know that when I started to pick up, Kasta shouted at me to leave. And when I didn't, he threw his last beaker into the wall beside me."

I hear the echo of it shattering as Jet's eyes turn to the sunrise. The first break in the rope that once tied them, and it was made by exactly who I suspected: their father. What a horrible way to discipline a son. I realize the Mestrah wanted Kasta to focus, and to learn early on that a king is not allowed his own passions over the needs of his country, but Kasta *was* researching a need, even if it had nothing to do with treaties or civil order. And poor Kasta. To lose all that work at the hands of the man who's supposed to support him.

"And that was it." Jet sighs. "From that day on, he wouldn't see me. And I . . ." He grimaces. "I just wanted back what we had. I thought—if I was stronger, if I trained hard enough to reach his level . . . he'd have to spend time with me again."

Understanding creeps like beetles' legs up my neck. "So you made it your mission to outdo him."

Jet lets out a long breath, and I finger the last bite of meat pie. What terrible years those must have been for the brothers, each chasing the approval of someone who would never give it. But even if Kasta couldn't see past his own hurt, Jet seems to have forgotten *he* did, when he realized how far apart they'd split. And looking at him now, shame darkening his face and his barely eaten pita in his fingers, I just see a sad boy who lost his brother far too young; a boy capable of forgiveness even after that brother tried to *kill* him.

And I have a feeling it's this boy, not the one who's the best swordsman in Orkena, that the Mestrah saw when he asked him to rule.

"Jet," I say.

"I know. It was petty, it was horrible, and I should have just let it go, but—"

"It's not your fault."

He shakes his head sharply. "It is. If I hadn't gotten so defensive about it . . ." He bites his lip, and when he speaks again, his voice is quiet. "I know things can't go back to what they were. But I'd always hoped that he'd forgive me."

The pain in those words aches in my bones. I don't think he'd tell me this if he was planning to face off with Kasta at the caves, and I feel myself starting to trust him again, just a little.

"You realize whatever changed Kasta happened before your rivalry," I say.

Jet shrugs.

"You just wanted back the friend you'd lost. Kasta wouldn't talk to you, so you tried something, and yes, it went wrong, but only because other things were going on that you couldn't control. Like your father." I say this with more disdain than I owe the god who runs our country, but I can't help it. In my mind, he's just as responsible for my being here as Kasta. "Kasta could have seen the change in you, or cared he was hurting you, but he didn't. Whatever happened, you'd already lost him." I hug my knees to my chest and gaze out at the dawn. "We all wish we could change how someone reacted in the past," I say, thinking of Gallus's sad smile. "Or that we could have seen it coming. It's not our fault for hoping things would turn out differently."

They're Fara's words, said to me when Gallus left, and my heart pinches to repeat them. He'll be waking soon. The sun will fill the little windows of the feed room and spill over our cots, and when he opens his eyes, the first thing he'll see is my empty bed.

Two days. Including the Choosing banquets, I've already been gone two days. How many more before something happens that he cannot fix?

"Zahru?" A warm hand touches my shoulder. When I look over, Jet's deep brown eyes are filled not with shame or anger but something lighter, something on the edge of disbelief. "I really am very sorry."

I nod, pushing my toes into the sand.

"And I swear to you, I will make this right."

My heart jerks at the conviction in his voice. I look over, and even if my heart still beats a warning, I allow myself to believe him, at least for today. For today, I'll trust that everything will be fine, and that I'm safe, and that it doesn't matter if I lean into Jet's hand or not because in a few more days, this will just be part of my story.

"All right," I say. "I mean, I'm still going to insist on my own horse and judge you on everything you do now, but with hope and optimism instead of scouring suspicion."

He snorts. "Progress. I'll take it."

I smile. "Goodnight, Jet."

"Goodnight, Zahru."

I leave him with the sunrise. Melia and Marcus offer me a smile as I shuffle toward the tent, and I manage to thank Marcus for cooking before crawling in, the sight of the woven sleeping mats like a feast for my exhausted brain. I can't tell if my head hurts from lack of sleep, making sense of Jet, or the wine, but it has definitely had enough. I think I could lie down on a bed of spikes right now and they would feel like feathers. Sleep pounces on me like a cat.

And yet, as I fall rapidly under, it is not Jet's warm eyes that flicker through my thoughts.

It's a picture of Kasta with a quill and scrolls, but no matter how many hours he works or theories he drafts, not one of them tells him how to please his father.

XV

WHEN I dream, it's of gardens being overtaken by spiders; clear rivers mixing with blood. Beautiful things falling to decay. But no matter how many webs I clear or jars of water I rescue from the river, the garden still rots. The jars crack, and the blood finds its way in.

After far too short a time, someone nudges my shoulder.

"Zahru, we need to get moving," Melia says.

"Mmph." I tuck my knees up and cradle my aching head more comfortably in my arm.

Melia shakes my shoulder, hard. "Bandits spotted us. They are on their way."

"What?" I say, jerking my eyes open.

"Pack quickly." Melia already has her sleeping mat and cloak under her arm. "We still need to take down the tent."

Thus begins day two of the race. Melia slips outside, and I put a hand over my heart, wondering if I'll ever again experience what it's like to wake up refreshed and not on the verge of impending doom. I tug on my ice shawl, shivering at the chill against my skin, and roll my sleeping mat with expert speed. In moments, I'm ducking out the door.

The heat hits me like an oven. Overhead, Numet's torch is blazing and bright in a cloudless sky, turning the sands a vibrant red-orange. I wince as my eyes adjust, and trudge over to where the horses gather beneath a crest of sand. Marcus and Jet stand to the side, a telescope raised to Jet's eye. Melia checks the girth on the gray gelding. Despite the dirt covering the rest of us, her purple tunic and silver armor somehow look as new as they did two days ago. I look down at the ruined mess that is my gown, and sigh.

"I thought we passed their camp last night without notice," Jet says, handing the telescope to Marcus. "Is there another one we didn't know about?"

Marcus shakes his head. "Whoever they are, they're not from the thieves' camp. Their horses are carrying more than a day's worth of supplies." He pockets the looking device. "They're following our exact trail."

"They're tracking us." Jet chews his lip but manages a weak smile when he sees me. "Let's get ahead of them, then. How are you feeling, Zahru?"

"Slightly run over," I admit. "But I'm all right."

"Good. Stay by the horses and out of sight. There are only four of them, and I don't think they realize how close they are to us, yet."

I nod my understanding and slip over to the horses while the boys pull the tent stakes. The geldings nicker in greeting, and Melia relieves me of the sleeping mat, latching it deftly behind the war horse's saddle. *Wrong?* asks the white mare, lipping my shoulder. *Sad? Why?* I try to repress my nervous energy as I stroke her velvet nose.

"I'm all right," I tell her. The last thing I need is for my anxiousness to get the horses riled before we've even folded the tent.

"If you need a drink, take it now," Melia says, offering me a waterskin. I accept it gratefully and take a long drink before handing it back. My head is still angry with me, but my stomach is much happier after a meal and some sleep.

Melia replaces the waterskin in the saddlebag and tilts her head at the mare. "She is yours today. Take care of her."

My heart warms, and I nod. The first of Jet's promises, kept. "I will."

"Everyone mount up," says Jet, approaching with the tent in his arms. "We're ready."

He stuffs the canvas into one of the war horse's saddlebags, and I pull myself lightly onto the mare's back. A surge of her sadness washes through me as I take up the reins, and I stroke her neck in sympathy. The horses didn't get long to rest either, and it pains me to think of how hard this has been on them, too.

Melia? the mare thinks, swiveling her head to look at me. *No Melia?*

"Oh," I answer, surprised. "No, not today."

I look over at the Healer, who tips a waterskin into the gray's mouth. So it's not the toil of the journey but longing for Melia that makes the mare sad. It takes a truly kind and gentle person to win an animal's attachment so quickly, and oddly it's this, more than anything the rest of the team has said, that makes me feel my trust is well placed.

"All right, Melia," Jet says, having pulled himself into the front of the gray's elongated saddle. "As agreed."

He reaches down, and Melia smirks as she swings up behind him.

"You are right," she says, settling into the saddle's wider back end. "It *is* more comfortable back here. And now we can spend all day going over the reasons you must stay!"

Jet grimaces, looking very funny smashed up against the pommel, but I can only snicker at the pleading look he gives me.

"Don't look at me," I say. "You still owe me a thousand *sorries*."

"Right," he says, forcing a smile. "Sorry, again. And trust me, I will be *very* sorry by the end of the day."

"This ridge will block their view for a kilometer," Marcus says, urging his war horse into a jog. "But then they'll be able to see us. Where are we headed, *aera?*"

"That's up to Zahru." Jet waits for me to move my mare after Marcus, then draws the gray up beside us. "I promised you'd get to choose your way, and so you will. We've been going east, and if we continue we'll be at the main river by midday. Those towns are the closest to the race route, though, so people will be watching for us, hoping we stop in. But if we can get you onto a boat, you'll be free." He turns in the saddle, nodding at the desert beyond my shoulder. "Or we can go west. There are a number of towns out there that follow the trade route, and plenty of merchants with their eyes on the northern cities. It would take longer, but we'd be well out of the path of the Crossing. It's your choice."

I nod, though I already know which I'll choose. West is the safer route, but the journey would span over a week, leaving far too much opportunity for my father's condition to be found out. A boat could get me there in two days, total. In two more nights, I could be back at Mora's table, crushing salt for our bread.

I mean, that's admittedly an optimistic fantasy, considering that in reality, I'll probably be taking many of those future meals scrunched in the corner of a wagon as Fara and I relocate to a new town. We'll need new names. New histories. I'm not sure how seriously the Mestrah will take my desertion—I'm sadly quite replaceable—but even if he sends no one after us, we can't risk word of my return reaching his ears. But as much as my stomach twists to think of leaving Atera for good, at least Fara and I will be together.

"We'll go east," I say.

Melia frowns, and I know she's thinking about the additional risk of being discovered, but Jet nods. "East it is."

Marcus gives his horse more rein, and the gelding responds eagerly, his great limbs churning into a gallop. Jet's gray gives chase, Melia holding tight to the prince's waist, and then it's just me and the white mare, left to choose if I'll follow.

Melia, the mare thinks, dancing sideways when I hold her back. I suppose this will be the true test. Jet will prove his intentions here for better or worse, and some strange part of me almost hopes he's lying again, if only to believe that when I do get free, it's completely without regret.

Because if this is truly the kind of king he'd be, I'm starting to see Melia's point.

The bandits follow us the entire morning.

No matter how many plateaus Marcus guides us around or how many kilometers we go without any sign of them, inevitably we reach an open section of the desert, and their distant shadows come back into view. They gallop when we do and slow when we do. Their casual pace makes Marcus more uneasy than if they had just attacked us outright.

But they begin to lose ground, and as the team relaxes, so do I. It helps that Melia and Marcus are good company. They speak of their memories from the palace: epic fights Jet has won; a snooty delegate Marcus scared off once with a single roar. Melia never misses an opportunity to comment on how each memory makes Jet the perfect leader, and Marcus and she agree on various supporting points until Jet loudly changes the subject, starting the whole cycle over again. Despite the shadows behind us, I find myself smiling most of the way.

Still, I try to keep my eagerness at bay. Cautiously optimistic, that's what I've determined to be. But as the bandits lose even more ground, and the scenery shifts from rocky plateaus to the green, spindly trees that only grow near water, it's hard not to think my days in the desert are over. When the first caravans come into sight, my excitement soars so intensely the mare starts prancing.

"All right," Jet says. "This is probably a good place to decide what we're going to do. Marcus, are they still following?"

The soldier lowers his telescope. "Think we finally lost them. We did a lot of weaving in that last stretch, and I haven't seen them since."

"Good," Jet says, sitting straighter. "Hopefully we'll be done here before they pick up our trail again. What are we up against?"

"Not much, fortunately. Elab is a fishing town, and on the small side." Marcus nods at the sprawl of low, distant buildings. "But that has its advantages. There's no upper district here, and people won't be expecting royalty to stop into a working village."

"So they won't be looking for us," Jet muses.

"They won't be *expecting* us. But if we show up dressed like this, we'll stand out like a leopard in a plum custard."

Melia purses her lips. Jet cuts a glance at my burned gown, but Marcus is looking at the prince's shining armor and vivid blue tunic. If Elab is anything like Atera's lower district, their fine clothes will stand out far more than my bedraggled dress.

"A leopard in a plum custard," Jet repeats.

"With a side of cheese," Marcus confirms.

Jet shakes his head slowly. "All right, that's going to top the 'weirdest Grekan sayings' list for now. So we'll change . . . into our sleeping robes, I suppose?"

Marcus nods. "With the cooling cloaks, that should suffice. The docks are on the east side, with the most direct route through the market." He raises the telescope again. "But that's the busiest area, with too great a risk someone might recognize you. I'd suggest the southern loop, past the town's inn. It should be nearly vacant at this hour."

"So we keep our heads low, get Zahru on a boat, get out."

"The faster you go, the better. But the horses will need to stay with me. They'll draw as much attention as your clothes."

"You're staying?" Jet asks Marcus, disappointment in his voice.

"Someone has to, and my size will draw notice. But I'll also be a surprise reinforcement, if you need it."

Jet nods in reluctant agreement, and I note that beyond confirming Marcus's plans, he hasn't questioned him on a single thing. For all their gibing, Jet trusts him implicitly.

"Where should we meet?" Melia asks.

"We'll ride to there," Marcus says, pointing to a far plateau speckled in desert brush. It's as close to town as Fara's stable is to Atera, just far enough outside to be apart from it. "The road passes on the other side, and you can join the travelers going in. Though you'll need to look like you've walked longer."

I brighten. "Hey, I look like I've been trampled by a wagon! I'm already ready!"

Marcus snorts. "You look like you've been through a bit *too* much. You'll need some of Melia's clothes."

My shoulders sink. "Oh. I thought I had that one."

"We're almost there, Zahru," Jet says, and the promise in his face sets dragonflies loose in my stomach.

Almost there.

The road into Elab is achingly familiar.

Unlike the proud paving stones of the capital, the roads here are dirt and packed clay, preserved more by the frequency of travelers than the work of careful upkeep. A small stable heralds the northern entrance, though it makes mine and Fara's look like an estate. Instead of a full building it's simply three mudbrick walls that form a shelter for camels and oxen, topped by a makeshift palm roof that barely shades the poor beasts inside. A section for small animals sits off to one side, a single cat curled in a shaded corner.

The Whisperer cleaning the stalls is a boy no older than ten. He wears only a stained wrap of cloth around his hips and a look of envy as a richly dressed traveler rides past on her camel. I'm sure he's thinking how much he'd like to go with her, how much he'd like to see the desert and the wonders of the palace, and I have the urge to shake his shoulders and tell him to stay inside for the rest of his life. Daydreaming is all fun and games until you're chosen as a human sacrifice, and having to sneak through a dilapidated town with a deserting prince and the risk of a treason charge.

Then again, I have a feeling this is the kind of thing that only happens to me. Everyone else who attended the banquets is home right now with stories about peacocks and marble pillars.

But even the smells here remind me of home, and I find my excitement building again as Melia, Jet, and I follow a wagon clinking with spice jars. There's the scent of the river, fishy and clean. The heady smell of the spices, of lotus root and hyacinth. Even the bitter stench of nettle weeds reminds me of my trips gathering water from the river, and I swivel my head as much as I did in the palace, latching on to every reminder of home as if each piece could ensure I'd be getting back to it soon.

A soft hand closes around my arm. "Stop looking like a tourist," Melia says, leaning close. "No one comes here for anything but work. Remember what Marcus said?"

"Look like I know where I'm going. Sorry."

The road splits, one sloping down to a small market whose stalls are shaded by ragged canvases. We take the road that arcs right instead, past a row of single-story homes. I drink in the familiar shape of them; the comforting sounds of people working and chatting.

"Looks like my father's rationing plan is doing well," Jet says, tugging his hood so it covers more of his eyes. Marcus thought it best for him to walk behind us, as then most people should focus on Melia and me. But I'll admit there's something about the mysterious tilt of his hood, or only being able to see the smooth, strong angle of his jaw, that I'm finding inconveniently distracting. "The people look well. And there are grain barrels in every home."

"An astute observation, *aera*," Melia teases. "Taking notes for what's working?"

"I didn't even notice that until he pointed it out," I say, slipping into Marcus's role.

Melia grins. "Would you say that's because he has a natural eye for his people?"

I nod. "I think it's his concern that really sets him apart. Not only that he notices, but that he's truly interested in the results."

"Hey," Jet says, poking my shoulder and sending a thrill down my arm. "I thought you were on my side."

"We are *all* on your side," Melia says.

I glance back. "My loyalty flexes. I don't think I've heard a single *sorry* from you this morning."

"Gods, that's right," Jet says, gripping his fist in mock distress. "Sorry. Sorry, sorry, sorry—"

"How long do you think he'll say it if I don't stop him?" I whisper to Melia.

"Sorry, sorry, sorry, sorry—"

"He's pretty stubborn," Melia says. "Maybe forever."

"I feel like that runs in the bloodline."

"Yes," Melia concurs. "I would say just in the men, but it got to Sakira, too."

"Mm."

"Sorry, sorry—"

"I think I'm actually going to miss it," I admit. Not that I'll miss the desert or looking over my shoulder for stabby princes, but something about Jet has always felt comfortable, our one (big) misunderstanding aside. I can't explain it. A day back with him, and I feel we've almost returned to what we were, each of us in our respective disguises, trading cheeky words for smiles. I mean, technically he wasn't in disguise before and I was just too clueless to recognize him. But it's easy to be around him is what I mean. It's easy to forget we're not friends and that these next few minutes are the last we'll ever have.

"Yes, I will miss him, too," Melia says sadly. Jet is *still* going on with his *sorries*. "I would have stayed in Orkena if he would be king. But I do not know if Sakira or Kasta will keep the Mestrah's agreements in place with Amian. I cannot risk being locked here, in case they decide I owe my services to my schooling country and not my own."

I look over in surprise. "Can they even do that? Make you stay?"

"That was the way of it, until Jet's father determined it unjust. Orkena has drawn far more scholars since. The Mestrah believes those with magic are the gods' children no matter where we are born."

I can no longer make sense of the Mestrah. I had revered him before we met, but I can't forget what he said in the throne room to Kasta, or how he turned his sons against each other. And yet he's the same god who has provided for Fara and me over all these years. The same who believes Melia should be free to return to her family, and did not force Jet to take the crown even when he believed him the best choice. The same who loves Sakira so dearly he fears letting her rule at all.

"I don't understand," I say. "Does the Mestrah put one face on for the public and another for his family? You know what he did to Kasta and Jet, right?"

Melia frowns. "What he did?"

"He turned them against each other. He made them compete for his love."

"No." Melia shakes her head. "He made them compete for the *throne*, and Kasta could not separate his father's love from his lessons. The Mestrah wanted the brothers to work together. To learn from each other. I heard him say it more than once."

"He never thought maybe he'd gone too far?"

Melia looks over her shoulder and swats at Jet. "*Aya!* Stop that noise! I can't hear myself think." She turns back, eyes wide with annoyance. I stifle a laugh. "Even gods are not perfect, Zahru. But I think he did something right if he raised this one. As annoying as he can be."

"Was that an actual compliment?" Jet asks.

"Yes, but this one is running away," I remind Melia.

"For now. We will see—"

"Hey, I'm talking to you!" comes a man's voice. We must be passing the inn, for it's the longest building on the road, its many small windows shaded with threadbare curtains. Three armored men stand outside the main door, their skin tanned and weathered, their bodies well muscled. The largest one crosses his formidable arms.

"What, too good to come over and say hello?"

"Gods, he's talking to us," I say.

"Keep walking," Melia says.

"Finest mead on the river here," the man tries. "Come on, give us a minute or two. I have stories that'll make your heads spin."

"I have something else that'll make your head spin," another snickers.

"Shut up, Des," the man snaps. "Ladies—"

"We are not interested," Melia says, lacing her arm through mine.

"I'm a Stormshrike." He starts to follow, and Melia closes her hand around something beneath her cloak. He leaves it at that for a moment, as if his power alone might make us run into his arms. "Do you like rainbows? Or maybe you girls are waiting for lightning—"

"I believe she said she wasn't interested," Jet snaps.

"And I believe this is none of your business," the man jeers, reaching for me. "Come on, *adel*. One drink, and if we haven't charmed you by then—"

He goes suddenly stiff, his head jerking as if listening to something behind him, though neither of his comrades has spoken. He winces, jaw clenched in pain, and brings his fingers to his head.

"Kale?" the shorter one says, his gaze darting to us.

"My . . . head!" the man gasps, dropping to his knees. "I can hear them screaming!"

"Jet," Melia mutters. "Is this wise?"

"Make it stop!" the man wails. "Apos have mercy!"

"What's happening?" I ask.

"Keep moving," Jet says, and Melia pulls me quickly along.

The man yelps again, then falls into the sand as if released, his hands dropping from his head. His eyes roll wildly toward us, and he scrapes back toward his comrades, panting.

"*Saxou*," the man curses. "Was that them?"

"You should not have done that," Melia says as we hurry away. "You have as good as announced yourself."

"And if you'd used blight powder on him, his friends would have stepped in. That was the least confrontation possible." Jet grunts. "Besides, I'm not sure they're the sharpest swords in the stack. Who knows if they'll ever sort out what happened."

"What did you do?" I ask.

"Just a little sound trick," Jet says, and for a moment the pressure in my ears flickers in and out, like a ghost moving through my head. "With just enough intensity to make a point."

"Oh," I say, shivering. Now I understand why the gods believe sound a fitting power for a possible king, if that was a *little trick*.

"Still, I do not like this," Melia says. "We need to get Zahru out of here before someone realizes what happened. They may accept a prince wanting to keep a low profile on his journey through, but they will know exactly what you're doing if they see you send her home."

We quicken our pace. The road stays mercifully clear as we go, save for a fisherman pulling a heavy wagon of fish, who nods politely as we pass. Something about the way he watches us bothers me in a way I can't place, but maybe I'm doomed to be overly paranoid from now on.

"There are the docks," Jet says.

The road curves and drops, and the houses end where the sand meets the mud. The smell of fish here is as thick as the wet air. But I'd call *docks* a relative term. There are no planks or special alcoves for boats. Instead, a smattering of wooden posts lines the shore, where ropes tether small trading canoes and mid-sized fishing vessels. Aging planks connect the bigger boats to the shore so people can carry barrels of goods up and down.

"There," Melia says, pointing to a trio of merchant canoes. "I will go ask about their destinations, and if they would take someone up the river." A glance at Jet. "No more showing off while I'm gone."

Jet crosses his arms. "I wasn't—" Melia gives him a look, and he scowls. "He deserved it either way."

Melia leaves for the merchants. Jet turns his back on the village, and I fidget with the sleeve of my cooling cloak, listening to the quiet lap of the water, the clicking cries of the storks wading through it. A crocodile slides away from the shore where we've stopped, a deadly log slinking through the reeds.

"Well," Jet says. "Took me long enough, but we're finally here." A sad smile pulls his lips. "I'm sorry again. A thousand times more than I can ever say."

His hood has fallen back from his eyes. The river's reflection flecks his irises with green, and I try to take in every detail of his face, this prince who will soon be no more than a legend, a rumor children will talk about like a ghost. They will know him only as a swordsman, a bastard prince, a talent lost far too soon to the desert. They will never know of the sacrifices he endured. They will never know how great a difference he made in one lying, buffet-sampling Whisperer's life, or the risks he took to help me.

For this, finally, is enough for me to believe him. I'm not sure how much closer I could be to freedom than actually on one of those boats, and despite what happened before, everything else he promised has come true. Somehow he's managed to fulfill his dying father's wishes, save his brother from condemnation, and rescue me, all without anyone the wiser. If I were feeling clever, I might have pointed out how this, too, is the mark of a good leader. But I can at least give him what his brother never did.

"I forgive you," I say, meeting his gaze.

My favorite smile crosses his mouth, and my heart twists knowing I'll never see it again. He reaches into his cloak and offers me a heavy leather pouch.

"Here," he says. "This should be more than enough to secure your way home, and for a little extra once you get there. Don't show it to anyone all at once. Take a single piece for your passage, and another anytime you need something."

I take it and peer inside—and almost drop it when I see the first wink of gold.

"Gods, how much is this?" I don't even think I saw this much at one time in the *palace*. Sapphire earrings, golden spiders with rubies for bodies, and more shining chains and precious gems than I could dream of glint in the noon sun, a small fortune in my hands. Half of this would buy Fara and me a house.

"Consider part of it my attempt to make up for what you've endured," Jet says, glancing at Melia. She's moved on to the second merchant now. "It's not nearly enough, but I don't know what else to do."

"This is more than enough," I say, shaking my head in disbelief. "You have more, right? For *your* new life?"

"I have plenty." But the way he says it, I have a feeling it's not much more than what he's given me. Which is still considerable, but seeing as this is all the wealth he'll have to live on from here forward, it's an incredibly generous gift.

"You can't give me all of this." I dip my fingers into the bag, freeing a few gold chains. "You have to take some back."

"Don't be ridiculous. I want you to have it."

"No, apparently what you want is for me to have a small panic attack on the ride home, thinking about you living in the streets of some faraway town because you were five gold chains short of paying your rent! Take these."

He grabs my hand when I pull the chains out. "Leave those in there. You deserve them."

"You have to take them. I don't even know how to value these. I'll use them to pay for bread or something irresponsible if you don't."

"Zahru—"

"Jet."

His mouth quirks. "I want you to use them on something irresponsible. Gods, you snuck into a palace to get a bite of chocolate! Buy all the chocolate you want." He looks down at our hands, where my sleeve has slipped away from the scar on my wrist. "Buy anything you want. And let that be the greater memory of this."

Warmth spreads from his fingers, and something restless stirs in my chest, until I remember I'm leaving and gently pull away.

It's just gratitude, I tell myself as I carefully tie the pouch to the belt of Melia's brown tunic. It's just the overwhelming feeling of this finally being finished, because under any other circumstance I wouldn't be talking with him at all. It's foolish to think it means anything else. Certainly not that he might be helping me for reasons other than wanting to clear his conscience, or that I'm just realizing *he* will be the greater memory I'll have of this.

"All right," I say, praying the heat I feel in my face isn't showing under my skin. "I can do that. I can spend all of this on ridiculous things."

He chuckles. "Thank you. I'm going to—" He clears his throat. "I'm going to miss the way you can be so agreeable *and* demeaning at the same time."

"And I'm going to miss the way you never actually act like a prince."

"Ah. There it is again."

I blink. "There what is?"

"Oh, Zahru." He rubs a hand over his face, and when he looks at me again, his eyes are sad. "You make me wish I could stay."

If I wasn't reddening before, I certainly am now. I struggle to think of something clever to reply, or something honest or wise, but I take too long and soon Melia's footsteps sound to our side, relieving me from saying anything at all. She pauses a little away and looks between us, one perfect eyebrow rising.

"Am I interrupting?"

"No!" I say, not wanting to embarrass Jet, or myself, for whatever Melia thinks she sees. "We were just discussing . . . chocolate." Gods, Zahru, stop talking. "I get really intense about chocolate."

What is *wrong* with me? Melia's suspicion turns to concern, so I suppose it worked, but I quickly look down before I can say anything else.

"All right," Melia says slowly. She turns and points behind her. "Here are your choices. The charm maker is going to Ziti, then stopping in the capital for more supplies. Though I would not suggest being seen in the capital." She points to a woman in a yellow *jole*. "The fortune-teller plans to hit every town on the way up, but she is willing to go straight to Atera for the right price. The potter was here to visit her nephew." She points to an older woman in a plain tunic. "She lives north of Atera and would be glad to take you."

So this is it, then. Time to say goodbye and to finally go home. I exhale as I consider the three merchants, anticipation buzzing beneath my skin. Two days, and the shore I'll be standing on will be Atera's. Two days, and I won't even remember the moment I was standing here, overwhelmed by the possibility of it, still not believing I was free.

"So I . . . I can just go?" I ask, looking to Jet. Why am I even asking? I should be running for the shore, throwing every piece of jewelry I have at whoever will get me home fastest.

"Yes," Jet says, that same strange sadness in his eyes. "And may Numet be with you."

"Numet be with you," Melia echoes. "Go live the life you are meant for."

I swallow and return their parting blessing, and turn slowly for the boats. It's so easy, it feels like a trick. I head for the potter, the woman who was visiting family, looking tentatively over my

206

shoulder. Jet and Melia watch me like I'm something dear they're setting into the wild. I square my shoulders and shake off the last of my suspicions, letting the reality of it sink in. I'm going home. I'm going *home*.

"Hail, child," the older woman says, smiling as I approach. "Your friend told me you need passage to Atera?"

"Yes," I say, slipping a jade earring from the pouch. "Will this be enough?"

"More than." Her brown eyes widen. "Are you sure? I only need enough to cover our food. I already have the spell that will move the boat."

"I'm sure. I insist on it, for your kindness."

The woman lifts the earring, inspecting the detailed face of the jade cat. She casts a curious look at me, and I'm sure she's seeing the contrast of my sand-coated hair and Melia's plain tunic with such riches, but she only shrugs and gestures to a few large baskets waiting on the shore.

"All right. Help an old lady with these and we can be on our way."

I cast a glance over my shoulder for Jet, but he and Melia are no longer by the far houses. Of course. They would want to leave quickly, before anyone has a chance to recognize them. I'm reaching for one of the baskets when I hear a familiar, cringe-inducing laugh.

I turn to see an entire group of armored men filing into the clearing between the shoreline and the houses, led by the Stormshrike.

Jet and Melia stand at their center, hands raised.

XVI

HE'S a prince, I remind myself. *He's a prince, and once they recognize that, everything will be fine.*

The men stalk closer, a collection of varying skin tones and muscles, and tighten their circle. The fortune-teller takes one look at them and hurries to finish packing her boat. The fishing boats are taking note, too, shoving their planks onto the shore, pushing out into the river.

The old woman waddles past me with a heavy jar. "We should go, too."

"Who are they?" I ask, not moving.

"Bounty hunters. If you leave them alone, they'll leave you."

This does not make me feel better. I remember the Mestrah asking Kasta what he'd do if he met bandits who wanted to hold him for ransom, and the sinking feeling in my chest pulls tighter as Jet jerks his hood back, and the men only smile in response. Surely they'll just talk. Surely the Stormshrike will remember what Jet did to him—what Jet's power could do to *all* of them—and back off.

"Make haste, girl!" the woman says. I shake myself and lift the last of her baskets, following her to the canoe. The river water swirls around my feet, cool and tempting. I place the basket beside the others at the front and pause in gripping the thick river reeds that bind its sides.

The armored men have put some kind of strange metal device over their ears. One of them lurches for Melia.

"No," I breathe as he yanks Melia to his chest, locking a knife close to her throat. The metal must be blocking Jet's magic. There's no way he would have let them near her otherwise.

"Hurry!" the woman says.

The man holding Melia shrieks as she turns her head and throws something into his face. He releases her, and Jet draws his dagger, and the circle of men converge—

"Girl, I am not waiting around to be leftovers," the woman snaps. "Get in, or I'm leaving you!"

I clench the reeds, tensing to get in. But can I go? *How* can I go? If Jet had left me with Sakira, he and Melia wouldn't be here. If they'd insisted on visiting the western cities and not cared how long it would take me to get home, they wouldn't be here. If they did not feel compelled to escort me through town to ensure this very thing didn't happen to *me*, they wouldn't be here.

They can handle themselves, the logical part of my mind argues. *They could have encountered this anywhere, with or without you. Go!*

But it doesn't look like they're handling themselves. The men have captured Melia again, and one drags her toward the buildings while another binds her hands. Jet holds five more at bay with his dagger and sword. Without his magic, it will take only one lucky strike, and he'll be theirs.

But if I don't take this boat, who knows how long it will be before I have another chance to escape. *If* I have another chance.

He could die, whispers the other part of my brain. *And Melia, too. Is your freedom worth that?*

"Girl!" yells the woman. "I'm leaving—"

"Help them!" I say, gripping the canoe. "Please, we have to

help them. Do you have protection spells? A sword?"

"Do I look like a mercenary? If you're not getting in, get out of the way!"

She slaps my hands with the canoe's emergency oars. I let go in surprise, and the woman shoves out into the river, shaking her head and muttering about fools.

And there goes my boat.

But I have no time to lament my continuing streak of bad decisions. I whirl to see Jet now surrounded by four men, the fifth writhing and cradling his bleeding arms outside the circle. I don't know where they took Melia, and panic seizes me that I might help one only to be too late for the other. That I have no effectual plan doesn't faze me, as usual. I run for their circle, hoping to be able to distract them long enough to give Jet an advantage—

A hand grips my arm and jerks me around. I slam into a core of hard muscle and the smug smile of the Stormshrike. The strange casing around his ears looks almost fluid in the sunlight.

"Well, hello there, beautiful," he says. "Thought any longer about that drink?"

"Obviously that's exactly what I was rushing over here to do," I say, aghast. I should probably have said something that would better serve my safety, but really? "Where did you learn about social cues?"

He chuckles. "It's hard to learn from the dead."

I have no idea what that's supposed to mean, and revulsion crawls my skin as his hand slides down my hip, splayed and searching.

"Stop," I say, jerking away. His grip tightens painfully on my arm.

"Don't get excited, I'm just making sure you don't stab me, like your friend." His hand closes around the leather pouch. "Ah, what's this?"

He rips the bag from my belt, and when he catches sight of what's inside, his eyes widen. He releases me to sift through the treasure, greed lighting his face.

Jet shouts, but the man catches me before I can turn.

"This is a lot of gold," he says, jingling the bag. "Does your prince know you have this?"

An idea strikes me in a flash of nerves. "If you spare us, I'll give you the rest of it."

"There's more?" A horrible grin works across his face, and he lifts a ruby beetle from the stash. "I knew I liked you. A smart girl thinks her way out of things."

More than you know, I think as he drags me to where two of the men have finally pinned Jet to the ground. The prince struggles and breathes hard, his eye purpled and a cut across his cheek. His arm bleeds where a hunter holds him, and I wince when his captor's fingers tighten around it.

Jet's eyes close when we stop. "You," he pants, "were supposed to run."

"See, if you'd just let us talk earlier," the man says, "we could have avoided all this. We're reasonable businessmen. Someone hires us to kidnap you; you hire us to look the other way. Luckily your girl knows how it works."

"You will burn for this," Jet seethes. "The Wraithguard won't care if you were 'doing a job.'"

The man scoffs. "Even the Mestrah's personal guards will have trouble finding us now. You might want to speak to us with a little respect, *aera*. You never know when you'll suddenly find yourself on the bottom." He shoves me into one of his comrades, who grabs my arms. Jet jerks and tries to stand, but his captor squeezes his injured arm until he gasps, and he stills.

The Stormshrike saunters over to Jet and squats, jangling the pouch of riches. "This is a good starting point. How much more do you have?"

Jet looks at me, and back at the pouch. When we pay them, his entire savings for a new life will be gone.

"Enough to never need another job," Jet says, resting his chin on the sand. "And then some."

"Where?"

"Behind—behind the first plateau. We have horses, too."

"Well, boys," the Stormshrike says, standing, "we should rob princes more often. No hard feelings, *aera*." He stands and motions to the alley where Melia disappeared, and turns back to the men holding Jet. "Let him up. No tricks, or I keep the girls, too."

"Hey," I say. "I was the one who made the deal!"

"Just business, *adel*. Maybe you should have spent more time defending your team and less trying to make off with a cut of the pay. *He's* the one with the gold, not you."

With a jolt, I realize he thinks I'm Jet's First . . . and that I intended to abandon the prince for a pouch of jewelry. Which means they don't know I'm the sacrifice . . . and they don't know about Marcus.

Maybe *he* should have spent more time learning about his target.

"Melia," Jet gasps as he's jerked to his feet.

"I'm fine," Melia calls, struggling against the grim-faced woman who drags her forward. Her hands are bound and her cheek bruised, but I'm relieved she looks otherwise unharmed. She catches sight of me, and her eyes widen. "Zahru."

"Lead on, prince," the Stormshrike jeers, pushing Jet ahead. Injured and with his hands bound behind him, Jet stumbles, but another man jerks him upright. Their blatant disrespect and lack of magic have me wondering where they're from. The Stormshrike clearly lied about his identity, since I have yet to see him conjure so much as a breeze. Magicless bounty hunters who would agree to kidnap one of the Mestrah's deadly sons . . . I mean, it worked, but it shouldn't have. Something is off.

The man holding me binds my hands, too, as if that will make any difference in what I'm capable of. Still, part of me is oddly thrilled at being taken seriously.

"Don't try anything," he growls as we follow the procession through the market. The locals shrink away or turn their backs as we pass. Like me at the banquet, I doubt many of them would recognize Jet, but I suppose that's for the best. This is a humiliating display for the son of a god, and a debilitating one if the people knew what they were watching.

Gods, I hope Marcus is ready.

We march past the sparse stalls and their wares; past a mother with two small children who hurries down an alley to escape us. Past the Whisperer boy who clutches the manure rake. I count the men around us: eight including the Stormshrike. I have no idea if Marcus would consider that many or few, but I hope it's the latter.

"We're around the back," Jet says, heading for the side of the plateau.

"Keep the girls behind," the Stormshrike calls. "And in front of you in case the prince tries to get crafty."

The man guiding me sighs as if this is a monumental request but does as he's told. Melia grunts as the woman shoves her forward. We pass a thick section of thorny brush and sage, and my heart lurches as we round the corner and the horses come into view. The town of Elab is almost entirely eclipsed by the hill now. In moments, anyone there who might start to feel like a hero will no longer be able to see us.

"'The Steel of Orkena' my eye," the Stormshrike grumbles. "We could have come back here and taken it while you were gone. What kind of fool leaves his riches unguarded?"

Jet only looks at him—and smiles.

The grin vanishes from the Stormshrike's face.

A twang sounds from above us, and the Stormshrike's eyes bulge as he grips the arrow now lodged in his neck. Another twang as an arrow hits the woman holding Melia in the side. Just as the bounty hunters shout and panic, a third finds its way into my captor's arm.

"Archers!" yells one of the men. Their employer must not have paid *that* well, because they run into each other in their haste to get away, more arrows sinking into the sand and narrowly missing heads. Melia pulls me in to her as the last of them tramples through, an arrow nicking his calf as he runs. He howls and doubles his pace, a cloud of sand drifting in his wake.

Then it's only the three of us and the Stormshrike, who will not be going anywhere ever again.

"Oh," I say, gagging. I turn away from his body and right into Melia, whose green eyes darken like a storm.

"And just what did you think you were doing?" she snaps. "You are supposed to be halfway home! You have no weapons, no sense of self-preservation . . . You could have been killed!"

Heat flushes my neck. "I—"

"Marcus would have handled it! That is his job. We already risked our lives taking you into one town. If we take you into another and you don't stay where we put you, so help me I will throw you into the river myself!"

She tosses her hands up and stomps past Jet to the horses. I stand there a moment, stunned, shame rushing through me like a burn. I thought I'd helped. I didn't think about them having to risk their lives again, I only—

"It's all right," Jet says, rubbing a hand through his dusty hair. "That's how she gets when someone she cares about scares her." He smiles. "Usually *I'm* on the receiving end, though."

Melia harrumphs and sifts roughly through the mare's saddlebag. Jet looks at the body and back to me.

"You came back," he says.

"Yes," I say, edging toward the horses. I want to put as much space as possible between me and the dead man.

"You were literally on a boat home, and you came back to help us."

I swallow. "I know. It was foolish of me. I didn't even think . . . Well, that's not true, I thought a lot, but I didn't think about *what* I was going to do, just—"

"Zahru." His hands steady my arms. I look up at his bruised face,

215

feeling embarrassed that he's the one in much worse condition, yet he's the one comforting *me*.

"Thank you," he says.

I blink back the heat climbing my neck. "I'd never forgive myself if they'd hurt you," I whisper.

Maybe I should have left it at "I wasn't thinking." But it feels like we've been through a lifetime in these two days, and now I know that Jet would do the same for me. That he's *still* doing the same for me. And as much as I'm trying to ignore it, as much as I'm telling myself I only feel this way because anyone would be appreciative of someone so dedicated to saving their life, I can't help but notice the way his hands soften on my arms and the safety I feel in this moment, like the world could explode and we'd still find our way out of it. I can't help but wish things could be different, and he wasn't a prince, so every moment didn't feel like I was losing something irreplaceable.

"Well. I *did* kind of deserve it," Jet says, lips twitching. "But I need you to promise you won't do it again."

I grunt. "As long as you promise to stop getting into life-threatening situations."

He smirks. "I'll do my best."

We stand there a moment, his hands on my arms and me leaning toward him, not moving away. What am I doing? This hasn't changed anything. Soon we'll head for the next town and I'll get on a different boat, and whatever this is will be as impossible as it was before.

Jet must see the sadness in my face, because he squeezes my shoulders. "We'll try again," he says. "Osjerg is only a day or so south. It's a bigger city, and much better regulated. We have another chance."

Maybe I should tell him that wasn't what I was thinking. But I still *do* need to get home, and what difference would it make anyway?

"And that," booms Marcus from above, "is how you clear a party!"

Jet drops his hands. Marcus saunters down the hill toward us, crossbow over his shoulder, that same joyous, brilliant grin on his face.

"I feel insulted on your behalf that there were only eight," Marcus says. "We need to work on your reputation. I was ready for twenty, at least."

Melia rolls her eyes and approaches Jet with a flask of healing water and a cloth. "Eight were enough. If Zahru hadn't bribed them, I'm not sure where we'd be."

"Hey," I say. "You just yelled at me for—"

"You are still on my list for putting yourself in danger," Melia snaps, but a small smile pulls her mouth. "But you did help us. And for that, I am grateful."

"They bested you?" Marcus frowns, and kneels by the body. "Were they some of Sakira's fanatics?"

"No," Jet says, holding his arm so Melia can tend the cut. "They're Nadessan, maybe. Or Pe. I think Wyrim hired them to hold me as leverage against my father." He looks over his shoulder. "Look at his ears."

I'm definitely not comfortable enough with death to watch Marcus inspect the body. I slink farther behind Melia, peering

217

around her just enough to see Marcus lift one of the strange metal casings.

"No," Marcus breathes.

"I think they've done it," Jet says, his voice tight. "I couldn't use my magic against them at all."

Marcus grits his teeth and stands. He presses the cup-like edges of the metal, and it crushes easily between his fingers.

"It's still fragile," he says. "But the Mestrah must know about this. We need the Metalsmiths working on how to counter this at once."

He stoops and grabs the other cup before retrieving the bag of gold the man stole from me. I spin away when his hand closes around the arrow, but a sound like squishing fruit fills the air, and even without seeing it I know I'll never be able to scrub that noise from my memory.

"Sorry, Zahru," Marcus says, collecting the other arrows from where they've stuck in bushes and the sand. "I don't like to kill unless I have to."

"It's all right," I say, my stomach roiling.

"First dead body?" Melia asks, wiping the last of the blood from Jet's face.

"And hopefully last."

"Yes. I always hope that." Her voice is sad. She rolls her cleaning cloth in her fist and evaluates me. "Are you hurt?"

"No."

"All right." She sighs. "Let's go, before they find brains or reinforcements. I suppose we are headed for Osjerg now?"

Jet nods. "But we'll need to take the long way around. I think the men following us this morning were scouts, and that's why they kept their distance. They alerted the bounty hunters to our position."

"Rie's blood," Marcus curses. "I knew we'd lost them too easily."

"And your sister is definitely out of it?" Melia asks.

"Of course she is."

Melia narrows her eyes. "Jet."

"What?"

"Check."

He sighs and pulls the listening scroll from his belt. His eyes slip down whatever's written inside, and he nods. "She decided to mark her name at the first checkpoint after all. She's hosting parties and parading through the streets buying people drinks and new clothes, and by the way, she hopes I'm having a terrible and boring time."

Marcus grunts. "Are you going to tell her what happened?"

Jet rolls the scroll. "Maybe later, when Zahru is safely away. For now, I'm much more concerned about what Kasta's doing."

"He hasn't reached the first checkpoint?" Melia asks, surprised.

"No. Sakira may be angry with me, but she would have mentioned it."

All of us go quiet. Sakira would have arrived at the first checkpoint yesterday if she didn't take any additional detours. That's more than enough time for Kasta to have caught up.

"Well, I'm ready to go," Marcus says. "Zahru?"

"Yup," I say, climbing quickly onto Melia's mare.

"No one panic," Jet says, though he and Melia stride toward the gray. "He's not any stronger than we are. We just need to be careful."

"Yes, but he has a Shifter," I say.

"That's not helpful, Zahru."

"Sorry."

"Don't worry," Marcus says, nudging my leg as he untethers his war horse. "Good ol' Adoni won't let us down."

He pats the crossbow, and I can't help but smile at the thought of Marcus's actual grandmother facing off with a Shifter—and chasing her away with her pitchfork. We turn the horses back to the desert, and another pang runs through me both for the thought of how close I was to returning to Fara, and for how easily I've fallen into this new routine. As though I am just another part of the team, too.

It's not going to be just Jet I'll miss.

XVII

WHEN the adrenaline from Elab has worn off, and the horses move sluggishly into their tenth kilometer, the relentless heat of the sun starts to feel like a comfortable blanket. Marcus stays steel-eyed and upright, but I nod off a few times, and Jet almost slides off the gray before any of us react and Melia pulls him up. None of us has slept a full night in two days. After Marcus scours the landscape and determines it's clear, we decide we have to stop for a few hours.

"You can tell it's bad," Jet says, "because Melia hasn't said anything about me ruling all day."

Melia smiles and lightly punches his shoulder. But she's too tired to argue with even that.

We stop in a cluster of bushes beneath a short jutting of rocks, where Marcus can watch the world from higher up but our horses and tent can stay camouflaged. Melia insists Marcus sleep, and he insists he can stay awake for a week. She doesn't press the point. We crawl into the tent like wet cats, and I'm asleep the moment I lie down.

I'm woken by someone jerking upright beside me.

"Gods, how late is it?" Jet says. He's no more than a dark outline on a barely lighter canvas. It's pitch-black, and crickets sing in response.

Melia rolls over on my other side, fingers pinched between her eyes. "Not late enough."

"We should have gotten moving hours ago. Marcus was supposed to—"

He bolts out of the tent. I groan and turn on my back, not nearly rested enough for another danger-filled day.

"That boy is going to kill me," Melia says, pulling herself up. "How does he even move that fast right now?"

"I don't know," I say. "I think I'll break something if I try."

"Ah, we should probably check on them, in case something *did* happen to Marcus." She pats my arm and pushes slowly to her feet. "If I had known. If I had known this was what I was signing up for . . ."

She grumbles and makes her way out. I yawn and stretch, every muscle in my body as tight as wood. My back feels like it's made of knives, and I'm certain my rear has gone completely flat from riding. But I push to my hands and knees, even if I swear I hear my muscles crying, and finally to my feet. Melia's low voice reaches me outside the tent, calm and chiding. Hopefully that means everything is fine, and I'm not going to have to resort to questionable tactics to save everyone again.

The night greets me with cold fingers. Overhead the stars wink and shimmer, and I rub my arms as I navigate bushes and climb the short path to where Marcus had set up watch. Jet and Melia are on their way down.

"He's asleep," Jet says, looking relieved. "We'll give him a little longer, then start off again."

"Yes," Melia says. "And next time, do your panicking outside of the tent so the rest of us can sleep." She pushes past him but winks at me. "I am going to rest a while longer. Let me know when mister 'awake for a week' is up."

She brushes by me, and I turn with Jet to look out at the desert. It's an entirely different landscape at night. Rie's pale lantern shines over the dunes like they're ice, picking up glints of silver in the sand. An ibis croaks nearby, but the wind is still, and I feel as though we've been captured in a painting. "The Last Night," the artist would call this one, the last time the Whisperer girl in the story talks to the selfless prince, who she is doomed to never see again. At least, it had better be the last night. Not the second-to-last night. Not the last-night-before-she-dies night.

"Are you still tired?" Jet asks.

"I'll probably be tired for the rest of my life," I admit. "But I feel better than before."

A smile. "Can I . . . would you walk with me? I don't think I can go back to sleep."

"All right," I say, my nerves needling under my skin. This will be the first time we've had the chance to be alone while not running from some danger or other. Gods, don't let me overthink it. It's just a walk, it's just talking. I pull my hands around my elbows, both to hold myself together and to ease some of the cold.

"You know," I say, "I never thanked you for coming to get me. I kind of thought you were going to betray me again, so, you know. Thank you for not doing that."

He grins. "Well, that's just because you don't know how seriously I take agreements. You still owe me a story about Nadessa."

I laugh. "Nadessa! You'll be lucky if I remember where *I'm* from after all this."

"Are there peacocks there? And ceilings made of ice?"

"In Atera?"

He snorts. "In Nadessa."

"You really want a story about Nadessa? Right now? You're going to be there in a week!"

"But I want to remember what you'd remember."

He looks over, and my blood leaps at the picture of him against the stars, his kind smile, his clever eyes. He could be the boy at the banquet again, coy and joking. And yet he is so much more than that boy now.

"Fine," I say, smiling. "Maybe you can write to me if you find out the stories are true."

"Maybe I'd like to write to you even if they're not."

This time when I look over he looks guilty, and I can't help but laugh at how ridiculous we are, edging this awkward line, both of us knowing it soon won't matter. But maybe hoping it will, anyway.

"All right," I say. We round the side of the rock outcropping, where a small pond of spring rain lingers among a few reeds and a dozen storks. It's already drying, the shore far receded from the original edges. But firebugs glint over its surface like tiny flames, and for now the water is glossy and perfect, a small piece of star-filled glass in an otherwise bleak landscape.

Much like my guilty-eyed prince.

"I only know a few stories," I say, leaning back against the rocky wall. "But the ones I've heard are amazing." I pull up my memories of the travelers with their gloved hands and gossamer wraps, fabric so thin it looked like sheets of light. "The Nadessan palace has an entire garden made of jewels. Garnet roses, sapphire ponds, topaz tree trunks, emerald leaves. One of the early kings captured a Wishing bird and made the wish as a gift to his daughter. Walking through it supposedly brings you peace for a week."

"A garden of riches," Jet muses, leaning on the wall next to me. "And the emperor shares it? Is that why we rarely hear of trouble from the east?"

I tilt my head, considering. "I don't know. The traveler said she stole a ruby from there, which makes me think she probably wasn't invited in."

"Ah."

"The other story was about the food." I don't know if it's the memory of it or that I'm just remembering how long it's been since we ate, but my mouth starts watering.

"I'm beginning to see a trend with you."

"They have the most amazing-sounding delicacies. Creamy drinks sprinkled with mint leaves. Spiced rice. Pears and moonmelon, cakes made with figs and cinnamon . . ."

"So, hypothetically, if I'd brought chocolate with me when I came to rescue you, you'd have forgiven me right away?"

I straighten. "You have chocolate?"

He laughs. "No, but if that will keep me in your good graces, I'll buy you an entire stall's worth at the next city."

I consider him carefully, as if he weren't already tethered in those graces. "Then I think you really have no other choice."

"Why?" His mouth quirks, and he leans closer. "Am I in danger of falling out of your graces again?"

I don't trust myself to look over. He's far too close, and I will do something rash. "No," I say, clearing my throat. "But I've decided that's the least you can do for keeping me out here another day."

He laughs in disbelief. "*I* kept you out?"

"If you could just handle yourself and stop being so popular with dangerous people, I could be home right now drinking juice and getting my hair braided."

"Drinking juice?"

"Well, I'd use your money to buy wine first, but then I have to throw it in my ex's face, for him thinking I would die out here." I shrug. "So, juice."

He chuckles and settles closer, his shoulder leaning against mine. "You know you could buy more than one bottle of wine."

His fingers trace my hand, and whatever I'd planned to respond scatters in an instant. I open my palm, and he draws circles in it, feather-like touches that send fire up my arm.

"Maybe I would," I say, swallowing. "If I had occasion for it."

"Like celebrating being home?" He twines his fingers through mine, and my heart pulls with wanting to pause this moment, with wishing it was the first of many nights like this, not the last. I close my fingers around his and look pointedly out at the pond.

"Like celebrating a good king," I whisper.

It's daring of me, and Jet stiffens as soon as I say it. But he doesn't pull away. I don't know where I get the nerve to go on, but I'm desperate to know whether I'm the only one who feels changed, or if he feels the same shift. Maybe this doesn't have to be the end. Maybe there could be a future for us that isn't spanned by a handful of letters and a few thousand kilometers.

"Jet," I ask, looking over. "What made you change your mind about ruling?"

I reason it's safest to start there, with the what, and not the why. Not to mention I've been haunted by the look he gave me when he said he'd never go back to what he was.

Jet exhales and rubs his thumb over mine. "I don't know if I should say. I feel like we just set my father in the right light again."

"It was something he did?"

"It was . . . yes and no."

"All right," I say, shrugging. "Tell me a good story about him. Then tell me what happened."

He thinks for a moment, his eyes on the dark horizon, and finally nods. "All right, well, before he was sick, my father liked to paint. He said every good ruler needs an outlet they don't share with anyone, so for the longest time, Sakira and I were convinced he had a thousand masterpieces hidden away in his rooms. We told him we wanted to inherit them." He smiles. "As you've probably gathered, my father is a very serious man. But when we said that, he burst out laughing. He said, 'Are you sure?' Of course we were sure. So he led us to his painting room and showed us . . . stick figures."

I snort. "Stick figures?"

"Hundreds and thousands of stick figures. Gods, he's an awful painter! But he let us each take one, under the explicit promise we'd tell no one who made it. That's the day I learned we came before his pride . . . and that you don't have to be good at something to enjoy it."

His grin widens, and I snicker. "You told someone right away, didn't you?"

Jet scoffs. "Have more faith in me than that." His lip twitches. "You know it was Sakira."

I laugh. "Of course it was."

"But he took it well." Jet shrugs, and his smile fades. "I still have that painting in my quarters."

Another piece of him he's left behind. I let the silence stretch between us, wondering if he'll answer the other half of my question, and suddenly thinking it might be better if I don't know. I like the image of the Mestrah laughing with his children, enjoying his bad paintings.

"As to what changed my mind . . ." His brow furrows. He pauses so long that I nudge his side.

"It was the same thing, wasn't it?" I say. "You saw those stick figures, and you thought, if *this* is my future—"

Jet laughs and squeezes my hand, but the sound turns pained. He leans his head back on the wall and closes his eyes. The moon silvers his brown skin; darkens the shadows beneath his brow.

"I want to start by saying my father is a good person," he says. "Most of the time. But sometimes a good person doesn't make a good king. And sometimes a good king isn't exactly . . . good." He looks at me, and whatever he sees there, he seems to decide something. "What did your tutors tell you of the Ending Drought?"

I grunt. "Absolutely nothing. Whisperers don't have tutors, Jet."

He winces. "Gods, sorry. Another thing I—it doesn't matter. The Ending Drought happened in our grandparents' lifetime. It was seven years long, and we lost thousands to starvation and thirst.

Hundreds more died in the fights over what we had left. And then one day, it just . . . stopped. My grandmother delivered carts of food to every city in Orkena, claiming the gods had answered her prayers."

A twinge of fear pulls my heart at his choice of words. "'Claiming'?"

He keeps his eyes on the desert. "The food wasn't from the gods. It was from the countries outside Orkena's borders." His hand tightens on mine. "Pe, Wyrim, Eiom. My grandmother sent our armies to raid them. We devastated their soldier ranks . . . civilians died, too. It was easy. We had magic, they didn't. Our remaining neighbors immediately approached us with trade agreements that promised food and other valuables, eager for peace, fearful of the consequences. *This* is the backbone of our reputation. Of why our armies are so feared." He sets his jaw. "To save us, others had to die. I can't make that kind of trade, Zahru."

I swallow and follow his gaze. "I wouldn't want to decide on people's lives, either."

"And another big decision is coming. Those men today? I know Wyrim hired them. It seems the guard towers along that border aren't worth much if they're finding others to do their work." He sighs. "Wyrim has never forgiven us for what we did. They've been rallying support against us for years, urging our trade partners to cut ties, saying we bullied our way into unfair contracts. They've made it their life's work to invent a metal that neutralizes magic. So far no one has joined them for fear of us, but if they've succeeded . . ."

"There will be war." A shiver runs up my arms as I imagine an army darkening Atera's horizon. "But couldn't you renegotiate the contracts? Make the terms fairer and appease Wyrim?"

He shakes his head. "That's the thing. The more I learn about politics, the more I learn nothing is as simple as it seems. If we back off on the trade agreements, those countries will think we fear Wyrim, and might press for unfair terms in *their* favor. Or we may lose them entirely. Especially if they sense I'm the kind of king who's afraid to go to war."

Gods, politics aren't nearly as straightforward as I thought they were. A friendly move should be met with friendly acceptance. It seems entirely unfair that even the peaceful solution could end in war, and I don't blame Jet for not wanting to be the cause of so much suffering. I'd much rather leave that to someone older and wiser.

But then I think of who those "older and wiser" people would be.

Kasta, who's paranoid everyone in the world is out to get him, and isn't above twisting the gods' will for his own purposes. He's already made it clear he doesn't care who suffers, so long as he gets what he wants. Or Sakira, who thinks ruling is parties, daring feats, and handsome company, and who can't even take the Crossing seriously enough to prevent *me* from riding away.

I can't imagine Kasta backing down on the contracts or doing anything but rising to the challenge of war. Neither can I imagine Sakira yielding, especially since she wants to prove she can bleed as much as any man. They will send our armies. I don't know much about war, but I know a magic-neutralizing metal would be devastating for soldiers who've spent their lives training in magic alone. And if the palace runs low on warriors, they'll draft anyone who can fight. My friends back home. Hen. And anyone no longer useful in their current station . . . like my father.

I could be getting home just in time to see them off. Forever.

"And this war is unavoidable?" I ask, realization gripping me like a python.

"Most likely. Even if we were able to renegotiate the contracts, Wyrim is out for blood. They've long boasted their science can outdo our magic. This would be their chance to prove that."

I look at him, wondering how he can risk his own life multiple times to save mine, but not see what fate he's leaving to the rest of his people. "So, instead of facing this responsibly, as someone who respects how serious war actually is, you think it's better to leave our fate to the boy who *cut a gods' symbol into my wrist* or the girl we left passed out in the sand?"

"I—" He gives me a betrayed look and groans. "Not you, too."

"Look, Jet, I was on your side until you started talking about unavoidable war. There are things I don't like about my job, either. I hate it when an animal is too sick or too hurt for me to help. It's the worst feeling to know there's nothing I can do. But if I quit, I'm completely forgetting the dozens more I've helped. The dozens more I *could* help."

He lets go of my hand and shoves off the wall. "It's not like I'm leaving the palace abandoned. Sakira will charm our allies into defending us, and Kasta . . . will do much better without me there. Orkena will pull through as it always has."

"Maybe, but at what cost? My father's life? Mine?"

"It won't get that bad."

"You don't know that. But you could know that, you could control it, if you were the one in charge."

Jet crosses his arms. "I'm not going to argue with you. I've made my decision."

"But you would be fair. You'd make the right decision when it came to Wyrim."

His voice sharpens. "I said I've made up my mind."

I cross my arms, too. "Well I don't think you've thought this through."

"And I don't think you're remembering the very reason I can't."

"All right then, what am I not thinking of? What are you really afraid of?"

The glare he casts me falters immediately. He kicks a small rock into the edge of the pond, and his arms drop in defeat.

"Changing," he says.

I blink. "Changing?"

"You asked what I saw in my father that changed my mind. And I told you he has a good heart, and he'd do anything to protect his country and his family." He rubs the back of his neck. "But I do mean anything."

The night freezes on my skin. "Like your grandmother?"

"Yes." Jet winces and looks down. "When I entered my fourteenth summer, my father took me to visit a Wyri prisoner." His hands tighten around his elbows. "The man was a carpenter. He had two young daughters he wouldn't stop talking about. But he was the brother of a woman who was researching the anti-magic metal, and he knew things." His voice cracks. "When we left, we had a name and a location, and the man was bleeding from his eyes." He closes his own eyes. "But it was my father's face I couldn't stop thinking about. How focused he was as he dragged the man's unwilling memories from his mind. As if the screaming didn't affect him at all." He swallows. "The information helped us set back Wyrim's research by years. But I can't do that. Look what I did to my *brother* when duty called for it." He shakes his head. "I can't fall again."

He looks ill, his fingers clenched around his elbows, and this time I don't care that we only have another day left—I move to him and slide my hands around his jaw, tilting his face to look at me. Reassuring him I'm here. That *he's* here, and not in that room.

"Jet?"

His jaw clenches against my palm. "I know. That's part of the job, too. I can't expect to protect people if I won't hurt the ones who would harm them."

"That's not what I was going to say."

He stays quiet, his brown eyes finally focusing on me.

"I was going to say, you only have to go as far as you want to. Torturing the prisoner was your father's choice. I know you love him, but you don't have to make the same choices he has."

He smiles like I'm being naïve. "That's what the job calls for. It's just the way it is."

"That's a lazy answer."

That was definitely supposed to be a thought that stayed in my head, and Jet blinks in shock, and I quickly drop my hands. "I mean, you already know that's not the kind of person you want to be. So make sure you don't become that. Go out of your way not to."

"But that's exactly what my father intended, too. He didn't used to be the kind of person who'd torture someone else."

"Then keep people around who know what you want! Who aren't afraid to call you out. Like Melia." I smirk, and finally a real smile cracks Jet's face. "The world changes whether we like it or not," I say, my chest pinching as I think of Hen and her job offers; of all the places she'll go without me. "But who you are is always something you have control over."

I don't know if it's surprise I imagine in Jet's eyes, but something shifts as he looks at me, like I've just shown him a door he didn't know was there. It's only then I realize how close we've drawn. How close our hands are, and how, if we clasped them, we'd be a breath apart.

"You're not going to call me a coward?" he says quietly.

I shrug. "Anyone who does is being hypocritical. We're all afraid of something."

He lifts a brow—and slips his hands into mine. "And what are you afraid of?"

I laugh, but more to quell the jolt of panic in my chest. At some point we crossed the awkward line into something else, and I've just realized why he feels so familiar. I've had warm brown eyes look at me this way before. I've felt power thrumming under my fingertips like this, dangerous and alluring, drawing me so coyly in I don't even recognize I'm falling until the day he'll decide to step back.

This is how it started with Gallus, too.

"That's not how this works," I say, looking away.

He laughs in surprise. " 'This'? And what is 'this'?"

"I'm just a part of your story, all right?" I draw back, though pulling away from him hurts as deep as a cut. "I don't have to answer questions. No one's going to care what my answer was."

He raises a brow. "I'm not entirely sure what you're talking about, but I wouldn't share your answer either way. This is just between us. And I assure you, I care."

"Fine, I—" I hate that it feels like I've already made a mistake. But I only need to remember what that first day without Gallus was like, and know I'm in no hurry to be there again. "I'm afraid to tell you what I'm afraid of."

"Now, that's cheating."

"Not if you consider I'm more afraid of you finding out what it is than I am of the thing I'm afraid of."

He thinks about that a moment, his smile weak. "You truly won't tell me? You know a lot of my fears now. At least assure me you have one."

He reaches for my hand again, and I draw back, pretending not to notice the flash of confusion on his face. But he doesn't insist. He waits, enveloping us in the smell of leather and sage, firebugs dancing at his back and the moonlight frosting his hair, and I know I can't enjoy any more star-filled nights with him. I can't notice how easy it feels to be at his side. I can't imagine him in the place of my mysterious rescuer, destined to be by my side through thick and thin.

Because it's all too easy to imagine him in a minute or a year, after he remembers he's a prince and I am nothing, giving me the same pitying smile as Gallus. *But you couldn't have thought this was serious, right? You're just a stable girl, Zahru.*

What am I afraid of?

Being broken. Being used. Being left behind, again . . . by someone exactly like you.

"Snakes," I say, clearing my throat. "I'm really afraid of snakes."

Jet gives me a look. "Snakes?"

"Have you changed your mind about ruling?"

He puts up his hands. "Snakes are a legitimate fear. Come on. We'd better check on Marcus, and then we really should get moving."

I nod, my stomach twisting at the careful distance he keeps between us, the start of a new line of my drawing. But this is the way it must be. We'll both be grateful at the end of it, and when he's settled into his new life in Nadessa and I am home, we'll smile over the small time we had, without any regrets for the time we didn't.

But as I help Melia ready the horses, my fingers sliding over the mare's soft hair, I can't get the first part of our conversation out of my head. Going home suddenly feels a lot more like running away. Like something much more important than me is dangling above a churning river—and all I'm doing is watching the water rise.

XVIII

THIS time, we stay closer to the roads.

Marcus keeps a careful eye on the distant travelers and wagons, but there aren't many people moving this late at night, and even fewer who turn their gaze to the dark. The only person we risk passing is an old oxherd, whose herd of oxen mill directly in our path. But she only nods her covered head and lets us pass without comment. I find myself lingering as we go, listening to the animals' quiet words. They think of food, of rest, of gratitude for their keeper. So unlike certain heifers I know back home.

And despite the ache that thought inspires, despite the distance between those heifers and me, I can't help but feel it's going to be a good day. It's almost the third morning of the race, leaving only forty-eight hours until the contest defaults. We'll reach Osjerg just as the city is waking and boats are readying for trips up the river. This time it'll be Marcus who comes with me so no one recognizes Jet again. In the meantime, Melia is going to write Fara to assure him I'm alive and on my way home.

This attempt will work. I will get to say "and they lived happily ever after" at the end of this journey yet.

Still, before I go, something in me itches to speak with Jet again about taking his place on the throne. Maybe there's no future for us, but that doesn't mean he can't have a future as our king. He'd only need to go to the first checkpoint and wait for the Mestrah to announce the default. He could restart with his siblings, then choose to save yet another poor soul from execution, becoming the most merciful, progressive leader we've had in a long time.

I just have to figure out a clever way to spin it. To get him to see he'd be the best ruler without him shutting me out and changing the subject.

"Hold up," Marcus says, pulling on the war horse's reins. "I need to save a cactus."

He dismounts even before the gelding has stopped, and strides toward a grouping of rocks. This is exactly the kind of cryptic thing I'd expect a hardened soldier to say, that perhaps truly means "I'm running reconnaissance!" or "I'm setting a trap!", and my curiosity gets the best of me.

"Save a cactus?" I whisper to Jet.

"He has to relieve himself," Jet says.

"Oh," I say, thoroughly disappointed. "Right."

I wait for Jet to say more, but he only draws the listening scroll from his belt, unfurls it, rolls it again, then asks Melia for the waterskin—all without so much as glancing at me. I wonder if he's thinking about how I pulled away from him. I hope he doesn't think it's something he did. I have the sudden thought that this is definitely not the way I want to leave things, and when Melia notices me watching them, I nod.

"Can I switch with you?" I ask her. Jet jerks his head up, and I give him a shy smile. "Is that all right?"

"Oh." He fidgets with the waterskin and recorks it. "Yes. Sure."

Melia casts a suspicious glance between us, but she dismounts in a single motion, her plum-hued tunic twisting around her legs. I get down and thank the mare for carrying me with a kiss to her nose. In return she itches her entire head along my side.

Melia, she rumbles as I give the Healer the reins. *Melia*.

"Yes, back to your favorite," I mutter. Melia smiles, a mischievous glint in her green eyes. I'm sure she thinks Jet and I did more than talk last night, and even though I know we didn't, I still feel heat bloom in my face. I turn away quickly, bracing myself for what I'll find in Jet's eyes, but his gaze is on the horizon, on the distant glint of city torches. And he looks *tired*. His riding cloak and tunic are frosted with sand; his eyeliner has all but worn off. The feathered metal of his armor, shiny and bright when we started, is dull in the light.

Despite this, I lean against the gelding and put on my best smile.

"You know," I say. "You look like you could take on a country right now."

Admittedly, subtlety is not my strong suit. Jet gives me a look. "You're going to make me wish I was still riding with Melia, aren't you?"

"I think you're not keeping a very open mind about this. What you should see is yet another opportunity to spend time with a delightful young lady who just wants to compliment your strengths."

Marcus snickers from behind the rocks. "We've converted her!"

Jet groans, though I catch a hint of a smile. "Gods, fine. But I'm sitting in back this time."

He sits off the rear of the saddle so I can pull up, and I smirk as I settle in, until he moves behind me and I remember there will be literally no space between us. Smirk: gone. It seems that just because I've told my head to stop wanting him doesn't mean my heart is listening in the least, and as he takes up the reins, I'm hyperaware of his stomach against my back, his arms around

239

my shoulders. Smooth, muscled arms that direct the horse with the softest touch of his hand. I concentrate on the life and luck symbols pressed into the pommel to distract myself, but I do not see this boding well in the long term.

"Whoa, easy," Melia says to her mare when the horse shies beneath her and pivots north. The war horse and Jet's gelding jerk their heads up, too. They look off past the distant oxen, who shift restlessly, mooing and breaking rank.

"What was that?" Marcus says, returning with his crossbow drawn.

Listen, the gelding says.

It's quiet, whickers the war horse.

They swivel their ears, and I get the uncomfortable feeling *it* is not in reference to our surroundings. They hear something moving whose thoughts are silent. And since, from my experience, no animal goes without thinking for longer than a few moments, that something must be human. They weren't alarmed by the old shepherd, so it can't be her. Someone must have followed us from the road.

"We should move faster for a while," I say, shrinking into Jet.

"Did you see something?" Marcus asks.

"They hear something."

I nod to the horses. They're still watching the northern dunes, nostrils wide. Marcus's gelding paws the sand.

Unnatural, he snorts. *Hyra.*

Stranger. The horses jitter at this, the mare sidestepping before Melia collects her again with the reins. Wariness crawls up my spine. The rational side of me reasons they only mean the person isn't someone they can see, but maybe being in the desert has heightened my sensitivity to their emotions, because I feel as uneasy as I did when I saw Kasta watching me at the banquet.

"Could be jackals," Melia says, running her hand on the mare's neck to soothe her. "I saw some slinking around back there, watching us go by."

"It's not an animal," I say. "It doesn't think the right way."

Marcus shoots a concerned look at Jet.

"She's a Whisperer," Jet says, pulling his hood up.

"Oh good," Marcus says, brightening. "That actually answers a lot of questions I had."

"Shall we run for a few kilometers?" Melia says.

"At the least," Marcus says, pulling onto the war horse. "Jet, can you keep us quiet?"

Jet nods. "I'll redirect our noise onto another path as long as I can. Hopefully whoever it is will follow the decoy."

We start off, first at a jarring trot that resurfaces all my concerns about sitting this close to Jet, and then into an easy lope that might be the end of me. Jet's weight shifts at my back, heavy and warm, and it takes reminding myself I made a decision, and picturing our pursuers as cannibalistic corpses, to keep my imagination from taking me to a place from which I'd never fully recover.

"It's a nice night, at least," I choke.

"It is," Jet says, his voice a pleasing tenor in my ear.

I clear my throat and remember I have a mission to attend to. "What will you do in Nadessa?"

"I don't know," he says, adjusting his grip on the reins. "I'm staying with Marcus and his boyfriend awhile, and then . . . we'll see. There are so many places I want to go. I don't know where to start."

"Well, there's a really nice place north of here, with a beautiful palace full of starlit pools—"

"Zahru."

"I know, but I can't help it. Don't you feel like you're throwing away an amazing opportunity?"

The sound of the wind fades, as does the hiss of the horse's hooves against the sand. We're in our own little bubble. But the saddle creaks when Jet shifts, so he must only be silencing the background noise.

"No," he says. "I feel like I'm finally free after years in captivity. Haven't you ever wanted anything else? Haven't you ever dreamed of what you could do if you weren't a Whisperer?"

And just like that, he's cornered *me*. It would be lying to say I knew my place in the world, that being a Whisperer was all I'd ever hoped for. After all, the very reason I'm in this mess is because I wanted something different. And whether I like it or not, Jet is just doing the same thing—living the life he wants, not the one preordained for him.

"She's silent," he says. "Gods, is it possible you have nothing to say?"

"Sometimes I think before I talk," I snap.

He snickers.

"That's not a fair question, anyway. I'm a Whisperer. Of course I've wanted more. You're a *prince*."

"But if someone handed you everything you needed to live a different life . . . would you take it?"

Somehow *he's* the one who's taken the clever approach to this argument. I can't answer that question without supporting him. Without acknowledging that in his position, I would do the same thing.

"I—I don't know," I say. "It's not the same. How did you turn this around already?"

He laughs. "Just tell me what you would do. No judgment. I'm honestly curious."

I sigh. "Well, before this"—I gesture to Melia's tunic and the horse—"I wanted to be an adventurer. I wanted to see different parts of the world. Find hidden treasures, sit in crowded taverns telling stories of all the things I'd done." I shrug. "You know, be someone interesting."

He's quiet for a long while. "You don't think you're someone interesting now?"

"I'm a Whisperer, Jet. People aren't exactly lining up to hear about camels and vengeful cats."

"Is that why you—" He relaxes as if he's gotten the answer to something. I don't like the knowing tone in his voice when he speaks again. "You realize after this, I won't be a prince. Not that it should matter, but any expectations you think are on me for . . . whatever . . . aren't going to be there."

I think he's telling me that *this*—*us*—might actually be possible, and now I really have to fight the careless part of my brain to stay quiet.

"You want to be an adventurer," he says. "You want to see the world." He leans around my shoulder. "Come with me."

All the sound dies except for his voice.

"We can go anywhere. See anything you want. It's probably ideal to be away awhile anyway, at least until the priests name a new sacrifice. They won't even bother to look for you if they think you perished with us. And you'll have every story imaginable when you return."

My heart jumps into my throat. "You're serious?"

"When else would you be able to do this? It's perfect. We could head straight for Nadessa's border. We'll be out of the Crossing's path within a day."

"But—" His face is alive with excitement, imagining where we could be tomorrow; in a week. But there's something more there, too. A hope. Not just for himself, but for me, and it's so real and raw and exactly the kind of thing I want to be true that my heart breaks just looking at him. Because of course this is what I want. Not just the adventure, but to feel like someone could want these things for me and mean it without caring what it looks like to anyone else.

I want so badly to say yes.

But whether I like it or not, I *am* still a Whisperer, one with responsibilities.

"I . . . can't," I say.

The excitement falls from his face. "You can't? Why not?"

"My father. He needs me. I can't just disappear."

"Well, what does he need until you can return? You saw how much gold I brought. We could send him anything. Food. Clothes. A new house, if he needs it."

I shake my head. "No, he needs *me*. He needs help running the stable."

Jet thinks about that. "All right, then we'll send for him. He can come with us."

My heart lurches. It's a more than generous offer, and so typical of what I've learned about Jet. He has a solution to please everyone. I want that to mean I could agree and things would work themselves out, but I think of what Fara would need to do to join us, and I know it's impossible. My father would have to find a replacement to tend the stable, a task that would be quite easy if I was there to help him translate each animal's needs—a task that might damn him if another Whisperer realizes he's lost his magic, and thinks he's leaving to avoid the service he still owes the Mestrah.

"My father runs the city's only stable," I hedge. "It's . . . complicated. But he can't just leave."

"He would only need to close it temporarily." There's a frustrated edge to his words now. "At least ask him before deciding?"

"The work we do is important," I say, more forcefully than I mean to. "I don't need to ask him, because I already know the answer. We have clients who are counting on us."

"He's just a Whisperer," Jet says. "Does it really matter who tends the animals?"

I can't even reply at first. It's silly I should even care, considering I'd been thinking that exact same thing this whole time. But apparently part of me still fervently hoped Jet didn't see me as "just a Whisperer" but actually valued what I do and who I am.

But here's the confirmation I needed that he's the same as Gallus. A boy who's happy to keep me around as long as our dreams align, but I'd wager the second he remembers he wants more, the silly little stable girl will be the first to go.

"I suppose anyone *could* watch them," I say, leaning away. "But my father believes in something called 'duty.' He's the best person for the job. And unlike some people, he wouldn't be able to live with himself if his charges suffered in his absence."

It's cruel of me, I know. But I'm angry at myself for hoping, angry at him for drawing me in, and so tired of being ashamed of what I do.

The sound of the wind and the sand roars up at a volume I suspect is twice as loud as necessary.

That's how we spend the rest of the night.

XIX

DAWN is silvering the horizon when I start to feel guilty.

Not for snapping at Jet, because I really am tired of being "just a Whisperer," but for the words I used to do it. Fara is always saying I need to be as patient with the animals as I'd want them to be with me. Advice that I think holds true for anyone. When someone is afraid of something, it's much better to build up ways they might overcome it, not to tear them down over it.

And no matter what I feel, Jet still has a kind heart and the right mind to rule fairly. Gods know he's been through enough already. He's probably as tired of hearing the comment I made as I am of the one he did.

By the time we slow the horses to rest, I'm bursting with regret.

"Jet," I say, turning.

He puts a finger to my mouth, which seems rather harsh, honestly, until I follow his gaze to the sky. High above us, barely more than a smear of ash against velvet blue, hovers a bird.

Jet's gelding pins his ears. Melia's and Marcus's horses freeze in place, and while they should be catching their breath, they inhale in bursts and hold it, listening.

Gods have mercy on them, comes a faint female voice in my ear. Chills prick my arms, and I hold my breath to listen, too. That sounded like a complete sentence, but no animal I've cared for has ever spoken so fluently.

Hyra, snorts Melia's mare. She tosses her head and lunges, and when Melia tries to muscle her to a stop, she rears. Marcus's gelding also moves, pulling his bit and circling.

"What's gotten into them?" Melia asks as the mare dances beneath her.

Go, the mare's thinking. *Must go. Let go!*

"I don't know," I say. "They're calling it *hyra*."

"That's an old word for 'Shifter,'" Jet mutters, and the chill on my skin bites deeper. Jet's gone rigid behind me. "How far is Osjerg?"

"An hour," Marcus says, his telescope already raised. "We can't run the horses that long."

"*Apos.*" Jet's gelding is getting antsy now; he shifts and sidesteps beneath us. "How did they even catch up to us? They had to have fallen for the decoy. We haven't seen them all night."

"Shifter?" I say, choking. "As in, *Kasta's First*?"

That's exactly why I can hear her but the horses can't, though I would have preferred literally any other explanation. I can sense the animal part of her magic, but the horses have no such abilities.

Marcus doesn't seem to be finding what he's looking for. He growls in frustration, pivoting to look along the entire horizon— until he faces the direction we were originally headed.

He jerks the telescope down. "Because Kasta wasn't behind us." He points as a galloping rider emerges from around a distant plateau. "He's been waiting ahead of us the entire time. The Shifter must have trailed us last night to see where we were going, then flown ahead to direct them."

"Tranquilize her," Jet says, gathering the reins. "We'll push the horses as long as we can, but when Kasta catches us, I don't want to be fighting her."

He turns our horse, but Marcus raises a hand. "Don't go yet. This is the clearest shot I'll get, and if you move, she'll follow."

Jet nods, metal grinding as he pulls his sword from his scabbard. Marcus shifts his crossbow from his back to his arms, and Melia mutters a prayer under her breath, her thumb worrying the charm around her bicep. The Shifter dips and descends, dips and descends. Something flaps in her talons that looks nauseatingly like a dead cat.

"Marcus," Jet says.

"She needs to come down just a liiiittle farther . . . *Tyda!*"

She dives. Marcus fires twice and reloads, but by the time he can raise the bow again the bird has plummeted to the ground in a spray of sand. The horses rear and scream. Melia's takes off in a panic—moving *toward* Kasta's horse—and Marcus's pitches so bad he can't aim for another shot. I nearly lose my seat when ours jerks after them, too blinded by fear to listen to my pleading.

"Go," Jet shouts. "Go!"

I look under his arm as the gelding sprints, where a dark shadow rises from the place the bird fell. It's grotesque at first—a jumble of too-long legs and beak and neck—and then the face fills out and rounds, and wings gather into powerful shoulders, and feathers to sleek, stippled fur.

A cheetah.

"Jet," I say. "Jet, we're not going to be able to out-sprint a cheetah."

"I know. I'm thinking."

"If this doesn't end well, I'm sorry. I didn't mean what I said."

"Zahru—"

"Well, I meant some of it. But I wouldn't have said it like that. I would have made it more like a suggestion, or—"

"And I would be thrilled to speak with you about this later. But right now I have to think, and I need to think in silence."

We might as well have turned our horses and opened our arms for the speed the Shifter is catching us. Jet's gelding is fast, and we quickly reach Melia and Marcus, but the cheetah is already on our heels. Marcus turns and fires. The cheetah feints left, and Marcus fires again and she screams, a horrible half-human, half-cat yowl that grates under my skin. She loses a stride but keeps after us, a bolt bleeding from her shoulder.

Marcus has to reload.

The cat shifts her yellow eyes to us and leaps.

Jet slices with his sword, but the cat stays low. Her claws tear into the vulnerable haunches of the gelding, whose thoughts explode with pain as he whinnies and falls, pitching us forward, throwing us hard into the sand. I land on my back, almost on my head, and gasp as I push to my side. Jet rolls to his feet, sword ready. Far past us, Melia tries to turn her mare but the horse gallops on, and Marcus tries to the same result, finally jumping off. But even at a sprint, it will take him time to reach us.

Jet's gelding lies in the sand, bleeding, whimpering.

The Shifter circles us, eyes darting from Jet's blade to me.

The girl first, she thinks, her lip curling over pointed teeth. *He'll move to protect her. And then—*

"Jet!" I cry.

She springs. Jet strikes, just as she knew he would, and she dodges with ease, coming under him and sinking her teeth into his hip—

"No!" I yell, but there's nothing I can do, because my magic is useless, of course, and I scramble to find anything I can throw, but there are no rocks bigger than my thumb. Jet grunts like something's off, and even though he could strike the cat he simply rolls to his back, a peaceful expression on his face. Did she hit something vital? I consider the sword, but it's still in Jet's hand, and she could easily strike me before I could reach it—

Something glints in the sand, twenty paces from where I'm standing. Jet's dagger. It must have come free in the fall, and I turn and sprint for it—

"Hold on!" Marcus shouts. "Zahru!"

Hoofbeats gather behind me. I'm ten paces away. Five. Marcus drops to a knee and aims his crossbow, but an arrow sings over my head and strikes his shoulder, sending him sideways into the sand. A black stallion slides to a stop in my path.

Kasta grips me by the back of my tunic and drags me over the saddle.

"Ha!" he shouts. The horse springs forward. I twist and push away, but his grip is iron on my shoulder and something sharp pinches my neck. His life-draining magic floods my veins like an army of beetles. My muscles go slack.

"Zahru!" Marcus shouts, his teeth clenched. "We'll find you!"

Kasta scoffs. The sand flies beneath us, spraying my cheek, and I can only watch as Marcus struggles and fails to raise the bow, and the cheetah lopes after us, limping, and the distant shadow of the city that would have been my freedom fades into the dark.

I no longer feel like this is a good day.

My worry for what's happened to Jet is a twisting pain in my stomach. He could be bleeding out right now. He could be poisoned. Melia will do everything in her power to help him, but Shifter magic is an unpredictable, twisted thing, and for all I know it could take a special kind of magic to heal him. I wish with every thread of my soul I could take back what I last said. If that's what he remembers of me, I will never forgive myself.

I need him to be all right.

But I might not fare any better. At least with Sakira, I had Kita to dote on me. I had the start of a plan. I had a sliver of hope I might change the princess's mind, if only I could find a way to guarantee her win without my death.

I had time.

Kasta will not be careless. Kasta may not even let me move while I'm in his charge, and I have a devastating feeling the only way I'll be escaping is if one of the other two pries me from his dead fingers.

And sometime during the attack, my mother's protection gem fell free. For more reasons than the hope it would save me, it's this thought that makes my eyes burn.

Kasta's Healer soon joins us on a brown gelding, from his hiding place behind a small plateau. We might have kept running then without breaking stride, except it's at this point the Shifter collapses. I could have told Kasta she needed help long ago if I had control of my mouth. A guilty part of me is glad I don't. Since my death seems closer than ever now, the last thing I need is to tarnish my soul by assisting such a cursed creature.

"Christos," Kasta says, jerking his head at the cheetah.

The Healer—Christos—casts Kasta a resentful look that surprises me with its venom. I suppose he's loath to use his magic on such a creature, just as I am to even remark that she's hurt.

"So close, yet so far," Kasta says, brushing my hair from my eyes. His fingers feel dirty against my skin. One side of me is coated in sand from where I fell, and there's something unbearable about his seeing me like this, as filthy and underdressed as I'd be at the stable. I wish he'd at least set me upright. I feel like a sheep laid over a butcher block, which I suppose is exactly how he sees me.

"The horse?" Christos asks, his pale, bony fingers digging through his saddlebag. He looks exhausted now that I see him up close, and also older, maybe even a couple years' Kasta's elder. I thought Healers prided themselves on their age, especially once they neared twenty, but he doesn't wear a single Healer's amulet.

"No," Kasta says. "The jackal."

Christos blinks, as if in a fog, before lifting something flat and furry from the saddlebag. I'm wondering what kind of code they're talking in when two long ears flop across Christos's arm and I realize, with a jolt of nausea, they're talking about animal skins. Shifters can only transform if they have the pelt of the animal they need to turn into. Kasta must have brought her a spread of options.

"Zahru, meet Maia," Kasta says, turning his stallion so I can see the cheetah. The Healer kneels beside her and examines the bolt in her shoulder. "Maia was a girl, once." The Healer grabs the bolt and jerks. The Shifter screams and snaps at him but quickly lays her head back in the sand, sides heaving. "In fact, she's one of the few I ever considered a friend. She was the daughter of a priest. Clever. Rebellious. Powerful, in that she could dream of things that would happen in years, not merely days. She was destined to be High Priest."

The Healer sets both hands over the bleeding wound and mutters under his breath. The cheetah grits her teeth and closes her eyes, and I have a feeling she's not enjoying the same painless relief I experienced with Kita.

"Maia claimed to be my ally, too," Kasta muses, and ice flushes through my veins. I don't like where this story is headed. I want to turn my head away, close my eyes, anything but look at this monster who used to be a girl, who used to have a future and a life and a soul, until she met Kasta.

"In case you're wondering if I'm the kind of person you can fool twice."

The Healer steps away. The Shifter looks at me, her poisonous yellow eyes not full of resentment or animalistic rage as I'd expect, but shame. She shoves her head beneath the jackal hide, and Kasta turns us away before I have to watch her transform.

The feeling returns to my fingers by nightfall. I'm afraid to give Kasta any indication it's come back, not wanting to be paralyzed by him again, but I don't know how much longer I can stand the silence. Unlike Sakira's laughing team and Jet's gibing banter, no one speaks here at all. The Healer alternates between sulking and dozing on the back of his gelding. Kasta is disappointingly unlike any of the villains I've heard of, for he hasn't boasted once about his victory or given me a single hint at how he might be overcome. The Shifter is a jackal, so that kind of makes the decision for her. But even her thoughts are few. Once in a while she'll look over her shoulder for Jet, but otherwise the same lines go through her head: *Only a few more days, be patient.*

Now that my initial panic has worn off, I've pulled myself together from earlier. I've come to terms with the fact that escape from Kasta and his Shifter isn't possible in a conventional way. And while I know Jet will do everything in his power to find me, I can't count on that to be my only strategy.

And so I've settled on a plan that's potentially foolish and comes with a lot of *ifs*. But I can't help remembering what Jet said about Kasta. That before the pressure of his father, before the messy competition for the throne, Kasta was a shy boy fascinated with science, with understanding the world and teaching his brother what he knew. I know that part of him is still there. I saw a glimpse of it when he said we could be equals; in the fire of his eyes when he admitted why he'd chosen me.

And if I can reach that side of him, if I can get him to see what he's become . . .

I wonder if he'd even be ashamed enough to let me go.

"Can I at least sit up?" I ask.

Too timid. Kasta doesn't even indicate he heard me.

"I can't feel my left side."

He glances down but makes no move to stop the horse. I inhale and remind myself he's no different from Jet or Sakira or any other living person, Deathbringer or not. He still has hopes and fears and dreams. And thanks to three nights ago, I know what two of those are.

"You know," I say, "if you really believed the gods let you do this, you'd treat me like a queen. Or are you just seeing how far you can push them before they smite you?"

Kasta draws up on the reins. He somehow looks as clean and perfect as he did at the banquet, his liner black and thick, his jaw shaven and smooth. A new bracelet circles his wrist, one of the stone runes bearing an eerily familiar symbol: protection. I have a twisting feeling I'm the inspiration behind it. His eyes are as blue and cold as ever, but where they were once indifferent to me, now they burn with something darker.

"Sit up," he says.

Progress. I try to move, but my numb side won't cooperate, and I've nearly slid off when he catches my arm and hauls me upright. It's a maddeningly careful motion, and he releases me as fast as if I'd struck him.

And I'm sitting. At my own request.

The firmness of his chest against my spine makes me stiffen. He's still shirtless, of course, a rather arrogant show of fearlessness in such a dangerous race, but where I should have been able to count on a cooling cloak to give us some separation, the only thing around his neck is a leather necklace whose square runes glow with red markings. It would take nothing for him to draw my life away; a breath from a candle.

"You're not allowed to kill me until the caves, right?"

A grunt is his answer, a puff of air by my ear.

"I'm really certain that's a rule," I say. "If you do anything to me before—"

"It would be a waste of energy to harm you now," he says. "As long as you don't do anything foolish."

"Like try to reason with you or be understanding. Got it."

"Like speak out of turn."

I swallow at the threat but remind myself where silence got me the first time I held back with him, and press on. "Can I at least have something to eat?"

The Healer curses. Kasta draws up on the reins, and the stallion sighs beneath us. I shift, eager to dismount, but Kasta catches my shoulder.

"Stay here. Christos will assist you."

The Healer drops to the ground, rubbing his eyes and muttering under his breath. Without him, his gelding dances to the side, eyes wide, where he can better watch the Shifter.

Demon, he's thinking. *Stay back.*

Calm, thinks Kasta's stallion. *She's controlled.*

Controlled. The gelding snorts, pinning his ears. *You not carrying Tira's skin.*

The horse skin. Discomfort pricks my neck as I wonder how new it is, since the horses know its name.

"Food is a waste of limited space," Kasta says when the Healer asks for my hand. "Especially when you have a resource who can produce the same results with a mere touch."

The Healer's jaw clenches, and he glares at Kasta but says

nothing. I stare at his palm, beetles crawling my skin as I realize why he's so exhausted.

"You're having him sate your hunger?" I ask. "*He's* generating the energy your body needs?"

"If you're tired or sore, he can heal that as well. We won't be stopping to sleep."

"But that's an enormous amount of magic." I look to the Shifter, who needed true healing, and the horses, who've probably run much of these three days without stopping, without sleeping. It's cruel. Christos's magic will exhaust his body as if he'd personally run those kilometers, and normally he'd have to sleep and recover, unless he uses his magic to heal *himself*, a feat that demands twice as much effort as usual.

This journey will take years off his life. I remember Jet saying one of Kasta's early experiments was to research how to prevent this, and my heart twists for what the Mestrah's discouragement has cost.

"It does seem unfair," Kasta muses. "But then, so is the reason he has so much more magic than his peers. Remind me, Christos, how old was that girl you let die? Seven?"

I jerk my gaze to Christos. The Healer swallows but doesn't refute it.

"One of the strongest powers in our world," Kasta says, his words edged. "And he would dare to resent it."

His older age. His lack of amulets. Suddenly it all makes sense, and a hot coal burns in my stomach. I know the price of Christos's magic is high. But it's one thing to use it as little as possible; another to let someone die in doing so. Fara and I couldn't afford a Healer for my mother, but if we could have, and we'd put all our hope in *him*—

Christos is still waiting for my hand.

I shiver against the flickering thought that he deserves this. Kasta is definitely merciless when it comes to people he thinks have wronged him—but it seems he's just as merciless with people who've wronged someone else. I quickly shake the thought from my mind. I'm supposed to be convincing Kasta that getting revenge on people like this is wrong, not agreeing with him.

"Forget it," I say. "I'm not that hungry."

"Suit yourself." Kasta presses his heels into the stallion's sides, and we lurch forward. "In a few days it won't matter what you did."

Over my shoulder, the Healer's still standing with his hand outstretched, watching me. He shakes his head as we move farther, and finally mounts up to follow.

I turn this newest revelation over in my mind.

"You realize you *can* actually be upset with someone without dooming them to their death," I say.

Kasta adjusts his grip on the reins. "Don't be so reductive. I chose him for a purpose, not for revenge. He'll still be alive at the end."

"Yes, except he'll resent you for it. I agree what he did was awful, but if you let him rest—"

"And risk my entire future for *his* sake?" Kasta shakes his head. "No. I'd rather claim my crown."

"Assuming you get that far."

He scoffs. "And who will catch me? It will take Jet's Healer an hour to neutralize the poison from Maia's fangs. Sakira is too busy parading to notice what's happening, and both of them will soon be long behind us."

I shrug. "That's assuming your team continues to cooperate."

"They will. Maia is bound to me, and Christos won't dare betray me with her as my guard."

"I wasn't talking about them."

I'm insulted by how long he takes to think about that, wondering who else I could mean.

He laughs. "And what have I to fear from *you*?"

I try to steel my voice, to make myself believe it as much as him. "Magic isn't the only thing that holds power."

"Perhaps you intend to annoy me to death."

"I only mean, a binding spell is all that holds your team together," I say, straightening. "They'd follow me as easily as you, because you've given them no reason to favor you. The same will hold true when you're king, but your enemies will be much worse than me."

This time his silence is satisfying.

"Are you threatening me?" he growls in my ear. "Or giving me advice?"

I clench my teeth at his closeness, resolved not to move. "I'm warning you that in all the stories I've heard, it's the kind kings who prosper. The tyrants meet early ends."

"Tyrant." He snorts, but the sound is sad. "You give too much weight to Jet's lies. I love this country more than he's loved anything in his life. I will do everything to see it prosper."

"Then start with its people." I turn to look at him, hope flickering in my chest. Is it possible this might work? "Send your Shifter to hunt. Let us rest without your Healer's magic. And *let me go*."

"I can't."

"Why not?"

"Because this is the only way." His eyes come alive, burning with how thoroughly he believes it. "This is bigger than this race. Than Christos's life. Than yours. I've come too far to turn back now."

"But you've already proven the gods allow exceptions. If you freed me—"

"Then you'd have power over me beyond measure. I'd have too much to answer for if I claimed to have killed you, and someone saw you alive. The questions they'd have—"

"Then don't claim it at all. Let Orkena see you spared me. That you showed a mercy no other Crossing victor has shown."

"Orkena does not want *mercy*," he says, and the horse stops, tossing his head as Kasta's grip tightens on the reins. "It wants a king who makes sacrifices for the greater good. If the court thought I valued you above my duties . . ." He shakes his head. "It's a waste of air to explain it to you. You'd never understand."

"I'm telling you there's another way to do this. You said you wanted to be better. Did you mean it?"

He searches my face, and for a moment a crease appears between his eyes, a glimpse of the prince beneath the darkness, uncertain and listening. He opens his mouth—and the wall builds up again, hardening his jaw.

He smiles like he's thwarted a trap. "I can see why Jet chose you.

He knew exactly what I'd—" His gaze shifts to the horizon. "This discussion is over."

"For the millionth time, Jet and I are *not*—"

He grips my neck, fingers pinching, and this time the world tips. One moment I'm gazing at an impossible expanse of silver desert and twilit sky, and then it's spinning, spinning . . .

And then it's black.

XX

TIME passes in ribbons. A flash of silken sand, a twirl of satin sunrise. Cold eyes lined with velvet. Rough hands against my shoulders, against my neck. Numet rises and the ribbons turn hot and gold, but a chill clings to my bones that I can no more shake than my dreams.

When I finally wake, it's to the sound of someone snoring and the feel of gritty sand beneath my cheek. A lump of gray clothing I recognize as the Healer slumbers to the side. Beyond his hooded head, the shallow mouth of a cave opens to the orange sea of the desert, the shadows long against the grass. Heat curls the rocks forming the opening, battling the cool trapped at my back. It's late afternoon, maybe. It feels too hot to be morning.

How long have I been out?

The black stallion and the brown gelding stand within view, scavenging for desert grass. I don't see the Shifter. I don't see Kasta, either, and I jerk upright, hope springing through me that the Healer somehow freed us, when rough fingers close around my arm.

"Easy," Kasta says, from where he's seated on my other side. "Don't make me regret letting you wake."

I still, not daring to breathe until his grip loosens and he releases me. I draw slowly to a sitting position, edging away from him in the process. But the cave isn't large, and Christos blocks a third of it.

I still don't see the Shifter. I look past the horses to a skeletal tree, where a hawk sits motionless on a branch. I assume that must be her, until the bird tucks its head under one wing and the thoughts that reach me are low in pitch.

Rest, it thinks. *Then hunt.*

The horses are relaxed. The desert is quiet, save for the occasional call of birds and Christos's snores. The Shifter is not here.

"She's scouting," Kasta says, taking up his dagger and lifting a thick piece of wood from the sand. He's carving something, but it's too soon to say what it is. I can only remember how he used that knife to carve into *me*, and I pull my hands around my arms.

"Are we near a bandit camp?" I ask, trying not to sound too hopeful. Clearly things have gone wrong if I'm hoping to be held for ransom over my current situation, but honestly anything that slows Kasta at this point is fine by me.

Kasta makes a long cut in the wood, his eyes on his work.

"Or the first checkpoint?"

This, I'm hoping, will tell me how long I was asleep. If we haven't crossed the checkpoint yet, then it's day four of the contest, and Kasta is running out of time.

But again, Kasta says nothing. I snicker, bitterly, and push my heel into the dirt. "Why did you wake me if you're just going to ignore me?"

Kasta pauses, his thumb between the knife and a thin shaving, and for a moment it looks like even he would like the answer to that. He glances at the Healer, and the knife moves again. "It was too quiet."

He leaves it at that. I watch him work a moment more, his movements careful and precise. It's taken me this long to notice he's changed from his *tergus* to a white tunic belted with rope, an outfit suited more for traders than princes. A loose hood covers his head and he's cleared the kohl from his eyes, leaving them bare. He's still too striking to pass for a commoner, but it's the closest I've ever seen to him looking normal, and it's several moments before I realize I'm staring.

Sapphire eyes meet mine, and I look quickly away.

"We *are* near the checkpoint, aren't we?" I say.

No answer. Of course.

"Why are you dressed like you don't want to be seen?"

The knife stops again. "Do you ever stop asking questions?"

"You're the one who said it was too quiet. Is it because of Sakira? You're afraid she'll take me from you?"

He looks over, and I know from the flash in his eyes I've hit on something he can't ignore. I grip the sides of my tunic. I need to press him just enough to get him talking, not to be put under again.

"No one will be taking you from me," he says.

I shiver at the conviction in his voice. "Then why go in disguise? Why not parade for support like she is?"

He glances out of the cave. Now that I'm looking, I can see the hazy silhouette of a city in the distance.

Kasta goes back to his carving. I'm thinking nothing I do will be enough to get him talking when he says, "The first checkpoint is not just a way to mark our progress. It's a test of the people's favor." He turns the carving in his hands. The piece is starting to taper at one end like the head of a rattlesnake. "My parading would not attract the same attention."

I remember Marcus asking if Jet's attackers were some of

265

Sakira's "fanatics" and consider the city again. Only someone confident in her people's support would go in so boldly . . . and only someone worried about it would try to hide.

And suddenly I realize . . . Kasta is *nervous*. The carving in his hands. Stopping to send the Shifter ahead. Waking me. His hands are steady as he works, but I see the restlessness in his fingers now, the twitch of irritation before he decides on a new line. Meeting with a group of Sakira's supporters, with the complete lack of his own, is just as dangerous for him as meeting bandits.

I want to ask if he's starting to see the value in allies, but I think that will get me put to sleep, and I remember him claiming Jet had turned everyone against him, anyway. I know only part of that's true now, especially since Jet stopped challenging him a while ago, and Kasta's paranoia is the bigger obstacle keeping people at bay. And yet, he woke me. He's letting the Healer sleep, he's pausing to rest . . . he *listened* to me.

Something he wouldn't have dared do if he fully believed I was against him.

I exhale at the realization and straighten against the wall. "Do you still think I'm working with your brother?"

The knife pauses. Uncertain. "You were on his horse."

"As the *human sacrifice*, if you'll recall."

"Perhaps you are far too forgiving."

"Perhaps you're not forgiving enough."

Kasta looks over, and back to his carving. "Who a king trusts is the difference between life and death."

I trace the dirt beneath me. "Says the boy who told a stranger she was his equal."

266

A muscle works in Kasta's jaw. The knife moves over the wood, but the cuts are slower, deeper.

"You told me you'd hoped to finally have an ally." I wait for him to deny it, but when he doesn't, I go on. "How long has it been since you've let anyone help you?"

"I'm starting to regret waking you."

"Because you think I have some nefarious motive?" I challenge. "Or because you're afraid I don't?"

His glare cuts to me. His fingers clench the carving as though he might put it down, a tiger flexing its claws, but he stays seated. "Your motive is easy," he says, relaxing. "You want to live; you think if you play innocent, my guilt will spur me into letting you go."

My heart lurches. "Because you *would* let me go, if you knew you'd made a mistake?"

The knife pauses. His expression echoes the one he wore when I asked why he woke me, but he doesn't answer. I shift and decide to leave it at that, for now. I don't want to push too hard, and it doesn't help my case anyway to simply ask for freedom.

I try something else. "I don't think your reputation is as bad as you think it is."

His jaw tenses, but his focus is back on his work. He's carving the smaller section into a curved point. Now it looks like a hawk, and I realize he's not glancing at the city outside, but at the bird.

"I'm serious," I say. "My best friend has dirt on *everyone*, and all she told me about you was that you keep to yourself. People don't know much about you, but I don't think that means they'd attack on sight, either."

He flicks another shaving from the carving.

"So if it's them you're worried about, you still have a chance to change their minds."

He drops his hands into his lap. "Why are you telling me this?"

"I don't know, because I have a conscience?" Maybe not the most strategic thing to say, Zahru. "And because I think you should know."

Well, I certainly have his attention again, though I'm sure he's contemplating why in the gods' names he woke me, not when it might be convenient to free me. But he's confirmed my suspicions thus far. I've stepped well beyond the appropriate boundaries, and he's let me speak my mind. I know it could mean nothing. I know I need to be careful even if he does start to listen. But I can't help but think that only someone who feels *guilty* about what he did would put up with my nettling for this long.

He doesn't quite look like he believes me. But he doesn't tell me that, either.

A screech breaks his gaze. The hawk bolts from the tree as an eagle lands outside in a puff of sand, the horses screaming as her feathered body seizes and contorts. Black boots form from her claws, and from her wings, tattooed fingers push out from fingerless gloves, the ink white and glowing against the warm beige of her skin. The Shifter stretches up, up before us on two legs, every bit of her covered in elaborate armor, notched metal as black and shining as a beetle's shell. It hums with power; with the subtle, shadowy runes that protect and bind her.

She pulls the eagle pelt from her head, where black silk hoods a masked face. A strip in the mask reveals the bridge of a slender nose and eyes that are venomously, piercingly yellow.

Those eyes hitch on me in confusion before sliding to Kasta. He ignores the question in them as he tosses the half-finished carving and sheathes the dagger.

"Well?" he says.

She jerks a cased scroll from her belt. I suppose her curse means she's not even allowed to *speak* with royalty. Kasta uncaps the case and slides the parchment from inside.

"Of course she is," he mutters, eyes shifting across the page. "Wake him," he tells me. "We're leaving."

This time, I'm not put to sleep.

Kasta rides behind me, still and silent as ever, and the Healer yawns on the brown horse, and the Shifter trots behind us as a jackal. But something still feels different. I'll admit I hoped there'd be a kind of ease now, some small reassurance from Kasta that would indicate he'd started to yield. But if anything, he's tenser than before. He keeps his hood up, his eyes forward, his hands tight on the reins.

We're not approaching the city from the usual route. Roads crowded with people and mounts color the desert on either side, I assume thanks to word of Sakira's presence. I can only imagine the kind of parties she's been throwing. I can't even make out individual buildings yet and I hear music. A great way to win the people's favor . . . not a great way to stay alert in case the race dynamics have changed. I hope Jet wrote her that Kasta had taken me. Not that I trust her to return me to him, but at least the company would be improved.

Our route takes us west, far out of range of the tall, expansive estates that make up much of the city, where rows of strategically placed palm trees block the residents' view of the storage huts we're approaching. Tents are set up outside of them, a dozen sunbleached squares closed tightly against the sun. A group of people converses before one with their eyes on the city. The patched state of their clothing and the worn tracks between structures make my chest squeeze when I realize what we're coming across.

Forsaken.

Wild rabbit skins patch holes in roofs; mud reinforces edges where tents are fraying against their frames. River reeds bind rough tables of driftwood topped with chipped, sunbleached bowls. There's no shade, and no well—they'll have to make the long trek to the river for water. Still, I'm hoping to spot one of the Mestrah's food barrels within the slit of tent doors, until I remember he doesn't provide for them. They're expected to leave Orkena when they're old enough. A journey symbolic of what awaits them in the afterlife, where they're destined to forever wander the sands between the mortal realm and Paradise, since tradition forbids them to be buried with the amulets that permit the rest of us to cross over.

Of course, considering how dangerous my escorted journey has been, it only makes more sense to me why even these conditions are preferable to braving the desert.

A girl in a too-large tunic, her ivory skin blotched from the heat, turns as we draw near. She can't be much older than sixteen. She tugs the elbow of the man next to her, who shakes his head, but whatever he's declining, she sets her jaw and starts toward us.

"Tanda," he calls. "Tanda, don't!"

The girl ignores him, striding for us like a soldier. The wind blows her hood back. Her long hair trails behind her, white-blonde and thin, and Kasta's hand slides to the hilt of his sword, and my heart lurches into my throat.

She draws closer, within striking distance.

"Please," she says, her eyes as gray as the dark circles beneath them. "They won't let us work during the race. We were barely scraping by as it was, and now we're out of food, and they're saying we can't work again until next week. Please, can you spare anything? Rice? A bit of gold?"

My throat clenches in pity. Even if the priests would tell us the Forsaken deserve this fate, Fara would say it's not for us to judge, and he wouldn't hesitate to help. I glance at the new leather saddlebags, useless as they are since Kasta didn't pack food, but he *must* have gold. I wish I could slip her some coins.

Kasta keeps his gaze ahead, of course. Royalty is not even supposed to acknowledge Forsaken, as unfavored by the gods as they are.

The girl clearly doesn't recognize him. Her gaze shifts to me. "A soldier shoved my mother this morning for trying to return to work. The fall cut her ankle, badly. I can't even buy a scrap to cover it." Her voice cracks, and she moves closer. "You have to help us. We have elderly, too … a week without food could kill them."

I brace myself at her nearness, but whatever threat Kasta feared, his hand moves away from the sword, and relief floods me that ignoring her is all he'll do. I force myself to look forward, heat prickling my eyes. I wish I could throw her the saddlebag. I wish

I wasn't more worried about what would happen to my chances for escape if I did.

The girl stops. We've gone past the last tent, and she knows we're not going to help her.

"Go on then," she growls. "Pretend you can't see us, like everyone else. And when you lie down tonight on your padded beds, after you've gorged yourselves on cake and thrown your leftovers to your dogs, you can thank the gods they gave you enough power to hide your cowardice."

Kasta stops the horse.

A sick feeling hits my gut. She'll pay for saying that. He'll have her whipped, or order her to pack up and leave, and then her mother will certainly suffer, if she can even survive the journey to the next town. But just as I'm bracing for all the terrible ways this will end, Kasta moves his hand to the saddlebag.

I hold my breath as his fingers hover over the latch. He can't be getting something for her, so what is he doing? Is there some worse horror he carries that would scare her more than a sword? But I can't think of what it would be, and when I look over my shoulder, I'm stunned by the expression on his face. It's pinched and uncertain, and goes smooth as soon as he catches my eye, but it's far from anger.

The moment passes. Kasta's fingers drop, and without a word—without a single reprimand—we ride on.

But Kasta does not relax until the tents are far behind us.

XXI

I can make no sense of what just happened.

It was such a small thing. A hesitation; a crack in Kasta's stone. If I hadn't been riding with him, I would have thought he'd almost had the girl punished. But the more I think about it, the more certain I am that what he intended to do wouldn't have harmed her. Kasta has never held back on the opportunity to doom someone who's wronged him.

I think . . . he almost *helped* her.

I remember Jet saying something changed with Kasta; something Jet had yet to understand. I had assumed it was the destruction of his laboratory, but what if it was something worse? Something to do with the Forsaken, for I'm certain now that the tension I felt was in anticipation of crossing them. He chose the route in; he knew we'd pass the tents. As though fearing something he might see.

Or perhaps, fearing to see some*one*.

"Kasta," I say as he pulls the stallion to a stop. "Did you lose someone who was Forsaken?"

"Get down," he growls, gripping my arm.

We'll revisit that later, then. I slide off the saddle, unsettled, and force the heartbreaking scene from my mind. We're on the edge of the valley of storage huts, dozens of little cake-shaped structures made of mud and topped in straw. The city rises behind them in a wall of white sand and brightly dyed canopies. People are just visible through the gaps in the houses, hoods up against the heat, their laughter ringing above the lively music.

"You're going without me?" I ask when Kasta doesn't dismount.

"Take her inside." He looks to the Shifter, still in jackal form. "We'll be back."

He turns the black stallion and sets off with Christos, who gives me a meaningful look that I can't place. Maybe it's simply a "thanks" for not using him, even if my stomach is now snarling in regret. Or maybe he's suggesting I take advantage of this time without Kasta. We *are* in a big city now, with lots of people.

And lots of travelers whose mounts have been all over Orkena. If I can convince one to take me home . . .

The Shifter growls as if she knows exactly what I'm thinking. She points her nose toward the nearest hut, and just as I'm pondering whether she could stop me if I ran, her fur begins to melt. Right off her skull.

I don't wait for her to finish transforming. I dart for the nearest huts, heart hammering as I decide how far I'll go and which I'll dive into, when a tattooed hand jerks me around and I look into a poisonous glare that makes it clear I will not be reaching the crowds. I will not be going anywhere without her permission ever again.

I force a smile. "It was just a thought."

In answer, she tugs me around the nearest hut and across its dark threshold. As my eyes adjust, I realize with a sickening pang that it's lined with wheat.

Bags and bags of it, enough in this single space to feed a small village, while the Forsaken starve outside.

"Gods," I say. "The city can't share even one of these with them?"

The Shifter grunts and releases me. *This girl and her questions.*

I freeze with my fingers around a spear of dropped wheat. That was a thought. Not something the Shifter spoke aloud, but a different voice in my head that pushed over my own. Did I imagine her answer? I could hear her thinking when she was in animal form, of course, but I shouldn't be able to hear human thoughts . . .

Except, she isn't human.

I swallow and turn around. "How long is he going to be gone?"

The Shifter lounges against the far wall, beside the open doorway. *Not long enough. Not that it matters, anyway. You're the last person in the world who'd be able to outrun me.*

"Hey. I'm not asking so I can escape. I'm just curious."

The Shifter's attention snaps to me. Her eyes narrow as they scan my body.

It's like she knows what I'm thinking. She's better at reading others than I expected.

"I know exactly what you're thinking," I say, feeling overly pleased with myself as her eyes widen. "So you may as well speak to me outright."

You can hear me? she thinks, her arms unfolding.

"Every word."

She straightens suddenly, a feral, jerky motion that makes my heart race.

Gods, she thinks. *All this time I could have . . .* Her eyes flash back to me and she snickers. *A Whisperer. Of course. Why didn't I ever think of that?*

"Think of what?" Her joy is starting to alarm me. If someone could read my thoughts, I'm not sure I'd be thrilled about it.

You can hear me, she thinks, definitively this time. *I have not spoken with anyone in* . . . She thinks a moment, brow creasing. *Four years.*

"Four *years*? Can't Shifters—um, is that part of the curse?"

It occurs to me that might be an insensitive question, but then I remember her dragging our gelding down and biting into Jet's hip, so I feel it's more than an even trade.

The girl's eyes glint with a terrible light. She clasps her metal mask and pulls it free, and I expect it to be like one of those travelers' tales where she's scarred beyond recognition or has knives for teeth, but she's so shockingly normal I actually feel a bit disappointed. She *is* pretty, but her cheeks also look hollow, as if she hasn't been eating well.

But her face isn't what she's showing me. She opens her mouth and sunlight glints off her teeth . . . off something dark at the back of her throat. I don't understand what she wants from me until I realize it's a stump.

Her tongue is missing.

I close my eyes and exhale.

It's not part of the curse, no, she thinks, replacing her mask. *Shifters can talk. We're actually very good at it. We can mimic anyone's voice we wish, simply by having heard the other person speak.* She sighs. *Which is why, when the Mestrah discovered what I'd done, it was the first thing his commander took from me.*

I shudder, remembering how Shifters are assimilated into the army—and suddenly I know what the runes circling Kasta's neck are. If caught, Shifters are sentenced for life to use their terrifying abilities to serve the Mestrah. The exception being that something has to be created to keep her power under control, as well as protect whichever general has her in their command. Maia's been bound to that rune collar for *four years*. By law—and for his own safety—Kasta would have to wear it for the race. I'm suddenly feeling lucky such collars are otherwise highly illegal. I have no doubt Kasta—well, probably Sakira, too—would have ordered one for me if they could.

"That's awful," I say.

Awful? She scoffs. *Aren't you going to say I deserved it?*

"Did you?"

She chews her cheek, gaze shifting as a hot wind slides into the doorway. *Not back then.*

"How did it happen?"

I remember Kasta speaking of who she was before, of how she'd been destined for great things. In my mind I'm conjuring all sorts of horrible explanations for how their friendship could have ended this way. He said she'd betrayed him, but what could have been bad enough to sentence her to *this*?

Her thoughts go suddenly flat, a subtle shift in silence like moving from a grand room to a closet.

I don't remember.

I have a strong feeling she's lying, but I can sympathize with not wanting to recount painful memories, so I let it go.

So what did you do? she asks.

"Me?"

I can feel the touch of the priests on things. Their magic makes me ill. She points a tattooed finger at my scar. *I don't feel sick around you at all.*

That's the kind of statement I feel I should thank her for, but I just lift my arm and rub the mark with my thumb. "I insulted the soup."

She grunts. *He's getting touchy.*

"I also accidentally talked to Jet, and now Kasta thinks we're conspiring against him."

You and the rest of the kingdom.

"There's got to be a way to get through to him," I say, pulling my cooling cloak back over my wrist. "He started to listen to me, at the palace. I don't think this is who he wants to be. If I can just make him see—"

The Shifter laughs; a hollow, bitter sound.

Let me save you some time, she says, leaning back against the wall. *Four years ago, I thought the same way you did. That if I was kind enough, supportive enough, I could pull the light from his darkness. Because it's there, maddeningly so. But believe me when I say it's a false light. You can't kindle it, because it's not really there. And even if you make an unspeakable sacrifice—*

Her fists clench over her knees, and she exhales. Her gaze shifts to the far wall.

The only person you should be worrying about saving right now is yourself.

The feeling of loss settles over the room like a weight. It's getting stranger and stranger to think of her as a monster. On one hand, the priests say Shifters are a temptation created by Apos, the god of deceit: a way to test if we'll defy the life we've been given when incredible power is only a murder away. Even if one finds *us*, we're expected to prove our purity by subduing it without killing it. On the other hand, she's not nearly as evil as I expected. I suppose the stigmas surrounding Shifters come because the kind of people who kill for power are already ruthless and wicked, but she's just a person. A person who refused—as I am—to accept death on someone else's terms.

I know Kasta already introduced us, the Shifter thinks. *But it's been too long since I could do it on my own. I am Maia.*

"Zahru," I say.

Footsteps scuffle near. The Shifter—Maia, I really should be calling her—tenses, but they march behind our hut without incident. When she relaxes, I settle onto a small stack of bags, rolling the spear of wheat in my hands.

"I don't suppose you can just let me go?"

Her brow pinches, and though I can't see the memories she's referencing, I feel her thoughts intensify. She drums her fingers on her knee. *Maybe. I'm bound to his will as long as he's wearing the rune necklace, and I can't go near it. But if you take it . . .*

"How?" My blood jumps that she might actually help me. "He'll know what I'm doing as soon as I look at it. And he's literally not planning on sleeping until the caves."

You might have to get creative. She raises a shoulder. *It should be easy enough. You're good with words.*

"But that's what I'm already doing. I think he's starting to yield, but asking for those runes . . . that's a completely different level of trust."

You don't need to get close emotionally, *Zahru.* I can't see it, but I swear I feel her smirking beneath her mask. *The runes are* around his neck.

It takes me a pause to realize what she means.

"You want me to *seduce* him?" I say this much too loudly in a hut Kasta will soon be returning to. But the thought of being that close to him again, and especially of lying to him when so many other people have lied . . . sounds like the makings of a very dangerous game.

He's conflicted about you. I can tell. He wants to believe you, and it's been a long time since he's let anyone close. Use it to your advantage.

"I—" I exhale, wincing. "I don't know. I'll get the necklace, but let me try talking to him again. If I'm still getting nowhere, I'll consider your way."

It might be your only chance. If you don't make your move soon—

Her thoughts stop, and she jerks away from the wall so suddenly that I crush the piece of wheat. Her eyes cut to me and she clenches her jaw, stooping to fit beneath the roof.

We have to go, she thinks. *He's calling me.*

She grips my arm and hauls me to my feet, and we stride into the blinding heat. My eyes don't adjust until we've curved around several huts, each as full as the first. All this food just sitting here, waiting for when the city might need it.

"*Sabil*," I curse as we pass a hut overflowing with corn. "Do they not know how badly off the Forsaken are?"

Of course they do, Maia thinks. *Orkena harbors little care for those not "blessed" by the gods.*

"This is cruel. Someone has to do something about this." I make space for a worker carrying another bag of corn, but Maia nearly drives me back into him. "Can we slow down? I can't walk this fast."

Then jog, Maia thinks, her grip tightening. *I have no choice.*

"Is something wrong?"

In response, Maia's gait quickens, and now I do have to jog to keep up.

"Maia, what is it?"

The mention of her name must stun her, for she looks down at me before pressing on.

He's in danger.

I'm ashamed to say part of me feels hopeful at this, because if someone else takes Kasta down then I won't have to do anything at all. Or he might be injured enough that I can break the necklace while he's being healed. They're terrible thoughts. I'm a terrible person, and I'll never be able to look Fara in the face again. Fara prides himself, and me, on the good we do in the world, the healing we bring. If I've become just as heartless as the person I'm trying to get through to, I may as well not go home.

But I can't help it. I want us to be too late.

I make a deal with myself that I won't hinder our progress on purpose, but neither am I going to rush to his aid. Maia drags me past the last of the huts, over a crowded bridge, and into market streets, where the buildings are taller and gleaming and filled with smiling people who've turned their backs on the Forsaken. A baker tosses a loaf of bread he dropped to a pair of fat hounds. I think of what the girl said to us, and my stomach twists.

Left, right, the Shifter thinks. *The Stone Chalice. Second floor . . .*

We weave deeper into the city, dodging hagglers and merchants, musicians and drunks. In moments I've gathered enough snippets of conversation to guess why Kasta chose now to make his move:

Sakira is throwing a party on a Dreamwalker's yacht, and everyone who goes drinks for free. The same information, no doubt, that Maia conveyed to Kasta in the cave. People are busy either making their way there or talking about when they'll go, and even with Maia's height and unusual armor, no one pays us much heed. One man even compliments her "costume" as we pass, then drunkenly explains to his friend he wants to go looking just like that.

We're in the heart of the city when Maia yanks me through a darkened doorway. A gleaming juniper counter marks a bar, and tenants squint at us from mudbrick benches built directly into the tavern's walls. Maia only has to look at the bartender for him to point frantically upstairs.

"I told no one he was here," he says, backing against the washbasins. "They must have followed him. I thought they were guards . . ."

Something solid hits the floor above. We cross the room and stride up tiled stairs to a large sitting area where tables cluster to one side and a rolled piece of parchment marks the area as closed. At the far wall, three masked men have Kasta cornered, two blades raised against his one. The third holds a ball of light that crackles and sparks like a twisting piece of lightning.

Kasta's gaze shifts over their shoulders, and one of the swordsmen turns. And freezes.

"Ivan," he mutters, nudging his companion.

"What?" Ivan snaps, his focus on the prince.

"We have a problem."

"The leopard," Kasta says, returning his gaze to his assailants.

"Foolish prince," muses the man with the lightning. "We were just going to hold you quietly awhile; give your sister a few days' head start. Now it's looking much easier to just kill you."

"Is that the sacrifice?" says Ivan, with a grin that makes my stomach churn. "What do you think Sakira's reward would be for *her*?"

Sakira's fanatics. Exactly as Kasta feared.

Maia reaches around her belt and unlatches a shimmering, spotted pelt.

"I don't know," chokes the first man who turned. "I'm too worried about the *Shifter*."

"Then kill the prince quickly, and we can handle her together." Ivan turns back to Kasta, leering. "Should have cooperated, *aera*."

He strikes. Kasta blocks and slices wide toward the other swordsman, who jumps back with a curse. The man with the lightning slings it at Kasta's chest, and the prince jerks his wrist to block it, the protective bracelet glowing white-hot as the bolt slams into the wall instead. Beside me, Maia is changing. The ears of the pelt meld into her crown, spots stretching down her back, fur soon covering every place that once was armor. Her tail twitches around her haunches and she snarls, fangs dripping with saliva.

The Stormshrike gathers another electric ball from the air. Maia races toward him and he heaves it at her, but it's a careless throw and she dodges, and in an instant she's on top of him. His scream cuts short as she rips into his throat. I gag and turn back to Kasta, who manages to evade a blow from one man only to be cut across the arm by Ivan. Kasta growls and swings wildly; the second man raises his sword for a killing blow, and Maia leaps on him from behind.

One on one, Ivan and Kasta are well matched. But the cut is to Kasta's dominant arm. He blocks blow after blow but isn't quick enough to attack; he nearly loses his head when Ivan comes at him two-handed, metal singing as a thin line slices from the top of Kasta's throat to his chest. The rune necklace falls with a *clack*. Kasta casts a panicked look at it and has to spin away to avoid another slice, but no matter how he tries to force his way back to it, Ivan blocks him at every turn.

Maia raises her head, jaw dripping with the second man's blood.

"Maia," Kasta says.

Ivan lunges. His attacks are frenzied now, wanting to finish Kasta before the leopard can finish him. Kasta is tiring beneath them. He blocks too late and Ivan smashes an elbow across his jaw, knocking his head into the wall. Before he can recover Ivan yanks his sword from his hand and positions both blades around his neck.

"Maia!" Kasta yells.

She casts a tormented look at me, and back at Kasta. Her muscles strain with indecision. She takes a hesitant step forward—

And sits.

XXII

I'VE dropped into a nightmare. I must have, for I can't be here, watching this happen, with two men dead and another—a boy who wants to kill me, a boy whose greatest fear is that he has no one left to trust—about to die. About to die because a girl who used to believe in him, who he clearly desperately believes still holds a thread of that loyalty, has given up. And is hoping, as I was not too long ago, that fate will take its course.

I thought that's what I wanted, too.

And gods, it would make things simpler. With Kasta gone, this could all be over—not *likely* over, as I've been hoping all along, but truly, definitively over. I could see Fara again. I could jump into Hen's arms. I would never, ever travel again in my life—

And I would always think back to this moment, when I stood here, unmoving, as a prince I lectured about mercy is cut down with his own sword.

"Oh, Apos," I swear, glancing around for a weapon. Ivan has noticed the Shifter's hesitation. He's jeering now, the blades grinding as he gloats.

"And when it comes down to it, not even a monster will defend you." Ivan chuckles. "What a favor I'm doing the world."

I sprint forward. Maia snarls when she realizes what I'm doing, but she's too far to stop me, and just as Ivan tenses to pull the blades, I grab a broken stool and smash it across his head.

Ivan stumbles sideways, dazed. Kasta grabs hold of the man's face and I gasp when the screaming starts, the sound like its own knife in my head, as Kasta pulls every remaining year of Ivan's life away and adds them to his own. I force myself to keep moving as the shrieks crescendo. The broken necklace is only a few paces away and I lunge for it, but Ivan's screams die as his body thunks to the floor, and just as my fingers snag the first stone of the necklace, Kasta wrenches my arm up and jerks it away.

He holds the necklace in a trembling fist, his glare shifting to Maia.

The leopard snarls and darts for the stairs.

Kasta doesn't stop her. He only looks at me with those same burning, bottomless eyes, like I was the one who betrayed him.

Now there is most certainly no talking.

Kasta grips my wrist as we walk the streets, low enough on my arm that the casual passerby would think we were holding hands. His white cooling cloak hoods his head and billows against his arm. Its steam makes the city look like a mirage. I have my hood raised as well, but I'm sure I'll still die of heat. Or maybe I'm just hoping I'll die of heat before something else happens to me. The fear burning my veins makes the day cold in comparison.

His grip on me tightens and relaxes, as if he can't decide what I deserve.

I can only think of his hands on Ivan's face.

"A necklace for you, lady?" calls a merchant. "The garnet holds a message from your loved one! Sir, you need only to whisper to it, and the stone will remember. Sir? Sir!"

If he chases us, I will start crying. I've seen enough violence in the past few days to last my lifetime. But Kasta pulls me into an alley, and the merchant finds another couple to prey on.

The storage huts slide back into sight. We follow a group of nobles across the bridge, close enough that we look like part of their group, then break off between buildings on the other side. Instead of weaving through the center as I did with Maia, Kasta keeps to the edge, looking over his shoulder every few steps.

We round a small group of huts—

And stop.

"No," Kasta growls. His grip tightens as he searches the perimeter, eyes locking on clusters of palm trees. Then he whirls, pulling me along, and storms back toward the city.

"Can't you just call Maia back?" I say, so quietly I'm certain he won't hear me. I'm not actually sure I want him to hear me.

"It's the horses," he says, anger curling his words. "He took them."

" 'He'?"

"Christos." He spits the name like a curse. We're back on the bridge again, exposed this time, but Kasta no longer seems to care about being discreet. "We passed those men on our way to the tavern. They were speaking of their preference for my sister . . . of how they'd kill for her." His jaw clenches. "I was distracted trying to find the scroll we mark to check in. By the time I found it, Christos had slipped away. I thought he'd only deserted me." He pulls left to avoid a wagon clinking with potions. "Then those men came up the stairs."

We slip back into the streets. I want to say this seems dangerous when the Healer could still be here recruiting the aid of more such men, but I suppose the absence of the horses means he's long gone.

"You warned me," Kasta says, a bitter smile pulling his lip. "I didn't listen."

I swallow. I fear I already know the answer to this question since I'm still at his side, but I ask it anyway. "But it hasn't changed your plans?"

He doesn't answer. A single stone of the rune necklace sways from a pouch near his hip, and I contemplate the chances of being able to summon Maia before he could get it back when he yanks me into an alley and behind an abandoned cart. He turns and grabs both my wrists, his gaze burning with my reflection.

"Why did you save me?" he asks.

He's cutting off the blood flow to my hands. I grit my teeth, and I don't know if it's my frustration or the sudden conviction that nothing I do will make a difference, but I meet the fire of his gaze with ice of my own. He's no longer as perfect as he looked this morning. Dirt streaks his face on one side, his jaw purpling where Ivan hit him.

"Let me go and I'll tell you," I say.

A grunt. "Of course." A sneer snakes onto his mouth, but his shoulders fall. "You thought if you saved me, I'd help you escape."

"I'm talking about my hands," I snap.

A skeptical line appears between Kasta's brows, and he looks down, at the place he grips my wrists.

"You'll run," he says.

"You'd catch me."

"You'll call for help."

I falter, not because that had been on my mind, but because it hadn't even occurred to me that was something I could do. He's right, though. I'd be bound to attract the aid of at least one of Sakira's supporters . . . but I think of the bounty hunters, and the men willing to kill for Sakira, and shake my head.

"They'd save me only to deliver me to your sister," I say. "I'd be no better off."

A frustrated growl. "Then it truly is that you saved me to save yourself."

"Oh, no," I say, my laugh bitter. "If that's what I wanted, I'd have let you die. Maia would have gotten me out of here before anyone else knew what happened, and this would be *over*. I'd be on my way home, back to people I dearly miss, instead of standing here trying to convince the world's most paranoid prince that maybe one person in his life is simply trying to do the right thing! Gods, why *did* I save you?"

I pull back, prepared for him to wrench me around for speaking in such a way, but he lets go so easily I have to use the cart to keep my balance. *Run!* screams every muscle in my body. But I've been good at ignoring my survival instincts thus far, so there's really no reason to give in now. In any case, I don't want to risk being back in Sakira's hands. At least Kasta will be slowed now without a Healer or horses, and that means much better odds of reconnecting with Jet.

And *Rie*, there has to be a part of him that was affected by what I did. Fara says good deeds are like sparks; when one lands, it catches fire to everything around it. I refuse to believe Kasta is so far gone he can't even feel its heat.

He looks at his empty hands and at me, as if someone else made him let go.

"I saved you," I say, "because even after all you've done, you didn't deserve to die like that."

He closes his fingers. His voice is quiet when he says, " 'Like that'?"

"Outnumbered. Unarmed. Alone." I press my thumb into my palms, rubbing feeling back into them. "Only tyrants deserve such a death."

A weak smile. "You said I was a tyrant."

"I said you're fast becoming one." I drop my hands and my gaze, turning to the bright street and its laughing people, at how impossibly unaffected they are by all of this. "But a person who mourns for children isn't a tyrant. He's incredibly frustrating, and it would be nice if he'd stop treating everyone like enemies, but he's not completely gone."

Kasta watches the distance between me and the street, and his hands lower, slowly. Merchants call to customers, and families laugh as they pass by. A pair of little girls races past us, nearly knocking into him, but his eyes stay on me.

Again he looks like he wants to say something but rethinks it at the last moment.

A shadow stretches behind me. Footsteps crunch the sand, and Maia steps into the alley, human again, her yellow eyes feral and searing. She clutches a large red pelt in one hand and a saddle in the other. The runes on her armor glow white-hot. She's fighting Kasta's summons with every grain of magic she has, but she cannot win.

Because of me.

The heat of the prince wafts against my shoulder, his voice gravel against my ear. "I'm not so sure."

Maia raises the horse pelt she's carrying and lifts its ears and nose to cover her own. Blood-red fur spills down her arms and legs, her teeth gritting as her bones break and thicken, until I have to close my eyes to block out the twisted sight of her. Kasta's hand rests on my shoulder.

But this time, his grip doesn't tighten.

XXIII

WE race from the city with eerie grace.

Maia's gait is too fluid, as if she were part snake and not entirely horse. Her chestnut coat flashes like copper in the sun. Kasta bends around me like a thorn bush, his hood low, his muscles tense. Those unfortunate enough not to move from our path are forced out of it by powerful shoulders and snapping teeth.

Maia's anger simmers beneath us like a current.

As if the gods can feel it, a storm builds on the horizon. It's far off now—little more than a smudge of darkness where the sand meets the sky—but they are the kind of clouds Fara would watch with nervous clucking, as if reasoning with them in another language. Sometimes the clouds would listen and stay north. Sometimes they grew, and before the wind started, Fara and I would rush to close the barn and cover it in protection spells, the ones that cost two months' work to afford. It wasn't rain we feared. The stable was built on a slope to withstand the storms that came each year, and they came with different clouds that Fara beckoned closer. These clouds didn't bring water.

"Please tell me we have a tent now," I say as Maia bolts past the last of the shops.

"We have one," Kasta says.

Or Maia stole one, more likely. "And spells?"

"A few potions."

I turn. "We're going into the desert without spells?"

He ignores me, his gaze on the sand. "I was a little pressed for time. So no, we don't have spells."

"We have to stop." I sit up, as if Maia could possibly listen to me over him. "We have to stay in the city tonight."

"No."

"Do you see those clouds? That's not rain. That's *sand*. If we stay out in it—"

"I know what a sandstorm is."

"Do you, though? Because I'm thinking your father may have a point when he says you don't take advisement."

His jaw tightens. "If we stay in the city, I could be dead by morning. What would you have me do?"

I'm so caught off guard by the presence of a question, I don't know how to answer. "I . . . well . . ."

"Our ancestors used tents before they had spells. Ours should be enough. The storms never last long."

"And if it's one Alette prayed for?"

A pause. "It would do Sakira no good to kill you. The gods would only give them a storm strong enough to slow us."

"So to be clear, if our tent rips to shreds, we have no backup plan."

I'm getting tired of important questions like this being met with silence.

"Of course," I say, "if you've changed your mind and we aren't going in the direction of the caves, we could avoid the storm entirely, because Alette would only pray to block your path to the next checkpoint."

He opens his mouth to answer—and closes it.

Thinking.

"True," he says.

"'True,' I'm right? Or 'true,' we're not headed for the caves anymore?"

"The Crossing isn't over because of this, Zahru."

"But you can change how it ends. Take me to safety, then win your race and tell the Mestrah you chose mercy."

More silence.

"Your way hasn't been working," I say, and finally his eyes shift to me. "Try mine."

He still doesn't answer, but he touches a hand to Maia's neck.

Maia swings her head and changes course.

We run until Numet pulls her lantern below the horizon and the stars stretch above us. We stay far from the roads. Distant campfires and caravan lights flicker around us, well out of shouting distance. It's clear Kasta won't risk meeting any more of Sakira's supporters. I only hope he doesn't take us so far out that I lose track of the roads entirely.

Maia doesn't once falter in stride. As a Shifter, her cursed magic doesn't tire her body as it's supposed to, nor will her abilities fade the more she uses them. Her only limitation will be the stamina she has for running. In this form, with more than twice the lung and heart capacity she's used to, she'll be able to sprint for hours. Or maybe she no longer cares if she runs herself to death. I've been listening for her thoughts beneath the sound of hoof and wind, desperate for a hint of forgiveness or understanding. But she knows I can hear her, and each time her thoughts drift to Kasta or the city, she rearranges them to focus on the desert. I've heard little more from her than *Never free, too late, traitor. Senseless girl. Now what?*

I close my eyes against the accusations, wishing I could send her my thoughts as easily as I can hear hers. I can't change what happened in the tavern, but I still have every intention of getting that rune necklace. We'll have to stop now that the Healer's gone. I can take it while Kasta's distracted or sleeping. Or I'll get him to break it himself. If saving his life wasn't enough to get through to him, nothing will be.

I will fix this.

Hold on, Maia.

When my legs ache from balancing and my stomach groans a reminder of its emptiness, I decide I've waited long enough. Kasta has to agree we've gone as far as we can. I sit up against him, tensing.

"We should stop for the night."

I expect a protest, and have already worked out my counterargument, when he simply sits back. Maia slows and then stops, her great sides heaving as she turns her head away. Kasta slips off behind me. I start to move as well, but he turns like he might offer to help, and I freeze, hardly daring to breathe, until I remember it's poor Maia I'm on and slide off without waiting.

We raise the tent in silence. Again Kasta surprises me by helping me do it instead of making Maia keep working. He slings the jackal skin at her instead, and as soon as she's changed she curls into a ball to sleep. Kasta's beside me as we stake the tent, driving the sticks deep into the sand. But his mind is far away. He hardly looks at me and never at Maia. The first time he meets my gaze is when he pulls open the tent flap and gestures inside.

I crawl onto the horse pelt—it's an awful thing to use as bedding, but it's better than the sand—my body begging for just an hour's rest, a moment's quiet. But I owe Maia more than that. I owe myself more.

I'm not sleeping until I have that necklace.

I sigh as I move to the back of the small tent, fretting over how I'll do it. A light potion hangs from the poles supporting the ceiling, the liquid illuminating the space like a tiny star, and I sit toward the head of the horse and unclasp my cloak, balling it as if for a pillow. Melia's tunic, with its mercifully reinforced linen, has held up for the most part. I can't say as much for the rest of me. My arms are stained orange from sand and horse sweat, and I doubt I smell much better. I grunt to think what would happen if I attempted this Maia's way. I'm lucky Kasta can look at me without grimacing, let alone as anything desirable.

Actually, I wish he *would* grimace, if only to reassure me he's still capable of emotion. His expression hasn't changed in hours. He sits opposite, just past my feet, his eyes far away as he pulls his cloak over his head. A fine stubble of hair blackens his jaw, and in the dim light he looks so exhausted I feel I know what he'll look like as an old man. Sand dusts his olive skin, and his trader's tunic is as filthy as mine.

He doesn't lie down. He watches me in a way that makes me increasingly aware of how alone we are, and I scrub some of the sand from my arm.

"We should bring Maia in," I say.

"No."

He folds his cooling cloak and sets it to the side, as carefully as he would a bowl of glass.

"The storm—" I say.

"Stayed to the south. It will miss us." He looks at his hands, at the blood dried across his chest and crusted on his bicep. The cut on his arm isn't healing well. It bled while we rode, and even now the red beneath the cut is bright. He pulls the tunic off, a prince once more with his bare chest and *tergus*, and pulls a small bottle from his belt that turns the air sour when he opens it. He soaks a clean section of the tunic and presses it to his arm with a wince.

I consider helping him, but the same eerie, deliberate calm surrounds him that did after we spoke with the Mestrah, and it feels wiser to give him space.

"You remind me of Maia," he says, nodding outside. "Before."

Or maybe it's not the same. His tone is quiet. Sad.

Broken.

"She wasn't as thoughtful as you. But she followed the rules. Even if the outcome wasn't what she wanted, she believed in something. I could always count on that. I underestimated . . ." He exhales. "I underestimated how much it's changed her."

It, as in her being condemned to a life as a demon. For a moment I can only stare, wondering how on earth he could think that *wouldn't* change her.

"You had to suspect she might never forgive you," I say. "The fate you left her to is hardly better."

He looks over. "The fate *I* left her to?"

"Yes, as you've been hinting at this whole time? And threatening me with? Have you lost that much blood?"

The prince shakes his head. "I didn't do anything to her."

"Then what, she woke up one day feeling suspiciously damned, and because she can't talk, you go around telling people you're the reason to scare them?"

"She had a choice." His eyes flash with the reflection of the potion, and he returns his attention to the wound. "She made the wrong one."

"There wasn't a right one. She either had to let a monster kill her, or kill it to save her own life."

"That isn't what happened." His fingers tighten. "She was supposed to stay home."

He doesn't elaborate, and I try to work out what that means. She wasn't supposed to be in harm's way . . . but he *was*? "Please don't tell me hunting a Shifter is some kind of royal rite."

He shakes his head. "No. Hunting one is against the law for royalty, too." He swallows, his gaze never leaving the cloth. "Which is why she was the only person I told about it."

A chill snakes through my veins as I realize what he means. This was no grave accident—he went *looking* for one. What had happened that would make him go after a *Shifter*? I think immediately of his destroyed laboratory; of the formulas he lost. Was he trying to prove his father wrong? Did he think he could catch one and unlock some secret in its magic?

"But . . . I don't understand," I say. "You needed it alive, and she decided she wanted its power?"

"No."

"Then—" I let out a frustrated growl. "You're not making sense. Obviously things went wrong, or she wouldn't have killed it. What happened that night?"

A muscle twitches in Kasta's jaw. His fingers flex around the cloth and the shadows shift in his face, warring against the light. "That's not a story I share with anyone."

"Are you *kidding* me?" I can't stop myself. Anger bursts through me, and I'm normally not a violent person, but I almost shove him. "After everything I've told you, after I *saved your life*, you still don't trust me? Gods, what's it going to take? Do I need to throw myself between you and the sword next time? Or maybe I need to be more patient. Maybe I just need to wait for the moment when you *stick a knife through my chest*."

He blinks, and as aggravated as I am, the shock on his face is very satisfying.

"Don't you ever get tired of being miserable? You can't go on like this, Kasta. Not as a king, not as a person. Have you really trusted no one since that night?"

He only looks at me, his face tormented, and I sigh and rub my palms into my eyes. I don't know why I thought getting through to him might work. Maia even told me I'd be foolish to try, and now it's looking like I'm going to have to wait for him to sleep, which I hate almost as much as Maia's plan to seduce him, because I feel *so close* to breaking through. I wanted this to end better, but I can't wait weeks for him to change his mind.

The tonic dips again; he lifts a new corner of the tunic to the wound.

"What age did you come into your magic?" he asks quietly.

I fluff my cloakpillow to lie on it. "What does that have to do with anything?"

"Do you want the story or not?" he snaps.

I look over, hardly believing my ears. "I was six."

"The same for Jet. Sakira was five." His voice is softer now, but something curls its edges, like the ripples of a crocodile under the water. "They used to practice together, when they got older. Sakira would transform fruit into birds, and Jet would give them voices. I could see them from my windows. Sakira would make them attack me if she caught me watching." I expect him to tense at this, but he goes on as if there's nothing strange about that at all. "As we got older, and my abilities still hadn't shown, they started stealing my food and ordering me around like a servant. They were preparing me, they said, for my future in the streets."

He folds the soiled cloth, streaking his hands in new blood. Things are clicking into place one by one, and a new sadness stirs in my chest.

"At that time, I still believed my father loved me. I sought his reassurance that he'd never cast me out like that. Do you know what he said?"

He's still speaking as though none of this affects him. I wonder how many times he's thought about this; how many times someone has to feel the pain of something before they feel nothing at all.

"That such a thing would be unbearable, and that he'd change the law?" I whisper.

Kasta grunts. "He told me I'd come into my magic, or I wouldn't.

300

That the gods would show their favor"—he swallows—"or he'd send me to the orphanages with all the other eleventh years who failed to show."

Everything he refuses to feel is seeking me instead, needling my heart like a hundred scorpions. I know the old families—the nobles—place an unreasonable amount of importance on magic, but their blood is so saturated with it that to have a child without magic is as rare as having a child born blind. I never thought about what happened to those children. I suppose I assumed, naïvely, that all of them simply grew up and found new lives outside of Orkena.

"Gods, please tell me you didn't," I say. "You went after the Shifter for its *power*? Knowing what would happen to you?"

He shrugs. "Nothing would, if no one found out. I would never have used the Shifter's obvious abilities. I only needed its strength, its endurance, and the priests would have thought I was a Dominator."

"But the curse—"

"The gods had already abandoned me." His eyes flash, shifting to mine. "You've seen the Forsaken. That would have been my life, now and for an eternity in the afterlife. Do you really believe I had anything to lose?"

My heart jerks in sudden comprehension. Maia's "sentence"; her betrayal.

I close my eyes. "Maia tried to stop you."

"Yes."

"She knew the only way to do so would be to kill it herself."

To take the curse before he could, because as a priest, she feared

Kasta's desperation would ruin so much more than his mortal life. But for Kasta, she took away what he thought was his last chance at having magic. She'd as good as sentenced him to exile.

I grimace. "You told the priests what she'd done."

"No."

I choke on my surprise. "No?"

"I wanted to." He closes his eyes, fresh blood dripping beneath the cloth. "I almost did. But in the end . . . I couldn't. Maia confessed to it herself."

"Then everything you said about being responsible—"

"I could have defended her." There's an old ache in his voice, but it doesn't reach his eyes. Another pain he no longers feels. "I could have confessed."

The silence after that is horrible. I can picture him in the throne room with Maia all those years ago, the priests holding her arms, Kasta standing at the Mestrah's side. Her future, and his, held in Kasta's mouth. But there was no happy ending. If he admitted to hunting a Shifter, she might have gone free—and he would have met his fate as Forsaken immediately.

I press my fingers into my temples. "All right, I understand now why that seemed like a betrayal, but . . . can't *you* see now that she was only trying to protect you? She stopped you from making an irreversible mistake. She thought she was saving your *soul*. How can you still fault her for that? Especially since you came into your magic soon after?"

Kasta watches me, something between torment and amusement on his face. He's quiet so long I wonder if he'll pull away again, and this is where the story will end, but after a moment he exhales, coming to a decision. He places the tunic to the side, as careful as ever, and reaches into the pouch at his waist. When he opens his hand, tiny needled bulbs clink in his palm.

"I don't know what those are," I say.

"They're scorpion stingers," he says, watching me. "Poisons."

A black feeling opens in my chest. As does the realization that Maia said she met her fate four years ago, when Kasta would have been thirteen.

"This one can make someone ill for a day." He touches a stinger colored a vivid green. "This one can render a person unconscious for hours." An amber stinger. "And this one . . ." He rolls a white bulb between two fingers, careful not to touch its tip. "Can kill a man in ten seconds."

The sting on the back of my neck. The man screaming in the tavern. The real reason he stopped for the blonde girl.

"You never came into your magic," I whisper.

And everything slides into place. His feverish need to believe a Whisperer—someone considered nearly as weak as the Forsaken—could be a powerful First. His jealousy of his Soundbending brother that went so much further than their father's attention. His fear he'd always be second to someone because of something he couldn't control.

His desperate need to prove them all wrong.

The laboratory. His research on magic. I remember Jet saying he couldn't imagine the Mestrah destroying Kasta's work, but I wonder if it wasn't him at all. If instead it was *Kasta* tearing up his own research, devastated by the realization that the subject he'd made his passion . . . would be something he'd never possess.

I hear the beaker shattering again beside Jet's head, and my heart cracks with it.

"But how is that possible?" I say. "The priests would have tested you. You'd have to demonstrate your magic to a panel."

"I warned the tester he couldn't draw my magic to sample it because I feared it would kill him. Then it was just a matter of diversion. If they're watching my target, they're not watching my hands."

"That's . . ." I can't stop a small smile. "That's brilliant."

"Brilliant?" He snickers. "Don't you mean disgusting? Unnatural? *Sacrilegious?*"

"No," I say, realizing I actually mean it. "I mean, I wish you'd chosen something that didn't hurt people, but you made up for a shortcoming with different skills. Your power is one of the most feared in Orkena, but you made it yourself." I search his eyes, a new thought breaking over me. "Can't you see? That's exactly what your father's wanted you to do all along. *That's* who you are when you let go of your bitterness. Resourceful. Ingenious."

He shakes his head. "It's not enough. For the Mestrah, it's never enough."

"Stop worrying about a man who was going to abandon you," I say, sitting forward. For the first time I feel like I understand him, like the good prince he could be is right there on the surface, the other side of a card waiting to be turned. "Look forward. Think of what you could change! A magicless king. You could redefine our entire system. Elevate the Forsaken and give everyone a chance at a good life, based on hard work rather than birth. No one would ever have to fear being cast out again." I'm getting lost in my own ideas, but I can't help grinning at the possibility. It's a sad beginning with a happy ending, as all good stories are. "You could save people from your fate."

"They'd never accept it." The shadows are taking over again. He lifts the cloth back to his arm, and the wound bleeds anew. "If they found out I was powerless—"

"You're not powerless. You made your own magic, you survived three assassins in a tavern, and if you'd start treating people again like you used to treat Maia, you'll find others who are willing to sacrifice for you, too. You just have to stop leading us into fates like soullessness and human sacrifice. Gods, here." I snatch the tunic from him and wet a new side of it with the tonic. "You're making it worse."

The eyes that watch me are a stranger's. They're lighter and wondering, filled with questions instead of hate, with hope instead of anger. "You think I could be a good king."

I work the dried blood off his skin, my fingers sure but careful, leaving the wound as an angry line. "Yes."

It looks like it needs sewing, but I don't have a needle or thread. A simple binding will have to do. I glance around the tent for anything clean I can use and spy a saddlebag just behind the prince. When I reach for it, he catches my hand. Gently, this time.

Leaving me balanced centimeters from his face, and practically in his lap.

"I need a cloth," I say, with the lurching realization that I'm getting through to him a little *too* well.

Kasta slips his thumb over my palm. "I couldn't understand why the gods would torment me with you when I'd already been through so much. But I was right the first time. You are the answer."

I swallow. "Then you've changed your mind?"

He kisses me. An impossibly soft, warm thing that sends a shock wave through my body, stealing the feeling from my fingers, the thoughts from my mind. I jerk back, as stunned that I let him kiss me as I am at the hum resonating in my veins. *It's only shock*, I tell myself, because I really was starting to believe he was too far gone. And now a sinking feeling pulls at my gut. Because whether I meant to or not, I've played right into Maia's strategy.

A stone of the rune necklace dangles from the pouch, and I steel myself. This is so not something I ever wanted to do to anyone, but I can't let another opportunity to escape pass.

I slip my arms around Kasta's neck and press my mouth to his.

The first kiss is easy to ignore. I can pretend it's nothing; a brush of my lips on someone else's, cordial and light. The second one is harder. Kasta gets bolder, his hand sliding beneath my hair, pulling me closer. And still, every movement is careful and quiet, laced with that maddening uncertainty that's so unlike him I almost wonder if this is some kind of strange dream.

Then his lips part mine, and I start to unravel.

Because he, of course, is not kissing me like it means nothing. He kisses me the way he looked at me as his First. Like I am everything, like I am *more*, and as the same heat flares in my core as it did at the palace, I start to panic that I'm not pretending anymore. His hands slide down my back; his thumbs into the grooves of my hips. Kasta, who has never once cared about my being a Whisperer. Who knows what it is to be judged on what he lacks. Who fears what the world will do to him because of it.

His arms flex, asking me closer.

I slip into his lap.

His touch is thunder and stone and wind. It sparks up my back as he presses me against him; as his mouth demands more from mine. *Closer. More.* I'm drowning in him again, at the mercy of his undertow, the desire in his kiss. I feel dizzy and drunk, the current pulling faster now, making my fingers clumsy as I try to find the necklace.

Kasta's hands drop to my knees. I gasp as they slide beneath my tunic, and when his lips move to my neck, I abandon my mission and grab his wrists. This is no longer a game. There's more here than I want to admit, and I don't know what it is yet. Maybe it's an entirely new level of exhaustion. Maybe it's the draw of how much he wants this. I don't want to entertain the third option, but if he really does feel this way for me, maybe there's still a way to end this where no one gets hurt.

"Kasta," I breathe. His arms flex beneath my fingers, but he pulls back.

"Yes?"

I almost forget the question. His eyes are startling in the light, vibrant silver in the center, river blue on the edges. Nothing like the cold, hard gaze I'm used to. This is who he is when he feels safe. When he lets go of his anger and fear, and lets himself free.

I swallow. "Are you still planning to kill me?"

His expression doesn't change. The only hint I have that he heard me are the shadows, slinking like oil back into his gaze.

"Say no," I say, my fingers trembling as I pull them from his wrists. He can't possibly say yes. After everything I've done, after he trusted me with his secret, after *this*—

"You know what I've been through to get here," he says.

"That's not an answer."

"I can't do this without you."

Revulsion builds in my chest, horrible and thick. I want to hit him. I want to scream and ask how nothing I did could make a difference; that I've given him the benefit of the doubt the entire time, that I've tried to help him—

"The magic in the knife is my last chance," he says, as if that's a better answer. "It's the only hope I have left."

"You haven't listened to anything I said!" I say. "Magic is still the only thing you want. And what, you thought I'd smile and let you stab me if we . . ." I pull at my hair. "What is *wrong* with you?"

"There might be a way to do it without you dying. There's a Speaker at the next checkpoint who knows more. They have centuries of knowledge, they're experts in the science of magic . . . maybe there's a way." He trails gentle fingers on my shoulder, coaxing me forward. "Give me some time. I don't know what this is."

"Gods, they're called *feelings*," I say. "Maia was right. There's nothing I can do. You'll never be anything but selfish and cruel and afraid—"

His gaze sharpens. "Maia?"

"I tried," I say, my voice cracking as I lift the poison I've grabbed from his pouch. My fingers shake so badly I nearly drop it. "I never wanted to hurt you. Just remember that I tried."

I stab an amber stinger into his back and squeeze the bulb. He has time to shove me away before the sleep poison works through his system, stealing the shock from his eyes, the disbelief from his hands, and he slumps back against the horse skin, as relaxed as if he's dreaming.

The boy who fears he'll never be enough. And in that, has done everything possible to ensure it's so.

I scream into my knees, angry with myself for how close I let him; at what he could be if he would just *let go*. I gather the supplies I want in a rage, half the potions and two leaves of dried fish, and the pouch of poisons from his belt. I start removing the protective bracelet, for only one of its runes is burned and used, but taking it would certainly doom him, and I curse him and leave it. I can't believe I was arrogant enough to think I could be different. That I could save him like in the stories, with faith and kindness.

That he could let go of his fear because of me.

And still, as I bite back my sobs, I stop to bandage his dratted wound and shove the bloody cloak under his head to raise it. I leave the light potion but take the horse skin and practically leap from the tent, where the cold air feels like breaking the surface of a well.

Maia raises her head, jackal grin wide.

I fling the rune necklace at her feet.

XXIV·

WHEN we're only a few kilometers away, and the glow of Kasta's tent fades among the dunes, my stomach has had enough of too little food and exhaustion and stress, and I make Maia stop so I can be sick. My anger has faded with the distance, leaving me with a horrible kind of emptiness. I'd reached him. I'd broken through a barrier he'd never let *anyone* through, and part of me questions if I even heard him correctly when I asked if he'd spare me, because the answer he gave makes no sense. What more could I have said? What more could I have possibly *done*?

You think I could be a good king.

It wasn't a question. He believed that I believed it, and even then . . .

It wasn't enough. Just as nothing has ever been enough for the Mestrah.

I guess I know who Kasta learned it from.

Maia, at least, has forgiven me. Not that she said so, but I can tell by the way she thinks, how her thoughts are no longer cloudy and muddled but light and quick. The same with her steps and the alert set of her ears, every piece of her looking forward. She's changed to the chestnut mare again—I told her she didn't need to and we could walk together, but she wanted to put distance on Kasta—and when she's not thinking about how far we should go before we rest, she's wondering how I can feel even the smallest sadness. I saved her. I saved me. I tricked one of Orkena's most merciless, untrusting powers into admitting his darkest secret and taking his own poison.

Those are good things, she says.

Because the deathly stingers in Kasta's pouch made me anxious, I kept two of the sleeping poisons for emergencies and buried the rest in the sand far behind us. The rune necklace lies in broken pieces in the saddlebag. When we reach the next city, we'll trade the individual stones for clothes and transportation. I'll go home. Maia hasn't said what she'll do, but I imagine it has to do with starting over, with having a life she actually owns.

Zahru the Silk-Lipped, Maia thinks, as her latest attempt at coming up with a suitable title for my heroism.

I groan. "Please stop before I choke myself on sand."

But you have to admit it's clever. It works for both—

"I know what it works for." I clench her mane without meaning to and make myself relax with a huff. "I'd be really happy if we never talked about it again."

I've already decided that when it comes to telling people this part of my story, I'm skipping the details. The last thing I need is for Hen to resume Maia's quest to find me the perfect hero name, or my neighbors thinking I'm some kind of lying succubus. I'll say we put up the tent, I knocked Kasta out with a stake, and I took the necklace and ran.

And ran and ran and ran.

Zahru? Maia asks, stopping. She turns to look at me, my reflection sad and dark in her yellow, starlit eye. *There's nothing else you could have done.*

My shoulders droop. "I shouldn't have talked to him. I should have just waited for him to go to sleep and taken the collar."

She watches me a moment, and I brace myself for the *I told you so*, but her gaze only softens. *For what it's worth, I was hopeful you could reach him, too. When he was with you, I thought . . . I started to recognize the friend I'd lost. I wanted you to be right about him.* She turns her attention east. *But it is done. Now we must move forward.*

I sigh and clutch her mane as she moves into a jog, but I know what she says is true. There was no other way for that to end. My alternatives were not talking to him, in which I wouldn't have known about the poisons and might have woken him trying to get Maia's collar, or believing Kasta truly would ask the Speaker about me, in which he still used the word *maybe* when it came to sparing me. I shudder at the memory of his lips on my neck; at the traitorous recognition with which my heart greeted his.

You're tensing, Maia thinks.

"Sorry," I grumble.

Hmm. Maia slows and her ears swivel back and forward, listening. *The clouds are moving.*

I squint at the horizon, at the darkness stretching into the stars. "Isn't that . . . normal?"

It would be. She swings her head, moonglow silvering her mane. *If there was any wind.*

A stone builds in my stomach as I realize it's as still as a tomb. The dark clouds aren't to our side anymore. They're in front of us, to the east. Maia has been following the scent of the nearest river, so I know we couldn't have gotten turned around.

"Alette," I say.

The storm is turning us back to them.

"Are there any outposts nearby?"

Maia breathes in and sighs. She has to be close to exhaustion no matter how excited she is to be free, and I can't ask her to outrun it, especially with my weight adding to her burden.

The pelts, she thinks. *We can huddle beneath them. They're stronger than fabric. They'll protect us just as well.*

"But that could ruin them."

She turns her head to see me. *Do you have a better idea?*

I don't. I slip from her back and remove the saddle as carefully as I can, turning away as she shifts from horse to human. We have no stakes to hold the pelts, so we wrap the horse skin around us both, the leopard pelt hooding her head and the jackal hooding mine. I watch her masked eyes as the wind picks up and realize that at some point, I started to trust her.

Strange, that I should free myself from a monster who looks like a boy and end up with a girl who looks like a monster.

What? she asks when she sees me staring.

"I don't think you're damned," I say.

A laugh threads her thoughts. *Tell the gods that when I die.*

"But really. How could you be? You're cursed because you were sparing your best friend from making a terrible mistake. That's an amazing, admirable thing to do. What fault could the gods find in it? That'd be like saying you were too kind, too selfless. It's not even possible."

She watches me a moment longer, then shifts her gaze back to the desert. *He told you what happened.*

"It's nothing to be ashamed of. Why did you say you couldn't remember?"

Mm. Her tattooed fingers tighten on the pelt. *Old habit, I suppose.* She closes her eyes. *I couldn't even tell the Mestrah, when* the priests were warming the knife to cut out my tongue. *He asked me, without Kasta there, why I'd done it. How Kasta had been involved. If I'd told the truth, he would have pardoned everything.* He'd have set me free. She laughs, bitterly. *But I said nothing. Ironic, isn't it?*

"Then you're definitely fine. True monsters wouldn't put someone else first."

Unlike monsters who do nothing when that someone is nearly beheaded.

I shrug. "I just used Kasta's poison against him and left him in the middle of the desert. If we're going down, we're going down together."

She laughs, her eyes crinkling. *Gods, I've missed this.*

"This?"

She shrugs, and it's a moment before she answers. *Having a friend.*

I smile in turn, snickering at the idea of us, the world's deadliest creature and a girl who talks to cats. "We make a decent team."

We do. Sakira doesn't know what she's in for.

Sakira. I sigh at the swirling sand and squint out at the dunes, but the storm has muddled everything outside a short distance. I reach into the saddlebag and pull free a strip of dried meat, offering half to Maia.

Thank you, she thinks. *But I can't eat that.*

"Don't tell me you're a vegetarian."

She shifts. *Not exactly.*

"But you can't eat meat."

I can. She hesitates. *I just can't eat animals.*

314

"Wait, *what?*"

She presses a dirt-crusted palm over my mouth and turns away, listening. The storm is nearly on us. Sand hisses outside the skins, and the wind presses us forward in bursts. It feels like fingers searching in the dark.

"Did you just tell me you have to eat human flesh to survive?"

Apos, Maia thinks, which is not an answer. *We have to move.*

"Look, Maia, this is a very important question—"

I hear horses. She's already pulling the horse skin toward her, drawing it over her face. *They must not have been far behind us. I've been so focused on the storm—*

"Wait!" I catch her arm, but her bones shift under my fingers and I let go with a shiver. "You have to be exhausted. I can't ask you to do this."

You're right. I should do the leopard.

"That's not—"

But I can't stop her. She's already switched skins, and pointed fangs jut from her mouth as she shrinks and thickens, her fur shining in the moon like loose gold.

"Please, gods, don't eat them," I say.

A snicker. *I'm not going to eat them. I fed right before the race started.* She shakes her shoulders and circles in front of me, tail twitching. *Relax. It'll be a few more days before I'm ravenous enough to eat whatever moves.*

A female "Whoop!" sounds outside the blowing sand, and my heart twists as three horses charge into view, headed by Sakira's dratted buckskin. A small dip in the dunes is all that remains between us.

I have a feeling Sakira isn't going to be as careless with me as before. And if Maia stands in their way . . .

"You should go," I shout over the growing wind. "They don't care about you. They want me. If they hurt you—"

What are they going to do, kill me? Maia flashes a toothy grin. *It's cute that you think I need protecting. Stay back, Zahru the Silk-Lipped.*

The horses break the closest dune just as the wind surges, needling me with sand. It sprays before the buckskin like water before a boat, flying over the trio of horses as though hitting glass, obscuring our view so it seems the desert itself is folding in on us. Maia lets free a scream that's met with terrified echoes of the horses' own. The protection around them shatters. The buckskin rears and the gods release the wind; the sand drops just as Kita's horse bucks and charges off into the night, and Alette struggles to hold her mount, who kicks and jerks, refusing to move closer.

Hyra! come their frantic thoughts. *Run! Run!*

"Kasta can't be far," Sakira says as the buckskin lurches beneath her. "Find him."

"But, Sakira—"

"I'll be fine."

Alette turns her gelding south. Sakira draws her sword, a long, curved blade, and drops down from the mare. For as slender a silhouette she makes against the sky, she makes up for it with the shadow of muscle in her clenched arm, the sharp determination in her blue eyes.

Maia snorts, and it sounds like a laugh.

"Mm, I guess I would be confident, too," Sakira says with a small smile. "If I didn't know what this was."

I remember too late that Jet gave Sakira his sword. She whips the Illesa to the side, and light fires from it in a wide scythe, slamming into Maia's shoulder and sending her spinning in the sand. I cry out, but Maia shoves to her feet in an instant, hissing, and Sakira slices the air again, sending two more blinding arcs toward the leopard. Maia dodges, leaving only air between the princess and me. Sakira lunges for me. I jerk away and Maia leaps; Sakira swings for her and the leopard darts away, snarling. The princess turns to me, eyes urgent.

"What are you doing?" she says. "You can't want to stay with Kasta? Let's go!"

"I . . . Kasta isn't really a threat anymore," I say.

"What?"

Her eyes widen with understanding as she turns—and dives out of the way of Maia, whose jaws click closed as she coils for another leap.

"Stop! Don't hurt her!" I say, and I mean for Sakira not to hurt Maia, but it's Maia who looks at me. Sakira fires another beam of light that slams into Maia's head. The leopard grunts and teeters, then collapses in the sand.

"No," I breathe, dread curdling my stomach as I rush to her. Why couldn't I have let her handle it? Why do I keep trying to save people who are much better off without my help?

"Don't touch her!" Sakira says, but I've already scooped Maia's head into my lap and am searching frantically for a wound to cover, a cut to mend. Something I can do that would actually be useful.

"What did you do?" I say.

"What do you mean, what did I do? I just saved you from a cannibalistic demon. Why are you touching it?"

"She's not an 'it,' she's a girl named Maia, and *what did you do to her?*"

"She's stunned." Sakira sheaths her sword, watching me like I'm coddling a python. "Gods, relax. Is this some kind of Whisperer thing?"

"It's some kind of caring thing. How long until it wears off?"

"Long enough." She presses two fingers into her mouth and whistles, and Alette and Kita start back over, their horses tiny shadows against the vast landscape. Sakira pulls her scribing brush from her belt and twirls it in her fingers. "I'm sorry, Zahru. I wish it didn't have to come to this."

My stomach drops at the glint in her eyes. "Come to what?"

She lurches forward and slams my head onto Maia, holding it there as the ink of her brush licks my shoulder. I gasp and twist, but in seconds she's done, smirking as she leaps back. I strain to see the mark she's left on me. It looks eerily like the symbol for Obedience, a mark I only know because Fara has a cloth drawn with it beside the doors of the stable, but before I can smear the ink, it's sunk into my skin.

"Now. Put this on her."

She throws a twisting chain at my feet. I lift it, stomach sinking, and turn it in the moonlight. "What is it?"

"Something to wake her up."

I don't like the look on her face. But I can't disobey her command, and my fingers move without my permission, looping the chain around Maia's neck. The links glow red and stretch as they lock around her throat, the metal steaming against her fur.

Another necklace, another chain. I stroke her soft cheek, regretting for her sake, as much as mine, how close we'd come to freedom.

"Good girl," Sakira says.

"I'll find a way to get it off," I say. "Your spell won't last forever."

"Ooh." Sakira grins. "You have some new fight in you. I like it. Kasta's influence, I assume?"

I bite the inside of my cheek. I'm most definitely not discussing either of her brothers with her—which brings me to the jolting realization that Jet must not be doing well if Sakira reached me first, and my heart twists anew. Gods, I hope he's all right, and that the poison from Maia's fangs hasn't been putting him through some otherworldly torture. I wish I could help him. I wish I hadn't—

I swallow and bury the thoughts. First I need to survive Sakira, then I can fret over what I should have done.

"You're happy enough to use Jet's sword," I say, nodding to the Illesa. "But not to respect that he wants to free me?"

"I told you, my obedience to the gods comes first. If you're not meant to be the sacrifice, you'll get free."

"Has it ever occurred to you that you could *help* with that?"

Sakira twirls the sword and replaces it at her hip. "I could, if that's what I believed the gods wanted. But we are far too close to victory for me to believe that now."

I bristle against the reminder that she thinks the gods mean for me to die. "Has he written you, at least? When I left him, he wasn't—" I swallow. "He wasn't well."

A pitying, crooked smile. "He's fine. He had a little trouble with my fans at the first checkpoint, but I told them he was harmless, so they eventually let him go. Other than that, I don't know. We're not really sharing our locations anymore."

I exhale in relief. Maia's attack just slowed them, then. I consider that Sakira might have had her fans delay Jet on *purpose*, and am about to ask when Maia groans, stirring in my lap—then her head convulses backward, punching me in the stomach. I gasp and reach for her as she jerks away, but she screams her horrible half-human scream and twists her jaw toward the collar, but it's around her neck, she can't reach it, and then her spine lengthens and her legs twist; her fur lifts from her skin, the pelt peeling off her arms—

"You said it would wake her up!" I yell.

"Yes. As you can see, she's awake."

"What else does it do?"

Maia cries out again—a human sound this time—and when I turn she's crouched on one knee, looking at her hands. The pelt drapes her head, trapped by the collar. Her yellow eyes flash at Sakira.

The collar must block her magic entirely, because I can't hear what she's thinking.

Her gaze shifts to me.

"I'm sorry," I say hurriedly. "I didn't have a choice—"

"Ah ah, no talking," Sakira says. "Let's go."

I try to say the rest of that sentence—that Sakira marked me—

but I can no more press words from my mouth than tell my arms to sprout feathers and fly. I hope she can see in my eyes that this is far from over. That we'll try again, and we'll both get free.

Maia only watches as I settle into the front of Sakira's saddle, her fists tightening around the chain.

XXV

THE desert stretches before us in a blanket of darkness.

We pass fewer and fewer campfires until there are none at all, and even the chirp of crickets and the scattered thoughts of distant animals fade to silence. Sakira doesn't seem bothered by the change of scenery. She questions me instead, asking how Jet stole me, how Kasta stole me again, and—to my horror—how I escaped. But maybe the Obedience spell isn't all encompassing, because I'm able to admit I poisoned Kasta without mentioning why he carries poison or how I got close enough to do it. She doesn't press the issue. At first I think it's because I've cleverly avoided rousing her suspicions, but when her weight slumps against me and soft breathing replaces her words, I realize it's because she's literally too exhausted to care.

The team decides to camp for the night.

Maia is left outside the tent. She's been following us at a distance, even though Sakira would've preferred to leave her where she was. But Sakira doesn't want to soil her brush on Maia's skin, nor does she trust her spells will work on a Shifter, so Maia has followed. Now I just need to figure out how to get her collar off. Sakira's bound to drink again, and when she does, that's when I'll strike. I'll get whatever spell or key I need to remove it. And when everyone passes out, I'll use it on Maia and off we'll go.

Rest tonight, I tell myself. *There's nothing more you can do right now.*

Alette hangs her priest's amulets over the tent's arched entrance, so that coming near it would make Maia ill.

And before Sakira goes to sleep, she draws a new Obedience spell on my arm and tells me I can't leave the tent unless she has.

◇

I wake to a soft touch on my cheek.

We can't have slept long enough. My legs are lead from another day of riding, my head pounds as badly as when I'd had too much wine, and the last time I woke to something I thought was soft and harmless, Hen had freed a coop of stolen chickens into my room. I pray it isn't a scorpion or a tarantula and turn over, stuffing my cloak back under my head.

"Zahru," a girl whispers.

"Mmph," I say.

"We need to get going."

Kita. She sits above me, her pale fingers brushing my bangs from my brow, a soft smile on her face. I wonder if this is how she wakes her children. I have the sudden urge to hug her, if only to comfort myself with the closeness of a parent, but I settle for returning her smile.

"I feel terrible," I say.

"Do you want me to help?"

I shake my head. "No. I'll manage." I sit up with a yawn. "I swear we just went to sleep."

"A few hours ago, yes. But I know what you mean."

Alette and Sakira are outside, their morning shadows passing over the tent as they ready the horses. Neither holds a flask— yet—but I'm sure Sakira will want to celebrate getting me back. Especially if I encourage her to do so. I comfort myself that I'll only be with them a few hours more as I shake my cloak free of sand.

And thus begins day five. I swallow a spike of worry for Fara and sling the cold cloak around my shoulders.

"Breakfast," Kita says, offering me a quarter loaf of bread and an entire dried apple. It's as much as Fara and I would share for a morning meal. I take it slowly, noting the food bag is definitely something I need to find before Maia and I go.

"Is everything all right?" Kita asks.

"Oh. Yes. Sorry." I take a few apple slices and break the bread in two, but Kita shakes her head.

"Take all of it. Sakira wants us at our strongest, and the next checkpoint isn't far. We'll restock there."

I nod in thanks and try to be civil about eating it, but it tastes like cake and honey after not eating with Kasta at all, and I devour each bite faster and faster. Kita watches me over her own apple, though her nibbles are hesitant and far between.

"Zahru?" she says.

"Mm?"

"Your companion is gone."

I stop with a slice of apple halfway to my mouth. "What?"

"The Shifter. Sakira said the collar was starting to break, so she marked her with Obedience and sent her away."

I drop my breakfast and stand. "Into the desert? Without water or magic?"

She reaches for me. "I'm sorry, I didn't know you'd be upset. Zahru, wait!"

But I've already stormed out the front of the tent, the cold

324

morning air swirling around me like water. Dawn smears the horizon like a broken yolk. Sakira is reading an unfurled map and looking as clean and collected as if she's just left the care of six handmaidens and not sent someone out into the sand to die. A fresh haircut shows off her pale neck; a blue skirt flashes at her hips instead of red. Powdered pearl glitters over eyelids that rise when she looks up, her mouth curving into a smile.

"Zahru. You look rested."

"How could you do that to Maia?" I say.

Her smile fades. She turns back to the map. "Without the runes that control her, she's a danger to us all. You should be thanking me. It was only a matter of time before you became her next snack."

"It wasn't like that. She helped me escape. Without her, I wouldn't have known how—"

"To free her?" Sakira gives me a pitying look and rolls the map. "She was using you. You can't honestly believe you'd *befriended* that thing."

I close my mouth and push back the heat climbing my throat. It's not even worth arguing that point right now. "You sent her to die."

"She's a monster."

"So is someone who sends a person out to starve."

Sakira purses her lips. "A person? You do know what she eats, right?"

"Yes! But she wouldn't have eaten me, she would've—" I've never considered what she would've done. But the sad reality is that the only way to end that sentence is with *eaten someone else,* and that hardly helps my argument. "I could have asked her what she was planning to do."

Sakira tips her head, her eyes softening. She presses the scroll back into the saddlebag and latches it. "I know what this is about."

"Basic human decency?"

"You were hoping she'd help you escape again."

I turn back to the tent, both for how very wrong she is, and so she can't see me acknowledge she's also very right.

"Zahru, when the time comes, I promise I'll make it as painless as possible. Kita will slow your mind until you fall asleep. You won't even know it's happened."

And that's the last straw. I'm tired of being disposable; tired of people talking about my death like it's just another item on a busy list.

"Wouldn't that make you seem too weak?" I say, whirling. "Gods, what if someone finds out you were trying to be half decent? You should probably make it take as long as possible so you can tell your father how horrible you really are, and how *that* makes you the perfect queen."

"Whoa, where is—"

"Because that's all that's important, isn't it? How cold and heartless you can be. How far you'll go to rule a country you hardly care about, so long as you can keep partying and prove your father wrong. If you cared about me, you wouldn't be looking for ways to make it painless, you'd be looking for ways *to not stab me*. Gods, what is *wrong* with your family?"

"I—" A flicker of something real breaks her composure, before that infuriating pity takes over again. "I care about this country. That's not the point of the sacrifice."

"Isn't it? Because even your brother, the one who cut *this* into my wrist, said there might be a way to finish the race without taking my life. So what is it you're really after?"

Sakira watches me, and finally the pity falls from her face—but the cold that replaces it reminds me so much of Kasta, I step back. She storms to the buckskin and pulls a soft, sapphire-blue pouch from the saddlebag.

"You want to know what I'm really after?" she says, shoving the pouch at me. "Here."

I take it, my nerves already prickling. Whatever's inside feels loose, like rocks, and smells strongly of smoke. I ease back the drawstrings, half expecting something to leap out—and my heart flips as I take in the charred remains of a wooden puppet.

"Maybe my warm and welcoming demeanor," Sakira growls, "has you fooled into thinking I'm not paying attention to anything else. But I'm going to give you the benefit of the doubt. You weren't raised in the court, so there are many things you don't see." She returns to the buckskin and pulls out the rolled map. "That's how it should be. I want my people to feel safe in their homes, knowing I can keep them that way."

A stone rolls in my stomach as I turn the toy. The child who owned this must have loved it very much. Its carved face is worn even where it isn't burned.

"But there is one thing magic can't fix."

Sakira opens the map. The jagged outline of our country shines back at me: the Amian plains and the Pe mountains bordering the west, Nadessa and the ocean to the east. Greka crowns the north, its many lakes feeding the rivers that flow south through Orkena before ending at the island kingdoms of Wyrim and Eiom. A crimson line traces Sakira's route south from the palace to the caves. But west of our route, beyond the skull that marks an inhospitable stretch of desert called the Barren, five dark X's form a jagged smirk. All of them line the border between Orkena and the southern mountains—the closest to Wyrim's islands.

"This is a small hunting village," Sakira says, pointing to the first X. "This is a prestigious school for the upper magics." She moves to the next X. "This is a town that refines lumber, this one was once a thriving trading post, and *this*"—her voice thickens as she moves to the biggest X—"was Quadra. It used to be a mining town."

My throat tightens. "Used to be?"

"All of these are supposed to be our allies." She points to each country, excluding Wyrim. "Even Wyrim is supposed to be neutral toward us, but that's quickly changing. Each of these X's has seen an increase in trade hostility in the past decade. Not just from Wyri traders, but Eiomites and the Pe, too. Fights have broken out over prices. People have gone missing. My father's soldiers now guard these towns day and night." She taps the biggest X. "Except for here."

Her gaze flicks to the puppet in my hands, and my heart twists.

"Quadra was made up of *Mineralists*, Zahru. Mineralists and their families, who harvested sandfire for our buildings. But they were close to the Pe border, and too small to be included on maps, so Wyrim started rumors that we were mining some new, deadly kind of rock. Mercenaries, Pe and Amian, took it on themselves to handle it. They didn't even question the rumors. They bombed the entire settlement in the middle of the night." She grits her teeth. "That's all that's left."

My eyes heat as I look down at the broken puppet. Mineralists can locate precious stones and minerals even through layers of rock, though they have no power to affect them like Earthmovers, and therefore aren't any higher in status than Whisperers. This could have been my toy. Quadra could have been a place I grew up, dreaming about boats and chasing travelers for stories, until it all came to an end in a flash of pain and terror.

"My father sent the Wraithguard to hunt every one of the people responsible, and to remind the world what war with us would mean. There have been no more attacks. But that's the very root of the problem." Her blue eyes shift to me, determined and glistening. "Our enemies fear us because we seem more than human. They must see us as people. They must see us as *friends*."

Suddenly I understand how much more this is to her than thrills. Sakira enjoys the parties and the challenges, yes. But her mind is on the future. On making everyone as comfortable as I am in her presence, not only to win their trust, but to show we are as capable of passion, laughter, sadness, and even mistakes as the rest of the world. To try to prevent the war by stopping the fear that fuels it.

"But they must also know we have limits," Sakira says, rolling the map. "If peace doesn't work, there will be war. And I will not sit back and let *this* happen to my people." She plucks the toy from my hands, sliding it carefully back within its bag. "I'm sorry,

Zahru. That's why I have to have the power in the knife, too."

I can't think of anything to reply. The girls ready the horses, and I can only stand there, watching, with smoke curling my nose and the ghost of the puppet's warmth like a weight in my palm.

◈

The heat is blistering.

Distracted as I was when Sakira showed me the map, I remember her route cutting through a corner of the Barren, and I have no doubt we've moved into it now. There are not even small rocks here. Just thousands of kilometers of deceptively smooth hills that radiate Numet's energy like a mirror, the sand hissing as it billows beneath the horses' legs. We don't press the horses faster than a walk, but we don't pause to rest them, either.

But just when I'm thinking the speech about Quadra has transformed Sakira into a responsible, quest-minded queen from whom I have no hope of escape, the princess declares that reliving depressing news makes her hungry, and out comes the food. Flatbreads with bean dip, dried strips of pork; some kind of candied fruit Alette bought at the first checkpoint. It's practically enough for a banquet, though I know our supply isn't nearly so infinite. Sakira even brings out the flasks as I'd hoped she would, but now that freeing Maia is out of the question, I decline. It only reminds me that yet another of my escape plans has failed, not to mention that if I do come across Jet, he's going to heavily judge me if he discovers me riding drunk. Again.

Jet. My insides twist with worry, and I panic now that something truly has gone wrong. I hope he's only behind because they've had to rest more than usual, and not because he's having trouble recovering. I close my eyes and breathe out, assuring myself that Marcus and Melia are taking good care of him. I will get another chance to see him. I will get a chance to apologize.

Because this time, my escape plan will revolve around the only person I have yet to trust: myself.

I know I can't best Sakira with magic or brute force. I know the Obedience spell on my arm will be a problem. But I also know we have to stop at the second checkpoint before we reach the caves— and Jet knows that, too. I can leave clues for him. When we reach the Speaker, I'll push the bounds of the Obedience spell. If Sakira doesn't specify how *long* I have to stay close to her, I might be able to sneak away while they're talking, or get a message to the Speaker that I'm not a real sacrifice and need help. If that fails, I'll try for the Illesa and stun them all. And if Jet isn't there by the time all this has passed . . .

Then I'll take my chances on my own. Even an outpost in the middle of the Barren has travelers and trade caravans.

It's long past time to go home.

Sakira has planned her entire crowning ceremony and selected half her officials by the time Numet sinks beneath the horizon. She marks me with Obedience every few hours, and I stay quiet and solemn, as though I've given in. I don't know if the act fools her. She's the one who claimed her brothers always underestimated her, but now that her win seems assured, she's hardly paying attention to me. Her head is full of sweet cakes and party silks and handsome suitors, and when she's not looking, I can't help but smile at the irony of it.

We spend another too-short night in the tent, and I dream of boys with silver for eyes and knives for hands. Day six of the Crossing begins, and passes the same as yesterday. The dunes shift like shadows, the sand whispering in rare breezes and slithering beneath the horses' feet. Numet charges across the sky. The stars wink. The spells that fill the waterskins fade, and our food supply dwindles.

But just when I'm fretting I won't survive long enough to put my plan into play, we wake the morning of day seven to see a shimmering cluster of palm trees and squat, square houses in the distance. The second checkpoint. Even the horses get excited about the sight of civilization, lifting their heads and prancing forward.

Shade, they think to one another. *Food. Rest.*

Sakira doesn't even pause to check her appearance. She pulls me into the buckskin's saddle and lets the mare charge.

I've seen many building-like mirages in the last two days, and even some that looked like caravans and riders, so I'm relieved that as we draw closer, the shops grow bigger and more solid and the haze of heat thins. It's a small town by the breadth of it, perhaps even smaller than Atera, and I find myself searching for a stable on its perimeter, for even the smallest similarity to cling to. It's certainly not as busy as Atera. No travelers mill about the well at the outskirts or come out with their hands shading their eyes to see us. Then again, when it's this hot out, I imagine everyone who can will stay inside.

"I can't believe we're actually going to meet the Speaker," Alette says as we slow outside the well. "*The* Speaker, who's advised every single team since the first Crossing. How did your father even find them?"

"You don't find the Speaker. They find you," Sakira says mysteriously. "But actually, after my *fara* announced the Crossing, they volunteered."

"They?" I ask. "I thought there was only one Speaker."

"The Speaker is neither a man nor a woman," Alette says. "They're more."

"Oh, right," I say, nodding.

"You'd have met them eventually," Sakira says. "They always attend a new Mestrah's coronation."

Alette fidgets. "Do you think I can ask them a question?"

"I don't know." Sakira shifts behind me. "They're mainly here to advise us. My brothers and me, I mean. But if there's time, you probably can. Why? What do you want to ask?"

"I . . . there's just this thing I need to know. And I thought, because they're thousands of years old . . ."

"I told you, you're overworrying. It doesn't mean anything that the gods are ignoring some of your prayers. All priests go unanswered."

"I know, but they're only answering me in regards to this race. Nothing else. The last priest they ignored died within the year."

"He was also as old as dirt and talked to statues."

"He wasn't *that* old—"

I don't hear the rest of her reply. A cold that has nothing to do with my cloak sinks in as I study the quiet buildings, the empty street, and the crumbling well, where a bucket dangles from a broken spindle. Half its slats are missing. It clanks against the spindle's post with a hollow, rhythmic thud.

"Sakira . . ." Alette says.

Sand billows into the buried street. The nearest house, which I could have sworn looked white and shining from a distance, is actually the first floor of something larger, with its roof and upper floor eroded away. Palm trees sway over broken fences and broken jars. The haunting echo of someone's long-forgotten wind chime sends beetles down my spine.

"I don't think there are supplies here," I say.

Or people. Or crowds.

The second checkpoint is a ghost town.

XXVI

I don't understand. That was the best plan I've ever made. It was realistic, it accounted for many different variables, and it didn't rely on anyone specific to make it happen. Except, I'm realizing, it did rely on *someone* being here. I don't know what to do if literally no people populate the town. There's no food here, no water, and certainly no one who can help me secure a ride home.

This isn't right. After everything I've been through, after everything I've learned . . .

"Is this the right place?" Kita asks.

"Of course it is." Sakira pushes off behind me, sandals scuffing the sand. "We've been following the Southern Viper. This is the only outpost between here and the caves."

"Do you think people lived here before?" Alette asks, sliding to the ground. "You know, for the original Crossings?"

Sakira doesn't answer. Her confidence has vanished. She lowers the hood of her cooling cloak as she moves forward between buildings, their mudbrick sides bleached and crumbling. Maybe she's realizing, like me, that nothing goes the way it's supposed to. That we ate the last of the rations last night. That all the alcohol and spellwork and daring feats in the world won't help us survive if she's led us to the wrong place.

"Sakira—" Kita starts.

"I know," Sakira snaps. She glares over her shoulder. "Someone has to be here. Someone has to know if we check in."

She stalks into the sand-blown streets, looking left and right, not bothering to give me a single command. Alette hurries after her.

And then I'm alone with Kita and the horses.

I could take the buckskin and go. Kita would probably even let me. Even if she followed, what would she do? She's not trained in combat, she doesn't have a stunning sword, and the buckskin is the fastest of the horses. She'd have to give up before she lost sight of the checkpoint. I could take the compass. Sakira just revealed what constellation she's been following, and I could use it to reverse direction.

But I have no food.

And if I leave, I fear the last of Sakira's resolve will break. She'll press her team back into the desert to find me, with two horses and no compass. She'll rely on Alette's prayers to save them, unless Alette's prayers *don't*, and then I don't know what will happen. She might get desperate like Kasta. And who better to trade years off her life for their survival than poor, sweet Kita, who let me go?

Thus leaving two little children in Juvel to visit her tomb each moon, wondering if it's their fault she died so early.

"*Adel?*" Kita says.

I sigh. "I wish you were a worse person, Kita."

She blinks. "Sorry?"

"You should be." I swing my leg over the saddle and drop to the ground, not looking at her as I start after the princess. "You're making my life very difficult."

"I—but . . ." She hurries after me, her Healer's tunic flapping in the wind. "Did I do something wrong?"

"No. That's the problem."

A pause. "I'm not sure what you're trying to tell me."

"I don't know, either," I admit. A new gust of wind pushes against us, as if saying *go back, go back*, and I have to grip my hood to keep it in place. The heat slinks under my cloak like fingers, like the breath of something monstrous. "This place is awful."

"It's a strange place for a checkpoint," Kita agrees. "But I guess it's just another test. We were only given coordinates for these, with no idea of what to expect. The first checkpoint must have favored the popular heirs, with the crowd able to help us and hold Jet. This must favor the resourceful ones."

The resourceful ones. Like Kasta. I'm almost to the point where I can think of him without my stomach twisting, but I press the pain away and try to see this place as he would. He wouldn't have been discouraged by its emptiness. He would use it, and he would find what was out of place.

"There's nothing here," Sakira says, emerging from between eroded walls. "How can there be nothing here?"

"You've checked all the buildings?" Kita asks.

"There's only this set of shops and a handful of houses." Her fist clenches on her scribing brush, the wood bending dangerously. The tip drips black. I have a feeling she's tried more than one Reveal spell and is using far too much ink to do it. "No one's been here in a very long time. There are no footprints, no wheel marks, no wagons. It doesn't make sense."

Kita fidgets, her voice gentle. "*Aera*, are you sure—"

"This is the checkpoint!" Sakira says, turning on her. "I'm not dull, Kita. I know how to use a compass." Her glare sharpens. "This is it."

She sets her jaw and marches past us without another word.

Kita sighs and starts after her. Leaving me with the sun and the sand.

And the ghost of Kasta, bending to the ruined street, scrutinizing the quiet buildings. What would he be looking for? Not a way out. Not a scroll to sign that would prove he'd checked in. Nor would he care about food or supplies, because the first thing he was going to do when he got here was—

The Speaker. That's it. He'd be looking for a person. A wise, magical person who wouldn't want to be out in this wind, in this heat.

But where would a whole person hide? When animals seek shelter—

My heart jerks. *The animals.* We've made a lot of noise tromping through the ruins, but even in the Barren, they must be here. A lizard or a family of mice, making the most of the sheltered walls and sparse grass. Even if we haven't seen them, they always see us.

They certainly would have noticed the Speaker's arrival.

"Look for Valen's symbol," Sakira says, shoving a scroll into my hands. Her grip tightens on my shoulder as she adds, "Once you find it, come back to me."

I glare at her as she pushes past, cursing her magic. But maybe all this sun exposure is making me stubborn, because I'm still convinced I'm going to find a way around it. If I can find the entrance to the Speaker's house first, maybe I can get far enough away from Sakira that I *can't* come back. And—as I consider the silent buildings and their possible inhabitants—maybe this is one instance my magic is actually more useful than hers.

I open the crumpled scroll.

I can't read, but I find Valen's angled face near the bottom and trace the looping coils of the rattlesnake beside him. The god of fortune and fate. Of course. I roll the scroll in my hand and wait quietly where I am, listening, holding my breath. Only the sound of dribbling sand and Sakira's complaints come to my ears. But I stay perfectly still, and when Sakira has moved farther away and the wind lulls, I hear it.

Food? Food. Food, food, food.

A light voice, inquisitive and fast. Some kind of rodent, probably. Or maybe a snake. I edge toward the crumbling structure on my left, careful to keep my steps silent.

It comes again, hardly a whisper above the wind.

Food. Food! Safe? Safe food?

I peer into the ruined building. It has no roof, but its mudbrick walls are large enough to have housed many people at once. Judging by the eroded shelves carved into the far wall, it was probably a tavern. In the corner, where a cluster of desert grass grows in the shade, a mouse noses around the wheat-like seeds dripping from the grasses' tips.

It sees me and darts back into the wall.

"Wait!" I whisper.

Fear tinges the air, and I press back with reassurance.

"I'm not here to hurt you," I whisper. "I'm looking for something. I wondered if you'd seen it."

Silence. It's too afraid to even think. I inhale, suppressing every thread of impatience jolting through me, and reach out again, this time with joy.

"I'm looking for a secret," I say.

Its fear ebbs. Mice are quite fond of secrets; at least, the ones in Fara's barn are always bragging about how they've hidden something or other. Curiosity flickers in the air like fire bugs. I finger one of the pearls sewn around the neck of Melia's tunic and jerk it free.

"I'll trade you," I whisper. "One secret for another."

Carefully, I move toward the grasses and leave the shining pearl at their base. Then I step back, almost to the doorway, and wait.

A small brown nose wiggles in the hole in the wall, then a tiny head pokes into the sun.

Secret? it thinks. *Secret?*

"Trade," I say.

It hesitates a moment more, then dashes out, grabs the pearl in its mouth, and darts back into the hole. *Pretty. Mine. Pretty.*

Somewhere across the buildings, Sakira curses. No doubt she's trying other spells to find the symbol and they're not working well. I can hear Alette comforting her. Kita must be elsewhere, performing her own search, but a quick glance tells me she's nowhere near.

This can't take much longer. This is faster than I like to push, but I have to take the risk.

"I'm looking for a snake," I say.

Fear cracks the air like lightning. I hastily rip another pearl from my tunic and hold it out.

"A secret one," I say. "Not a real one. It looks like this."

Slowly, I unfurl the scroll until Valen's symbol is visible. I leave the second pearl at the base of the grass and the scroll behind it.

"Have you seen it?" I whisper.

Whiskers twitch in the hole in the wall. The mouse pokes its head out, just enough to see the scroll.

Seen, it thinks. *Yes.*

"Where?" I ask, struggling to hold back my nerves.

The mouse considers me and disappears again.

More, it says.

I . . . have no idea what that means. There's more than one symbol? More than one snake? "More what?"

Pretty.

Oh gods. It wants another pearl.

"Fine, but this is robbery," I hiss, pulling off another and setting it by the first. "Now, where is it?"

A pleased squeak, and the mouse darts out, takes both pearls, and disappears again into the hole. And stays there. Thinking about how jealous its friends will be. I'm beginning to suspect I've been conned by a rodent when it peeks out again and thinks, *Below.*

"Below?" I say. "Below us where?"

It tilts its head, struggling with how to describe it. *Water. Stones. Below.*

"Water?" I whisper. "But there is no—"

I whip around, my heart lurching against my chest. *Water, stones, below.*

The well.

"Thank you," I whisper before darting out into the sun.

I may leave this part of the story out when I tell it, too. If it wasn't embarrassing enough that I got hustled by a mouse, the number of times I've had to explain to the buckskin what I need her to do is bordering on absurd. I know horses get bored with long sets of instructions, but I only have three: stand next to the well, don't move, and if I tug on the rope connected to her saddle, pull the knot free. I have yet for the mare to look at me when I give that last instruction. She's too concerned with how much more grass the geldings have than her. Which, to clarify, is the exact same amount.

But I'm out of time. Sakira, Alette, and Kita are moving closer, and I need to disappear.

I check the knot for the last time and make my way slowly down the inside of the well, hoping the mouse understood what I was looking for and there's not a real snake waiting for me. I tossed an old brick down before I started, so I know there's a bottom and that it's dry. But I haven't been out of the sun long enough for my eyes to adjust. I can only go hand over hand, step by step, praying the mare doesn't move, praying the knot holds.

The air changes as I go. From hot and choking to hot and dry, and as I sink farther, to damp and cool, until finally the sandy bottom of the well comes into sight, and my heart quickens with hope. I let go a meter above it and land softly, the sand cold beneath my feet. The well is just wide enough that I can stretch both arms out and touch the sides. It's been dry for some time. Rough, waterworn bricks encircle me, the mud set between them so thin the stones blend into each other without pattern.

"Valen," I mutter, searching the walls. But my nerves buzz as I make one full circle, then another, and nothing stands out from the brick. Not even an interesting collection of stains. Did I misinterpret the mouse's words? Frowning, I draw my fingers along the stones, but everything feels the same. Smooth and cold. If there's a secret passage down here, it's well concealed.

"Zahru!" comes a distant shout.

Sakira. She's either noticed I'm gone or is about to. I whirl in the space, cursing my lack of luck, and consider the rope. If I tug on it, the buckskin will pull the knot free and Sakira won't know where I've gone. I'd have more time to search for the symbol . . . and absolutely no way out if I'm looking in the wrong place. Sakira doesn't have another rope.

And then I see it. It's barely visible in the layers of wear, but toward the base of the bricks, no higher than my ankle, coils the inked body of a sleeping rattlesnake.

Valen's symbol.

"Zahru? Show—"

I cover my ears and hum to block out the command. I don't know if it will actually work, but when a few seconds pass and my mouth doesn't feel compelled to shout or my legs to move, I suppress a wild laugh and frantically rip the tattered fabric of my tunic. Still humming, I stuff two pieces of the linen into my ears and find the symbol again in the brick.

Now or never.

I jerk toward it—and my mind jerks back. *Once you find it, come back to me.* I gasp in frustration as my fingers tremble centimeters away from the symbol, refusing to push it. I can't believe this is how close I'm going to get to escaping only to have my own body pull me away. I try again. And again. It's no use. My fingers deflect toward the rope, stubbornly grabbing it every time I try to use them for anything else.

My hands itch to climb. They want the rope because it's the fastest way out. The symbol is right there, *right there*, and if only I was stronger, I could probably—

I stare at the braid in my hand, and up at the rim of the well.

The rope is the fastest way out.

Unless it's not.

The mare will release the knot if I tug. I jerk on the braid as my arms compel me to climb, biting my cheek as my feet start up the brick, one step higher, then two, three—and finally I feel a soft pull on the other side, the mare acknowledging my request.

"Yes," I whisper.

The rope loosens in my grip. I fall back to the floor as it loops over my legs, and just as Sakira's yells penetrate my earplugs, I jam my thumb into Valen's symbol.

XXVII

THE ground shudders. The coiled snake glows and the earth itself slides sideways, pulling me closer to the wall, a circular edge opening over darkness.

There's nothing underneath it.

It's possible I should have considered something dramatic like this might happen after activating an ancient symbol.

I scramble to my feet and press against the wall, kicking the rattlesnake brick with my heel, telling the trapdoor to stop, please, but the grind of it sounds like a laugh, and soon there's so little to stand on that I have to accept I'll be falling into the abyss. All I can do is pray there's something soft to land on.

The last edge slips beneath my feet.

I drop into frigid air. It leaches the warmth from me so suddenly it's hard to breathe. The wind rushes by my ears and I pull my arms in, gasping—

SPLASH. Freezing water engulfs me, surging into my mouth and nose, tearing the plugs from my ears. I flail and kick, trying to determine which way is the surface, but the current spins me and I have no light to follow. Water burns my lungs and throat. I'm fighting every instinct not to choke, not to take in more of it, when it dumps me over some kind of ledge, and I land on my back, hard, on—

Soaked pillows.

The waterfall dumps over my back, down into a grate beneath the cushions, and I crawl out of the spray, coughing and sputtering.

And *free.*

I'm in a tomb. A very important person's tomb, from the look of it. The dustless floor shines in the light of the torches, the polished bricks painted with different blessings in silver and gold. Murals of Mestrahs, of princes crossing the desert, of a sacrifice bleeding before a princess line the walls in full color, and glowing prayers wrap the many pillars. At the far end, beneath the curved ceiling, gleams a life-sized painting of Numet astride the white mare that takes her over the sky in the day. Statues of Rie's winged servants hold braziers filled with fire.

Through a short forest of vases, glass statues, and other priceless tributes stands a painted throne with lion's paws for feet. A person sits atop it in a fine tunic of red silk, a golden belt wrapping their waist. Their bronze cheeks are unshadowed by stubble, their eyelids a bold, glimmering scarlet rimmed in thick kohl. But instead of gem-laden hair they wear a formal hat atop their bald scalp, a square of red fabric circled by small golden skulls.

"Well," they say, their voice a welcoming tenor. "You're not who I was expecting at all."

"Are you the Speaker?" I ask, as if I'm completely unfazed by falling down a trapdoor and entering a tomb via waterfall. If nothing else, the Crossing has made me adaptable.

"Some call me that," they say, lifting a lazy shoulder. "Some call me strange. Or freak. Or liar." They smile. "I consider all of them compliments."

They don't look like they're thousands of years old, but I suppose having the gift of immortality extends to a youthful appearance, too. "*Liar* is a compliment?"

"It means I've told someone something they're afraid to hear. I know I speak the truth, so why should I be offended by it? I like to make people think. I like to make them afraid." They lean forward, elbows on their knees. "Do you want to know what you're afraid of?"

"Oh, I already know that," I say, shivering as I push to my feet. Drenched as I am, the tomb is freezing. "But how would you? I thought only the Mestrah could read minds."

"When you've lived as long as I have, you pick up a few things along the way." They smirk, like the ability to master a god's power is no more remarkable than coming upon a rare cloak. "But I think you should consider my question. I don't think the answer is what you think it is."

"Then I definitely don't want to hear it. Then I'll have something new I'm supposed to be afraid of, and I'll wonder if I was afraid of it before you said something or if I became afraid of it because of you, and honestly I'm really tired of being afraid of things." I shiver again, running my hands over the prickles on my skin. "Do you have a towel?"

The Speaker laughs. A loud, surprised sound, and they shake their head. "I could answer any question you want, and *that's* your most pressing inquiry?"

My teeth chatter. "Please?"

The Speaker shrugs. They navigate the riches on the floor with fluid grace before fetching a scribing brush from the back of their belt and gesturing for my arm. They hold my hand firmly and draw a waving symbol on it in red ink, the spell glowing as it sinks in.

"You're *trielle*, too," I say. "Is there anything you can't do?"

"I should hope not. I've had two thousand years to learn how the world works."

"But you should be in the palace, then. You should be Mestrah."

Their laugh is amused. "And have to deal with endless generations of the same problems over and over? People squalling over land and magic and who insulted whom? I have better things to do."

"You do?"

I realize too late this might be considered offensive, but what could a person who's seen and done everything have left to do?

"Oh yes. I have an immense family, as you may imagine. It takes most of the year to visit them all. My extremely great-grandchildren and their grandchildren and my current children and their children . . . family is the most important thing, you know."

"I know," I say, my heart aching for Fara's warm arms and Hen's clever smile.

"Then you're wiser than some I've met." They press their fingertips together and study me. "So. You have two thousand years of knowledge at your disposal and half an hourglass left." They nod toward the throne, where an hourglass dripping real emeralds is indeed half emptied. "Surely you didn't come all this way to ask me about a towel."

"Oh. But . . . am I allowed? I'm not . . . I don't belong to a team."

"I know who you are. And you do belong. You simply haven't figured out where."

A line like that makes me hopeful, because if the Speaker thinks I have enough of a future left to find where I belong, then the Crossing can't be the end of my journey. "I can ask anything?"

"Of course."

"And you can read my mind?"

"To an extent."

"Then you know I'm not supposed to be the sacrifice. You know I'm telling the truth when I say the priests didn't make this mark." I raise my scarred wrist.

They nod. My heart beats harder.

"Can you send me home?"

Their smile is slow and sad, and my hopes wither even before they speak.

"I'm afraid that would be breaking the rules," they say. "The priests have declared you the sacrifice, and so the sacrifice you are. But this has been a most unusual Crossing. I would not be surprised if it comes to an unusual end."

Disappointment settles over me like a weight. Maybe it's time to accept this is meant to be. I've had multiple chances to escape. All of them have been thwarted. This is the third time I've found myself free of a murderous heir, and the third time I'm meeting a dead end. *But what did you expect, Zahru?* Gallus pops into my mind, his pretty mouth turned down. *You're just a stable girl.*

"Zahru." The Speaker rests their hands on my shoulders, and I look into violet eyes. "There are still two important questions you need to ask me."

I grit my teeth. Now that I know they can't help me, I just want to leave. "I only have one."

"If you insist."

"Will it be painless?"

This wasn't a question they were expecting, because they frown. "Leaving here?"

"No."

I don't have to say I'm referring to my death. The Speaker's brow softens, and they shake their head. "I can't see into the future. Call it my only flaw. But it doesn't matter, because that's not the right question."

"I don't want to know anything else. It won't help, anyway."

"Zahru."

"I can't keep doing this. I thought if I found Jet, I'd be safe. But that wasn't true. Then I thought if I saved *myself* I could make it, but Sakira caught me. And then I used everything I'd learned, even my *magic*, and I found Valen's symbol on the well, and I thought . . . I thought finally, this had to be it—"

"Zahru—"

"But it's not! What did I do wrong? What did I do that's so unforgivable? I help my father. I care for the animals we have, not because I have to, but because I can't stand for them to be hurting. I tried to help Kasta . . . I tried to help Jet and Sakira. Because I want to be a good person. But it doesn't matter." I've started to shake, and I grip my elbows to try to stop it. "No one cares if you're good or not. They care about what you can do for them. But I'm no one, I can't change anything, and what I am will never be enough!"

Kasta's words from my mouth make me cover it with both hands. I swallow the heat climbing my throat, resolved that if I'm going to spill all this out on a stranger, I'm not going to cry as well. The Speaker's hands squeeze my shoulders. I wonder if they're used to sacrifices breaking down in front of them. I wonder if the other sacrifices felt like this, that they'd tried to be obedient and good and helpful, that they'd wanted to show the gods they were wrong not to bless them with powerful magic, that they were still worth something anyway and in the end—

In the end it didn't matter.

The Speaker lets me catch my breath before they speak.

"Do you know why it's important to face our fears?" they ask.

I shake my head.

"Because that's the only way we can change them."

Tears burn my eyes. The Speaker is a blur in front of me, but I bite my cheek to stop from looking away.

"You think you've been chosen because you have nothing to offer." A pause. "Have you considered you've been chosen because what you have to offer is different?"

I can't reply.

"You think what you've done doesn't matter? You think kindness has no power?"

"Not here," I blurt.

"Especially here." The Speaker lets go of my shoulders. "The ones who seem the most impervious to it are the ones who need it the most."

I sniffle and wipe my palms beneath my eyes. "But it's not working."

They grin. "If you'll forgive the comparison, kindness is like a poison. Sometimes it takes time to work." They fold their hands.

"You have the kind of power that stays with someone for a lifetime. Magical fire awes, magical swords cut. But not a single person on their deathbed remembers those things. They remember the people who loved them. And believe me, I've stood beside many deathbeds."

I consider the Speaker with a new appreciation, mulling over the words. I don't think they'd say that just to be flattering. They have much better things to do and much more powerful people to flatter, like the heirs, but they've gone out of their way to help me. To show me, by example, how much of a difference words can make.

"That was actually a terrible choice in comparison," I say. The Speaker smiles, and I wipe my eyes again, willing myself to believe their words. "But thank you. I'm sorry to burden you with that."

"You're not the first. Now. Are you going to ask your second question or not?"

I blink, thinking it would be much easier if they'd just tell me what I should ask, until I remember Kasta's urgent eyes. "Is there a way to get magic in the caves without killing someone?"

The Speaker sighs. Maybe that was the wrong question. "The knife demands blood. Great magic cannot be born without great sacrifice."

"But you have many types of magic."

"And I have made many sacrifices." Their jaw clenches. "Some I would not make again. But that is the nature of my power, and no one else's."

I can't stop my shoulders from sinking. That was my *last* last hope, because if Sakira knew she could get the magic without taking my life, I feel like she'd consider sparing me. I might have to go into hiding for the rest of my life, but she'd have the most important part of her victory. She could even claim she brought me back to life or something. Sakira would like to be sensational like that.

"Oh." The Speaker's brows rise, and a small smile pulls their lips. "You're not asking for yourself, are you?"

I shrug.

"I tell you what. I like you, young Zahru, so I will give you one more question. Think carefully this time. I'm not allowed to send you home, but what could you ask that would remain within the race, that would be almost as good?"

I let out a shaky breath, considering what they've hinted at. They can't send me home, but they *can* send me somewhere?

"Can you send me to another team?" I ask, hope like lightning in my veins. "Can you send me to Jet?"

The Speaker grins. "That, finally, is the right question. Farewell, young Whisperer. Remember what I said. Remember where your true power lies."

"True power?" I ask. "But I don't—"

The torches extinguish. The gold and glitter vanish into pitch-black, and suddenly I'm outside beneath a night sky brilliant with stars, the dunes as dark and endless as an unmoving sea. The abandoned town is nowhere in sight. I spin in the sand, panicking that the Speaker miscalculated and sent me into the middle of the desert, when hoofbeats fill my ears. I freeze, hardly daring to hope.

A gray horse and hooded rider break the closest dune, flanked by two more horses, one of whom is twice as thick as the others. The leader pulls his horse up so hard it nearly rears. His partners do the same. He jumps off the saddle and pulls back his hood, revealing a shadow of close-shaved hair and a look so troubled, so hopeful, that I sob in relief.

"Zahru?" Jet says.

XXVIII

"JET!" I cry.

He runs for me and we crash together, his arms tight around my back and mine clutched around his neck, worried that if I even think too hard he'll disappear. But he's warm and he's real and we hold on to each other, me trying very hard not to cry again, him apologizing over and over.

"I'm sorry, I'm sorry, I should have been paying attention, I should have been watching for Kasta—we tried to find you." Jet pulls back, his lovely eyes stricken. "We paid some mercenaries to tell us where you'd gone, but they lied and I—I thought we could never catch up . . . I'm sorry. I'll never be able to say it enough."

"I'm here," I say, squeezing his shoulders. "It's all right. I'm here."

"How?" he says, threading a lock of my hair through his fingers. "Are you real? Am I dreaming?"

"The Speaker. They couldn't send me home, but they could send me to another team, and . . ." I shrug and smile. "Here I am."

"Numet thank you," Jet says, embracing me again. "I won't forget this second chance."

I hold him as long as I dare, gratitude for the gods flooding my heart for my second chance as well. I may not have the power to get myself out of this alone, but the gods are helping me all the same. Guiding me to the right people. To *good* people, who believe I'm someone worth saving.

And whether the Speaker intended this or not, they're helping me face yet another of my fears. Because maybe it took bounty hunters and mild heatstroke and getting way too close with the wrong prince, but at least now I realize how unfairly I judged Jet. He's been attacked and poisoned; beaten and nearly kidnapped. If he truly believed I was "just a Whisperer," he wouldn't dare risk his life for me in so many ways. He may not understand what I do, but until we talked about the coming war, I had no idea what he had to deal with, either.

He just wanted to find a way I could break free, too.

And so I won't be afraid anymore of what the future holds for us. I won't worry about how it will end, because then I'll miss out on *this*. On the chance to enjoy someone selfless and wonderful; someone who's practically given up the world for me, who puts me above himself no matter the cost. *This* is how the good stories are supposed to go. This is how they're supposed to end.

Melia moves her mare up beside us, looking as flawless as ever.

"I am very glad to see you, Zahru," she says. Marcus grunts, and though clouds veil the moon, I'm certain I see him wipe a finger under his eye.

"Don't mind him," she says. "He took losing you very hard."

"Yes, well." Marcus clears his throat. "I'm the most decorated soldier in the capital. I should be able to protect a single person in my care."

"Thank you for coming after me," I say, looking between them, and finally at Jet. "Again."

"Just remember where I'm putting you if you risk your life again for us," Melia says, but she smiles.

"New plan this time," Jet says, ushering me toward his horse.

"We're going to take you all the way home, and if anyone reports us, I'm going to stand up to my father."

My heart jerks, and I look at Marcus and Melia. "But they'll try you for treason." They nod. "No, I can't let you do that for me. We'll do the same plan as before. Get to a town, stay hidden, and I'll find my own way back."

"This is not just about you, Zahru," Melia says. "Though it is very much about your safety."

She nods to Jet, who exhales. "I've had a lot of time to think about what you said. About what all of you have been saying." Marcus gives him a look, and a guilty grin pulls Jet's lips. "You were right. We're each born for something, for a duty our skills are meant to serve. I've been afraid of mine. But that's a part of any job worth doing." He takes my hands, pressing them in his. "And if it means I can save even one more person like you, it'll be worth it."

I gasp. "You're going to try to win?"

Whatever he sees on my face makes him smile. "When the race restarts, yes."

"Jet!" I yell, laughing. I can't help it. I throw my arms around him and squeeze, so proud of him that tears brim my eyes, that he's already becoming the person he wants to be and not the person he thinks the station entails. He will be all the good parts of his father . . . and so much more. "Gods, I'm so happy to hear it. You're going to be a phenomenal king. And you'll know what to do if the war comes. You'll do the right thing, like you are now."

The smile those words inspires is both shy and genuine, and if my dratted mind wasn't already latching on to new worries, I would have kissed it.

"But you don't have the advantage," I say. "And we know Wyrim will make another move to kidnap someone, and this time they'll be more careful, and you'd have to come all this way again . . ."

I stare out at the endless Barren, at the sweat drying on the horses' sides.

"Don't worry about us," Jet says. "We know better what to expect now. All that matters is getting you home."

Which are the words I should have wanted to hear most. It's exactly what I pleaded for from the Speaker . . . exactly what I hoped to hear when they sent me to Jet. Fara must be worried sick. Mora and Hen might have already been arrested for attempting to come after me, and I ache to be back in the stable again, tucked away with the quiet sounds of the animals, enjoying the safe, predictable routine of home.

And gods, I still want that. I want to tell Jet that yes, absolutely, let's go before anything else happens, because haven't I been through enough?

But I think of the bounty hunters and their strange metal. The blackened puppet from Quadra. The war crouching on our borders like a hungry lion, waiting to spring on the new Mestrah, its mouth open for the thousands Sakira and Kasta would send at it. All to prove they're hard enough; that they're not afraid.

And looking at Jet now, at the grim determination in his eyes, I'm reminded that sometimes what we want isn't as important as what we need to do. Melia's right: this isn't just about me. This isn't about helping Jet see who he could be, or going where I'm most comfortable, or doing what I'd rather be doing. This is about ensuring Orkena stays out of harmful hands. This is about the fate of thousands of people . . . people like Kita, like Maia. Like my father and Hen.

"I don't want to go home," I say.

Jet gives me the same look he did when I first told him he should rule. "What?"

"Too much could happen if you restart the race. We're almost to the caves. You have me. Let's finish it."

"Zahru—" Marcus starts.

"You said there was a way to win without killing me, right?"

Melia looks to Marcus. "Yes, but—"

"Then let's go. This is the best chance you have." I turn to Jet. "I want you to win. Don't even try to argue with me, because you know it won't work."

Jet snickers, but his smile quickly fades. "And I'm absolutely honored to have your support. But I can't let you risk this for me, either. Yes, I can refuse the sacrifice, but I don't know what will happen when I do. I don't know what will happen if Kasta or Sakira is there. There's still too great a risk to you."

"I don't care."

"*I* care. And as your prince—"

And that's as long as I can resist. I kiss him, my hands twisted into his hood and his surprised hands at the curve of my spine, just long enough to feel him press back, even though pulling away is like taking only the smallest bite of cake. But I'm sure Melia and Marcus would appreciate me expressing some restraint, and besides, I have an argument to win.

"You're taking me there," I say, our faces still centimeters apart. "*Aera*," I add, with a smirk.

Jet swallows, his gaze flickering from my eyes to my lips. "I feel adamantly like that was cheating."

"You do remember I'm the same girl who snuck into a palace banquet?"

"I think we need to argue about this a little more."

Marcus loudly clears his throat. Jet and I look over, my hands still grasping his hood and his on my back. Marcus and Melia watch us with raised brows, looking both amused and slightly uncomfortable.

"I'm going to call the lady the victor," Marcus says. "With the note that I, too, would prefer Zahru go home, but"—he raises a hand when I start to protest—"we all made a choice to be here, and you deserve to make that choice as well." The war horse dances beneath him, and he pulls him steady. "But if we are going to try for a victory, we need to get moving. We only have one more day to bring Zahru to the second checkpoint."

"Are you sure?" Jet says, turning to me. "I know it's been worse than terrible, and your family must miss you dreadfully—"

"Jet." I slip my hands to his shoulders. "This is more important. *You're* more important."

His smile tugs at the edge, and he folds his arms around me with a sigh. I swallow and hold him, turning my head into his neck, letting the steadiness of his arms and the calming smell of leather and sage burn into my memory. For now there's certainly no chance of us traveling the world together. Not for a short time, not even with my father's blessing. After the race is through, I won't see Jet again. He will be the Mestrah, and I will be a girl from Atera. But despite the ache that pushes through me, despite how

I assumed such a thought would break me after all my hoping, I know it's the right thing.

Until then, I'll just make the most of the time we have.

I wonder if Jet is thinking the same, because when I lift my head, his eyes are sad.

"You're an amazing person, Zahru," he says. "You make me believe the gods could be out there after all."

I swallow and drop my hands to his chest. I'd just told the Speaker how I thought the gods had abandoned me, and looking at Jet now, I'm ashamed of even thinking it. But some part of me holds back from admitting it. I may be resigned to losing him, but I don't want to make this harder than it already is.

I smile weakly. "Now let's go get your crown."

After I fill the team in on Sakira's and Kasta's last whereabouts, Melia decides the best chance for arriving at the caves first would be to travel without a break, as we could reach them within a day at such a pace. She will heal the horses' fatigue, hunger, and thirst as needed, and ours as well. It's a lot of magic to use, but Melia insists we allow her to do it. Much of our success depends on reaching the caves and refusing the sacrifice before the other teams have a chance to get there.

The only caveat is that Jet still needs to visit the Speaker.

They hadn't been far from the second checkpoint when the Speaker relocated me. (More concerning is how an entire afternoon passed in what I thought was my short visit with the Speaker, but Jet says time always moves strangely around them, and there's nothing we can do about it.) The moon has only sunk the distance of my hand when its white buildings come into view like low clouds. We slow the horses, all of us on a knife's edge as we look for evidence of Sakira's team, but nothing shifts between the shadows. The horses are gone from the well. Melia and Marcus go ahead to scout the buildings while Jet and I wait a distance off, until Marcus waves his saddlebag in the air, signaling the path is clear.

Jet urges our gelding forward, the horse's hooves beating a comfortable rhythm in the sand.

We haven't spoken of the moment we just shared, but we don't need to to know we've reached the same conclusion. Jet has sat behind me with a different ease than before, and I've leaned against him, enjoying his warmth and the sound of his laugh when I admit I was almost conned by a mouse at the second checkpoint. At least I know now what to look for in the future. Not for the heat of a fast-burning candle, but for the ordinary moments, for how easy it is to imagine myself with Jet every day, saying things to make him smile, seeing myself in eyes that reflect me and nothing else.

"Did the Speaker make you solve riddles or anything?" Jet asks, tensing for the first time since we started riding.

"No," I say. "But anything you want to ask you should think of now. You only have a set amount of time."

His fingers shift on the reins. "I have no idea what to ask."

I place my hands over those fingers, steadying them. "That's all right. I didn't, either, but the Speaker knew what I wanted anyway."

He gives me an appreciative smile and laces his fingers through mine until we reach the well. Melia frets about leaving the horses, but I have a feeling the Speaker is someone I'm only meant to see once, and when I say I'll watch them, Marcus immediately volunteers to stay with me. The plan makes Melia grumble—she'd rather we stay together—but there's a new fire in Marcus's eyes that Jet doesn't dare challenge.

"Numet's speed," I wish them as Jet starts down the well.

"Be here when we come back," he says.

"We will," Marcus promises.

Jet disappears beneath the well's rim. The light potion he wears illuminates the stone in a ring, and we watch him sink until it vanishes beneath some impenetrable darkness, where only the scuff of his sandals against the brick remains. A thud vibrates up the walls—Melia must have landed. A second thump sounds, and just as the silence is worrying me, a voice travels up.

"We've found the symbol," Jet yells.

"*Ammon*," Melia curses. "It's glowing."

Silence. Then, from Jet: "Is the floor supposed to be moving?"

"Yes," I yell. "You'll drop into a pool."

"Of course we will. I hate water," Melia grumbles.

"Good luck!" I call.

No reply. The well has gone as quiet as the buildings around us, and I strain to hear a splash or the grinding of the trapdoor, but it must be enchanted for silence. Marcus exhales and turns his gaze to the desert, his fingers tight around his crossbow. I think he could take out an entire army right now, the way he glares at the sand.

I miss his smile.

Marcus's tension makes me feel safe but also anxious, and I gravitate toward the horses, finding comfort in their quiet company. Jet's gelding nudges me for water, and I draw the horses' waterskin from the saddlebag. He closes his lips around the nozzle and drinks, tossing his head to keep the Water spell active.

Good human, he thinks.

I smile and stroke his silver neck.

The night stretches on around us. I want to ask Marcus more about his family, about why he enlisted in Orkena's army and how his magic works, but I don't want to distract him from his watch. I spend the hours with the horses instead, watering them and sprinkling the strange grass-growing potion into the sand, brushing their sleek coats with my fingers. These would have been bothersome chores if I was at home, but here I feel full. Transported, however briefly, back to the stable and its comforts, the smell of hay and dust wrapping me like a shawl.

I stare off into the horizon, imagining Fara at work in the stalls, speaking gently to his charges. *I'll be home soon*, I promise, convinced that if I think hard enough, my words can travel the distance between us and find him.

Dawn is breaking—day eight; gods watch over Fara—when voices stir Marcus and me from a breakfast of dried lamb and beans. They drift from the center of the ruins, and Marcus raises the crossbow, a bolt poised as Jet and Melia jog into view.

"How long has it been?" Jet asks as Marcus jerks the bow down.

"A few hours," Marcus says. "Numet has just risen."

"We have to go. We need to leave now."

"What's wrong?" I ask, packing the food. "What did the Speaker say?"

"More than I can repeat. But that's not it." He holds up his listening scroll. "Sakira's scroll has been destroyed. My writing won't sink in anymore."

My heart lurches. "Do you think she destroyed it because she's upset?"

"She wouldn't. I haven't told her I'm back in the race, or that I have you. I'd planned to beg her forgiveness later." He strides to the gray, and I follow in haste, stuffing our breakfast in the saddlebag and pulling myself onto the gelding's back. Jet swings in behind me. "Last she wrote, she mentioned the Speaker gave her interesting information, and she'd write again when she'd won the crown. If the scroll is destroyed, something else destroyed it."

I think of Sakira keeping the scroll on her thigh, and cringe to think how close the threat would have to be to crush it. But I'm a little surprised at what else he's revealed.

"She's going to try to win without me?" Maybe something I said finally sank in with her, too.

"I don't know. She didn't mention having lost you. She's understandably a bit less trusting of me now." He sighs, and turns the horse south. "Whatever the case, we need to find her as soon as possible."

He digs his heels into the horse. In an instant we're off, charging past the ghostly buildings and the sad wind whining through them, back into the blazing dunes.

Toward the caves.

My nerves grow with the rising heat. I hold the hood of my cooling cloak in place, trying not to think too hard about what might have happened to Sakira. I may be glad I'm away from her, but that doesn't mean I like to think of her hurt or lost in the desert somewhere. Or that I want to think of what might happen to *us*, if we meet whatever attacked her.

"What did you ask the Speaker?" I yell over the wind, desperate for a distraction.

Jet is quiet a moment, but soon the wind and hoofbeats fade, locking us back into our small slice of the world.

"If I was making a giant mistake by trying to win," he confesses. "And if there was anything I could do to save my father."

My heart jerks. His tone has already revealed the answer, but I ask anyway. "And?"

Jet exhales slowly. "They said if I valued my life, I *was* making a giant mistake." His voice quiets. "But not if I valued anyone else's."

That's not what I was asking about, but I let the silence stretch, wondering if I dare ask again.

"No magic in the world can save my father," he says.

My shoulders sink. His hands have tightened on the reins, and I cover them again with mine. Jet sighs, his chest relaxing against my back. No matter the outcome of the race, his struggles are far from over.

"I'm sorry," I say, twining my fingers in his. Watching my father lose his magic has been hard enough. I can't imagine what it would be like if I knew his condition was fatal. "At least you're giving him one very big thing to be happy about before he goes."

"Hmm?"

I smile. "He's going to burst with pride when he sees you."

Jet grunts, but I catch the hint of a smile. "Yes. Provided I can remember everything I've been desperately trying to forget about ruling."

"*Aera*," Melia calls. She's drawn her mare close, breaking our bubble. "I don't see anything."

Jet sits up behind me as the sound rushes back in, turning as he scans the dunes.

"We can't have missed her," he says. "How far are the caves?"

Melia points at the horizon. Just beyond the shimmer of heat, rising like the backs of hyenas, juts a range of hills tall enough to eclipse the royal city. Against the orange sands they look ashy and dark, much more like the entrance to the afterlife than the lush green paradise travelers speak of when they refer to mountains. As if my body can sense this is a very bad place to be, my pulse ticks up, the hairs on my neck prickling in warning.

"She must still be ahead," Jet says. "Keep your guard up."

They do, Marcus with his crossbow over his lap, Melia sitting straight and watchful. But though we run the rest of the day, pausing only for Melia to tend the horses, the only clue that anyone else has been here is a fading group of horse tracks and a heavy, restless feeling in my chest that something is very wrong.

XXIX

WE reach the mountains at twilight. We have yet to see anything of Sakira but her horses' tracks.

The restless feeling in my chest deepens.

As does my immeasurable disappointment. When travelers speak of the mountains, they talk of trees bustling with songbirds, of grass so fine and clipped it covers the earth like a carpet, of sheep with coats long enough to shear and horns that curve like hooks over their backs. Nothing green grows here. No birds flit between branches, no flowers grow in the shadows cast by the hills. There are no trees, no bushes. The black soil shimmers in the dying light, clattering over itself when a breeze rises, a silver wave running up the hillside like a shiver.

"Is that ash?" Jet asks.

Marcus dismounts, his heavy weight sinking into the dirt as he bends to lift a piece of it.

"Yes," he says, crushing it between his fingers. Black smears his pale skin like ink.

Of course the dark, depressing place where so many innocent Forsaken have died would be made of ash.

"She made it this far, at least," Jet says, urging our horse on. Sakira's tracks curve to the left around a stable-sized mound, down a dug-out path that makes the horses jumpy with how close the walls come to their flanks. And finally into a clearing that was probably large and circular at one time but is now no bigger than the base of a small home. Ash trickles over almost-buried stone walls, stretching like claws toward the center. Sakira's buckskin stands at the base of an enormous pair of carved sandals. She lifts her head as we draw near, her only company one of the two geldings, who doesn't acknowledge us at all.

Above them stand four giant figures carved from black stone, stoic brows circled by Mestrahs' elaborate crowns. Two women and perhaps two men, but the statues on the right are too worn to decipher their faces. Between the two middle figures stands a doorway as tall as their knees and twice as wide as a horse. The diminishing light hardly reaches into it. It's a square of black, as menacing and quiet as the deepest parts of a river.

"One of the horses is missing," Jet says, pulling our gelding to a stop. He slides off behind me, staying close as I swing my leg down to join him.

"It could have gone off on its own," Melia says. She leaps nimbly from the saddle, her Healer's charms swinging against her bicep. "Maybe the scroll was crushed by accident, and they are all right."

"I don't know," I say, moving for the buckskin. The gelding's lack of responsiveness is worrying me. "He wouldn't want to leave the herd. Either they'd all go, or he'd force himself to stay here."

The gelding still makes no move as I approach. His head is low, his eyes closed. His thoughts are empty, but I don't think he's asleep. Dried sweat coats his entire body like a film, and both horses' manes are matted and tangled. They've been ridden hard without tending. I wonder if that means something happened to Kita, and my heart clenches as I lay a soft hand on the gelding's shoulder.

He quivers beneath my touch but still doesn't move.

"What happened?" I ask the buckskin.

Water, she thinks. *Water. Water.*

Her saddlebag is still intact. Whatever Sakira survived, it was harrowing enough for her to rush into the caves without thinking of the horses' care. I slip the largest waterskin out of the pack and offer it first to the buckskin, letting her drink enough to sate her thirst, but not enough to twist her stomach, before offering it to the gelding. His eyes flutter and he moves his lips to take the skin, but he's too exhausted to swing the bag up, and I have to hold it while he takes concerningly small sips.

"Where's your companion?" I ask them.

The buckskin paws the ash. Her dark eye turns to the path we came from, ears back against her skull. *Gone,* she says.

My chest tightens. "And your riders?"

She shudders, then bares her teeth and kicks backward, screaming so loud that ash trickles around us.

No leave, she thinks. *I'll die here. I'll die!*

"Hey, hey, it's all right!" I say, backing away. "We won't leave. We won't. Melia, can you help them?"

"I'll do what I can," Melia says, taking the buckskin's reins. The mare jerks back and strikes at a mound of ash, but Melia raises a hand, waiting, until the mare stops dancing and stands, head high, nostrils wide. Melia approaches slowly, laying a gentle hand on the mare's cheek, and the buckskin shivers and quiets.

"You two stay with Zahru," Jet says, his hand on the hilt of his dagger. "I'll figure out what's going on here."

"Jet—" I start.

"*Aera*—" protests Marcus.

"Only the heirs are supposed to enter," Jet says, talking over us. "And the sacrifice, for obvious reasons." He turns to Marcus. "There were only two sets of horse tracks leading in here. That means Kasta is still out there. Take Zahru and Melia out of view and wait for me."

"Sakira didn't go in alone," Marcus grumbles, "or her teammates would be out here, too. You know what this feels like? An ambush. She's stringing you along with false clues, hoping you'll race in without thinking."

"Sakira wouldn't do that to me," Jet says, though doubt threads his voice. "And she's not going to hurt me, especially if I don't have Zahru."

"Well, it's reckless to go by yourself." I cross my arms. "If I'm the only other one who's supposed to go, I should go. I can at least run for help if something happens."

"Zahru, please. If it *is* a trap, and she gets to you before I can talk to her—"

"Then I'll defend myself. I'm not helpless." Especially with two sleep poisons.

His face falls. "I didn't mean to imply that. But we don't know if she still plans to kill you. You may not have the chance to react."

"Are you telling me I've been cut, kidnapped, poisoned, soaked, and dragged across the entire desert so I can sit outside while you walk into an ambush and die?"

He grunts. "I'm not going to walk into an ambush and die."

"You don't know that. Kasta would be dead right now if it wasn't for me." I wince. "He also might be dead right now because of me."

Jet blinks, which is the moment I realize I didn't tell him about the first checkpoint—or that my claim of "sneaking away while Kasta slept" was massively more complicated than I made it sound.

"The point is," I say quickly, "people aren't expecting me to be a threat, which is why I'm the best weapon you have. Two sets of ears and eyes are better than one."

Jet shoots a helpless look at Marcus, who puts up his hands. "I'm with her. And if you want to follow the Crossing rules, fine. But Firsts also have a rule: that we put our heir's life before all else. Melia and I will stay for a count of three hundred, then I'm claiming I heard a commotion and we're coming in, too."

"Fine," Jet says, agitation twitching through his jaw. "But for the record, I never liked this, and if Zahru gets hurt, it'll be on your consciences, not mine."

"As will the fact that this was my choice." I approach the massive doorway and turn, steeling myself. "I'm not changing my mind, Jet."

Jet gives me a helpless look, something on the edge of appreciation and concern, before reluctantly handing me a stringed light potion from the gray's saddlebag. I settle the little star around my neck, the light silver in my hand.

"Jet." Marcus removes his sword and scabbard and hands them over. Flames curl the handle when the prince takes it, though I can see in Jet's face that he's missing the Illesa. "Be careful."

"Be safe," Melia says, offering him her own glowing necklace. "And know we are here for you." She smiles and squeezes his arm. "Numet be with you."

"Numet be with you," echoes Marcus.

"And you," Jet replies before turning to me, worry etching his brow. I'd be lying if I said I was feeling very confident right now, either. Even if it turns out Sakira *is* safe, I don't know which side of her we'll meet in here. I want to believe it will be the side that chose Alette over a legendary horse, but I also remember the Speaker's pitying eyes when they confirmed the knife can't create magic without taking a life. Sakira would have been foolish not to ask them about that. She'll know, now, that there's no other way.

And gods, the last person she's expecting to challenge her for her dream is the one who's been her ally all along. Jet isn't just going against his own preference. He's betraying his sister, and any love they once shared will be shattered with this choice.

But when my eyes meet Jet's, the doubt and uncertainty harden into something else, and I know this is what must be done.

He draws Marcus's sword and reaches for my hand.

"Whatever happens," he says, "I want you to know I'm thankful for you. I couldn't see myself clearly before. And I . . ." He squeezes my fingers, his gaze flickering toward the darkness. "If I don't survive this, I want you to know I have no regrets."

"Don't survive?" My blood chills. The blackness deepens as we move in, the light of the potions shining across faded murals, across chariots and archers and nobles bowing to newly crowned Mestrahs. "What did the Speaker say, exactly?"

"We should be quiet. Sakira could be anywhere."

"Jet," I whisper. "On a scale of one to ten, how worried do I need to be about you?"

"Zero. Shh."

I don't appreciate being shushed, and doubly when he's just given me the kind of heartfelt confession heroes give before something bad happens, but I don't want to be the reason we're ambushed. My sandaled feet barely make a noise against the cool stone floor. His steps, oddly, are just as quiet. When I remember why, I squeeze his hand, hard.

"Ouch, what?" he says.

"You can control sound!" I say. "I could scream right now and no one would hear it!"

"Ah. Well. If I'm talking, I'm not concentrating on the ambush, am I?"

"But you could cloak us long enough to answer my question!"

Maybe I wasn't clear when I told him he was more important to me than returning home to my father and decidedly having no risk of being sacrificed, that his safety and ability to survive this are of utmost concern. But just as I'm opening my mouth to say that, Jet raises his hand, his face slackening at whatever he sees ahead. I squint into the darkness. A ghostly light grows in the distance where the tunnel curves, illuminating an enormous carving of Rie driving his carriage of souls.

And a real person lying below it, prone and unmoving.

"Sakira?" Jet says, rushing forward. He must forget to mask our sounds, because our footsteps echo from the widening walls. Dread crushes me from every angle. I don't want to see who it is. I don't want to have a memory of Sakira dead at my feet, her fierce eyes dull and sightless, her capable hands limp at her sides. But it soon becomes clear that whoever it is, they're too large to be the princess. My breath catches when Jet kneels beside the stained linen of a Healer's *jole*, and Kita's strong face comes into view.

Her eyes are closed. Jet touches two fingers to her neck and exhales.

"She's alive," he says. "But someone else is hurt." He studies a spackling of blood across her chest. The fabric isn't torn, so it can't be hers, and aside from dirt and sand, her arms and legs look clean. "I think she's been knocked out. We should—"

His gaze locks on something behind me. The air has changed here, the dampness exchanged for something empty and open, and I know, even as I turn, that what's behind me won't be another hallway.

The Glass Caves open before us like a massive hourglass dropped and broken on the earth. Ash climbs the smooth walls, splattering the black glass, the statues of gods around its edges drowning in it even though their heads reach the ceiling. Their faces and bodies have been hacked to ruin. The cavern's builders must have adorned them in gold and jewels, for crude tools have chopped and shattered the glass about each god's neck and face, a show of blatant disrespect that turns my stomach. I had expected the caves to hold the same reverence as a tomb—where, even though I walk among the dead, I see the gifts left behind by their loved ones, and I know they are satisfied and peaceful. This does not feel satisfying or peaceful at all. I feel uneasy and *watched*, as though the shadows are moving just out of my vision, hungry and restless.

The only thing untouched is a rectangular skylight in the center that opens to the stars, and the altar directly below it, its surface hazy and chipped with age.

"No," I breathe. Jet inhales, and slowly, slowly rises to his feet.

Kasta looks up from where he sits at the base of the altar, a gleaming white scorpion in his palm.

XXX

"YOU can't be real," I say. "You can't be *here*."

Kasta's expression doesn't change. He simply rises, smoothly, slowly, so as not to alarm the deadly creature in his hand. The starlight shines against the blood splattered across his chest. Sand frosts his skin and the dulled armor of his *tergus*, and I curse myself for leaving him with the protection bracelet. It gleams about his wrist, charged and ready.

His eyes are twin points of darkness, burning as hot as the fires.

Jet tenses beside me. "Where's Sakira?"

A smile twitches Kasta's mouth. "I don't know."

"You have her horses and Healer. Where is she?"

Kasta starts toward us, unrushed. The Illesa glints at his hip.

"Alive, maybe," he says. "The desert is a vast place without a compass or companions or a horse."

His fevered gaze shifts to me, and I shrink into Jet, wishing a million times over I'd listened and waited outside. I knew leaving Kasta in the desert might come back to haunt me, but this is so much worse than I imagined. The boy with the light in his eyes may as well be dead. This is what rose from his bones, a shadow with someone else's blood on his chest and rage crawling his skin.

"And Alette?" I say, though with a sinking feeling, I already know the answer. Kasta needed a new Healer, so he took Kita. But as to Sakira's friend, who could go on to pray for his failure . . .

Kasta ignores the question. "You are the worst mistake I've ever made." The scorpion twitches in his hand, and he stops in place.

"I knew you were his. And yet you were so *convincing*. I thought about it, after you left. How you made something so innocent, so . . . *harmless*, into a weapon that destroyed every wall I'd ever raised. I couldn't even be angry. It was brilliant. You showed me I still had a weakness, and now . . ."

"I wasn't pretending," I mutter, though I may as well be speaking to the statues for how much difference it seems to make.

"Kindness isn't as quick as a sword, but it's twice as effective. The merchant who found me fell for it easily enough. All I had to do was listen. Carry his bags. Help him with his camel, his tent. I accidentally woke him before I could slit his throat." His brow creases. "He thought I was alerting him to a threat."

His eyes slide back to me, and I stifle a gasp, the feeling leaving my body from my shoulders out. This is all my fault. Every kind thing I did for Kasta, everything I told him, he thinks I did for my own gain. Now a man is dead because of it, and Alette—

"You killed him," Jet says, shaking his head. "Was it that easy?"

Kasta swallows. The muscles in his jaw twitch, and despite the calm in his voice, I see the shake in his fingers. "I had to prove," he says, finally looking away, "that I could do it."

That he could kill. That he could kill *me*. Maia said the day he went after the Shifter was the day he crossed the point of no return, but she was wrong.

This will be the day he crosses it.

"And Sakira?" Jet says.

Kasta's eyes flit to me. "I knew if I skipped the second checkpoint, I could head off the lead team before they reached the caves." He lifts the scorpion by its tail. It wriggles in his fingers, but it can't bend its body to pinch his hand. "But you weren't there, Zahru. I didn't understand. It was only with much convincing that Sakira confessed the reason." He snaps the scorpion's stinger from its tail. The rest of the creature he tosses aside. "And then everything aligned. The Speaker told her you'd arrive *willingly* at the caves, at Jet's side. Just as I always knew you would."

"Because he chose me," I snap, with more venom than I mean to. "Because *that* doesn't matter to him at all." I point to the altar.

"I trusted you with *everything*." Kasta's blue gaze flashes, and an ache wraps my throat that threatens to choke me. "But at least you've made this easy."

"Stop this," Jet says, stepping between us. "You've involved her enough. You're a murderer and a disgrace, and your place is in chains, not on a throne. Yield the win."

"No."

"I will not hold back this time, Kasta," Jet says, raising his blade. "You cannot win this, even if you take her life. You skipped a checkpoint. The priests will disqualify you."

"Ah, brother," Kasta says, slowly drawing the Illesa from his belt. "But if you and Sakira are gone, what other choice will they have?"

He rips the sword across the air. Jet tackles me as light bursts from the blade in a fiery arc, the magic slicing over us, blinding hot and crackling, and shoves me away just as the tip of Kasta's sword slams the ground between us. Kasta stalks after him. Blades screech as Jet parries another attack, and I push to my knees and search the room, and it's a terrible, terrible sort of déjà vu, except this time I have no protection runes, no conveniently abandoned stools. *Think, Zahru, think—*

Jet curses. Light slams a mound of ash, spraying me and half the room, shaking the floor. I bolt for the exit, intent on running for Marcus, but Jet cries my name and I turn just in time to dive beneath another slice of light. The magic crashes into the tunnel before me, tipping the braziers at either side. Flames rush across the exit in a scalding *whoosh*. Horror twists my stomach as the fire licks higher, burning too hot and too high to be normal, and it's then I notice the sparkle of burning powder across the exit, carefully hidden beneath a layer of sand. *No*. Kasta has already thought of this. Without a Water spell to counter it, none of us will be leaving.

"Marcus!" I shout, though my voice is barely louder than the fire's roar. I press closer, and the immense heat presses back. "Marc—"

An explosive *BOOM* splinters the glass near me, showering me with shards and sending white cracks up the stone. I whip around, confused. There was no light before that attack. Jet can only cast me a panicked look before blocking another of Kasta's strikes. He must have tried to use his Soundbending against Kasta—who used the bracelet to redirect it at me. The warning is clear. Jet won't be able to use his magic at all.

Gods, if I had even a little power, I could crack the wall and bring the ceiling in. Or turn their blades to straw. Or at least do *something* that would give Jet the upper hand so I wouldn't have to wait here with my life on the edge of their swords, knowing that if the wrong prince wins, I'll be dead in minutes. Helpless to change anything. Except perhaps to make it worse, like when I distracted Maia.

I'm afraid to move.

But Jet has already changed strategies. He stops attacking and dodges a blow that sets Kasta off-balance, and his blade finds Kasta's ribs. Kasta gasps. His blood splatters the floor, and with a sickening lurch I realize what Jet meant about not holding back. If he wins, I'll be spared, but he'll still end up with blood on his hands. He'll still have to sacrifice someone he was trying to protect; someone he lied for, someone he loved.

Kasta squares himself and strikes again, but he strains his bleeding side and the blow falls short. Jet knocks his sword aside and kicks him where the blood runs heaviest. Kasta coughs, clenching the wound.

"Yield," Jet says.

Kasta grits his teeth. He blocks Jet's next strike and fires another bolt of light, but Jet ducks and slices his bicep. Kasta grunts and recovers, but he's weakening. He misses the next block. Jet slices his leg.

He's winning, but with the Illesa's stunning light, Kasta only needs one opening. I'm dreading the moment Jet falters. The moment he's even a fraction too late.

I can't watch this.

I turn away, my hand over my eyes. I think of anything else— of Hen at home, making dresses out of reeds. Of Fara stirring his morning tea. Of the river in Atera at night, as full of stars as the sky. Of holding Jet's hand—

Kasta shouts, shattering my escape. It's a war cry, a death cry, and blades clang and a blinding flash of light explodes a mound of ash, splattering me with debris. The world trembles and then it's silent—terribly, terribly silent—and I turn as slowly as I dare, praying Jet was merciful, praying it was quick.

But it's not Jet who stands leaning on his sword, using the blade like a cane.

Kasta got his opening. Jet lies sprawled against a hill of ash on the far side, his eyes closed, his bloodstained sword loose in his hand. With his head tipped toward the ceiling, he almost looks peaceful. Kasta straightens, slowly.

He limps toward his brother, gripping his side, his sword dragging against the floor.

Oh gods. Oh gods oh gods oh gods—

"Stop," I say, but it's a weak sound, and Kasta ignores it. He knows he's won. He knows there's nothing more anyone can do to him. Jet will never beat him at anything again. Jet will never sneak down from another balcony or ask about Nadessa or make me believe I'm worth crossing the desert for, or look at me like he did last night, and say I make him believe in the gods—

"Stop!" I yell.

Kasta doesn't. I could scream at the unfairness of it all, that I have to be the one who has to watch this, that no decision I make will end this happily. Kasta's ten steps away. Eight. He's injured. Maybe if I tackled him, if I used a sleeping stinger before he could react—

Something glints at the center of the room.

And that's when I realize I've been looking at this all wrong.

All this time I've been pleading with the gods to rescue *me*. I thought each time I failed to escape was a sign I was worthless, that I was meant to die, that I'd landed here only because I wasn't powerful enough not to. That I could never be enough, not for anyone else, and certainly not myself.

But magic isn't the only thing that holds power.

And I've never been the one who needed rescue.

Do you know why it's important to face our fears?

I'm the rescuer. Because what I have to offer is different. Because what I have to offer is far more potent than bringing the caves crashing to the ground or twisting rivers to my will. I can be a Whisperer, and I can convince runaway princes to take their place on the throne. I can be a simple girl from a simple town and still know exactly how to make Orkena's most merciless royal yield without a sword. I don't need stronger magic, because I take the time to listen. I take the time to care. I have people I'd die for, and people who'd die for me. And that . . .

That is more powerful than any magic.

I sprint for the altar. Atop the glass jut two small gold supports, upon which a beautiful, terrible knife lies, its edge rusty with old blood. Sabil's balancing scales form the hilt. I look over my shoulder, at Kasta standing over Jet's prone body, his blade raised.

I lift the knife and turn.

And lower the blade to my arm.

"Kasta," I say, and this time it's not a plea, but a command. "If you don't stop, I'm going to drag this blade across my wrist, and you'll never get your magic."

The Illesa quivers in midair. Kasta turns, finally acknowledging my presence, skepticism pulling at the shadows in his face. He doesn't stab his brother, but he doesn't lower the sword, either.

"You won't," he says finally. "You're afraid to die."

"Yes," I confess, gripping the hilt. "But that's going to happen either way. So you decide. You can kill your brother and get your vengeance, or you can have your magic."

I pray I haven't misjudged him. That his hate for Jet is not so strong he'd make the trade. His good arm flexes on the sword. He looks down at Jet's peaceful face, and a frustrated snarl escapes his lips as he lowers the blade and turns, blood oozing from his side.

"You realize after you're dead, I'll kill him anyway," he says.

"No, you won't. Because you're going to give me your word that you're never going to hurt him again, not physically or otherwise, and the same goes for Melia and Marcus. In case you're considering a false promise, I'll remind you of where we are. I wouldn't push the gods any more than you already have."

His gaze shifts to the statues behind me, broken and shattered. He wavers, perhaps judging how serious I am, but his eyes lock on the knife.

"Fine," he says. "I promise it."

"Promise what?"

"That I'll bring them no further harm, if you give me that knife. Do you agree?"

I shiver and bite my cheek. "I agree. But leave the sword there."

"No."

"You will," I say, gritting my teeth as I push the blade harder against my skin, just enough to bring a bright line of blood to the surface.

"Fine! Fine. Stop." I've never seen him panicked. It's a strange thing on his face, a strangely honest thing, and his weapon falls with a clang. His other hand presses hard against his bleeding side, and I ease the pressure on the knife.

He starts toward me.

It's at this point I realize what I've done is something I won't return from. I won't get to say goodbye to Fara. I will never tell this story to Hen. It won't matter how many clothes I memorized or types of food I learned, and fear pulls at the wildest threads in me, begging me to run, to use the knife against *him*. But I can't lose control. If I break the agreement, Jet will suffer the consequences. This has to stop. I have to face the real reason I'm here, and I have to say what needs to be said.

Kasta pauses just outside of striking range. He seems to consider, too, that I might use the knife against him, and his eyes search my face, looking for the lie.

I haven't lowered the blade from my wrist.

"When you kill me," I say, choking back my fear, "you will honor my memory by being the king I wanted you to be. You'll help the Forsaken. You won't hurt anyone ever again, not on purpose, and you will never, ever use kindness as a weapon as you did this week. You will look for the good in others, as I tried to. You will not use your suffering to make others suffer, but to save them from it. Do you agree?"

He tenses, waiting for the strike. As though I am the greatest threat between us.

"Do you?" I shout.

His gaze flickers from the knife to my eyes. "I agree."

My fingers shake so badly I nearly cut myself deeper. I sob and swallow, refusing to be afraid, trying to find an ounce of the strength I felt moments ago. It doesn't make this any easier. I want to protect Hen and Fara. I want Kasta to think on this moment when the war comes and show Orkena the mercy he couldn't show me. But I'm still not ready to die. I don't want it to hurt. I don't want his face to be the last I see.

I pull my wrist away from the knife.

And offer him the handle.

Hope, terrible and raw, breaks across his face. The darkness pulls back, smoothing the harsh planes of his cheeks, softening his eyes, until he's just a boy standing before me, a boy who's afraid, a boy who can't believe this moment is real.

He takes the knife from me as carefully as if it were made of glass.

And watches me.

I clench my fists and return his gaze, and I try not to tremble, I try not to shake. I try to be as strong as Fara would want me to be. Kasta steps closer and rests a bloody hand on my shoulder and the tip of the knife against my heart. He's still waiting for the trick. Still tensing for me to poison him, to cut him with a hidden blade, to reveal my real motive. Even I think desperately of the sleeping stingers in my tunic, but I can't risk failing. If I miss, it will be far more than me who suffers.

He flexes to stab me—

And hesitates.

I gasp in frustration, in the wild hope that maybe he won't, that finally this is enough. My head buzzes so loud I can see the noise in my vision, great dots of black and white, the world swimming behind them.

The light is in his eyes, silver-blue; uncertain.

"You can still choose me," I say, reaching for that light, and I don't mean in the same way as before, of course, but if he would give this up for me, if he could trust me . . . "Does it matter what your father thinks if I'm there? Let me help you. Whatever happens, you'd have me." I shudder, trying to keep control of my voice. "You wouldn't be alone."

His grip loosens, ever so slightly. I don't know how much longer I can stand this. I don't know how much longer I can go before I crumble entirely, but I can't lose it now, not when he's listening, not when the knife is moving slowly, infinitesimally, away from my chest.

Kasta shivers, and the shadows in his face surge and ebb.

"Choose me," I whisper.

His jaw clenches. The blade trembles. Indecision winces across his face and I swallow, waiting. He's considering it. He's considering it and gods, I might survive this, I might finally have made a difference—

The knife steadies.

But it's the regret in his eyes, the pain, that frightens me more than his anger ever did.

"I'm sorry," he whispers. "I wish I could."

His hand tightens on my shoulder, and he drives the blade in.

XXXI

AT first it feels like nothing. The pressure of the hilt against my chest, of something wrong within my skin. Static builds in my core like a gathering of clouds.

Then it explodes into my body.

My strength rips from me in a single breath, my legs buckling, my chest screaming as I drown in the fire of it, the finality. The caves brighten as white as the sun and back to black. Kasta holds me against him, his flesh hot and slick, his hand gentle behind my head. Muttering something. Cradling me like I'm the dearest thing he has, the dearest thing he'll ever lose.

Until he rips the blade back out.

I scream as white-hot pain surges through my chest, crippling my muscles, sending me to the floor. Or I try to, but the sound is gurgled and confused. Blood pours beneath me in a rising pool. Red on black, mixing with the ash. There's too much of it. I try to stop it, I try to move my hand to cover the wound, but my body won't listen. The caves blur and tilt. My eyes want to close. I swallow and let them, and my fear fades with the minutes, until it's almost pleasant to lie here, to give in.

The pain stops. All that remains is the heat, tempered to something comforting and warm. Light builds behind my eyelids. The lantern of Rie's carriage, I hope, come to deliver me to Paradise. The souls of those already in his vessel chatter and argue. I've been told ghosts whose bodies haven't been buried are often disagreeable, but it seems silly to be complaining already, especially since Rie's carriage will be far more impressive than even the glass boat I took to the palace. I try to turn toward the voices, to call out that I'm here, but pressure keeps my head firmly in place. The voices grow closer.

"I'm aware of how much blood this is," a woman says.

"She's trying to move," says a man. "That's good, right? Is that good?"

"Bodies twitch after they die," she replies. "But I don't think I've lost her yet."

"You have to go faster. Melia, you have to go faster."

"I know."

Melia? I choke trying to say her name, and at once the light fades. Melia leans over me, her weight on my chest, both hands bloody and pressed to my heart. Marcus paces behind her. I try to smile—

The pain returns like a lightning strike.

I gasp as it twists through me, a new knife splitting me in two. Melia calls to Marcus, who holds me steady, but Melia's laughing and sobbing, wiping her cheeks on her arm as she says something in Amian. The pain ebbs to an ache, then a twinge.

Then I'm lying there, Marcus's hands on my shoulders and Melia weeping into her hands, impossibly alive.

I sit up slowly, my core protesting every motion, and yank Melia into a hug.

"Thank you," I say as she sniffles and curses. She hasn't dropped her hands from her face. "I don't even know how to thank you enough. I—what happened?"

"Reckless girl," she mutters, sagging against me in exhaustion. But soon she drops her hands and hugs me back. "You are lucky we are not close to a river."

Marcus's shadow covers us, an unconscious Jet over his shoulder. "He's still breathing. But I can't wake him."

"I'll tend him outside," Melia says. "Let's go. Can you run?"

She helps me to my feet, but aside from an uncomfortable soreness around my ribs, the rest of me feels fine. "Yes. But what—?"

"No!" Kasta snarls. I whirl, pain twinging my chest as I focus on the figures across the room. Kasta stands cornered by a girl covered from head to foot in black, her masked face unreadable. The Illesa's curved edge smiles in one of her hands. The sacrificial dagger glints in the other, dripping my blood.

"Maia!" I cry.

Melia pulls me toward the exit. The Shifter turns away, and relief floods through me that she's alive, that she came for me. This was not exactly how I'd hoped we'd meet again, but it gives me hope our brief friendship isn't over.

Go, Zahru the Silk-Lipped, thinks Maia. *Leave the monsters to monsters.*

A strange numbness pulls at my heart. "She's going to kill him."

"Likely," Melia says. "And us as well, if we stay."

I know that isn't true, but I let her pull me away.

And so we run. Over the smoldering remains of the fire and past the carving of Rie. Past the bleeding sacrifices on the walls. Past Kasta's shocked cry—something horrible and sad, that grates against me despite my anger—and into the coolness of the night, where I collapse into the ash, exhausted, and look up at the stars while I thank every god in existence for my life. For their grace. For seeing me as someone worth saving.

"Gods, what on earth?"

Jet is awake. Before I can blink he's at my side, yanking me upright, searching for the wound, the source of all the blood.

"Where are you hurt?" he says. "Melia, what happened? Is she healed?"

I can't help it. I laugh.

Jet's shock transforms into firm disapproval as Melia tells him how she and Marcus had run into the caves, alarmed by the commotion, only to find themselves blocked by flames. Melia had sprinted back out to fetch Water spells, and as she was returning, Maia swooped into the caves as a falcon and dove through the fire. She must have gotten there just as Kasta stabbed me. By the time Marcus and Melia dampened the flames, she was human again, and though they hadn't seen her strike him, she'd kept him cornered while I healed.

Marcus got Kita out in the meantime, and the Healer took the buckskin to the other side of the mountain, where the race officials are waiting to greet the heirs. Marcus says a good portion of the army will be there, too, to protect the heirs on their way home, and so there will also be soldiers who can go looking for Sakira.

"You *handed my brother a knife*?" Jet says, gripping my shoulders. "Didn't you promise me you'd never risk yourself like that again?"

I lift a shoulder. "I did, under the condition that you started making better life decisions. Honestly. That's the third time I've had to save you."

He snickers. "Well. Maybe I fear you'll run off with someone more interesting otherwise." His laugh is quiet and pained. "Oh, gods. I'm going to owe you even more apologies now, aren't I?"

"Oh, far more than that. I want weekly shipments of chocolate, my own horse, salves for the stable, a kitten, a job for my best friend—I'll make you a list."

Jet smirks. He drops his hands into mine, his thumb a feather over my knuckles. "Good. Because actually, I wanted to ask you if—"

Marcus shuffles at our side. Melia watches us with a raised brow, and Jet seems to remember where we are, because he laughs at himself and helps me sit.

"Would you rather talk about this when we're not both covered in blood?" he asks.

I laugh. "Gods, yes."

"Right." Jet bolts to his feet and helps me up, his eyes warm and bright. "Let's get out of this desert, then."

XXXII

DESPITE my fear that we'll have to journey a week *back* across the desert to the palace, we follow the buckskin's hoofprints around the mountain of ash to three glass carriages waiting at the temporary camp. There, we're given fresh clothes, an inspection by one of the palace Healers, and all the fruit, fish, and honeyed breads we can eat. But the luxury that brings tears to my eyes, alarming Marcus so much he draws his bow, is that they also have a bath. I spend hours in it, soaking in the warmth and the smell of jasmine, enjoying the feel of water and weightlessness and *clean*. I scrub away every mistake I made in the desert, every regret. A soft golden *jole* awaits me at the end of it, and I emerge feeling like an entirely new person.

But our joy at surviving Kasta is cut short by the lack of news from the recovery team. Jet paces the edge of camp, waiting for the soldiers to return, but hours later, the listening scroll they gave him still reads the same: no sign of Sakira. Kita has miserably tried to convey where Kasta ambushed them, but the Barren is merciless in that way. There are no landmarks or towns she can give them for reference.

It's only with much prodding that one of the captains convinces Jet there's nothing more he can do, and we must return home before our own safety is at stake. The captain promises to send for reinforcements, and soon I find myself on a cushioned red seat within the grandest of the carriages, Marcus and Melia crammed in across from me and our future king at my side, looking uncomfortable every time a servant addresses him as *dōmmel*— Divine One.

"That's excessive, isn't it?" he grumbles. "Can't they just call me by my name?"

"Ah, the burdens of being a future god," Melia says, examining manicured nails. The boys look immeasurably improved in fresh sets of armor, and though I know Melia must have been as weatherworn as all of us, she looks practically the same. Save that she's no longer covered in my blood.

"That's not confirmed," Jet says. "Kasta was the one who completed the sacrifice, not me."

"Not really," I say. "I'm still here, and he skipped a checkpoint."

"And the recovery team did not find him," Marcus says. "If he was alive, you know he'd be here."

Jet chews his cheek. I feel the same pull in my chest as when I realized what Maia was there for, and I know Jet feels the same. In each of our ways, we tried. In each of our ways, we failed.

"I just wish there was more I could do for Sakira," Jet says quietly.

He drops his head to his hands, and I put an arm around his back, offering what little comfort I can. I pray Sakira is resourceful enough to make her way out, even without her team. We may not have met under the best circumstances, but I would never wish *this* on her.

"Maybe the Speaker told her something we don't know about," I say. "Maybe they gave her something that will help."

Melia nods. "She is *trielle*. Even if Kasta broke her brush and spilled her ink, she will find a way. Magic is drawn to her as a river to the sea."

Jet gives us a weak smile, a sign of thanks more than agreement.

"And you can do more when you're home," I add, resting my chin on his shoulder. "That can be your first order: finding Sakira and bringing her back."

He smiles and looks over, and the sadness in his face shifts as he takes me in. "Actually," he says, "I have my first order planned already."

◇

Jet could have gone straight to the palace. It's an entire day closer than Atera, and with his father ailing, his sister missing, and an entire city waiting to welcome their new crown prince, it would have made sense to see to his affairs first. Even *I* wouldn't have minded pausing on solid ground after the days it takes an even bigger glass boat to parade us past the southern towns. But we must drift by the palace and the waiting crowds in the dead of night, because when I wake on the fourth day, it's to the light of dawn atop the thatched roofs of a humble little town.

"Oh!" I say, bursting out of the cabin and clutching the rail. My heart swells at the sight of Fara's stable on the closest hill. I'm desperate to catch a glimpse of him working, and I fly to the front of the boat, where Jet leans against the rail, watching us come in.

I settle next to him, my shoulder against his.

"Thank you," I say. "I thought I'd never see it again."

He looks over, and the sight of him hurts my chest. He's dressed in a vibrant blue tunic, a crown of Numet's swirling suns encircling his head, his deep brown skin gleaming with fresh oil. Never has he looked so much like his father, and while the thought brings me incredible pride, it also reminds me we each have a duty to attend. No matter what we feel for each other, he's going to be king. I have no regrets about anything we've been through.

But I wish I didn't have to lose him.

"It's the least I can do after everything you've done for me," Jet says. He tries, and fails, to smile. "I only wish I could have spared you the journey."

"Me too. I'm never leaving home again."

"Ever?"

There's a playful tone in his voice, but it doesn't reach his eyes. He knows this moment has been coming, too. But I will cherish every small memory we've made. I will never forget what he did for me, what he sacrificed when he had nothing to gain from it, just the conviction in his heart that I deserved better. I will never forget how he helped me see I could be both a Whisperer and a girl worth dying for.

But even a girl worth dying for knows when she's met her limit. I've lived the story of all stories, and while I'm glad I had the chance—mostly glad, anyway—that's more than enough to last my lifetime. Now it's time to enjoy what I have here. Good work, a safe place to sleep, food and water when I need it. Fara and his wisdom. Mora and her grudges. Hen, when she's home from her assignments. This is what I was made for.

And it's more than enough.

I shrug. "At this point, I wouldn't even leave for chocolate."

"Now, that's extremely serious. Not even chocolate crème?"

I shake my head.

"With raspberries?"

Another shake.

"How about a cake that melts when you bite into it, with this delicious strawberry drizzle—"

"Not even if an entire palace was made from it," I say, though my traitorous stomach growls in disagreement.

Jet chuckles, and a deep sadness nestles into my bones. His smile fades as he looks over, but his eyes still glitter with mischief.

"What about for a coronation?" he asks.

"Absolutely not."

He laughs in surprise. "*My* coronation, Zahru."

I almost reply that after everything I've been through, it *better* be his coronation, but the look on his face stops me. He isn't looking at me like someone saying goodbye. He's looking at me like he did at the starlit pond. Like I'm the answer to a hundred questions; like I could make or destroy him with what I say next.

"I just thought . . ." He covers my hand on the railing, his eyes gold with my reflection. "Well. I thought, that was a terrible first impression. You were kidnapped, you were stabbed; we've yet to do anything together without being covered in dirt or blood . . . maybe you'd give me a second chance?"

My heart jerks. "But is that . . . I mean, can we? I know your father wouldn't approve. And I'm just—"

"A stable girl, I know." He smiles and traces my knuckles, his face now close to mine. "And the fiercest, bravest, most incredible woman I know. I would be so lucky that you'd consider me."

Joy bursts through me. Of course this will mean leaving Atera again, but I remind myself of what the Speaker said. Just as with Gallus, no two adventures are alike. One can cut and sting, and the next can be wonderful and glorious. This is definitely one I don't want to miss.

"Of course," I whisper. "Yes."

"Thank you," he says, squeezing my hand. "There are some formal processes to go through, but the ceremony should be in a moon or so. I'll come for you."

"I'll look forward to it."

His smile quirks, and he looks very close to saying something cheeky when his gaze flickers over my shoulder, and he stiffens. The stench of smoke reaches me just before I turn.

I'd been so excited to see my home, so focused on Fara's stable, I hadn't looked at the town. Unlike the other river cities we passed, no one lines the shores here to greet us. No one fishes in the canoes that bob, scattered and half sunken, across the river. Certainly no one comes down from the market, where the buildings are caved in and black.

"No," I whisper, dread plucking my ribs as I look toward the two-story estates, where the crumbled remnants of a house lean against the broken bones of Mora's haven.

"Hen!" I yell. "Mora!"

I grip the railing, not caring how high we are, but Jet grabs me around the stomach before I can jump. "Gods, Zahru, the river."

A snake twists through my ribs as I see what he means. It's not just canoes broken and bobbing in the water. Our boat drifts forward, and bodies stir beneath it, bumping against the hull.

Crocodiles scatter as we interrupt them, and horror needles into me as I realize what I nearly jumped into.

"Hold the boat!" someone orders. "About face! Guards alert!"

In an instant, the guards around the railings double. The boat jerks to a stop and starts pivoting the way we came. We're not going to dock.

"*Dõmmel*," the captain says, his many amulets glittering on his biceps. "I realize you wanted no one to know our destination so we wouldn't be interrupted, but I desperately request permission to contact the Mestrah about this."

"Yes," Jet says, swallowing. "Right away."

"But we're still stopping, right?" I ask, clutching the rail. "The stable's intact. There must still be people here."

"The threat may be here, too," the captain says. "I'm sorry. I don't feel safe letting anyone go to land."

"But my father—!" I whirl on Jet. "I can't just leave. We have to check."

"Stop the boat," Jet says.

"*Dõmmel*—"

"Does the Mestrah know about this?" Jet asks.

The captain consults his listening scroll. We stand for a few harrowing moments, me trying not to picture my family bobbing beneath the water, Jet gaping at the broken remnants of my home. Melia and Marcus soon join us, rubbing sleep from their eyes, but the sight of Atera snaps them awake.

"No . . ." Marcus says.

"Gods have mercy," Melia mutters, rubbing her thumb over her Healer's amulet.

"The Mestrah says they received word an hour ago of the attack," the captain says, with a pitying look at me. "He can only surmise Wyrim wanted to coordinate it with your return."

"Gods," Jet says, pressing his fingers around his eyes.

"Please tell me there were survivors," I say.

"There were," the captain assures me. "This is the worst area, as most took to the river to flee. Two-thirds of the city evacuated safely. They're taking survivors in Kystlin and Apolis."

Two-thirds. I close my eyes, begging the gods that my family is among them. Grieving for those whose families are not.

"We have to find them, Jet," I whisper, as he folds his arms around me. "Please tell me this isn't how it ends."

His arms tighten, his troubled eyes on the shore. "It won't be, Zahru." There's an angry promise in his tone. "It won't be."

EPILOGUE

—*Maia*—

BEFORE my parents disowned me, my mother used to sit with me each night by lamplight and read to me the stories of the gods. I would be High Priest one day, and I needed to understand them. But as much as she insisted these sessions were for educational purposes, she never moved away when I curled under her arm or begged her to read one scroll more, and at times she would even lean her chin against my hair, the scent of rosewater drifting around us. My mother was first and foremost a servant of the gods, and to covet me was to dishonor her duties. During the day, I addressed her as *adel* and kept my eyes on her careful hands, her gossamer-covered shoulders, mimicking the smooth way she lit incense for Rachella and knelt before the goddess with bread and wine. Those who saw us in the temple knew me only to be her apprentice and nothing more.

Perhaps she dreamed of my fate when I was still a child. Perhaps that is why she always looked upon me with sad eyes, and turned me toward the gods anytime I craved her arms. So that on the day I would betray everything I was meant to be, she would not miss me.

It was over the distance of our parents that Kasta and I found each other. We were eight when we met, and I was gathering soft mums from the royal gardens to honor Sabil, the god of magic, and the prince was cursing him. His anger fascinated me. Here was more emotion than my mother had ever shown, and it was not the only one Kasta had. He felt everything intensely—joy, excitement, sorrow, pain—and so being with him was like living inside a dream, where everything burned brighter and sharper. In me he found an anchor, the stone to his fire. I would hold him when he was upset, and he would make me things: small wooden carvings of gods and birds, as real as if they might come to life when I touched them. He was always calmest with a knife in his hands. At first I thought it was because of his siblings, but once I realized Jet and Sakira would never do him true harm, I came to understand it was for something else. For a shadow he could sense but not see; a shadow that thrived on his fear.

When his eleventh year arrived and he had yet to show magical ability, the shadow and he began to trade places.

I couldn't lose him. He had become to me what my mother was not—an ear to listen, a shoulder to lean on, a way to understand emotion on a level I couldn't grasp otherwise. I vowed to do everything in my power to save him from the darkness.

When I failed, I vowed to do everything in my power to destroy it.

And so I understand perfectly the calm that falls over his face as I stand before him, a blade in my left hand and a dagger in my right, the buried gods cracked and broken around us. It is a fitting place to die. Among the ruins of what should have been my life, just the two of us after so many confused years, the start and the finish of it all.

He does not run. With the magic gone from his grasp, he would rather I drag a blade across his neck than have to face another day in a world he cannot have, a world that will not bend to the will of his hands. I have lived four years a demon, and still I have found joy in the heart of my curse, freedom in the speed of my paws. He cannot see the light anymore through the darkness.

So I do what I should have done that day so long ago, before I traded my soul for his.

I will get out of his way.

I drop the sword. I slam him against the wall and raise the dagger to his neck, and aside from a heavy grunt, his eyes do not change. They lack the fear they should have. The desperate desire for life that makes a person human.

He thinks I am bringing him the mercy of death.

He is wrong.

Death is not punishment enough for what he's become. If I kill him, he will pass into Paradise a prince, revered and worshipped. And I will remain here, to be blamed and hunted; to be sent to the Burning Fields a murderer and a beast. No. It is time the world, and the gods, knows which of us is the true monster.

Perhaps he will find it ironic, that Shifters are still outcasts.

Have your magic, then, I think. *And may it be your ruin.*

I jerk his hand up and trap it beneath mine on the hilt.

And I make him plunge the dagger into my heart.

ACKNOWLEDGMENTS

FIRST and foremost, I would like to thank God not only for blessing me with the ability to pursue my wildest dream, but for putting the most incredible people in my life, without whom this book would not exist:

For my husband, who works early so I can work late, and who has helped me brainstorm solutions to all kinds of plot issues. He would like it to be known that he is actually the mastermind behind my books, and like a good partner I am inclined to let him believe it.

For my daughter, who joined our family and broke my heart open in the most amazing of ways, and added an incredible new depth to my life and my writing. You make me want to be better.

For my parents, who told me I could do whatever I put my mind to, and who unabashedly burden strangers with my books, pictures, and life story.

For my second parents, Rob and Kathy, whose enthusiasm for my work and help with my daughter are instrumental in giving me the time I need to write. To my siblings, Brent, Ty, Gentry, and Bailey, who I know I can count on for anything.

For Nicolette, Lauren, Danielle, and Sarah, who are the inspirations for the friendships in this book. You bring so much joy to my life.

For my critique partners Lori Goldstein, Bailey Knaub, Chelsea Bobulski, and Tatum Flynn, who are not only exceptionally talented in their own right, but invaluable readers and tireless cheerleaders. Your support and time have meant more than I can ever say. For Julie C. Dao, who has talked me off many proverbial ledges and continues to inspire me with both her accomplishments and her resilience. Without all of you, this would be a lonely journey.

For my agent, Brianne Johnson, who never once lost faith in me, even when I started losing faith in myself. Thank you for your pep talks and your career-saving guidance. For Allie Levick, whose smart edit notes and excitement made this a story a joy to revise.

For my editorial team at Razorbill: Marissa Grossman, Chris Hernandez, and Alex Sanchez, who took this stick pile of ideas I had and built them into an entire world. Dear reader, if you enjoyed this story, it is entirely due to their brilliant suggestions, encouragement, and patience. Also for Casey McIntyre, who made me feel like I'd joined a family and not just a publishing house, and Krista Ahlberg, who put the finishing touches on the book and made it look like I actually know something about math and navigation.

For my cover designer Theresa Evangelista, who made this book look damn good.

And last but certainly not least, a huge thank-you to the rest of the team at Penguin Random House and Razorbill, for pouring so much time and energy into *The Kinder Poison*, for taking a risk on me, and for sharing my words with the world.